SIPPING WHISKEY IN A SHALLOW GRAVE

MARK MITTEN

SIPPING WHISKEY IN A SHALLOW GRAVE

For information about special discounts for bulk purchases, please contact Sunbury Press, Inc. Wholesale Dept. at (717) 254-7274 or orders@sunburypress.com.

To request one of our authors for speaking engagements or book signings, please contact Sunbury Press, Inc. Publicity Dept. at publicity@sunburypress.com.

FIRST SUNBURY PRESS EDITION
Printed in the United States of America
November 2012

Trade Paperback ISBN: 978-1-62006-146-6
Mobipocket format (Kindle) ISBN: 978-1- 62006-147-3
ePub format (Nook) ISBN: 978-1-62006-148-0

Published by:
Sunbury Press
Mechanicsburg, PA
www.sunburypress.com

Mechanicsburg, Pennsylvania USA

"Nothing like being drawn back into another time! Old West Colorado comes alive in this novel. Depicting the many different lives, of Lawmen, Thieves, and true working Cowboys out on the Range. All done with the authenticity that makes you really understand what life might have been like back then. Not the glorified romance of many tales of the West, but bringing alive the true hardships, of an untamed Country. While letting us realize what tough, rugged individuals, they must have been, all in the name of survival. A great read, that completely revived my Western Spirit!"

Fred Hargrove
Western Cowboy, Singer / Songwriter

"Sipping Whiskey in a Shallow Grave is a fun and enthralling read! Mark Mitten has managed to create both an authentic voice, filled with western flair, and a freshness. The characters are so alive that you expect them to walk through the door as you put the book down. A great first effort for this wonderful new author!"

Carol Heiden
Executive Director, Colorado Therapeutic Riding Center

"While reading Sipping Whiskey in a Shallow Grave, I found myself in the middle of the action both mentally and emotionally. Mark does a great job developing the characters and the story so that readers are in the center of it all. Anyone who has an interest in the western world should read this one!"

Dr. Clint Unruh, DVM, Colorado Equine Veterinary Services

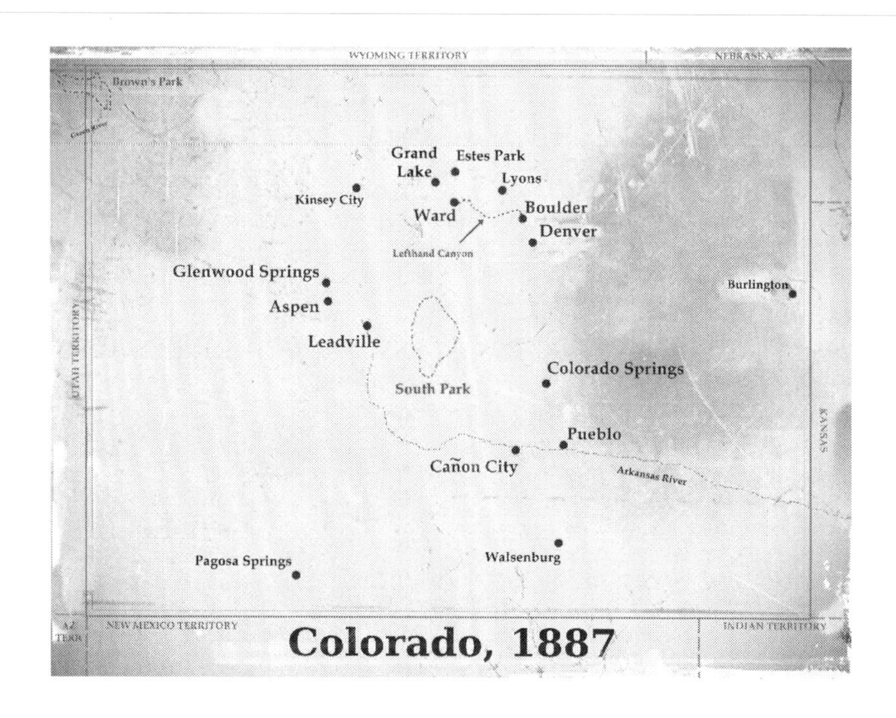
WYOMING TERRITORY
NEBRASKA
Brown's Park
Grand Lake
Estes Park
Lyons
Kinsey City
Ward
Boulder
Denver
Lefthand Canyon
Glenwood Springs
Burlington
Aspen
Leadville
UTAH TERRITORY
Colorado Springs
South Park
KANSAS
Pueblo
Cañon City
Arkansas River
Walsenburg
Pagosa Springs
NEW MEXICO TERRITORY
INDIAN TERRITORY
Colorado, 1887

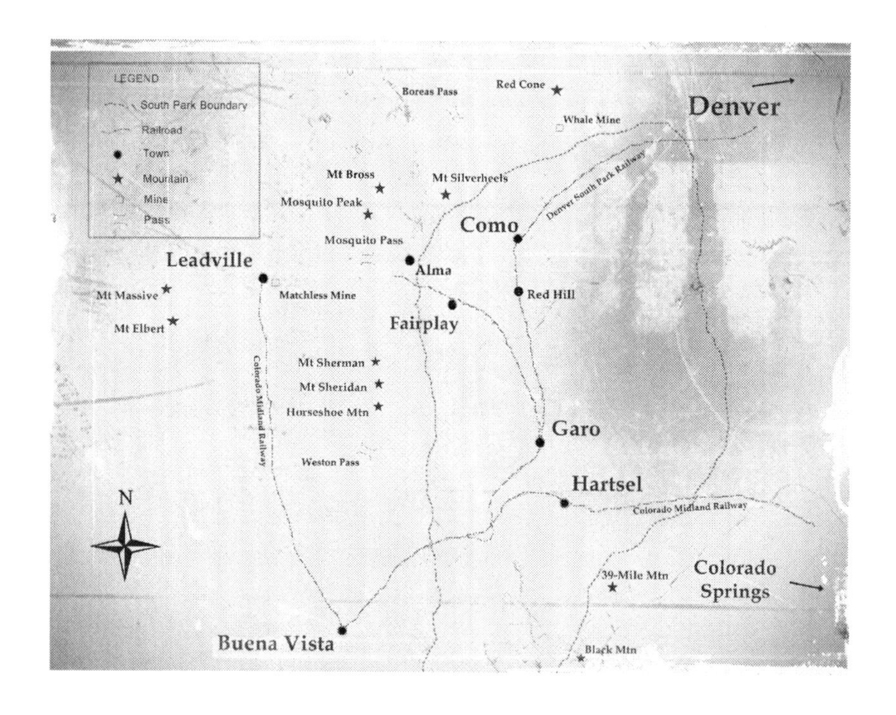
LEGEND
South Park Boundary
Railroad
Town
Mountain
Mine
Pass
Boreas Pass
Red Cone
Whale Mine
Denver
Mt Bross
Mt Silverheels
Denver South Park Railway
Mosquito Peak
Como
Mosquito Pass
Leadville
Alma
Mt Massive
Matchless Mine
Red Hill
Mt Elbert
Fairplay
Mt Sherman
Colorado Midland Railway
Mt Sheridan
Horseshoe Mtn
Garo
Weston Pass
Hartsel
N
Colorado Midland Railway
39-Mile Mtn
Colorado Springs
Buena Vista
Black Mtn

Part 1

CHARACTERS

PART 1

Cowboys of the B-Cross-C:
Til Blancett – owner of the "B-Cross"
LG Pendleton – top hand
Casey Pruitt – top hand
Edwin
Emmanuel – cook
Ira
Lee
Davis
Steve McGonkin
Rufe McGonkin
Gyp – wrangler ("jigger boss")

The Grand Lake Gang:
Bill Ewing
Vincent ("Judas Furlong")
Granger
"Ned Tunstall" (Charley Crouse)
Poqito
Caverango
Will Wyllis
Lem

The Grand Lake Posse:
Griff Allen – deputy sheriff
Ben Leavick – mercantile store owner
Roy Caldwell – owns apothecary
Red Creek Mincy – Civil War veteran
Merle Hastings – ranch don

Other citizens of Grand Lake:
Sheriff Emerson Greer
Caroline Greer – Emerson's wife
Bonnie Allen – Deputy Griff Allen's wife
Meggy Leavick – Ben Leavick's wife

People of Ward:
Julianna
Josephine
Prescott Sloan – banker
Hugh Hughes – owner & operator of The Halfway House
Jim Everitt – stage driver
Ian Mitchell – rides shotgun for the stage
Mr. James – the telegrapher
Zeke – farrier/blacksmith

Chapter 1

Colorado
Continental Divide
April 1887

Griff shivered. He knew Emerson wasn't happy about all this. On one hand, the snow gave them hoofprints to follow. Tracking bank jackers in the backcountry was tougher when the ground was just pine needles and dirt. They already had one tied to the pack mule — at least something to show for it all. On the other hand, by the time they made it back to Grand Lake and dumped him in the jailhouse the snow might melt down and tracking would be unprofitable.

There was a groan from the direction of the pack mule. Their prisoner was face-down across the animal's back and a long string of slobber trailed from his mouth. It had dribbled and frozen down the mule's side.

"Well, dern Em," Griff said with a glance to the sky. "Mebbe we should head on back then."

The sky was a gray ceiling, right over the treetops. Looking up at it, the lanky dark pines seemed to be pointing out the problem. Snow tufts were just starting to float around them. Big white flakes, light as the air.

"Either somebody spilt a sack full of cotton," Griff went on. "Or else that's snowin'."

Emerson Greer never looked up at the sky once. He knew the sun was gone and the clouds were low and snow was in the air. He also knew it was better to head back. He just wanted to give the chase a fair shake.

"Know I winged one," Emerson said quietly. "Got his arm purty good."

In addition to the horse tracks, Emerson kept noting drips of cherry red blood. Not hard to see in the snow. But hard to see in the dark. And it was almost dark. And the temperature was dropping pretty quick. Even the stalwart Emerson Greer wasn't immune to the cold. He was wearing his heavy winter coat and thick wooly gloves. His hat kept the snow off his neck.

He looked back at Griff.

"Shoot, let's call it."

Thcy were up near treeline. The forest was thinning out. The tracks led upslope onto the talus and Emerson didn't want to head up into the open rocks in the dark, horseback. It was slow going in such difficult terrain. Snowy rocks meant slickery footing, and a horse with a twisted hock would be a chore.

Emerson stopped his horse and sighed. He hated turning back. The sun would be out tomorrow and melt most of this off. Tracks would melt out, too, but he couldn't do anything more about that. They weren't provisioned for a long haul — plus they had one of them anyway.

"Those ki-yotes are probably making for Kinsey City."

"Mebbe they will," Griff agreed. "Get collared by the very men they stoled from."

Emerson Greer was the Grand County sheriff. While Griff was his deputy and friend, there was still an etiquette to decision making. Griff knew five miles back the pursuit wasn't likely to pan out. Since Emerson shot one of them in the arm, the men they were chasing were burdened with a wounded man and were likely heading for a safe place to hole up. Their tracks seemed to indicate that, too. However many there were, four or five perhaps, they were headed in a crow's line and weren't taking any breaks.

"Well, then," Griff nodded. He turned his horse and started back.

The pack mule's lead line was tied to his own saddle. The mule was responsive and followed without any nipping or pulling. He was a good mule — Kodiak was his name. Some trapper from up north sold him to Griff a couple years back. It was anybody's guess why he got that name. He wasn't mean, and Kodiak was sure-footed and confident on any trail. On occasion, Griff's wife Bonnie made carrot cakes. Griff inwardly wished those occasions were far more infrequent. Bonnie wasn't a good cook, especially when it came to sweets. Her most tasteless enterprise was her carrot cake. But Kodiak liked them. Griff always made sure to smuggle several slices out to the barn whenever Bonnie was out visiting — made it disappear from the pantry quicker.

"Untie me, you fools."

Griff glanced over his shoulder and smiled.

"Sure thing, boss," he said with a wink to Emerson.

The sheriff stepped his horse up by the mule.

"What's your name?" Emerson asked him.

"Bill," Bill said.

He slurped a bit — his chin was cold, since frozen spit was caked all over it. Bill twisted as best he could but the best he could see was Emerson's tapadero.

"Where's my hat? It's quite cold and there's snow in my hair."

"Long gone, amigo."

Their horses slowly plodded on. The light was fading fast now and it was getting hard to see through the trees very far.

"My head hurts," Bill went on.

"I'm not surprised none," Emerson replied. "Buffaloed you square on."

"You tied me to a godforsaken mule — that's thoughtless."

"Don't know how salty that mule is," Emerson said without much conviction. "Hope she don't roll."

Bill twisted again to throw a look up at him but could still only make out the tapadero.

"Damn you. Rather inhumane, I'd say," Bill muttered. He relaxed and hung his head tiredly. He was not lying — his head was hurting. In fact, Emerson had hit him with the barrel of his . 45 so hard it split the skin and knocked Bill's lights out.

Emerson leaned over and pressed his finger into Bill's torn scalp. Bill winced and jerked around violently but the knots were well-tied and he didn't go anywhere.

"Curse me ag'in, and I'll crack your skull ag'in."

"Best to just lay there and make do," Griff suggested.

Chapter 2

Beaver Creek
South of Estes Park
Colorado

A few of the cows were just starting to stir in the dim morning light. They rose up and started to root through the snow to get at the cold grass, but most were still bedded down.

Casey Pruitt rode slowly around the herd. He had given up trying to whistle a long time ago — his lips were too cracked. He was huddled inside an old yellow slicker with two sweaters layered up underneath for added warmth. Casey reached up and pulled his wide-brim hat even lower onto his head. It was frosted over. Then he readjusted a knit scarf that was wrapped around his ears and chin. It had been a long night, and he was more than ready for the sun to come up over the ridge.

Up and down the valley, patches of spring grass had managed to poke up through the white crust. It wasn't much yet but it was coming in. The season had begun.

"High summer graze," Casey muttered. "And I'm freezing my cantle."

The valley bottom was a mountain meadow blanketed with snow and walled in on both sides with bare-branch aspen and ponderosa pine. Winding right through the middle of it all, willow bushes sprouting up on both sides, was Beaver Creek. The creek was barely a foot across at its widest point, except the beaver pond, and was glassed over with thin ice from the night's lows. Casey could hear it trickling below the ice whenever he rode by. He knew it was just a brittle layer and would shatter pretty easy when the cows stepped on it. They could water that way — he didn't need to get down and break it.

It was a mixed herd: steers and mommas, yearlings, and even a couple babies out of season. It was mainly Polangus, but some Durham, too. Til, the ranch boss, bought them in Dallas and shipped them by rail up to Denver just the week before. Casey received them from the stockyards himself.

As he made his way slowly around the herd, Casey's dog limped over to the creek and sniffed the ice. The dog was close to a hundred pounds and had a coat so thick the winter air didn't get through. Casey called him Hopper — he had a busted leg from several years back but it never healed up quite right.

"Hope there's slap-jacks."

The big dog cocked his head to one side.

"I could do with just a hot cup of coffee. Although the way Emmanuel makes it, it'll just burn up my insides."

Catching some movement from the corner of his eye, Casey glanced up. Someone was heading his way, riding alongside the willows. That would be Edwin — taking his sweet time. He walked his horse, just ambling along. At one point he angled away from the willows to get around the beaver pond. The sound of hoofsteps in the crusty snow carried up the valley.

It had been another bitter night. It was April in the Rockies so that was no surprise. Casey shook his head impatiently. It was chilly, and his night shift was over and all he wanted to do was ride into camp. He was flat out tired. Also, his horse needed to be grained, and the bay knew what time it was, too.

Edwin rode past the pond and finally kicked it up to a trot. Casey watched him jostle about in the saddle, his white hat bobbing like a ghost in the dim light. Edwin was just a kid in his late teens, maybe. He had only hired onto the B-Cross the week before.

"Hey ya, Case. It's damn freezin' cold to be riding nighthawk — your pecker snap off yet?"

Edwin's grin was lopsided and his breath came puffing out in clouds.

"Boy, your mama musta had a pantry full of soap. Can you even taste anything but lye?"

Edwin let out a sarcastic, high-pitched hoot.

"Makes them beans go down. And that's what's waiting for you back at the cookfire."

Casey pulled off his rawhide gloves and rubbed his hands together to get the blood moving. His skin was so dry his knuckles were about to split.

"Kidding me? That same batch has been sitting in the Dutch oven for three full days."

He shook his head.

"Last time I ate 3-day beans," Casey went on, "I was belly-aching for three days beyond."

"Well there's paper in the shitter this time."

"What happened to your eye?"

Edwin's smile faltered. He reached up and touched his eye very carefully.

"Roped a bronc from the remuda, crack of dawn. It was that cranky ol' sorrel of LG's. Belly full of bedsprings."

Casey looked down to see which mount the boy was riding. It was not LG's cranky sorrel. It was a soft-eyed paint called Sugar.

"Ought be condemned!" Edwin added ruefully.

"LG can ride anything with hair on it. And his string's nothing but mean," Casey told him. "Likes it that way, I guess. Certainly makes a statement."

Casey walked his horse a few steps while he tried to work his gloves back on. They were frozen stiff and just too cold to make it worth the effort. So he gave up and tucked them in his belt. Behind him, he could hear Edwin mumbling to himself.

"Cows. Piss-stinkin' cows."

Casey pointed his bay back up the mountain valley. Hopper ran after him. The dog's limp turned into a smooth lope as he picked up speed. Casey glanced down at him. Ever since he got his leg squished, that poor dog always did better at a run than a walk.

Chapter 3

Grand Lake
Colorado

The blood had clotted and was clumped up in Bill's hair. He tried to run his fingers through it, but they got snagged and made his eyesight flash white.

"Your brainpan is all rattled. Just sit tight — ain't going nowhere."

Bill looked up and glared through the iron bars, but Emerson was not moved by it. At that moment, Griff came walking down the hallway and into the backroom where the jail cell was. Behind him was Ben Leavick, who owned and ran the Leavick Mercantile.

"Hoo-ee," Ben said and whistled. "Get the gold back, too?"

"No, I did not," Emerson told him.

"Let's go get it then."

"When is a man so privileged as to eat around here?" Bill inquired sullenly.

"Got your horse ready?" Emerson asked Ben.

"Yessir."

"Don't know how many are out there," Griff pointed out. "This one won't say."

Once more Bill picked at the dried blood in his hair but only made himself wince. He looked at his hand. He must have pulled the scabbing loose that time since there was fresh blood on his fingertips.

"Probably ain't nowhere about anyhow," Ben commented.

"Griff, you stay here," Emerson said. "Me and Ben will head on out, although I am not confident we'll catch up to them today, or at all."

Griff nodded. He already knew the chances were slim. This was more a formality than anything, which was why he wasn't too disappointed Emerson asked him to stay behind and watch over their prisoner — or too disappointed he would not be eating salted elk and cold beans tonight.

"Those tracks were angling right back toward Kinsey City and straight as an arrow, too."

"We'll head out that way and see," Emerson said. "Maybe Kare Kremmling has heard tell by now."

"Hell, maybe he's got 'em locked up for us," Griff suggested. "Or strung up."

Stepping over to the cell door, Ben Leavick smirked at Bill.

"Your compadres left you for the wolves. How's that make you feel?"

"You ain't no wolves," Bill replied with an easy smile.

"Kare's still mad at them Kinsey brothers," the sheriff went on.

"What for?" Ben asked him.

"One day they tell everyone the place is called Kinsey City. Just a couple alfalfa farmers, but it was Kare's store bringing everybody in."

"He was hot over that," Griff mentioned. "Still is."

"Hey," Bill said. "When a man is incarcerated, he is supposed to be fed rightly."

In the backroom of the courthouse, there was only one window. It was small and set up high in the wall. The morning sky was getting brighter outside, but with such a small window hardly any light got in. The room was dim and chilly. Bill got up and grabbed the cold bars.

"I'm expecting a fine breakfast this morning."

Emerson ignored him, but Griff was starting to get irritated.

"You eat when I say you eat."

"The hour's getting long," Emerson said to Ben. "We need to get on with it."

They both turned around and headed back into the hallway. Griff waved his hand at Bill to let him know he didn't care about his breakfast expectations and followed the other two men. Since it was early on a Sunday, the courthouse was empty. Their footsteps echoed on the hardwood floors as they crossed the room.

"Why don't you get that woodstove going in here?" Ben Leavick said smartly to Griff. "Keep your nose all warm while I help Em do your job for you."

"You *this* desperate for company, Emerson?" Griff asked.

"I'm that desperate for another pair of eyes and another working Winchester."

"Well, then. While you're making your way on salted elk, I'll head on over to the Grand Placer and see what's on the menu," Griff told them pleasantly. "Be thinking of you, Ben, with that moose-steak and potato plate on my lap."

Outside, the morning air was bitter and dry and there were no clouds in the sky yet. It was too early and too cold for anyone to really be out. Main Street was empty. Ben Leavick had hitched his horse right outside the courthouse, but Emerson's was all the way down at the livery.

"Caroline stayed up late and baked us up a big batch of her famous Cajun tomato bread," Emerson confided. "So we may not be suffering as much as you think."

The town of Grand Lake was white with a layer of fresh overnight snow. It seemed like every chimney on every building and home was pitching out smoke. They could smell it in the air, along with the scent of lakewater even though the lake itself was still frozen over for the most part.

Leading his horse by the reins, Ben walked with Emerson down to the livery stable to get his horse tacked up.

Watching them through a spyglass, Vincent smiled thoughtfully.

"That them?" Granger asked.

"Yeah, that's them," Vincent said, and kept watching. Granger held his hand out but realized after a minute that Vincent had no intention of passing the spyglass over. Granger gave up and stomped his feet in the snow a few times to get the circulation going in his toes. The town was straight across the lake. The four of them were camped in a thick stand of pine. The winter snow had drifted up pretty deep in places but they had managed to dig out a little area to watch from. Granger's toes never warmed up properly and they hadn't dared to light a fire overnight since they were so close to town. It had only been one night without a fire, but it was a hard night since Granger's boots were thin.

The two Mexicans, Poqito and Caverango, quietly observed Granger stomping around in the snow. Neither of them liked the gringo. It was clear Granger wasn't fond of the Mexicans either and let them know it whenever he could. Poqito wished they had not split off from the rest of the group the day before. Vincent made them both come along, otherwise they would have kept riding with Ned, Will Wyllis, and Lem — who were busy leaving a nice set of horse tracks for the sheriff to follow.

"They're at the livery now," Vincent told them, still looking through the spyglass.

The sun was coming up but it would be a couple hours before it was high enough to get above the mountains and actually shine on Grand Lake.

"Maybe we could light a fire now," Granger suggested.

"Don't waste your time."

"Why not... my toes are about froze."

Vincent lowered the spyglass and glared back at Granger impatiently.

"Soon as that sheriff rides out, I'll go get Bill. So saddle your horse and double check the cinch. That whole town'll be riding hard after us once they realize."

He pointed at Granger for emphasis.

"No fire. If you get cold, just rub your teeth together."

That, of course, was a reference to Granger's front teeth which contained a sizable gap. Granger's face tightened up. He did not like it when Vincent spoke down to him. Since Bill had gotten captured, Vincent's condescension seemed to recognize no boundaries. Of course Granger didn't care for Bill much either — but at least when Bill was around Vincent was less prone to goading remarks.

The gold and the gold dust they pulled from the Kinsey City bank were right there, in their saddle bags. Granger privately wondered why they were spending the effort to get Bill out of prison. What did they need Bill for, really? That was one less person to split it with. But Granger knew Vincent would not go for that kind of talk, as the two of them had been compadres for many years. But Granger also knew that, if it had been himself in that courthouse cell, Ned wouldn't be out leaving a false track and Vincent wouldn't be circling around to bust *him* out.

"Fine," Granger grumbled and began to stomp around again.

Poqito and Caverango did not move or speak. They merely continued to watch Granger, warily but patiently. Both of them were nervous that once Vincent left to go spring Bill, Granger's civility towards them would deteriorate.

Poqito glanced at Caverango. They both understood one another's worries, and sneakily unbuttoned their coats — if things went south, they could make a grab for their gunbelts a little easier. Poqito knew Granger's gun was already in the man's pocket, where he had his hands buried at the moment. He hoped Vincent would not be gone long.

Chapter 4
Beaver Creek

Shifting the reins to his right hand, Casey rode near the willows. He held out his free hand and let his fingers graze along the willow branches as he passed by. Casey had worked for many outfits over the last ten years — all in Colorado. And he loved willows and aspen and orange dirt and bits of quartz, and the pale blue sky. This was his country. Nighthawk on a winter shift would not change that high opinion.

His dog ran alongside, trying to keep up with his horse. All Casey could hear was the bay's breathing and the crunching snow beneath his hoofs. Casey tucked his chin into his scarf.

In a bend of the creek, he caught sight of an orange flicker. It was the cookfire. Beyond the fire was a one-room log cabin — the ranch headquarters. The walls were dark pine chinked with white mortar and nearly invisible in the dim light. He could also make out the covered wagon parked by the corral, where the remuda was lined up at the rail watching him.

On the potrack was a large steaming kettle. Tucked in the coals were two Dutch ovens, round and black and speckled with soot. Casey knew one of those was the 3-day beans. But there were no slap-jacks as he hoped.

Casey rode up to the fire and just sat there for a minute smelling the woodsmoke. Hopper caught up and ran right over to Emmanuel, a large black man with a filthy apron around his waist. He welcomed the shaggy dog with a big grin.

"Here ya go, pard," the cook said and gave him a biscuit. "How's that taste?"

LG Pendleton stood in the shadowy doorway, leaning against the doorjamb with his hat in his hand. He used his fingers to comb through his hair and seated the hat firmly on his head.

Finally, Casey dismounted, moving very slowly. He was sore. He immediately knelt down to a crouch, stretching. Sitting in the saddle all night made his legs cramp up but he only really felt it when he got back on the ground. LG lit a cigarette and called to Emmanuel:

"How about this tough ol' puncher riding in. Looks like he's been wrastlin' injuns and a-tustlin' grizz. Big night on the graveyard watch, I can read that sign."

"LG, sleep all cozy again?" Casey said wryly. "Never seem to get that short straw, do you."

LG laughed at him.

"And chipper as a lark!"

"Casey Pruitt," Emmanuel announced. "There's a-beans and biscuits fo' ya. Pipin' hot."

"Oh, them biscuits are looking mighty tempting, Emmanuel."

Emmanuel tossed a yellow biscuit to Casey.

"Gonna cut my night horse loose and I'll be back for coffee."

Reins in one hand, biscuit in another, Casey walked heavily towards the corral. The horses inside hung their faces curiously over the fenceline, ears perked up. They hoped he was bringing them grain but he wasn't. Casey's bay nickered. He was eager to get turned out and fed some grain himself.

"How come no one be a-eatin' my beans?" Emmanuel asked LG. "There was a time when my beans was second to none."

"Camp cookie sure ain't your calling," LG said and clapped him on the shoulder. "You can rope a steer with a blindfold on, but you can't seem to get a loop around a can of beans."

"If it weren't fer my damned ol' black face, I'd be a-runnin' my own outfit a long time ago."

"I know it, you know it. Every hand here knows it."

LG stepped up to the fire and flicked his cigarette in the hot embers.

"You kin cook up some biscuits — least you got *one* redeeming quality."

"Gonna keep me 'round now."

"Gonna keep you around."

Casey cut his horse loose into the remuda. He took the reins and headstall, and lugging his saddle by the horn, dropped it all inside the cabin door. He came back out and blinked in the smoke. He stood there for a long moment staring into the yellow flames.

"Case. Get some coffee in you," LG said. He picked up a tin cup and poured some in.

Gingerly, Casey took the hot cup and blew at the steam.

"How's the boy?"

"On that creampuff paint. Composing verse when I left him."

LG snickered and looked over at Emmanuel, hoping to get him riled up. The cook had a laugh that sounded like a donkey, so LG liked to get him going. But Emmanuel merely shook his head at the thought of Edwin's riding abilities.

"I hope he learns himself a lesson," LG observed. "Hurricane deck of a bad horse ain't for a greenhorn. Poets or none."

"That boy put his hand in the fire, if you tells him not to," commented Emmanuel.

"Shoot, he'd crawl right in and pull on a blanket," LG said.

Chapter 5

Grand Lake

Bells tolled. It was Sunday and most of the townspeople were either sleeping the morning away or sitting in a pew. Main Street was empty. Blacksmith, livery, bank, assayer's, feed & seed — no one was outside; they were all inside where it was warm.

Griff himself had spent most of the morning in the small sheriff's office in front of the woodstove. He finally decided it was time to feed the prisoner, so he put on his coat, pushed open the door and stepped out into the brisk air. A cold front had certainly rolled in. His nose had developed a drip, and he felt the wetness crystallize in his nostrils the moment he breathed in. Large flat-bottomed clouds were crawling slowly across the sky. It was not even noon yet. One glance at the sky and Griff knew snow would be falling in a couple hours.

The sheriff's office was stationed straight across the street from the courthouse — where Bill was locked up, probably shivering the morning away. All Griff did was push a wool blanket through the jail bars, once Ben and Emerson left. That big old courthouse was just too cold to sit around in.

Griff glanced up at the sky again and squinted, tipping his hat to shade his eyes. The sun had just crept up over Mount Craig and was shining brightly in the small space between the mountaintop and the thick gray clouds.

He started walking but paused for a moment to button his overcoat. Just walking from one place to the next gave him a sharp chill, even in the direct sunlight. But the direct sunlight was about to disappear behind those clouds and the temperature would drop once it did. He knew he should have buttoned up his coat before he stepped outside, but sometimes he just didn't think about it until he was already out the door.

A green hummingbird flew close by, drawn in by his red silk scarf. It buzzed around his shoulders for a moment and then flew off.

"Go hole up," Griff told the bird kindly. The calendar might have said spring, but the sky still said winter.

He glanced over at the courthouse. He did not feel bad for Bill. If it wasn't for Bill and his pards, none of them would be out riding horses in the bitter cold backcountry.

The Grand Placer Saloon was empty except for Otto the barkeeper, who was toking on a cigar. Griff wasn't much of a saloon patron these days. Marriage had domesticated him. Griff could admit that. His wife Bonnie was a churchgoing lady and was staunchly opposed to drinking and dancing. So Griff gave it all up. But he did yearn for a good cigar every now and then, especially when he caught the sweet scent of aromatic tobacco.

"Morning, Griff."

Otto was a heavy-set man and quite bald. He was sitting on a tall stool behind the ornate mahogany bartop playing solitaire. The Grand stayed open all day and all night: all day for the drinkers, all night for the gamblers.

"I believe spring actually got here. Saw me a hummingbird right outside that door."

"Not attending service this week?"

"No, sir. Got one in the jailhouse."

"*Wish* you were attending service this week?"

"No, sir."

Otto grinned. He knew Griff, and he knew Bonnie.

"How can I help you on this fine Sund'y morning?"

"I best get some feed over to the courthouse."

"Tell the Missus you got one in a cell next Sund'y. How does ice fishing suit you?" Otto suggested, disappearing into the kitchen. He knew Griff would not tell the Missus anything of the sort, but he thought he would mention it anyhow.

White lies on a Sunday would not go over well with Bonnie Allen. Griff tried that once in the first year of their marriage — in order to do some regular summer fishing. It in fact had *not* gone over well, and afforded a memorable conversation once he returned home that day.

Griff leaned up against the bar and looked around the room. He spotted a man sitting quietly at a window table. So quietly that Griff had walked right past him on the way in.

"How do," Griff said.

"Morning there," Vincent said. "Couldn't help but overhear. Are you the sheriff?"

Griff shook his head.

"Deputy Sheriff of Grand County."

"Judas Furlong," Vincent introduced himself, untruthfully. "Rocky Mountain News."

Vincent took one last bite of fried egg and scraped backward in his chair. He rose with a friendly smile. A sunbeam angled through the window pane and lit up the dust in the air. It was always odd to be in the Grand on a Sunday morning. It was so quiet compared to a regular day.

"Not much to write about," Griff informed him. "Last year all the mining camps basically shut down. Seems like a ghost town up here now."

Vincent straightened his neck tie, and then they shook hands.

Griff noticed he was dressed sharply. When they shook hands, Griff also noticed a fine turquoise ring. He wondered what kind of salary a newspaperman got. A deputy sheriff could not afford nice turquoise rings. Of course, Bonnie's shopping habits tended to whittle into the family finances quite a bit.

"Not here about the mines. Heard you have a man in your jail."

"Word must travel. Just came in night before last. How did you hear about that already?"

Vincent pulled out a notebook and pencil from his vest pocket. "Word travels."

He wagged the pencil in his fingers.

"Like to do an article on you and your sheriff," he continued. "Write up the story how you captured this unruly brigand."

Just then Otto came out carrying a tin plate. There was a cloth napkin on top, covering it over. He walked carefully around the bar towards Griff.

"It's too hot to hold...except beneath the applesauce."

Griff lifted the napkin so he could find the applesauce. There was toast, fried eggs, applesauce, and half the plate was filled with hot chili. Griff took hold of it by the cool side and covered it back over with the napkin.

"Dern, look at all this. Who we feeding...the President?" Griff asked him. "Still got that celestial working the cook stove?"

"Yep."

"Dish me up a full plate when I get back."

Vincent fell into step behind Griff, and they both left the Grand Placer. The street was still empty, and it felt even colder than it had a few minutes before. Griff glanced down and realized he must have unbuttoned his coat again, inside the Grand, but he could not button it back up with a hot plate in his hand. He decided to just walk quickly. Up the street, he could hear hymns being sung in the Methodist church. Even though the words were muffled too much to pick out, Griff knew the tune.

"What can you tell me about this prisoner?"

Vincent held up his notepad as if he was ready to write, but Griff was not paying too much attention to him. It was too cold with his coat unbuttoned, plus he had to take care not to slosh hot chili onto his thumbs and scald himself. He angled for the courthouse at a fast clip.

"Well, this one ain't talking too much yet," Griff answered, over his shoulder. "His crew robbed a little bank down in Kinsey City last week."

"What else do you know?"

"Sheriff Greer caught this one himself." Griff smiled as he thought about it. "We happened to be right there, as luck went. Eating dinner at the Kinsey Inn right across the river. Heard the dynamite go off. Smoke was rolling out the front door of that little bank. This fella ran out the door at that very moment. Greer buffaloed him — just like Wyatt Earp."

Pretending to be a newspaperman was easy, Vincent realized. All you have to do is scribble down some notes and people think they'll be in the papers. He glanced up and down the street. No one was around, and the deputy was too busy with the plate of food to even notice the effort Vincent was putting in, so he tucked the pencil in his vest and put away the notebook. He was just pretending to write things down, anyway.

"Let me help with that door."

He held the courthouse door open. Griff was being careful with the soupy plate because he didn't want to spill on himself. But Griff was also being careful, because he did not want hot chili slopping onto the nice hardwood floors. The courthouse clerk, the elderly — and quarrelsome — Betty Anne Hartworst would go into conniptions if she saw chili spilled on her floors.

"That is quite a feat. News worthy."

"Right place at the right time. Sheriff's out with Ben Leavick right now, tracking the ones that peeled off."

"Any official prognostications I might write up?"

"I have no idea what you just said."

"Criminal predictions?"

"Aw, they could be halfway to Steamboat Springs by now," Griff told him. "You might be interested to know they've got a printing press up there. Started their own paper, year before last — *The Steamboat Pilot.*"

"That so?"

"Yessir," Griff said, arching his eyebrow. "How'd that one get by you? Being a newspaperman yourself, Mr. Furlong. Kind of ironic."

Vincent shrugged.

"Life is full of ironies, Mr. Allen."

Chapter 6
Beaver Creek

Emmanuel took a branch and stirred the embers around. Gray smoke and ash swirled up and LG stepped back to avoid it, but Casey stood where he was and just closed his eyes. The warm blast of air felt good, and he didn't seem to mind that ash got in his coffee. It had enough coffee grounds in it as it was. He had to drink through his teeth to strain it. Casey figured that he could strain ash along with the grounds, one just as easy as the other.

Crickets were chirping by the creek even though the clouds were thick overhead and the sun had only made a brief appearance. The cookfire was a Godsend given the cold front that was rolling in and they all huddled close to the flames.

"Someone comin' in," Emmanuel said and pointed to the far end of the valley.

In the distance, they were able to keep an eye on Edwin circling the cattle. Just then, another rider came out of the trees and headed his way. The two of them met up and stopped to chat for a moment.

"I'd say that is Til," Casey said, straining to see. "Wonder why he's back at the ranch. Only been two days now."

"Coming back from a 2-days' drunk," LG guessed, in his wry way.

Emmanuel chuckled softly, shaking his head. LG sure had a brazen sense of humor. Til was not the drinking type, much less the kind to ride in to camp drunk at six in the morning. Emmanuel chuckled again. That LG sure was quick to poke fun at a man. Even the boss!

They watched Til ride across the snowy valley floor, head up to the cookfire, and draw rein. Steam was coming off his horse's neck and sides.

"Morning, boys. Cold enough for you?"

"Howdy, Til," said Casey.

"Cold enough," LG affirmed.

"Coffee, Mistuh Blancett?" Emmanuel asked.

"Appreciated."

Til stepped out of the saddle, rowels jingling as his boots touched down. He was wearing a heavy white calfskin coat with a pile collar. It was a warm coat, and he was glad to have it in weather like this. He bought it one winter down at a stock show in

Denver one January. Cost him forty bucks, but it was an investment. He let the reins slip out of his hand, ground-tying the big bay while Emmanuel poured him some coffee.

"What's the word, Til?" LG asked him. "It's a mite early to be riding in."

"And a mite briskly," Til agreed.

He took a quick gulp from the tin cup and immediately lolled his mouthful onto the ground.

"Yow, damn it!"

"Watch you'self, suh," Emmanuel warned him. "May be hot."

"Well by jove, it surely is," Til said in a genuine tone. Breathing heavily, he wiped his mouth with his sleeve.

LG turned on the cook with a dramatic flair and stared hard at him.

"You should try saying that *afore* a man scalds his'self."

"Careful, LG," Til warned him. "Crossing a cook be as risky as braiding a mule's tail."

LG gave him a sanguine smile.

"I've bull-dogged brahmas and I've broke mustangs… reckon I can handle this mossy horned steer."

Without warning LG gave a sharp slap to the bottom of Emmanuel's tin cup sending steaming coffee flying high. It spattered into the flames and the fire hissed. But Emmanuel only broke into another wide grin. LG turned back to Til and picked up the conversation where they had left off.

"Thought you were in Denver till the first week of May."

"Heard some news you boys need to know. Down at the stockyards last evening. Got to talking with Ab Blocker."

Emmanuel perked up at the name.

"Rode with 'im in '77. Good trail boss, one of the best."

"Last night? Gee, you musta rode straight through, then," Casey said with surprise.

"I did. The man's already bringing his first beef herd up from Texas, driving to Wyoming. Twenty-five hundred head."

Til paused and blew hard across his coffee. He tried a cautious sip before continuing his story.

"Word is this past winter was hard…and not just on us. Worse up north, from what Blocker says. Much worse. Every cattle range in Montana was hit hard. They're talking 75% losses."

"*Seventy-five* percent?" LG said and whistled. "That is hard to imagine."

"Same story in Dakota and Wyoming. Worst winter ever to hit them northern ranges."

Casey shook his head in disbelief.

"Unheard of," he said under his breath.

"Seems January was the worst," Til continued. "Forty-five below zero, sixteen inches of snow, blizzard conditions. Cattle even froze to death standing up...they say many of 'em were found bunched up against the fence-lines, dying in piles."

"Now that is why I loathe barbed wire," LG stated. "On open range cattle can drift with the wind, find some shelter. Good Lord."

The sunlight broke through the clouds and washed over the cow camp. The men blinked in the brightness as they absorbed what Til was saying.

"Ab tells me with the beef price down so damn low, musta been hundreds and thousands of cattle being kept up there. Holding out for a better price — now they're all in a bind. Whole market is in a bind."

"What can you do? When the price of a steer barely covers your freight charge?" Casey said in a sober tone. "You can't blame 'em."

Til knelt down. He picked up a rag hanging on the end of the potrack. Using it as a buffer, he pinched the lid on the nearest Dutch oven and raised it. Several biscuits were still left, and he pulled one out.

The crew all stared into the flames, lost in thought but soaking up the moment of sunshine. They knew it would not last long with the sky looking like it was.

"Soon as can be," Til stated. "Market's gonna need beef."

"And we're moving on it," he added.

Looking beyond the fire, LG silently quantified the herd in the distance. They were grazing peacefully. Til chewed thoughtfully. The biscuit was warm and tasted good after a long ride through the mountains at night. He glanced over at his horse. Bit Ear was still standing quietly. Til knew the bay was just as hungry and figured he better cut him loose in the corral soon. Get him some grain and hay first.

"Sooner we get them to market, better off we'll be," Til mentioned. "Crisis like this, we're in an ideal position to sell. Make some seed money — expand the operation."

Casey shook his head hesitantly.

"Boy, not even summer yet."

Til nodded at that. The season had indeed only just begun, but the fact was, time was getting away from them.

"Just can't wait for November. Ship all of them by rail back up to our Wyoming range for a month. We'll leave the yearlings there, sell the beeves."

"Seems like we just drove them all up here yesterday," Casey said.

"I know it. But we're just too far from the market up here. Need to know what's going on, be ready to sell when the short-iron is hot."

LG knelt down and took the last biscuit out of the oven.

"We'll bring the herd down Spring Gulch to Lefthand Canyon, and then on down to the foothills along that stage road," LG said. "We're a slow seven days' drive outta Denver as it stands. Can start the roundup right away."

"First thing in the morning," Til instructed. "LG, get the tack and the irons sorted today. Emmanuel, if you would get the chuck wagon loaded, I've already hired on a few more cowhands. They should be riding in sometime this evening."

Chapter 7
Grand Lake

The floor in the courthouse was dirty, as it was. Betty Anne Hartworst, the quarrelsome clerk, swept it out every day — except on the weekends like this. When Emerson and Griff brought Bill in the day before, muddy from the trail, they tracked it all in. In addition to being elderly and quarrelsome, Betty Anne was a behemoth rotund lady with white hair and a snippety tongue. Even without any spilled chili on those hardwood floors, Griff knew the woman was going to pitch a fit when she saw the mud. But that was part of her job, and Griff had other chores to do. He couldn't be sweeping out the courthouse every time he tracked in mud.

Griff led Vincent inside past the reception desk.

"Hoping for anything from this prisoner," Griff warned him, "is hoping for plenty. He ain't been speaking with me."

"It is my experience that men of this frame often seek the posterity of namesake."

"Good luck," Griff told him.

He set the tin plate on the big oak desk. It was getting too hot to hold. His thumb came out covered in chili, so he licked it off. It was spicy, and Griff suspected it was made with venison. Otto's celestial tended to use a lot of deer and elk. Sometimes they had moose. There were moose in the area. He found a cool spot again, picked it back up, and then led Vincent down the dim corridor. The hallway was lined with photographs of judges, Supreme Court justices, and senators. They all looked solemn, and Vincent thought it was amazing what a little lying could accomplish. Maybe he should have been a play-actor, a thespian. He thought that he was doing pretty good at it, which was not a real surprise since he did enjoy Shakespeare. Vincent saw a production of *King Lear* in Creede once and enjoyed it thoroughly — even though he never discussed the event with Bill at the time, or any of the boys for that matter. Bill would have seen it as a weakness that he even went in the theatre in the first place. Not now, of course. His play-acting was serving a useful purpose, one that Bill was certainly profiting from.

"It is possible he will speak," Vincent suggested to Griff. "If nothing else than to rant self-accolades. Seen it before."

Griff didn't acknowledge the comment. It was possible but unlikely. They came out of the hallway into the backroom where the jail cell was. With the cold front and the low clouds, the room with the high tiny window was rather gloomy.

"Breakfast time," Griff announced.

Bill was lying on a cot huddled in his blanket, and he didn't seem to notice or care. Griff suspected the man was still angry over being caught, being thumped on the head, and being tied to a mule. Not to mention they lost his hat on the trail somewhere — which was an insult to any man.

"Got some chuck," Griff said again. He stepped up to the cell door and stared down at the man sternly.

"What're you serving?" Bill finally asked in a lazy voice.

"What it is don't matter...ain't a buffet."

There was a tray slot in the otherwise vertical bars. Griff stuck the plate through and held it expectantly, but Bill did not make a move or even bother looking up. That was irritating.

"Got two seconds, then you're eating off the floor."

With a big sigh, Bill got to his feet and stared dully at Griff. Then he noticed Vincent. He raised his eyebrows and brightened noticeably.

"Paper's come along," Griff told him. "Wants to hear tell — all about your zest and truculence."

Bill strolled across the jail cell, stepping up close and faced Griff through the bars. Griff did not care for his look.

"Mebbe you'll make the papers."

Bill reached out for the plate.

"I'll draw the headlines in this pissy little town."

Feigning for the plate, Bill grabbed onto Griff's wrist instead. Griff dropped the plate, and chili and applesauce fell on the floor as he jerked around. But Bill had a tight grip and would not let go.

Vincent, the faux newspaperman, came up from behind and rammed his weight hard into Griff's back, pinning him against the bars.

"Dammit!" Griff cried out in surprise.

Bill pulled hard on the deputy's arm to keep him in place. Vincent grabbed Griff's hair and began smashing his head against the cell. The bars rang loudly with each percussive hit. Griff's brow split open, his nose made a loud *crack* and blood poured out.

"Got you, you rube!" Bill shouted.

But the Deputy Sheriff of Grand County was no longer conscious and sagged. Vincent relaxed his grip and stepped back.

Bill let go of Griff's wrist and let him drop heavily onto the floor. Blood continued to ooze from his nose and brow.

"Keys."

"Right here," Vincent replied, digging into Griff's vest pocket. He quickly opened up the lock and swung the door open. The two men looked at each other quietly for a moment.

"Mr. Judas Furlong, I presume," Bill said with exaggerated politeness.

"Mr. Bill Ewing," he answered, equally as cordial. "That'll cost you thirty pieces."

"Bleeding a little there," Bill noted.

Vincent followed Bill's eyes down to his sleeve. There was a red seep coming through the fabric.

"Now I have to dress that *again*," Vincent complained bitterly. He turned and kicked Griff in the side. But of course, Griff was not aware of anything and did not feel it.

"Pecker shot me," Vincent added and spat on Griff. Back in Kinsey City, after Emerson Greer had waylaid Bill, Vincent had managed to dash through the thick dynamite smoke and make for the woods — but Griff took a quick shot and caught him in the forearm, though it did not slow him down as he ran.

"Let's get him inside," said Bill.

However, Vincent knelt down, took Griff's gun from its holster and pressed the barrel against the back of the deputy's head.

"One shot," Bill warned, gritting his teeth. "And this whole town's upon us."

But Vincent did not move. He kept the gun pressed against Griff's skull and tapped his finger on the trigger guard. Vincent really wanted to shoot him. Not only to return the favor but to make him pay for ruining his good clothes. Blood did not come out easy once it set and Vincent went to great lengths to make sure he was dressed properly every day. He had barely gotten it out the first time and even hand-stitched the sleeve with a needle and thread. That was no easy feat for someone riding the trail, dodging the law — and there was clearly no chance of finding a launderer in this town under these circumstances. Vincent had no intention of looking unkempt like Granger or the Mexicans, or most of the boys for that matter. He preferred to maintain a sense of nobility about his appearance. It set him apart from the common criminal, and in his mind he was better than the others — better at robbing, killing, and better at getting away with it. A blood-stained sleeve made him feel like he was no longer set apart and that was something he could not abide.

"As it stands, they got no impetus besides a bunged up deputy," Bill reasoned. He kept his voice low as he spoke. He was hoping Vincent would listen to good sense and stay calm. All they had to do was get out of town without causing a ruckus.

Vincent relaxed suddenly and tucked the gun into his belt. "Fine."

Working together, Bill and Vincent dragged Griff into the cell and dumped him on the floor face down in the chili and applesauce.

Chapter 8
Beaver Creek

When his arms locked around its horns, the steer bawled and writhed but Casey twisted and dropped his body weight and they both came down as one.

Casey held the steer down on its side. Behind him, LG rode past him on his sorrel. The sorrel was LG's good cutting horse. He had the rope dallied around the saddle horn. It ran out taut behind him to a resigned calf, which was being dragged along by its hind legs.

"Hook 'em cow!" LG called down to it. Casey ignored the taunt. He was waiting for Edwin to apply the iron and while he waited, he glanced up at LG and shook his head.

The herd was a continual noise of lowing and bellowing. The sky had closed in over the sun again. Dark clouds had bunched up over the peaks to the west and rolled out overhead as far as anyone could see.

One of the new cowhands, Steve McGonkin, bent down and grabbed onto the steer's hind leg. With a grunt he pulled out it straight for a clean brand.

"Hold him tight, Steve."

Pulling on his thick leather gloves, Edwin took one of the irons from the fire. He hustled over to the animal and applied it quickly. The hide sizzled and blackened with the heat and smoke twisted up into the air. It read: *B + C*. The smell of burning hair was strong.

"Alright now, take 'em off," Casey instructed.

Letting go of the steer's leg, Steve picked up a handsaw lying near the fire. It took a few passes on each side to dehorn the unhappy beast.

After Steve got the horns off, Casey relaxed his hold and let the steer jump up. It ran right back into the herd, kicking at the air.

"How many are we taking to town?" Steve asked him.

"Everything in the cow line that can walk," Casey said, wiping dust from his eyes. "Little calves, big calves, mama cows, bull stags. The lot of 'em."

Edwin propped the spent iron back in the fire so it could get hot again. There were several irons in the fire, ready to use.

"We done cut out the yearlings and the 2-year olds, mebbe the last one right there," LG said from the saddle. "Rest of them beeves are branded already."

Casey stepped up to the black calf LG had roped and easily bulldogged it to the muddy ground. The whole area was a cold muddy mess. With a quick movement Steve unlooped LG's rope from its hind feet. He took hold of a leg and stretched it out for the brand. Edwin took a new iron and stepped up to use it.

"Hey, Ima!" LG called out over the herd. "Any mavericks over there?"

A hired hand named Ira sat his horse quietly. He turned and frowned deeply at LG. On impulse, he reached up and twisted the end of his trailing mustache.

"It's *Ira*," he called back. "Name's Ira."

Ira was a droopy-hatted cowpuncher who spoke in monotone — and often monosyllables. He stared forlornly at LG. Ira was from Tulsa, Oklahoma, born in the saddle. His father was a horse breeder, and horses were all Ira knew. At the cookfire, LG told Emmanuel that Ira must have been kicked in the head at least once at some point, which must have knocked out his smarts. Emmanuel knew he was teasing but like usual chose not to josh back. Emmanuel was always careful not to josh around too much, especially with hired hands he did not know. He never met Ira before. Of course, neither had LG, but that did not stop him from joshing the man.

Casey let the black calf go. Jumping and kicking, it ran straight back over to its mama.

Not so quietly, LG said to Casey, "Not sure where Til pulled these waddies from. Must be slim pickings down at them stockyards. I suspect Blocker hired on all the good 'uns."

Casey gave him a sharp glance from under his hat brim. Ira was barely twenty steps away, still twisting his mustache forlornly.

"LG, I swear."

"That ole boy can't hear us! Don't look so guilty," LG said with a smile. "He'll suspect you're talking about him."

"Ain't you just the clown," Casey muttered dryly.

Edwin stepped up to Casey and took off his hat. His hair was matted and dripping. A clear line could be seen where the dirt and sweat stopped and his clean white scalp started. Half of his forehead was pale as the moon.

"Fire sure burning me up."

The kid was breathing pretty heavily. He wiped his forehead with the back of his hand. Even with the cold front, all the men were drenched in sweat from the morning's work — but Edwin had the added burden of standing over the branding fire all day.

"What's the count?" Steve asked. "Lost track after three hunnert head."

"Ain't broke no record," LG said flatly. He waved irritably at the flies.

"Bliss enough, it's a fairly pleasant day," LG continued. "Last year we fought hail storms into June."

Edwin picked up a tin cup and headed off toward the creek. "Guess I'll go count my damn blessings."

The sun never got a chance to melt off the creek ice, and the beaver pond was still frozen over. Crouching on his heels, Edwin smacked the tin cup against the ice and broke through, then dipped his cup into the running water. As soon as it was full, he wasted no time draining it. He dipped it right back in and downed it again.

After four cups, Edwin stood up. Cold water dripped off his chin. He started to walk back towards Casey but swayed and checked himself.

LG was watching him from the saddle with an amused look.

Edwin ran a hand over his face, eyes widening for a moment. He took a step towards the other cowpunchers, but then bent over and folded his arms across his stomach.

"Alright?" Casey called.

"Dizzy. Hard to see."

Casey went over and helped him straighten up. Together, they walked away from the herd, Casey holding him up as they went along. They made it to the forest edge and in among a stand of budding aspen where Edwin promptly collapsed and did not move.

"That crick was mountain snow a couple hours ago," Casey said when he came back.

"Here comes Lee," Steve pointed out.

Lee, another one of the hired hands, rode up just then and halted his horse. He crossed his arms over the saddle horn and relaxed for the first time that day.

"Rufe out there still?" Steve asked him. Rufe was Steve's younger brother.

"Riding herd. With Davis."

"Well, boys, we're gonna get a late start tonight," LG announced. "We'll spend the rest of the afternoon tallying — probably start this herd around supper time at this dandy pace."

All the cowmen looked up in surprise.

"Tonight?" Lee asked. Til had said the B-Cross was in a hurry when he had hired on, but he thought they would at least get a night to rest up before trailing the cattle.

"Yep," LG said.

Lee dismounted. All of them took tin cups over to the creek, but were cautious after watching Edwin drink too much too quick after such a hard morning. They took care to sip it slow and easy.

Casey went over to check on Edwin. The rest of the crew trailed over to the trees to sit for a few minutes. Even LG got off his horse. He brought over a sack full of jerked beef, which he passed around. After spending half the day branding, they all managed to stay pretty warm with the work — but now that they were sitting still, the chill crept right in.

"This is Colorada, boys," LG said in a proverbial tone. "One day it's winter time cold. Next day it's summer time hot. You don't like the weather? Wait a bit and it'll turn."

The sack of beef strips made its way around the group. Another rider trotted up just then and got off his horse. It was Davis.

"Have a bite, Davis," Steve said to him and passed the sack over. "My brother heading in?"

"Not too far behind me."

Several magpies swooped in and perched on the tree limbs overhead. One came down and hopped right up to Edwin, cawing at him for something to eat. It clearly expected a handout and was not shy about asking. Edwin tore off a tiny corner and flicked it at him. The other birds immediately flew down to the ground near Edwin.

"Hear what Til was saying about Blocker?" Casey asked.

"Yep — the XIT," said LG.

"What's that?" Lee asked them. "What exit?"

Casey began drawing letters in the snow as he spoke.

"X, I, T...the XIT."

"New brand," LG explained. "Down in Tejas. Largest cattle operation I ever heard of. Three million acres! Had to ask Til twice."

"That's half the Panhandle," Casey added, nodding for emphasis.

Edwin sat up, still looking unwell. Casey's dog, Hopper, came over to the magpies to see if they were eating something he wanted. The birds spread their wings and swooped back up into the tree, cawing at the dog.

"Well, damn, what else did Til say?" Edwin asked weakly.

"Apparently, just here in November they bought up over a hundred thousand cattle," LG explained. "Get this...paid out one an' a third *million* dollars."

"Who on God's green earth can afford something like that?" Edwin asked, unable to get his mind around the sum.

"Syndicate up in Chicago, story goes," Casey told him. "Rounded up the funds. Folks all the way in England buying up stock."

"It's big, boy," LG told him. "They're stringing fence right now. Digging wells, putting up windmills. Nothing like it."

"Til's worried," Casey said. "Thinks with the Great Die-Up in Wyoming and Dakota, the XIT's gonna move quick to take over the market. And the King. Small outfits better move now if we hope to keep up with the game."

At that point Ira walked up to the group, having emerged from the herd on foot. His side was smeared with mud and snow and the crown of his hat was mashed in.

"LG, ain't no more yearlings," Ira announced. "Looks like we done roped 'em all."

Davis looked him over.

"Where's your horse?"

Ira flushed. He removed his hat, slapping at his legs to knock the mud off. He was silent for a few moments, pulling at his mustache. The breeze kicked up for a few seconds, causing the budding branches overhead to stir. LG grinned broadly, knowingly.

"Where'd he throw you?"

Ira looked abashed.

"Somewhere betwixt the first n' second jump. I cannot recollect."

Chapter 9
Grand Lake

"Bet there's a slew of ordnance locked up in there," Vincent mentioned to Bill, indicating the sheriff's office. "No one's going to bother us. This town is quiet."

He smirked, adding, "Quiet as a church."

Bill wasn't sure what the time was, but he suspected people would be letting out of church at any moment. The Methodists were right there on the corner, and he could guess this town had its share of Baptists and Presbyterians. This seemed like a churchy town to Bill. All morning long he was forced to listen to hymns humming through the thin courthouse walls.

"Jailbreak on a Sunday morning," Bill cooed and smoothed his hair, checking his reflection in the glass. "Lord have mercy! Where are the boys?"

"Out by the lake. Granger probably gut-shot them Mexicans by now. Ned's leading that sheriff to the wrong side of nowhere, even as we speak."

Pushing open the courthouse door, Vincent strolled nonchalantly into the brisk air. The clouds were certainly darker than they were an hour ago, and collecting fast. The sun had disappeared entirely and Mount Craig's summit was gone now, too, cut off by the lowering sky.

Digging his hands deep in his pockets, Vincent headed straight toward the sheriff's office. Bill let him lead the way — he wanted to get his bearings. Those lawmen had brought him in tied to the back of a mule. Not only was that a humiliating mode of travel but it also prevented him from getting a look at where he was.

"No one's about," Vincent said, feeling good. "Let's go knock."

It took a minute to cross the wide street, then up the short staircase onto the landing. Bill turned and looked around. A cold breeze blew across the frozen lake. He watched swirls roll off the white surface. The swirls swept right towards them. Bill hunched up as it hit, but Vincent wasn't paying attention and hooted with the shivers. Bill frowned at his old compadre. At least the man had a coat on. Bill didn't know where his was and wasn't sure what that damn sheriff did with it after they locked him up. And of course his hat was long gone.

The front door was locked up, but Vincent had Griff's keys. The first six he tried didn't work.

"What's taking so long?" Bill asked impatiently. He cupped his hands and blew into them several times.

Vincent finally found the right one, and they went inside immediately. The sheriff's office was so hot, it was like entering a sweat lodge. Bill saw why. A cast iron woodstove sat against one wall — and it was pumping out the heat! Bill went right over and nearly hugged it. He could imagine the deputy relaxing here all morning long — while all he gave Bill was a ratty wool blanket. They could have at least left him his coat!

Vincent peeked out the front window. The street was still cold, windy and empty. He pulled the thick green curtains closed. Bill turned so his backside could thaw. Curiously, he studied the office. It was not much of an office, really. There was a desk, a cabinet, two benches, a coat rack, the wood stove and a closet. He saw a nice coat hanging on the coat rack and tried it on. It was a thick rancher's coat with what appeared to be buffalo lining. There were gloves tucked down in one sleeve, and they would certainly be helpful. What a pleasant surprise. It was a nicer coat than he had in the first place. Given his poor treatment, and the fact that his breakfast was on the floor back in the courthouse cell, at least he was getting a decent coat out of all this.

Vincent wasted no time and went to the desk, yanking open both drawers — one with each hand. The drawers slid right out and dropped heavily onto the floor, spilling paper sheaves and pencils everywhere.

Bill gave Vincent a reproachful look.

But Vincent merely shrugged off Bill's reproof.

"No need for tippety toes," Vincent told him. "All the good folk are in their pews."

The buffalo coat seemed to fit Bill fine. Maybe a little tight when he stretched his arms, but it would work. He found a pipe in one pocket and a leather pouch in the other. He opened the pouch and smelled the tobacco. It had cherry undertones.

"And in their bide," Bill mused, "*Hell is empty, and all the devils are here.*"

Vincent held his breath. Bill was quoting Shakespeare! Did he know Vincent had gone to the theatre in Creede that one time? Vincent thought he had gotten in and out of there without any of the boys knowing. He glanced at Bill who was sniffing the pipe bowl. Or was this coincidence? Bill *did* seem to know most of the things that went on. Vincent watched him from the corner of his eye, but Bill did not seem interested in taking the reference any further.

Vincent relaxed, and returned to ransacking. He scattered the papers around with his boot and then went to the closet and turned the knob but it was locked. He picked up the desk chair and smashed it against the door. The door knob fell off but the door still would not open.

"Here we go," Bill said.

In one shadowy corner was a tall walnut cabinet. Gently, he ran his fingers over the smooth veneer and black iron latchwork. It was a tall cabinet and ran all the way to the ceiling.

Giving up on the closet, Vincent came over to get a closer look.

"Gun cabinet?"

"Keys."

Vincent handed Griff's keys to Bill. There were about ten keys on the ring. Bill fanned them out but they all looked the same in this light. He picked the first one and tried it in the lock. It did not fit so he tried another. Vincent leaned in over his shoulder. He had already been through the keys once at the front door, and remembered one of the keys was black and fancy.

"Try that one," he said, pointing at the fancy black key.

The front door opened and two men walked inside the office.

Bill and Vincent turned around.

It was Sheriff Emerson Greer and Ben Leavick, the mercantile store owner and operator.

They stopped in midstride.

The moment wore off.

Emerson Greer suddenly bolted across the room and tackled Bill, knocking him hard to the floor. Bill rolled around frantically, trying to break free. He landed several punches, but the sheriff grabbed onto Bill's wrists and hung on. In the scuffle, Greer's sidearm clattered out of its holster and was knocked under the desk.

Ben Leavick was absolutely shocked. The very same prisoner they locked up in the courthouse cell was standing right there, rooting around the sheriff's gun cabinet. He didn't know who the other fellow was, but it didn't matter. The shock dissipated, and Ben made a run at Vincent.

But Vincent remembered he had Griff's pistol tucked in his belt, so he pulled it out as fast as he could. He had just enough time to club Ben on the forehead. Ben's knees gave out — but he fell into Vincent's legs and knocked him down like a bowling pin.

Blood leaked down Ben's forehead and ran in his eyes. He reached up to feel his face, and his hand came away slick with blood. As soon as he saw it, Ben felt his stomach turn weak.

Somehow, Vincent managed to hang onto Griff's gun. He scrambled up to his knees and noticed that Ben was distracted by his bloody hand, so he leaned right over and clubbed him on the head a second time. Ben crumpled to the floor.

Getting to his feet, Vincent went around the desk to check on Bill — who was still wrestling with the sheriff on the floor. Vincent pointed the gun at Greer, but he could not get a clear shot and wasn't sure he should shoot even if he got one. What if the bullet passed right through the sheriff and hit Bill? What about the sound of the discharge itself? Bill had been fairly adamant about not shooting the deputy back in the courthouse.

Vincent was not sure what to do. He tried waiting for the struggle to play itself out, but they were still rolling around fighting and it did not look like it was going to end. While he thought it over, Vincent uncocked the hammer and lowered the gun. Perhaps Bill should just fight this thing out himself. He sat on the corner of the desk and watched.

"What's wrong with you?" Bill said through gritted teeth. "Shoot him!"

"Don't want to plug you in the process."

From his position on the corner of the desk, all Vincent could see of Bill was his angry eyes peering over the sheriff's shoulder. The room was basically quiet, except the sound of bootheels thumping against the floorboards.

"Shoot him!"

"Would be nice," Vincent said.

Emerson Greer realized another man was standing over him with a gun. Twisting, he kicked out and caught Vincent's shin, causing Vincent to slip off the desk.

On the other side of the room, Ben's eyes fluttered. He slowly got to his knees. His vision was blurry. Ben wasn't sure where he was or why he could not see clearly. Ben heard the scuffle and suddenly remembered he had blood in his eyes. Using his sleeve, he wiped his face so he could see better.

Vincent did not notice that Ben Leavick had gotten up. He had taken his place on the desk corner again, and was enjoying the fight. Every few seconds, the two men rolled across the floor one way or another. Bill would roll over and carry the sheriff along with him. Then the sheriff would roll and take Bill with him. It was entertaining.

"Shoot him!"

"What if it goes on through and I end up shooting you? You won't like that, Bill."

Emerson did not want to be shot in the back, so he rolled on over once more, dragging Bill around on top of him. Emerson thought it would be better to have Bill between himself and Vincent's gun. He realized what a bad situation this was.

Emerson broke his grip and grabbed Bill by the throat. He squeezed as hard as he could and Bill's face turned red and he sputtered.

"Alright…seen enough of this," Vincent said in a tone of exasperation. He stepped forward and wriggled the gun between the two men's bodies. He pressed the barrel against Emerson's chest and fired.

The discharge was much louder than he expected — the small room and everything in it seemed to rattle.

Emerson's grip loosened at once. He collapsed on the floor.

Bill staggered up to his feet, coughing, and hunched there trying to breathe. He pressed his hand over his left ear.

"Blew my hearing!" Bill shouted angrily at Vincent.

"I'm shot!" Emerson called out.

Ben snapped out of the fog that had filled his head. He wiped his eyes once more on his sleeve and looked around. He saw Emerson Greer lying on the floor near the desk. Bill and Vincent were standing over him and the acrid smell of gunpowder filled the room.

"Black muley son of a bitch!" Ben yelled. He leaped to his feet and ran headlong at Vincent.

Bill saw him coming.

"Watch out!"

Vincent turned around and pounded his fist into Ben's eye. Ben went down for a third time, hitting his head on the desk. Outside, they heard a door slam.

"Quiet, quiet!" Vincent whispered sharply.

He immediately crossed the room, parting the thick green curtains with his finger.

People were coming.

He took a deep breath to compose himself, ran his fingers through his hair, set the gun on the window ledge and stepped out into the chilly air.

The barkeeper, Otto, was running up from the Grand Placer Saloon. He had a look of clear concern on his face. Vincent knew he must have heard the gunshot. Someone else was coming up the street from the opposite direction, from the apothecary. It was Roy Caldwell.

It was play-acting time. Vincent stood on the landing and leaned far over the rail, making a big show of peering around the sheriff's office, down the side street, as if the gunshot had come from there.

"Hear that?" Vincent called to Otto.

Both men ran up to the bottom of the stairs and looked up at him questioningly. Vincent pointed down the side street. They followed his gesture but did not see what he was pointing at. That was, of course, because there was nothing to see.

"Everything alright?" Otto asked.

"Heard a gunshot!" Roy Caldwell exclaimed.

"We did, too!" Vincent said innocently. "Came from down there, somewhere. Your deputy just went to check on it."

Otto and Roy looked at each other. Something did not seem right to either of them. The gunshot sounded like it came from inside. Not outside.

"Griff?" Otto said uncertainly. "Well, then."

Vincent gave them a confident smile.

"That's right. Griff. He just ran off down there to see about it."

"Who is this?" Roy asked Otto, pointing at Vincent.

"He was in the Placer earlier."

"Mr. Judas Furlong — Rocky Mountain News," Vincent said. "Doing an interview with your deputy. Quite a fellow."

Once more, curiously, Otto looked down the side street. He did not see or hear anything from that direction. Griff was nowhere to be seen.

"Probably someone oiling their gun and it went off, you know how it goes," Vincent said, tipping his hat. "Take care now."

"And you, sir," Otto replied. "Come with me, Roy. I've got chili on the menu."

"Chili?"

Roy was confused. Why would he want chili? He had a nice stove in the apothecary where he cooked all his meals. He was a lifelong bachelor and did not even own a home. Roy lived in the apothecary — he had built a nice room in the loft — and had everything he needed right there.

"White-tail deer. Best take of the season. Come on,"

For some reason, mainly the look in Otto's eyes, Roy decided not to argue. They walked down to the saloon together. Vincent watched them for a minute and then stepped back inside the sheriff's office.

Bill stood near the window, watching through the curtains.

"Don't know if they took that or not," Bill supposed.

He stepped over Sheriff Emerson Greer, whose chest was bubbling with blood. Greer was not making any noises, but he was alert — his eyes followed Bill wherever he went in the room.

Kneeling, Bill picked up the keys from the floor and noticed Emerson's gun under the desk. Bill looked down at the sheriff and shrugged.

"Sorry, bud."

Bill took the gun, stepped over Greer, and went back to the gun cabinet. He tried the black key that Vincent had pointed out earlier and the lock clicked. Bill was relieved to find a variety of Colts, Winchesters, and a sizable cache of ammunition. Vincent leaned in and whistled.

"Pick your treats," he said. "And off we go."

Chapter 10
Ward
Colorado

"Julianna Purcell!"

Josephine's face sparkled, and she waved one arm high above her head.

The Miser's Brewery was a tempest. So many people were inside that no one could even hear the three-piece band. Between the banjo, mandolin or violin, none of the strings made it over the chatter. It was snowing outside, and the shawl covering Julianna's head was flecked with white powder. She pulled off the damp weave and ran her fingers through her long chestnut hair. It was much warmer inside the building than it was outside in the chilly air.

"I've found gossips and crows," Julianna announced lightly. Besides Josephine, there were two other women at the table. "Josephine. Vera, Hazel," she counted aloud. "Ella is absent."

"Corralling a young maverick," Josephine said.

"Spinning the wedding ring," Hazel added with her quirky smile, twirling her finger around in a circular pattern — she was miming a trick roper's loop.

Julianna sat down in a chair they had saved for her. It hadn't been easy to save the chair, either. Many people in the big room were standing, it was so crowded. Sipping coffees and teas, the ladies were enjoying the overall bustle of the restaurant when Julianna arrived.

"If anyone can take the snarls out of a rope," Hazel went on, "she is as sportsmanlike a woman as any of the cowboys on the range."

Vera shook her head and muttered, "Cutting more than she can brand."

Julianna just smiled. These were all friends here, even if they chided one another.

"Look over there," Josephine said, nodding toward the far corner.

The Miser's Brewery was one of the few two-story buildings in town. The eatery was upstairs, which afforded a view. A large picture window filled up half the south wall and overlooked the wooded mountain valley. White blots of snow dropped past the glass.

"What should govern my attention?" Julianna asked, her eyes searching the crowd.

"Corner table."

With a smile and touch of curiosity, Julianna shifted forward in her seat to see better. Vera and Hazel leaned apart so she could see past them.

"I see a solitary man," she observed. "Platinum blonde hair. Leonine mustache."

The man she spotted was dining alone and dressed immaculately. He looked pretty gaunt. She noticed his dark eyes were very direct, and he was quietly measuring everyone around him as he ate. He had not yet noticed the ladies watching him, or if he had he was ignoring them.

"Thin frame. A very fine-looking suit," she went on. "And the gentleman likes his whiskey."

He lifted a kerchief to his mouth and started coughing violently. They could hear the fit, even over all the noise. Julianna still couldn't hear the band, but she *could* hear the sandy cough.

"And the gentleman is wracked with consumption," Hazel pointed out in a hushed tone. She was obviously excited.

"Must I trace it out plainly?" Josephine said impatiently. "John...Henry..."

Julianna turned to her sharply.

"Holliday?"

The women all shushed her at the same time — their collective hush drew several sidelong looks. But Julianna only giggled. She knew they were trying to be coy, and she was deliberately being louder than she needed to be. It was fun.

"A dentist in Ward! How novel."

Julianna's voice was playful, but Josephine's face went red.

"That's really him. I'm *not* mistaken!"

Somewhere outside, a dull explosion echoed through the mountains. Ward was one of the many mining towns in the backcountry of Colorado — and detonations were so commonplace no one noticed.

"Maybe these miners need dental exams," Julianna said with a spritely look around her. "Hygienists they are not."

"Something tells me he's not pulling teeth these days," Vera muttered, darkly. Vera was a mutterer. She twisted around in her seat, frowning at Holliday.

Julianna sighed. They were all obsessed with this subject. In fact, the ladies seemed to be in an unalterably serious mood. Julianna didn't want to be serious. She had driven her buckboard all the way up the canyon from Gold Hill. It had been a month since she was in Ward last — the biggest town in the area, and the closest thing to big city culture she had. The Miser's Brewery served a delicious roast and scalloped potato dish, and she had been looking forward to an easy time with good friends and a tasty meal. She sighed a second time.

"This is not a terminus town," she told them, giving up. "No railroad, no gambling house. Why would such a man alight here?"

"Avoidance," Hazel offered. "From pursuants...men of darker intent."

From her tone it was clear Hazel hoped that was not the case. Julianna hoped it *was*. A little excitement sounded appealing.

"Heard about that fellow Ryan?" Vera said in her muttery voice. "Denver — last fall. Holliday dealt cards at Babbit's house. Ryan pulls a gun. But Holliday has a knife hidden on a lanyard, hung about his neck and no one knew it was there...until Ryan got cut up dead."

How delightful. Where was the waiter? The miners at the next table had big plates of roast and it smelled good. Julianna looked hopefully toward the bar.

"Ward's no boom town. Probably on his way up to Leadville," Josephine reasoned. "Faro. Man's a vulture. Feeds off those poor souls trying to scratch out a living in the placers and dredges."

Hazel turned and threw Holliday another curious look.

"Doesn't look too healthy to me."

Across the room, he was still trying to suppress the coughing fit. Holliday's face was white and his frail-looking body shook with the effort. It seemed like it was not going to end.

Finally, the talk turned.

"And how is the Commodore this month?" Hazel asked her, suddenly polite and proper.

"Well enough," Julianna replied, brightening. "Still the reclusive curmudgeon we all know and love."

Josephine was still put out over her friend's lack of interest in Doc Holliday. Josephine had been the first one to recognize the man, and the other two had gotten excited about it. Why didn't Julianna? Things like this did not happen in Ward. It was a boring little town. It made her mad. Plus, Julianna and Josephine were closer friends than they were with Hazel and Vera. She felt a mean streak coming on, leaned over and looked Julianna in the eye.

"This world is rapidly changing, my dear. Your father is stuck in the old days — he needs to get with the program."

Julianna felt her stomach tighten up. Usually when they all got together like this, the talk was lighthearted gossip. But sometimes it was bickery — times when it took a sour turn and rolled on like a runaway train. Julianna realized this was one of those runaway train talks. Any good humor she had when she came in the door drained away.

The other two joined in with Josephine.

"Colorado is a state now," Hazel said crisply. "Custer's dead."

Vera nodded and said, "Sand Creek was over *ten years* ago."

Julianna frowned. That fluttery feeling in her stomach got worse.

"Well, now. I'll try and remember to pass on your sentiments. I'm sure my father will appreciate the good news."

She tried to wave down the bartender, since the waiter was on the far side of the room. Julianna didn't want to talk about her father with these women anymore. Why were they all in such an abrasive mood, anyway? She did not care one whit about Custer, Sand Creek or Doc Holliday or his dry raspy cough. All she had wanted was a good meal, one she didn't have to cook — and some light conversation with friends. But now what she really wanted was a big glass of wine.

It was true her father was a colorful figure. Up until last year, the Commodore used to spend time in Ward and succeeded in making a spectacle of himself. Everyone knew who he was. That didn't help. He was a little eccentric and Julianna knew it, but the subject of her father was still very delicate for her anyway.

The look on her face must have conveyed what she was thinking.

"Oh, honey," Josephine said gently, deflating. She shot Vera and Hazel a harsh glare. She touched Julianna's forearm in a kind way. "We meant nothin' by it."

But Julianna turned her eyes to the large picture window and the snow falling outside. It was late in the day and only a matter of time before the sun went down.

"The tea is splendid this evening," Hazel said. "Codfish on the menu."

Chapter 11
Beaver Creek

Whenever the cloud cover was low and dark like this, Casey knew it was just a matter of time before it either sleeted, hailed or lightninged. Just as he started to say something to LG, it started spitting sleet up and down the valley. All the early wildflowers sagged with it — the larkspur, lousewort, the astor. April sure was a fickle time of the year, Casey surmised, and slid off his horse.

"Need me one of these," Edwin told Casey, indicating his slicker.

He came over to where LG and Casey were standing, with his hands jammed in his coat pockets. Edwin had lost a button somewhere and was using thread from the chuckwagon to hold it together.

"Need you a thump on the head," LG said to him.

Just the day before, it had been sunny and bright. Now here it was, damp and gray, with a stillness hanging in the air. LG and Casey both unfurled their slickers. Edwin noticed Casey wearing his the other night and had been wondering about it ever since.

"What is this damn thing anyways?"

"Fish slicker," Casey told him.

He ran his arms through the sleeves and thumbed the buttons into place. The entire thing ran from his neck to the tops of his boots, camel-yellow with a narrow red collar. LG's was identical except black.

Edwin reached over and touched Casey's sleeve.

"Feels waxy or something."

"They wear these on the high seas, them sailors," LG told him.

"Keeps the rain out purty good," Casey said. "Snow, too."

"This time of the year, up here in God's country," LG went on, "surprised we ain't got hail pecking on us."

Their hats were getting matted with wet sleet. LG flicked his hat brim to dislodge what he could. Edwin could see the hired cowhands loitering near the herd. The cattle were bunched up in a wide bend of the creek. Even from this short distance, the falling sleet made the herd look blurry.

"Not the best weather for this," Casey said, looking back at the herd. "But I suppose we best string 'em out — up the valley. My note papers gonna be soggy."

"Could have been *branding* in this shit," Edwin observed, sagely.

"Yep."

"Gotta swap my cutting horse for my circle horse," LG announced. "A'fore we get to tallying."

LG remounted his sorrel, careful to drape the billows of his slicker to cover over his saddle. He clicked his tongue, and the horse carried him away. Edwin and Casey watched him go. The sleet quickly blurred him out, too.

"Come on," Casey said to Edwin. "Let's watch this."

The two of them climbed back on their horses and followed LG to the corral. When they got near the bunkhouse, they caught sight of the orange cookfire flames, sputtering. Emmanuel was huddled over it, feeding in branches to keep it going. He was too busy to even notice them go by.

"Hey Gyp!" LG called. "Lend me a hand."

The new wrangler, Gyp — an older man with thin silver hair and a tall sugarloaf hat — came over to help while LG got the tack off his sorrel. He released the cinch strap, pulled it up and draped it over the saddle. He carried the saddle over to the wet fence and perched it on the top rail.

"Got that ol' boy?"

"I got him."

Gyp had a purple polka-dot silk neckerchief wrapped loosely around his neck. He dipped his chin down into it for a minute to warm up. His nose was red with the cold, and he had been sneezing all morning. So much so, that Emmanuel had given him a bottle of *Famous Francis' Cure-All Ointment* to sip from. Emmanuel bought the ointment at a traveling circus in Omaha two seasons prior from a dark man named Suneil. Suneil told Emmanuel he was born in Calcutta but raised in Boston, before joining the circus as a snake charmer. He also told the cook that the ointment cured him of snake poison, after all frequent bites were hazards of the trade, so surely it would work on arthritic knuckles and the backdoor trots.

LG took his rope and slipped into the corral. Shaking it out, he stepped towards the remuda. The horses were wary — none of them ever liked being caught.

Gyp held the sorrel by the bridle, watching as LG moved slowly into the horse herd.

"How's our jigger boss?" Casey asked him.

"He's doing alright," Gyp replied, talking about himself in the third person.

The horses skittered around like fish in a stock tank.

It was good to have all this help. Whenever Til brought on new hands, he frequently chose pairs who were already friendly. Lee and Davis used to ride together up in Estes Park. Rufe and Steve McGonkin were brothers. Gyp knew Ira — at one point, they both worked down at the Iliff Ranch and knew each other from those days. Til hired them in pairs, which was his normal practice.

"I can see this cavvy has the lion's share of half-broke broncs and spoilt outlaws," Gyp said and smiled.

"Aw, just our winter mounts," Casey told him. "Of course, half of them ought be condemned."

"This sorrel right here — one of the finest cutting horses I ever saw," Gyp said with genuine admiration.

Casey nodded.

"The man knows his horseflesh."

The horses suddenly broke into a run, circling the corral and kicking up clods of mud as they passed by. LG stepped after them quietly. He shook out a loop and had his eye on one horse in particular: all black except a stark white face.

"Going after Specter," Casey rightly noted.

LG slowly rotated the wide loop over his head several times. On the final turn he whipped it hard and stepped in to let it fly. The loop dropped around the horse's neck, and immediately Specter bolted. But LG leaned into it, holding on tight and digging in his heels. The other horses scattered, but LG had the one he wanted.

"Someone hold him down."

Gyp brought LG's sorrel into the corral and cut him loose. Then he eared down the black so LG could go get his saddle on him. LG cinched it tight and slipped a bridle on. Then he took a wide step over Specter's back and settled into place, gathering the reins in his hand.

"Sorriest horse I ever forked!" LG shouted and nodded.

Gyp let go and ran for the rail.

Specter, the black horse with the stark white face, wasted no time in scrambling up. Crow-hopping, twisting about, the horse went at it — trying hard to throw LG. But the cowman just waved his hat and whooped, sitting easy in the saddle.

The capering went on for some time. Edwin, Casey and Gyp watched in amusement.

"*Hoo-ee!*" Edwin shouted.

Specter pitched high and twisted. As he did, LG's slicker flapped and popped — which of course just made the horse pitch even harder. He wanted to shake the rider off and wasted no effort to make it happen. Quite suddenly, Specter quit pitching and began racing around the corral — hoping to rake off LG's knees on the fenceline.

As they came around, Gyp pulled open the gate so LG could ride on through. The horse shot out the gate and took off into the sleet. As soon as they passed through, Gyp closed it tight so none of the other horses could escape.

It did not take long and LG disappeared in the gray sheen.

"Got a *number* of pitching horses in there," Gyp reflected. "Any gentle ones?"

Casey shrugged.

"That may be the worst one we got."

Riding back up the valley, LG came back into view. As he got back to the corral, the horse finally resigned himself to a controlled trot, nostrils flaring and breathing heavily.

"See that?" LG asked them as he rode by. "This ol' boy pulling cork screws and side-throws."

He kept right on moving and circled toward the cattle with a wave.

"Let's go see about some coffee," Casey suggested.

Casey, Edwin and Gyp left their horses tied to the willows and headed through the slushy grass to the cookfire. Casey's toes were already cold and wet — the soles of his boots each had a matching dime-sized hole. He meant to find a cobbler once they got to Denver, but that was still a week away.

Big snowflakes were starting to come down with the sleet. Any grass in the valley they could see yesterday was gone now. Only the thistles were unhampered by the weather, standing tall like fenceposts.

Chapter 12
Grand Lake

"Emerson Greer's been shot!"

Ben Leavick stood in the doorway, calling out. But the wind blew his words away. Main Street was empty and he didn't see anyone in either direction. He heard a hammer banging at a horseshoe several streets over and there was organ music in between the gusts.

He reached up and touched his forehead again. It was sticky and his legs felt like they were filled with water, which made standing hard. How many times had he been hit in the head? He leaned on the handrail to get his balance. The courthouse and the apothecary seemed to switch places and he rubbed his eyes, but his knuckles were bloody and it only made things worse.

The winter wind did help to clear his head. When Ben first came to, inside the office, he felt overheated and too dizzy to even get to his feet. Crawling outside, the cold wind gave him a little clarity — enough to get up and call out for help.

Ben heard the front door of the Grand Placer bang open. He watched Otto slip in the slick snow and go down, banging a knee hard on the ground. He got right back up and ran towards the sheriff's office, almost sliding the whole way in his flat-bottomed boots.

"Leavick!" Otto yelled. "What in God's name?"

"He's been shot! Get in here, Otto."

Leavick turned and teetered back inside.

"I knew somethin' was wrong with all that!" Otto berated himself. "I sure did suspect it."

"What's the trouble?"

Merle Hastings was dressed sharply and still held his hat in his hand. The noon bell was ringing, the service had just let out, and a procession of churchgoers was filing outside. The steeple rose up in a tall silhouette against the storm clouds.

"Greer's been shot," Otto told Merle, and rushed up the landing.

"I should've come right back with my shotgun. I should have," he added.

Merle Hastings wondered if he had heard right. Merle owned the biggest ranch operation in the county — he had 3000 acres outside of town. Every week he brought his wife, kids, and all the hands that worked for him to Sunday service. Before most of the mines shut down last year, Merle had been a major beef supplier for the area. Now he had a great deal of cattle but only a fraction of the buyers. Most of the eateries had shut down except the Grand Placer and Sherman's, but he sold to both of them. They offered choice cuts of steak at reasonable prices. The citizens who still remained in Grand Lake ate well, even if much of the mining had petered out.

Betty Anne Hortworst had been bickering with Merle Hastings about how best to get wine stains out of fabric, and the virtues of parental discipline. Merle's two young sons had been sitting next to Mrs. Hortworst during the service, and their inability to sit still caused a communion tray to overturn in her lap.

But, as soon as she heard the sheriff had been shot, Betty Anne Hortworst became stone silent. Merle looked at her sideways. He had never seen the woman with nothing to say. Being the courthouse clerk, she spoke with Emerson Greer almost every day. This was quite a shock, even for the crotchety Mrs. Hortworst.

Sleet started to pelt them from above. The church crowd congregated around the landing and everyone spoke in mainly tense whispers. Sheriff Greer was well known and well liked. It was hard to imagine anyone shooting Emerson Greer — and on a Sunday morning of all days.

"Stay with the boys, Nettie."

"Be careful, Merle!"

Their two young blonde-haired boys, Walter and Remington — or Wally and Remmy as they were called when there was no mischief — huddled against her billowy skirt. They could tell something serious was going on and intuitively understood any further antics would be severely reprimanded. But that was okay, since they had the fresh memory of the communion fiasco to bask in.

Merle put on his hat and rushed up the steps into the office. Otto and Ben were kneeling over the sheriff. Merle crouched down beside them, trying not to step in the dark pool of blood.

"Emerson!" Merle said loudly. He reached down and softly tapped on his cheek. Emerson's eyes focused for a moment and he nodded at Merle. When he tried to speak, red bubbles came up instead.

"Let's move him," Otto said to Merle. "They got a cot in the back."

Emerson groaned sourly when the three of them lifted him up. Blood oozed from his chest wound, and his shirt and vest were completely soaked.

"He's been shot good. Need to call for the doctor," Otto said.

They set the sheriff down on the narrow bed in the other room. Otto wiped his hands on his thighs, pushed past Merle and Ben, and headed back outside.

As Merle and Ben watched, Emerson's breathing got even more raspy. Thinking how he could staunch the blood, Ben wadded up a corner of the sheet and pressed it on the wound.

"Who the hell shot him?"

"That prisoner they brought in," Ben muttered. "And another fellow was with him...they were here when we rode in. *Right inside* this very office."

The shock of it all was wearing off and Ben's anger was rising — he still could not believe what happened.

"Em and I were out tracking the getaways. Lost the trail above timberline out west a day's ride."

His face pinched up as he spoke.

"Must've circled around and come for town. Sprung their man."

Otto stood on the landing. He placed his hands stiffly on the rail and gripped it as tight as he could. His knuckles turned white. Looking down, he saw Nettie Hastings holding her two blonde boys while the chilly gusts blew the snow and sleet around in the air. Merle's cowhands were all there, too. They took it upon themselves to spread out around the building with their six-shooters drawn. Looking at all the faces, Otto did not see the doctor among them. Perhaps, like Otto, he was not a churchgoing man. Or perhaps, he was still inside the church and simply had not come outside yet. Glancing up the street, Otto saw there were still a few people trickling out of the building, completely unaware anything was wrong.

"Doc still in church?" Otto asked.

"No. I'll check his office," a young man said. Otto recognized him as the blacksmith's apprentice. He ran off.

The sleet came and went, spotty at times.

Otto glanced down at the blood smeared on his hands. Some of it had dried and some of it was wet and starting to freeze.

"Sheriff's been shot bad," he said quietly, mostly to himself. Otto felt dazed. The sense of urgency he felt was wearing off, and now he was getting queasy in the stomach. He held onto the rail even tighter, hoping it would pass.

Across the street, the courthouse door creaked open. From the doorway, slowly, Deputy Griff Allen inched his way out into the cold. Roy Caldwell followed him outside, trying to support his arm, but Griff kept shaking him off.

Griff looked bad. His forehead was split open, his nose pointed awkwardly off to one side, and he had blood and chili crusted all over his face. Bonnie Allen turned around at the sound of the courthouse door and gasped. She pushed past Betty Anne Hortworst, who was still standing silent as a stone, ran up and threw her arms around her husband. Being a deputy's wife, she always worried one day Griff would be killed. It was a stress that weighed on her mind quite frequently. Griff wasn't a soft man, she knew, but even the toughest men could be killed by a stray bullet or some other unexpected measure of violence. Her husband's safety always topped her prayer list every Sunday morning, as it had that very day.

"Griff!" she cried out. "Oh, Griff!"

"I'm alright, Bonnie."

"Heard him shouting and banging in there," Roy told her, and cupped his hand under Griff's elbow.

"Had me locked up. But I'm fine now, I'm fine. Quit fussing," Griff said. "Roy, don't lay a hand on me again or I'll knock you down."

He looked around and noticed that a surprising amount of townspeople were grouped around the sheriff's office, as if they were waiting on something. No one ever gathered around the office like that on any day he could remember.

"What are you all doing out here?"

"It's Emerson," Bonnie started but immediately choked up. She wanted to say more but found she could not find her voice. She was horrified to hear Sheriff Greer had been shot — but seeing Griff in such a state was even more horrifying. She began to sob and shake.

Griff noticed Otto up on the landing by the office door, clinching the rail. Then he noticed Otto's sleeves and shirt were dark with blood. Griff shook loose from Bonnie and rushed up the stairs.

"Don't look good," Otto said to him.

"Where is he?"

"Cot in the back," Otto told him quietly, and then repeated himself. "Don't look good."

Griff went inside. The office was a mess. Papers were strewn about everywhere, the desk was slid out of place and the chair was on its side. Looking over at the gun cabinet, Griff saw the door was wide open. His eyes went to the floor. Bootprints glistened in the dim light, leading into the other room. They traced back to a puddle of dark blood on the floor behind the desk.

Behind him, the front door came open again. It was the town doctor, peppered with sleet. Mrs. Caroline Greer, Emerson's good wife, came in with him. Bonnie was right next to her, supporting her by the arm. Roy Caldwell came in last with a look of general concern in his eyes.

"In here!"

Griff recognized Merle Hasting's voice calling from the back room. The doctor led the way. A wave of dread washed over Griff, but he went ahead and followed them back. There was Sheriff Emerson Green, lying on the spare cot, bleeding out.

Mrs. Greer let out a cry and rushed forward. She collapsed on the floor next to the cot and clung to her husband's arm. The doctor, whose name Griff could never remember, gently worked around her, checking the wound. He glanced up at Griff and shook his head grimly.

"Lord have mercy," Griff muttered.

The sheriff looked up at his deputy with red-rimmed eyes and began mouthing something.

"Can't hear you, Em."

Griff leaned in close. But Emerson could not get it out, whatever he was trying to say. Griff squeezed his shoulder in a brotherly manner. He could guess.

"They ain't getting far," Griff said to him in a rough whisper. "There will be hell to pay, I can assure you that."

"Shot a man while he's down," Ben Leavick complained bitterly. "Held him down and shot him point-blank. Couldn't even defend himself!"

Bonnie knelt down behind Caroline, placing an arm around her. Her face was flushed, and she was shaking. Bonnie said nothing. What could she say? This could just as easily have been her own husband. She turned her head slightly and glared up at Griff, to convey her disapproval of his job choice. But he did not catch the look and might not have interpreted it correctly even if he had. She frowned even more, making a mental note to impress upon him her firm opinion once they were alone.

Coughing heavily, the sheriff spat up a good deal of blood. Then he grew silent and his face seemed to relax. With that, Emerson Greer expired.

Outside in the cold street, all the people who were gathered around the landing heard a rising wail. It was Mrs. Caroline Greer, mourning her husband's passing.

Nettie Hastings was still standing in the same place, in the cold wind and sleet, in her billowy skirt, still holding her two blonde boys when she heard the wail. She pulled Wally and Remmy even closer. Nettie was sick to her stomach. She wasn't sure if she was shivering from fear or from the cold. Flakes of snow were twirling slowly through the air. She watched them thoughtfully. They reminded her of angels dancing, solemnly — angels who had come to carry the sheriff away. The wind picked up again and raked across the frozen lake. It blew the angels away, scattering them into the sky.

At that moment, Griff came outside and looked down at the people of Grand Lake.

"Sheriff's been shot. Whoever is with me, get guns. Get horses."

Chapter 13
Ward
The Halfway House

"T'was early in the summer."

Father Dyer leaned forward on his elbows.

"The Mosquito Mining District was instituted at that time. But having congregated just briefly, the miners neglected to agree upon its moniker."

"Now when was this, Father?" Prescott Sloan asked. The two of them were seated across from each other. A thin line of white smoke snaked up from Sloan's cigarillo.

"June of '61," Father Dyer replied without having to think about it.

His fingers were wrinkled, although they were sinewy and still very strong considering his age. He leaned back in his chair, removed his worn patched hat and set it on the table. Throughout the Halfway House, there were kerosene lanterns on every tabletop. The entire room was filled with yellow lantern light.

"It was quiet up there in those days. Buckskin Gulch was so overrun, some of them miners just up and moved four miles northeast. Hit a lode. But they forgot to name the area that first meeting."

The minister smiled at the memory. He leaned forward again, eyes sharp with the retelling.

"When the boys got together next, they opened the minutes of that first meeting. On that blank spot, precisely where a name was to be written — they discovered a skeeter. Finely pressed amidst the pages!"

He sat up straight, folding his arms. Sloan smiled politely. He did not really care to hear the old man's story. He was waiting for the stagecoach to get into town — it should have rolled in by now. When Dyer came in and sat down, Sloan realized he was in for another long-winded story. His eyes went out the window each time a figure passed by. It was almost dark outside, but still light enough to tell when someone went by.

"And how is Lucinda?" Sloan asked him.

Father Dyer looked down into his coffee cup. The black surface was still. He could see his own silhouette in the coffee, looking back up at him.

"She passed," he answered and sighed. "Been two years now. Happened almost as soon as we got to Denver."

"Sorry to hear that."

"Jehovah Jireh, my Provider," Dyer spoke with conviction. "It is well with my soul, Mr. Sloan."

Sloan raised the thin cigar and puffed at it. Ashes dropped onto his fine suit vest. He brushed at them with his fingertips. Someone walked past the window — it was Ian Mitchell, finally. The door opened and the man came inside.

"My soul as well," Sloan said. "Mr. Mitchell! Take a seat."

Stomping the mush off his boots, Ian Mitchell looked down at Sloan with little interest. He rode shotgun on the postal stage. The Halfway House was not only a public eatery, it was an official stage stop. It was also the place where Sloan liked to surprise him when he had a special message to deliver to Boulder.

"Father Dyer," Sloan said by way of introduction, waving the cigarillo in his direction.

"How do," Ian said and tipped his hat. "Jim'll be in soon. Untacking the jerk-line."

"Ian and Jim Everitt are our finest stage drivers."

"Jim manages the reins," Ian specified. "I manage the scatter gun."

He removed his duster and draped it across the back of an empty chair, then sat down heavily.

"How's your route looking?" Sloan inquired.

"Lyons to Estes to here today. Lake's still froze up there," Ian said, yawning without concern. "Gold Hill in the morning. Jamestown. Boulder by the twilight tomorrow — then start the whole thing over again."

The owner of the Halfway House, Hugh Hughes, came up just then wiping his hands on a towel. The Halfway House was situated in Ward, which was halfway between Boulder and Estes Park.

"Supper's being served," Hugh said. "Beefsteak, onions, bread and gravy. Pickles or dried apricots?"

"Beats sop n' taters," Ian told Hugh. "Jim's coming in, too. Apricots."

Hugh nodded and worked his way back towards the kitchen.

The door opened again and they all felt the cold air swirl in. Sloan hunched against it. He was an indoor man and disliked the elements. Father Dyer sat unmoved — he preferred the outdoors and favored the elements. He was also frugal. Once, he walked all the way from Fairplay to Denver just to avoid the cost of a stage ride.

“Gloomy out,” Jim said bleakly. “Feels a lot later than I know it to be.”

“Take up a seat,” Ian said, kicking out a chair from under the table.

“Father Dyer,” Jim said and shook hands. Then he noticed Sloan at the table and sighed.

“Sloan.”

“Well, I best carry on.”

Dyer got to his feet, buttoning his overcoat and replacing his hat.

“Prescott. Gentlemen. Good day.”

“Father,” Sloan replied. “Best in your travels.”

The old man stepped out the door and into the lightly blowing snow. Sloan’s smile faded as he watched Dyer, through the window, drift off into the evening.

“The lion and the lamb,” Jim quipped with a wry chuckle.

“Is that a commentary regarding my moral disposition?” Sloan asked, eyes narrowing.

Hugh returned to the table carrying two plates of food. He placed them in front of the stage men.

“Fifty cents,” Hugh stated. “Each.”

The two men paid up and turned their attention to their food. It did beat the standard feed the stage service provided for their drivers. After a long day up on a coach top, bundled up against the weather, it was a welcome break to get inside and eat a warm meal.

“Banker and the preacher, supping at the same table,” Jim continued. “The Good Book says: *Ye cannot serve both God and mammon.*”

Sloan shook his head and laughed awkwardly. Who did these two fools think they were speaking to?

“Well ain’t that the gospel truth?” Sloan mused.

The stage men eyed him blankly over fork-fulls of beef.

Sloan leaned forward and glanced around to see who was watching. From his coat, he pulled out a small buckskin pouch and slid it across the table. Inside there was a PO Box key and a note to Soapy Smith, the most notable crime boss in Colorado. He was opening the Tivoli, his most ambitious racketeering operation to date, and Sloan was getting in on it. But these fools didn’t need to know any of that. They were no more useful than the mules they drove. In fact that’s what they were. Mules. Carrying a load from one place to the next.

“This goes to Boulder on the morrow’s stage. Keep it under close perspective.”

Jim paused mid-chew.

"Close perspective," he said without much subtlety, "requires effort."

"Effort," Ian added, "requires recompense."

Sloan's face spread into another one of his empty smiles.

"And so it does."

The banker produced a roll of cash money and tossed it to Ian Mitchell.

"For your troubles and woe."

Chapter 14
Beaver Creek

"Didn't slacken his gait any. It was the durndest blizzard but he was a frisky coot."

The leather creaked as LG shifted in his saddle, adjusting to keep from getting too sore in any one place.

"But I made the line shack!" he said. "Could barely see his withers it blew so thick. He was an ol' devil, pulled some rodeo work ever time I saddled. But he right found his way through that whiteout."

Casey could understand the value of a good trail horse.

"Hard to throw a cowman off his trail — when his neck relies upon the trace of it."

"Snow blowed up against the doorframe up to my knees. I banged on that door and I banged again."

LG chuckled as he remembered the great relief he felt that day.

"Tell you, them sour-dough biscuits and hot black coffee had a place for me. That day and forward."

"Mercury's low," Til said. He rode up, his breath visible in the air.

LG cocked his head to one side to examine the sky.

"Looks like it's letting up."

Only light flakes were falling now. Casey reached inside his coat and produced a small battered notebook.

"Final count: two thousand thirty-three," Casey told him. "That's everything that can walk."

"I'll ride on down to Ward," Til said. "Wire the stockyards…let them know what we're bringing in. Get us scheduled with the depot."

"You're heading out tonight?" asked Casey. Til was no procrastinator, that was for certain. When he did something, he did it right away and he did it well. Still, the thought of a cold night's ride in the pitch dark was not something that appealed to Casey.

"Yep," Til replied. "Hate to say it. Weather not cooperating and such. But time is slipping on us, boys."

"Alright then," LG said. "The herd will hit the trail, too."

Even though the winter was technically over, it didn't feel that way. Casey had supposed they would be driving the herd during the daylight and bed down at dark. Not only was Til going to ride through the night, they all would.

"Gambly, I know," Til admitted. "Get her started. Head on down Spring Gulch, you should make Preacher's Glen by three AM. Camp there. I'll try and catch up to you in the canyon sometime tomorrow."

Casey glanced around. There was a cold fog closing in. Everything was gray and getting harder to see by the moment. The cattle were nosing through the soft snow to find the grass again. It had been there yesterday, and they knew it.

"Casey, tell Emmanuel to pack up right after supper and take that chuckwagon on down the mountain. Get 'er set up in the Glen. Have a hot fire waiting for you boys."

Til headed east, down Beaver Creek, out of the valley and into the trees. The big bay left a line of dark hoofprints in the thin layer of wet snow. The light was starting to disappear. Dusk came early when the clouds were low and the fog rolled in.

Chapter 15

Mining Encampment
Continental Divide
11,800 ft.
Near Grand Lake

Almost as soon as the sun dropped below the horizon the wind picked up. It whistled and weaved across the snowy rocks long after dark. Tiny ice crystals blew across the ridge and stung their skin. Bill and Vincent turned their backs to the wind and braced for the chill. The ridge was exposed and there was nothing to stop it.

"Stand right there behind me," Vincent told Granger. "Block the wind."

They were above timberline — the last few trees were just downhill from where they stood, maybe a hundred steps. At this altitude the trees that *were* there were short and scrubby, twisted from the rough conditions. Vincent could guess why, with weather like this.

Granger hated Vincent. They had traveled together for about a year now, mainly robbing banks, stages, and the occasional homestead. But it had been a long year for Granger. Vincent, primly dressed at all times and overly fond of personal grooming in Granger's opinion, continually patronized him and spoke with frequent derision. It had grown tiresome.

"I said block the damn wind."

Granger muttered, but then moved around behind them.

"There she goes! Poq and Cav got it down," Bill told Vincent triumphantly. "We'll soon have us a verifiable inferno."

Bill rocked back and forth, rubbing his hands together. The moon had just risen above the ridge. In the light, Bill watched the two Mexicans successfully uproot a stunted pine. Poqito quirted the mule while Caverango pulled on the halter, and the pine came twisting up out of the rocks.

The mule was not pleased about being the only mule on the windy ridge. The other horses and mules were corralled further down in the forest, out of sight. The mule wanted to be down there, too — perhaps eating some tasty grain, which he knew was packed in heavy satchels that he had hauled himself earlier in the day. Even now, the mule suspected the other stock animals were eating that very grain.

The moon disappeared as the wind pushed some clouds across the sky.

"Those mex'kins worth their weight in gold right about now," Granger said, shivering. He turned and shouted in the darkness. "Hurry up, you gall-dam mex'kins!"

His breath hissed in and out of the gap in his teeth. Granger had lost a front tooth several years back. Drunk outside a saloon in Silverthorne, he commenced to banging on an outhouse door. The occupant became irritated and flung open the door after completing his business. It caught Granger in the face. This was not only an unfortunate loss of a front tooth, it was also the moment he developed a deep-set fear of outhouses. From that point on, Granger preferred to relieve himself in the open. This was not always an easy option, especially in towns. Horse stalls and hay barns were his favorite places, if he could find them. They afforded the right amount of privacy.

"Leave them two alone. They're getting us a backlog," Bill told him. "That thing will burn all night. Sooner they get it up in that hearth, the sooner we all warm up."

Vincent rearranged his neck scarf to keep the wind out. He rubbed his upper left arm carefully. The wound was still raw. He needed to change the bandage every day now — by the time the sun went down, it became a sticky scab pile. He was not sure if it would heal properly on its own. The deputy had gotten him good for a near-blind shot through the haze of dynamite smoke. And it might be awhile before they were far enough away to find a doctor's office where there would be no worry about the law recognizing them.

"That sheriff won't last long," Vincent mentioned. "Township will be none too pleased I'm sure. Question is...how much of a lead do we have?"

"Better to be safe than dead, I suspect," Bill said. "We've got what we took from Kinsey City and it's a good haul. But those bricks have weight. We bury all that here. Travel light."

The moon came out of the clouds again, brightening the whole ridge like it was day — and then everything went dark again. In that moment, Bill could see Poqito and Caverango were leading the mule up the boulder field.

"If anything does come to pass, light out," Bill told Vincent and Granger. "Spread far afield, so they don't know who to follow. Then make for the apple orchards at Hall's Ranch. By the next full moon."

"Lyons ain't near far enough," Granger muttered.

Bill turned to him, and his eyes became hard. Reaching out quickly, Bill took a cold ear between his knuckles and tweaked it around. Granger buckled to his knees and screamed in pain. Bill hung on and shook it around a bit.

"How hard is it to just listen?"

Vincent watched calmly. He removed his gloves and began massaging the circulation back into his chilled fingertips. The wind kept sweeping over the ridge in cold bursts, and with each gust Vincent tucked his face deep into his neck scarf.

"If I say ride into Fort Smith and 'fess up to Judge Parker himself, you'll by God do it. And if I say ride hard to the bayous of Alabamy and wrastle a gator, you'll by God do that."

Giving his ear a final shake, Bill let go. Granger got right up to his feet, pressed his hand over the ear and stalked off across the talus without a word.

"Well damn, Bill," Vincent said with a light chuckle.

Bill shrugged casually. He could barely make out Granger moving across the rocks, heading toward the two Mexicans and their mule.

"How's that arm healing up?"

Poqito and Caverango were again trying to get the mule to move, to drag the little pine up the last few feet into the cabin — but the mule had planted itself firmly. He was determined to go down into the forest instead. Caverango tugged at the halter. Poqito quirted him.

"Aw, barely pains me — merely an irritant."

Vincent was lying. It hurt terribly, but he was not going to say that to Bill.

Up above them on the stony slope was a small mining camp. Someone had built a little cabin with one window. At the moment, it was dark and silent. The door was standing open. Granger still cupped a hand over his tweaked ear. He went straight up to the two men fighting with the mule.

"Drag that log in there! Now!" Granger demanded.

They glanced quickly at each other, uneasily. Granger was angry with them, they could tell, but they were not sure why. It was dark enough that they couldn't see much of his face. Granger waited for them to say something in response, to argue or complain — he wanted an excuse. But neither one spoke. They both stood there looking at him blankly. Granger glared at Caverango, who was closest, and threw a punch. Caverango's head popped back and he collapsed among the big rocks. Poqito leapt at Granger, but Granger kicked out the smaller man's feet.

Poqito fell down next to Caverango, yelling out in pain. The rock was sharp and loose.

Pulling open his overcoat, Granger gripped his Colt by the handle. The two Mexicans waved their arms pacifically. Bill was watching the whole thing in the dim light. For the most part, he did not care if the men fought. There was nothing wrong with a little fisticuffs now and again. But he certainly did not need Granger shooting the Mexicans. They were still in the process of hauling the scrubby pine up to the cabin. The wind was getting stronger and colder by the minute and they needed a fire as quickly as possible.

"No you don't!" Bill yelled. "Don't you shoot them. Get that fire going, you hear me?"

Granger looked hard at Caverango, then over at Bill. He let go of the gun handle and pulled his coat tight again. The wind picked up. They all leaned into it and held on to their hats. Granger hustled through the cabin door, disappearing inside.

"Our wind block is volatile," Bill said, referring to Granger.

"When the wind stops, we won't need a wind block anymore."

"That is true."

They made their way carefully across the talus and angled up to the dark cabin. They passed Poqito, who was rubbing one elbow gingerly. Caverango was back on his feet. He had resumed tugging at the mule's halter. They said nothing to Bill as he passed by.

Walking through the open doorway, Bill nearly tripped over a sprawled body. It was a dead miner.

"Would you drag this out of the way, at least far enough so we can close the damn door?" Bill scolded Granger, who was seated at a square table in the middle of the room.

"It bothers me that you don't think of these things by yourself."

"Jail's made you ornery," Granger told him sullenly.

He got up from the table and grabbed the dead man's wrists. He dragged the body further inside and closed the door. It was dim inside the cabin. Vincent found a lantern hanging on a nail. He struck a match and got it going. The only furniture in the room was the square table and four hand-built chairs. He set the lantern on the table, then settled into Granger's chair before he could sit down again.

"Could have gone the other way with it," Vincent told Granger. "Gonna stink in here."

"Fresh kill don't stank," Granger replied. "Be gone by the time it does."

At that moment, Caverango and Poqito opened the door and dragged in the small tree. It left long white scrape marks across the wooden floorboards. They dropped the root end into the fireplace.

Poqito took a hatchet and whacked off the limbs. The tree had long since died — the wood was dry and ready to burn. He was pleased they finally got it up the rocky slope despite all the problems with the disagreeable mule, the bitter wind, and Granger.

"Don't stink?" Vincent asked him. "You kidding me? When a man is shot dead, he shats himself."

Granger stared at him angrily. He was getting sick of Vincent's talk. All that man did was criticize him, no matter what was going on.

"I *know* they shat themselves."

"You a killer, Granger?" Vincent asked. "Because a killer would know they shat themselves."

"Boys, boys," Bill cautioned. He took a seat at the table and began checking the loads on his gun.

In a lull between gusts, Bill heard the mule whinny. He got up and moved quickly to the window. The clouds were streaming across the sky and the moon came in and out. He caught sight of three people riding up out of timberline. It was hard to make them out — the riders were indistinct in the gloom. But Bill easily recognized the tall white stockings on the lead sorrel.

"Well, Ned finally made it," he said.

Poqito lit a wad of newspaper in the fireplace and sprinkled pine needles over it. While it smoked and caught flame, he paused to rub his bad elbow. He glared over at Granger, but Granger was not looking in his direction.

The tree trunk was much too long for the fireplace. It stuck out from the hearth halfway across the room, one end resting on the rug by the table. As the night wore on and the trunk started burning down, they could inch it further into the fireplace. This was much better than wasting the time to saw it into sections.

Chapter 16

Ward
General Merchandise

Standing at the window, Julianna was uneasy.

"Miss, there is a room available at Hugh's," the man said. "Or you are welcome to spend the hours across the way. Hammet's Theatre is open. They got a Negro minstrel lineup. Be strummin' till the sunrise."

Julianna held her shawl close, cupping a hand to the window so she could see through the thick glass. She sighed quietly and turned away. It was dark outside and she was not going to drive the buckboard home after dark on such a cold night.

"Thank you for thinking of my well-being," she said politely.

The owner of the General Merchandise was Terrance Tillamook. Terrance Tillamook was a husky middle-aged man whose hair was salt and pepper gray.

"My wife would ream me if I did not think to ask," he mentioned kindly.

"It would be the ruination of you," his wife Joyetta said, her voice carrying authoritatively. She had just appeared from the stock room. "Weather and chill! Traveling at this hour in the cold? No, no, no."

"Thank you, ma'am. I do concur with good judgment."

The room was stacked with bags of flour, kegs of lard, dried meats, textiles, fabrics, racks of clothing, blankets, tin cups and plates, iron pots and skillets. Julianna walked slowly back through, stopping at the linens.

The door opened, and Josephine stepped inside the store. She looked around the room until she caught sight of Julianna's brown hair.

"*There* you are!"

Julianna ignored her. She pretended to examine the colorful linens. Josephine came over and joined her at the fabric rack. A salmon-colored silk caught her eye.

"This would make beautiful drapes for my kitchen. Don't you think?"

She glanced at Julianna, who was ignoring her.

"Come with me," Josephine pleaded in a regretful tone.

Julianna set her jaw but allowed the other woman to link arms and lead her out the door.

Through the big storefront window, Terrance and Joyette Tillamook watched them go.

"I wonder if she wants that salmon silk or not?" Joyette asked.

"If she wanted it, she would have bought it."

"Now, Terrance, maybe she would like me to set it aside for when she comes back."

"She didn't say anything of the sort. And what if someone else walks in lookin' for salmon silk?"

Josephine and Julianna walked down Main Street. The road was situated on a steep hill and in the evening hours it could be difficult to navigate on foot. The wheel ruts were lost in the shadows and it was easy to trip. There was light shining from the various businesses they passed: the Halfway House, the Miser's Brewery, Ezekiel's Blacksmith & Farrier Shop, Hammet's Theatre, the telegraph office.

Looking out over the forested hills around Ward, they could see all the lanterns and lighted windows scattered about in the darkness. There were only a few electric lights in Ward, and only the more prosperous businesses had them. All of the residential homes relied on lanterns and candles. Julianna still liked the homey glow of a natural flame. She thought the electric lights, though progressive, gave her a hollow feeling. She was still feeling hollow from all the sour dinner table talk.

"Samuel wants to move us to Horseshoe," Josephine mentioned.

Julianna gave her a side-glance.

"What? Why?" she asked.

Josephine sniffed indifferently.

"They just opened the Hilltop Mine. Samuel thinks his claim is all played out here."

The two women walked along quietly. The wind was swishing gently through the treetops and there was a little snow in the air.

They passed the Haw & Gee Saloon and could hear people talking and laughing through the open doorway. They even had a piano in there. It was the only one in town. The evening had just begun for a lot of people. Julianna liked Ward. It was a nice town — much bigger than Gold Hill. All her friends lived here. Sometimes she wished she lived here, too.

"He thinks he'll have an easier go. Hears talk about a big chamber inside. They call it the Ice Palace," Josephine rolled her eyes. "All glittery with mineral."

As she said it, her voice cracked. Julianna knew she was about to cry.

"Working inside a mountain is different than an open placer on a river," she continued. "Dirty, dark. Dangerous."

Julianna listened patiently.

"The mine sits way up top of Mount Sheridan," Joesphine said sadly. "He won't be coming home for supper every night, I can tell you that."

The road angled steeply downhill. The noise and bustle of downtown dimmed with distance. Several riders went by in the darkness, hoofsteps clopping loudly.

"Julianna, I am sorry about earlier," Josephine said softly. "I had no cause to say such things. Family is family."

"My father's an old Indian fighter," Julianna pointed out. "Your Samuel mines the earth. No one's what we want them to be. But they are what we need them to be."

They turned up a small road and stopped at Josephine's front door. It was a small frame house with bright yellow paint and white eaves and evergreens towering on each side. A lantern burned in the main window.

"Life seems to be rushing me," Josephine said, her voice unsteady.

The women stood quietly in the cold evening air. A few flakes fell on their shoulders and hats.

"Come inside. We'll be eating soon," Josephine told her. "Please stay. We've got the spare room all ready for you."

Chapter 17
Spring Gulch

"Keep an eye out for Ol' Mose."

LG's voice was solemn. He left it at that. Specter took off and it wasn't long before LG was out of sight in the pine up ahead.

The cattle were strung out in a long line. The herd was slowly winding its way through the trees. Ira and Edwin rode together — Ira had an appaloosa named Berry Picker and Edwin was on a dark bay they just called Dark Bay.

Ira's face crinkled up with the information, but Edwin was confused.

"Now who in the hell is Ol' Mose?" Edwin shouted after LG.

But LG was gone.

Ira became fidgety with this new information. He twisted in the saddle, looking sharply to the left and right. He squinted and stared hard into the forest. It was hard to see very far in the dusky shadows.

Edwin was almost waiting for an explanation, but by this point he knew Ira wasn't the sharpest knife in the drawer.

"Ira. What on God's green earth is LG talking about now?"

Ira broke from his trance and glanced over.

"Ol' Mose," he said knowingly, head dipping to add emphasis.

"Yeah, heard that part, dumb-bob."

"Ain't you heard of Ol' Mose, Edwin?" Ira asked, incredulous.

Ira waited for an answer to his own question but Edwin refused to respond to what he considered a dull query. He merely stared hard at Ira.

"I always thunk Ol' Mose kept his company up on 39-Mile Mountain," Ira said finally.

Edwin looked back down the line and caught a glimpse of another rider. It was Steve.

"Hey, McGonkin!" Edwin called out loudly. His voice seemed to get absorbed by the forest.

Steve trotted towards them, cutting around the tree trunks to catch up.

"Ira here can't make his words and it's ticking me off squarely."

"Ol' Mose!" Ira whispered tensely to Steve.

Steve cracked a smile and chuckled to himself.

"Ain't gonna get et tonight, Ira."

Edwin looked across the cows at Steve expectantly.

"Mose is a grizz," Steve explained. "Prob'ly the last one in South Park."

"We ain't *in* South Park," Edwin stated.

"Damn straight, and good thing we're not," Steve replied. "That grizz been eatin' cowboys...upwards of, well, since the '60s I suppose. Before any of us was born, except maybe Ira here."

"Ain't no grizzly out here," Edwin said contemptuously. "You're stupid, Ira. LG's just playing a gag on us and like a simpleton you fell for it."

"Now, you heard about poor Jake Radcliffe," Steve cautioned. "That was just three years ago."

"No, I ain't heard of no Jake Radcliffe," Edwin replied.

Steve's face got serious.

"Ain't fooling. Radcliffe went after that ol' bear, all around Black Mountain. Tracked him for ten days straight."

"Got et up," Ira added.

"Just about," Steve said. "Clawed up bad. Took him down to the Mulock ranch — the IM. Sent for the doc...but the man didn't live that long."

Edwin rode silently. He shifted his eyes toward the dark trees.

"Kilt near 800 head o' cattle," Steve said and nodded thoughtfully. "Well, over the years."

A few snowflakes pittered past.

"Well, look at me all puckered!"

Edwin's sharp laugh was meant to convey sarcasm and bravado. But it was pretty thin.

"Gonna shit me a penny."

Chapter 18

South of Beaver Creek

Except for Bit Ear, who was a faithful and rather stoic quarterhorse, Til was his own company. A thin crust of fresh snow made following the path difficult. It was barely more than a deer trail to begin with. The bay's hoofs broke through the crust with each step, making a loud gritty sound in the stillness.

The shadows got deeper as the evening settled in, which made the trail even harder to see. Ever since the sun went down, Til had not seen any wildlife. But that was no surprise. With this spring storm passing through, most of the forest critters were surely waiting it out.

"Bedded down or holed up," Til told the big bay. "Which is where we ought to be."

He reached down and patted Bit Ear's neck several times. The smell of damp horseflesh was strong. A chilly fog had begun to roll in, too. The treetops soared up overhead and were lost in the mist and the fading light.

Sitting up straight, Til yawned. He wiggled his toes inside his boots to get the circulation going.

Two thousand head did not constitute a large herd, but it was a decent size. And it was all he had at the moment. Til knew he could cut out the yearlings and two-year olds, continue to graze them at the Wyoming pasture. It wasn't too far away from Cheyenne, and he could be at the railyards in a matter of an hour or two. It was far more convenient than Beaver Creek, but then Beaver Creek was just the high summer grazing pasture. Normally the cattle he took up there, stayed up there until fall. With the market in such a bad state, this was not a normal season. He knew he would get a top price. But he had to be in the right place at the right time to get it. He was racing the big cattle companies now, and it was important to lock in all the buyers he could find.

A bat flew right past the crown of his hat, made a choppy turn and flapped off into the gray fog.

"Well there's at least something breathing besides me."

But the bat did not come back.

The trees opened up, and he found himself in a small alpine meadow. Til had been through here a couple times over the years, but the ground was normally dry enough by then that he could see where the trail went. But given the heavy winter, it was still under snow, and — if he was being honest — Til wasn't even sure where he was. Fir and pine gave way to aspen, and the slim white trunks were evenly spaced. The trail could be anywhere.

Til brought Bit Ear to a standstill.

Scanning the far side of the meadow, Til tried to remember anything familiar. He shivered. When he was not moving, it got cold quick. It was going to be a long dark night, and in these conditions it was not wise to stop for long — even if he knew exactly where he was.

"You figure it out," he told Bit Ear and urged the bay on with loose reins. His hoofs crunched along the ground as he stepped forward hesitantly.

It soon became obvious the trail was a lost cause.

Til spent a few minutes chewing it over. He knew the general lay of the land well enough. He was travelling down a forested gully, so really there was only one way to go. Plus, the stars would be visible once it got dark enough — if this fog would just lift.

The aspen grove petered out, and he was soon surrounded by evergreen again. The snowbanks got deep where the trees grew close together, especially on the north-facing slopes.

Til was wet from getting sleeted on back at Beaver Creek. The fog didn't help. The sunlight was gone now, although he could tell there must be a sliver of a moon somewhere up above. He wore his thick sheepskin coat — which was helpful — and even had a special pair of fur-lined gloves he bought off a trapper several seasons back.

Bit Ear kept moving along at a slow walk. They worked through the underbrush and tree trunks, past granite outcroppings and boulders. Whenever he felt pine needles rake across the brim of his hat, Til ducked low in the saddle. More than once, he nearly lost a kneecap when the big bay pressed on between tree trunks. If he hadn't been wearing thick angora chaps, he would have.

The terrain curved steeply downhill. Descending slowly in the darkness, Til continued to let the bay have his head. He always chose Bit Ear for journeys that ran late — he was a reliable night horse.

Looking rather ghostly in the fog and moonlight, Til could make out a white line somewhere up ahead. He thought it might be a stream. The slope steepened and he leaned back with it. The saddle leather creaked.

The white line grew wider as he got closer. Soon, it was right in his path. That was odd. Til was expecting to hear running water the closer he got — but it was silent.

The forest was black all around him. The fog was thinning.

Sliding down the last few steps heavily, the bay stepped out onto hard-packed ground. The white line was not a creek after all. It was a stage road, glowing softly in the silvery moonlight.

It was a welcome sight. Til knew exactly where he was now.

Collecting his reins with certainty, he pointed Bit Ear down the road. Ward was only a few more miles away. The road was fairly straight and stretched on into the night. As he lost elevation, the fog kept thinning until it was gone. In what little moonlight he had, Til noticed wheel tracks in the thin snow. There were also hoof prints and spats of manure. The road was well-traveled and just being on it made it seem like there were people around. In a big forest in the middle of a cold night, even Til could appreciate the feeling that he wasn't alone.

Another hour passed before he caught the unmistakable scent of woodsmoke. The road made a twisty curve and the trees thinned enough he could see the eastern horizon.

He knew Ward was right down there. He had made it.

Most of the homes he passed were tucked back in the trees. They were all dark.

The stage road led right through downtown Ward. The Haw & Gee Saloon was the only place open. The door was closed but light shined brightly through the windows. Til decided he was too tired to stop for even a cup of coffee. He went straight to the livery barn between the Halfway House and the corrals. The aisle door was sealed up tight. He pulled it open and led his horse inside.

Til put Bit Ear in an empty stall, then double checked the aisle door. On a cold night, just closing up the barn trapped in the body heat of all the animals. It kept everything warm inside.

As soon as Til closed the door, he lost the moonlight. He untacked and groomed the bay by touch. Taking the saddle and Navajo blanket with him, Til walked blindly down the pitch-dark aisle. The hay was easy to find. He could smell it. He set his saddle down against the wall. His Navajo blanket was damp with horse sweat, so he draped it over a beam. Til spread out his bedroll in the hay stack, but before he laid down he took an armful of hay back for Bit Ear.

Chapter 19
Mining Camp
Continental Divide

Someone upslope slipped. Stones skittered past Bill's head and rolled off into the darkness. He took a deep breath, gripping the rope even tighter. The last thing Bill needed was to get cracked in the skull because one of those fools kicked a rock loose. If he slipped, he wouldn't stop until he hit the ice pooled at the bottom of the shaft. He knew there was ice, because he had just pushed an unlucky miner down here a few hours earlier.

"Get that light near me."

Bill's voice echoed. Granger edged down the slope so he could get close to Bill. He held the lamp up high. Shadows danced along the walls.

"A lot warmer in here than up on that damn ridge," Granger said.

Bill's eyes glistened in the harsh light. He reached up to the lantern knob and adjusted the wick where he wanted it. Granger irritated him. If the man was going to stick the lamp in his face, he could at least turn it down a bit.

Granger could tell Bill was irritated. He tried to keep the lantern as steady as he could. It was hard to hold onto the rope and the lantern at the same time. The mine shaft was steep, too, like a ramp.

"Welcome to nest," Bill suggested.

Just below, Bill could tell the floor leveled out. He scooted down the slope until he could stand upright safely. Barely ten steps across, the shaft dropped abruptly straight down. Granger came down awkwardly. He slid the last few feet down the slope. Shadows flickered all over the place.

"Watch it!" Bill warned him. "Don't bump me."

He knelt down and examined the wall. He had brought along a pickax from the cabin. He spotted a convenient cleft and chipped away to make it wider.

Ned came down the rope and stood by Granger, watching Bill work. Bill glanced up at him.

"This'll do."

Ned put his fingers in his mouth and whistled sharply. Lem and Will Wyllis started making their way down the shaft. They brought down two heavy saddle bags. It was all the gold they stole from the Kinsey City bank. Bill sighed. He wished they had stolen paper cash money instead. Gold was too heavy to ride far with. And he suspected the sheriff Vincent shot was most likely dead by then. That meant there would be lawmen coming. Distance was the most important thing now. And distance meant traveling light.

"Take your time...don't drop them bags!" Bill called, glancing at the dropoff right behind him.

Poqito and Caverango were standing guard up at the mine entrance. Lem and Will each strapped one of the bags around their shoulders so they could hold onto the hemp line with both hands. The bags were very heavy. Neither one of them was overly excited about inching down such a steep tunnel with so much weight tied on. But they did it anyway.

Bill took the lantern and leaned out over the edge. Down there, the mine was flooded and frozen solid. He could see the ice and the dead miner splayed out on the glittery surface. Bill had expected the miner to tumble a hundred feet or more — but the poor fellow just thumped onto solid ice twenty feet down. Oh well, Bill thought. He's dead and that'll do.

Lem and Will finally made it down with the bulky saddle bags. Bill held the lantern high so everyone could see. There wasn't much room for all five of them. Crouching side by side, Lem and Will pushed the bags inside as far as they would go.

"Cover them up," Bill instructed.

Using their hands, they scooped up pebbles and grit, and heaped in all the dirt. They could hear the wind pick up again outside, roaring past the entrance.

"Here you go," Bill said and handed the lantern back to Granger. "Lem, bring that ax."

Grabbing onto the rope, Bill hauled himself up the slope, hand over hand. Ned followed, then Granger went up. Lem went next with the pickax tucked in his belt. Will was the last one — he hated being last. It was spooky watching the lamp float up the tunnel. It was pitch dark without it. Plus there was that dead miner right down there. Will did not like caves. He did not like train tunnels and now mine shafts were on the list. His chest felt tight. He was starting to breathe heavily. If he slipped even once, he would slide right on down that hole with nothing to stop him.

"Alright, then," Bill said as he passed Poqito and Caverango. "Bring it down."

Bill moved out into the night and turned around to face the mine entrance, enjoying his new buffalo coat. It was perfect for weather like this. All the boys were envious when they saw him wearing it.

Ned came out of the mine, then Granger — Bill had given him the lantern on purpose, in case there might be a shooter waiting for them. Bill watched him closely for a minute but no shot came. Lem gave the pickax to Caverango and hustled towards the cabin. He wanted out of the wind.

Will Wyllis felt a great sense of relief. Dark places made him antsy. The whole time he was clawing up the rope, chills kept afflicting his spine. The first thing he did when he walked outside was to plant himself next to Granger — just to be near the kerosene flame.

Bill observed Will and shook his head. Will was not smart, standing so close to the gun bait.

The Mexicans began pulling and chopping at the support beams which framed the entrance.

"Glad to see everything stands in our favor," Ned mentioned to Bill.

"Let's go inside and get warm," Bill said.

They headed across the snowy talus. Bill was glad for the wind. It was strong enough to carry away any sounds they were making. Bringing down support timbers was a noisy business. On a calm day, the sound of a pickax striking stone could carry for quite a distance. Plus, it was such unfavorable weather, he suspected that if anyone *was* tracking them, they were likely cozied up in a warm cabin of their own.

"How was your stay in Grand Lake?" Ned asked as they walked.

"Didn't stay long enough to really form an opinion."

"I led that sheriff quite far afield," Ned told him.

"No, you didn't — that's why we're in this mess."

Ned grinned and slapped Bill on the shoulder.

"Aw, you did fine. Nothing a little gut-shot sheriff won't fix. That ol' boy's walking with *Santa Muerta* by now."

They took their time crossing the rocks. As they got closer to the cabin, the door opened and they could see Vincent outlined in the doorway. The fire was crackling in the hearth directly behind him. It looked inviting.

"Bill?"

"We're coming."

"Hold up," Vincent said.

He held up a butcher's knife. It caught the moonlight when he angled it around. Bill looked at it thoughtfully.

"Mark it," he said.

Vincent made his way downhill, taking the butcher's knife. He walked towards a sad looking tree just below the mine. It was stunted — stripped bare by the exposure on the ridge. He jabbed the knife blade deep into the bark. It went in solidly. Stepping back Vincent observed his work. The knife's handle pointed directly uphill where the mine entrance was located. Or used to be.

Walking slowly and counting his steps, Vincent hiked straight up to the mine.

"Fifty paces," he called over to Bill.

The wind was clearing the sky, blowing all the clouds toward the eastern plains. The stars were bright as could be. Bill turned to Ned.

"I don't know about you, but I want a beer."

They went inside the cabin. Bill was ready to relax. Tomorrow was going to be another long day on horseback and he was pretty washed out. The past few days had been nonstop. At least the two miners they killed had stocked the cabin. Cans of food lined one shelf and bottles of beer lined another.

Vincent came back in. A minute later the others began filing through the doorway. Will was the last one to come through — but Granger gave him the lantern and pointed him right back outside.

"Last one in the door has to check them horses."

"Aw damn," Will said. "Last *again*."

But Granger had already closed the door.

Chapter 20
Spring Gulch

Rufe turned up his collar. After a couple hoofbeats, it curled slowly back down into its original place. Rufe turned it back up again. That collar was a nuisance. Once they got somewhere he could buy one, he aimed to pick up a new coat.

"Hope cookie be setting up that chuckwagon."

Rufe looked back at his brother. Steve just shook his head hopelessly and shivered. The crew had been on trail since they ran the tally. It had to be three in the AM by now — and the coldest part of the night. The McGonkin brothers were both exhausted and chilled to the bone. So were the cows.

"Can't be much further," Steve told him. "Cattle ain't in no shape to walk the night away."

"Hey watch this," he added.

Steve steered his horse right into the cow line and drew up. Normally, cattle would stop if a horse blocked their way. But instead of stopping, the cattle plodded slowly around the horse, mindlessly moving on into the dark. Steve removed his hat and waved it at them. But the cattle showed no interest in his hat either.

"How 'bout that," Rufe frowned. "So ding dang chilly, ain't paying no mind to a cowhorse."

The silver moonlight cast clear-cut shadows on the powdery ground. Rufe wasn't sure how much further they had to go to get to Preacher's Glen, like Til told them. Spring Gulch seemed to stretch on forever. There were all kinds of trees everywhere. Conifer, pine, spruce. He could have sworn they passed the same beaver pond about three times, but his older brother disagreed.

Steve turned his horse around again and kept moving with the herd. The Polangus were black as it was, and hard to see at night. At least they had the moon.

Rufe yawned. Steve saw it and yawned himself.

"Can't wait for the bedroll," Rufe mumbled. "Cows, cows. Movin' so durned slow."

Hunching forward, Steve squinted his eyes. It was an effort. He pointed two gloved fingers up ahead.

"Now, Rufie...see it?"

Rufe looked up from under his hat, breath hanging in the air. Lying beneath the wingspan of a big blue spruce was a dead steer.

"Ain't Polangus," Rufe noted. "Or Longhorn."

"Durham," Steve said. "But not one of ours. I'll check the brand."

He trotted his horse up to the carcass. Sliding out of the saddle, Steve knelt and examined it. There was hardly any snow under the big tree.

"Looks like one of Sprague's. From last fall, I bet."

One side was torn open right in its belly.

"Cat did this," Rufe said and put his hand on his .45. He looked around warily.

"If that's last year's kill, ain't nothin' to worry," Steve told his brother.

Rufe rode up close and looked down at the dead animal. It was dried out and covered in needles and cones. The skin was just a stiff layer of canvas. The eyes were gone, the legs angled out — it looked deflated, dried out and long since dead.

Sliding off his horse, Rufe unhooped his rope from the horn. He chuckled.

"Let's take a better look at this thing."

Kneeling down, Rufe tied a loop around the carcass's legs. Uncoiling the rope, he stretched it out and dallied the other end around his saddle horn.

Steve shook his head in a big-brotherly fashion. Rufe was always looking for something to liven up a dull ride. When they used to work up in Wyoming, Rufe liked to ride down wolves. Wolves were big pests and could set off a stampede. The range boss had put them on wolf patrol, but shooting them wasn't sporting enough. Rufe liked to ride them down and rope them, drag them to death. That was a pretty common thing. Most of the cowhands up there did the same thing.

Steve got his own rope out and tied it off around the steer's horns. They both remounted and began backing their horses in opposite directions.

The ropes unwound, the slack kinked out and the rope got tight. They dragged the carcass out from under the evergreen. It scraped across the cold ground.

"Here, now," Rufe shouted. "Walk way back!"

Steve shrugged and began backing his horse. His horse obeyed but clearly did not like it. He was a reliable trail horse though and did like he was asked — although Steve had to keep close control of the reins to make it happen. Rufe was doing the same. The ropes pulled taut and the stiff carcass lifted slowly off the ground, suspended between the two horses.

Rufe laughed out loud.

"Well how about that!" he said. "Floatin' beeve."

"Hey now, a ghost steer!" Steve said. "Wish Ira could see this. Eyes be big as saucers...he'd ride straight for Tejas!"

Ira had some easy fears to play on. That *would* be fun. Rufe hoped Ira would ride back and see this! He leaned over his horse's withers, grabbed the rope and began tugging at it. He got the carcass swaying.

"Lookie here, Steve!" he yelled. "Ghosty beeve, a-floatin' for blood! Wants him some Ira!"

Steve's horse decided this was too much. He hopped and capered about. As soon as he did, the rope went slack and the steer hit the ground. Inside the canvas shell, its dry bones rattled loudly with the impact.

The cattle erupted. There was no longer a cowline. It was now a rush of Polangus and Durham racing full out — kicking up clods of snow, mush and dirt.

Chapter 21

Mining Camp
Continental Divide

A gun went off outside.

The sound was almost obscured by the high winds, but instantly Bill and Ned dove out of their chairs and flattened themselves on the floor. Everyone else froze and listened, trying to determine if that really was gunfire they just heard.

Vincent and Lem were sitting at the table, cards in hand. Seeing Bill and Ned drop to the floor, Vincent realized that not only *did* a gun go off, but it might have been aimed at the cabin where they were all playing cards and drinking bottled beer. And there was a window not six feet away from where he sat. I've already been shot once this week, he thought, slapped his cards on the tabletop and slid out of his chair. He scooted away from the window on his knees.

Lem watched him go. He was still seated, with his cards fanned out. The wind had been howling like a banshee ever since the sun went down. The cabin walls shook with every swell. It could have been rock fall. Or a tree blowing over. Besides, it was cold out there. Bitterly cold. Who would be out there in this bitterly cold wind, Lem wondered. And if they were, why couldn't they wait until the sun came up before they started shooting?

Several moments passed. Maybe it was a tree or rock after all. Lem reached over and peeked at Vincent's hand.

Then another gunshot went off, louder than the first. A bullet hit the front of the cabin, but it didn't make it all the way through the plank wall.

Everyone scrambled. Lem jumped up and grabbed his shotgun, disappearing into the darkest corner of the room. Bill got to his hands, and shuffled over to the wall. He drew his .45 and began checking it over.

"Stay quiet!" he hissed.

Firelight flickered. No one spoke. Poqito and Caverango stood like statues on both sides of the hearth.

"Cover that door," Bill said, nodding to them. The two Mexicans brought their rifles up, ready. Bill was sure it was the deputy from Grand Lake. He knew they should not have shot anybody in that town — least of all the sheriff. When he first broke out of the courthouse cell, he was adamant about getting out of town without a killing. But then the sheriff walked in on them. It was a lung shot. The man probably died. Vincent had been impertinent, shooting him right in the chest. And Bill was still upset because his hearing was dull in one ear now. Vincent should have just winged the man in the leg or shoulder, or choked him till he passed out.

Embers popped onto the floor, sizzling — but no one moved to stomp on them. The window in the front wall might as well have been painted black. It was too dark to see through the glass and no one wanted to risk being shot in the head. Ned crawled over and blew out the lantern on the table. He hesitated thoughtfully, staring at it.

"Hey Bill?" Ned whispered. "Will is still out there."

Granger, bending low, hustled over to the door and grabbed the handle. He glanced over at Bill, as if for approval. Bill arched his eyebrows with interest. He was always interested in what Granger would do next. Slowly, gingerly, Granger pulled the door open — just a sliver.

He waited.

Nothing happened.

He put an eye to the crack and looked out into the darkness.

Then the door banged open — right into Granger's face. He was knocked off his feet and rolled sideways till he hit the table. The lantern slid off and shattered on the floor, spraying kerosene everywhere. Ned was glad he just blew it out or this little shack would be on fire before they could blink twice.

Will Wyllis stood in the doorway. He was shaking visibly. His stomach was shiny, wet with blood.

As soon as he saw the guns and rifles pointed at him, Will raised his hands and opened his mouth to speak. But instead of speaking, his head snapped forward and a spray of dark blood flipped up from the backside.

Will took a step forward and stopped unsteadily, wavering on his feet. His eyes went wide and lost their focus. His legs gave way and he fell back out the door. All they could see were the bottoms of his boots flickering in the firelight.

Two more gunshots went off. Splinters exploded off the doorjamb. Granger knew he was in a bad place, right there in plain view. Scrambling to his hands and knees, he scurried wildly from the open entrance. Granger kneed his way frantically past Bill and huddled beneath the window. He put a finger into his mouth. There was a floppy tooth, swaying like a hinge. Son of a bitch, he thought.

"Close that door! Close that door!" Bill yelled.

Lem popped out of his dark corner, ran over and kicked it shut.

The window shattered. Granger threw his arms up over his head. Thick shards of glass rained down.

Poqito and Caverango grabbed onto the twisted tree trunk in the hearth and began pulling it out. Smoke buckled up into the room, and the fire fluttered. As they tugged it out, Poqito bumped into the table and lost his grip. Caverango couldn't hold onto it alone, and the trunk landed hard on the floor. Embers scattered everywhere. There was a round wool rug under the table and several big pieces landed on it, smoldering.

Ned watched in disbelief.

"What the hell are you two doing?"

"*Killing el fuego!*" Caverango explained hysterically. "*Están mirando*! *En la luz!*"

"Forget the fire! You're gonna get us smoked and burnt out!"

Ned had to yell to be heard over the wind and the gunfire.

Gray clouds churned out of the smoldering wood even as he spoke. The smoke rolled right up to the roof and billowed around. They all began to cough. Poqito started stomping at the embers, especially the ones that had fallen on the wool rug under the table. One of the glowing embers got kicked instead of stomped, and skittered right into the kerosene. It ignited and the floor lit right up.

Vincent stuck his sixgun through the broken window and fired off several shots.

"Lem! Blast out that back wall," Bill shouted.

Lem's dark corner was no longer dark. The big fire in the center of the room cast too much light. But Lem tipped his shotgun towards the back wall. He discharged the first barrel — it was loud. The room shook. But it worked. There was a platter-sized hole in the planks.

"Do it again!" Bill yelled.

Lem fired the second barrel and blew more of it away. Caverango and Poqito gave up on the fire and began pulling frantically at the splintered boards.

Chapter 22

Spring Gulch
Preacher's Glen

"Must be nearing eleven o'clock. According to that Ladle."

Casey took off his hat so he could look up easier. The sky was clear, the constellations sweeping. Up above them the treetops swayed in the wind, but down in the gulch it was fairly calm.

As a point of pride, LG only took off his hat when he absolutely had to. Craning his neck awkwardly, LG studied the night sky.

"Quarter sliver," he said. "Horsethief moon."

They rode at an easy walk. They were on point, guiding the lead cows and keeping them moving in the right direction.

"*The night is as clear as a bell,*" Casey began.

LG completed the old trail proverb.

"*And cold as Hell.*"

It was true enough — certainly at this elevation, at this time of year. Casey's dog walked over to a dark seep near the willows. Casey and LG could hear him lapping water in the dark.

Behind them the lead steer followed along, keeping pace with their horses but clearly in no hurry. The rest of the herd was strung out in the trees. LG figured it might stretch as far back as a mile. But that's what the other riders were for. If they were doing their jobs right, they were keeping the herd moving, and catching any strays that might wander off. Since he did not know the hired hands very well, he could only hope Til had picked a competent group. Of course, LG had joked about it at the branding fire — but he knew full well that Til was a good judge of character.

The gulch began to open up. The forest gave way to a large meadow. In the moonlight, they could see a fresh wagon track in the powdery snow. Two dark lines led straight across to the far side. That would be Emmanuel. He had gotten a good headstart after dinner.

"There it is," LG said and pointed.

There was a small orange light twinkling up ahead.

"Mess wagon," Casey said appreciatively. "Let's see if Emmanuel has anything to chaw on."

His trail horse, Boot Sock, a bay with tall white stockings up to his hocks, lunged into a sudden gallop. Hopper began barking at the same time and made straight for the trees. Casey held on tight, looking back as he rode. He knew what was happening.

"They're running!" he yelled.

LG was right behind him, bringing Specter to a gallop and then an all-out run as the cattle came rushing at them. It was like a dam had broken somewhere. The two cowmen raced to stay with the lead steer. It was a big animal, racing blindly ahead.

LG rode up next to Casey and called over to him.

"Mill 'em!"

Both riders pushed hard to keep their horses moving just ahead of the lead steer. They guided him across the big meadow they called Preacher's Glen.

Specter's gait was powerful. His black mane waved wildly with the speed. Despite the unwelcome surprise, LG could not help but smile a little. How many times had he been right there — riding a good horse with a loose herd.

Lamming his spurs in, LG pushed ahead of Casey and began turning the lead steer.

The ground was lit up by the moon, LG was glad he could see where he was going. The stampeding cattle began circling all the way around the meadow. Preacher's Glen was soon filled with two thousand cattle, all running like the devil was on board.

Casey's bay was not as fast as LG's black, but Boot Sock held his own strong pace. Keeping to the outside, Casey followed behind LG. The cattle did not act like they were going to stop.

LG pointed the lead steer all the way around the meadow and joined up with the drags — the herd became an immense rotating circle. The sound of their pounding hoofs was as loud as thunder.

Edwin, Ira, Steve and Rufe all made it into Preacher's Glen and spread out. They tried to contain the milling herd, to keep it turned in on itself. Lee and Davis, who had been riding drag, were the last to arrive.

After what seemed like forever, the herd finally slowed down to a walk. The riders kept the cattle together, riding outside the circle.

LG loped up to Edwin, whose hat had come off back in the trees somewhere.

"Lose anybody?" LG asked.

"We need to. Those McGonkin brothers...what damn suckers."

Without his hat Edwin looked very boyish. His cheekbones were rosy red with the chill, which didn't help his appearance any. LG thought he looked like Pinnochio. Edwin pushed his fingers through his mussy hair, suddenly self-conscious that his hat was gone.

"You're not gonna believe this," he said, trying to catch his breath. "They roped a dead cow and thumped the ground with it."

The cattle were bawling and lowing. It was loud, and LG wasn't quite sure he heard right.

"A dead…they did *what*?"

Edwin hawked and spat on the ground.

"Antics about took us to the grave. No-account teat-licks."

Chapter 23
Mining Camp
Continental Divide

The mountainside glowed and popped like the 4th of July.

Opening another pommel bag full of cartridges and shells, Roy Caldwell hustled across the slippery stones. Weaving through a clump of weather-beaten ponderosa, he crouched down behind several men in the darkness.

“Creek?” Roy whispered, holding out the bag to Red Creek Mincy.

Red Creek reached in and pulled out a handful of .45 caliber rounds. He examined one to see if it would work in his gun, which it did, so he filled up his coat pocket. Roy took a moment to admire Red Creek’s rifle. It was an old British Whitworth. Roy had never seen any gun quite like it. The rifle looked heavy, with a long barrel.

The rest of the posse all carried Winchesters. Most of them were identical guns, firing the same caliber. This was because Merle Hastings bought brand new Winchester Model 1886 repeating rifles for each of his ranch hands — right out of Ben Leavick’s mercantile store. Merle told everyone he wanted his men to have reliable firearms if they were going to run down Emerson Greer’s murderers. This was a consolation for Ben, since he had been closer friends with Emerson than most of the townsfolk — except maybe Griff. He gladly sold them to Merle, taking pride in the thought that one of the rifles from his store would be the one to put a bullet in Bill or the newspaperman who sprung him. It was clear now that the man was no columnist.

Almost every member of the posse was taking shots at the mining shack, except Roy Caldwell. Since he never considered himself an accurate shot, he took it upon himself to be the supply man. He left Red Creek and hurried over to Ben Leavick, who had his rifle barrel propped in the nook of a tree limb so he could shoot straight. He was not concerned with wasting ammunition and was burning through rounds as fast as he could chamber them.

From this angle, they could all see the rooftop rising above the ridge-line. Moonlight made the little mining cabin even easier to locate, but it was still the middle of the night. The one clear target they could all spot was the window. It was a distinct square of red light — and it gave them something to draw a bead on.

Taking the bag, Roy hunched over and made his way across the talus to another group of men, who were firing from behind some large boulders.

Ben Leavick fired twice more before his rifle was empty. Roy's timing was perfect. Ben scooped out several handfuls and put the rounds in his pockets. At that moment, Griff moved out into the open and waved them on in the moonlight.

Everyone quit firing at the same time. After so many guns going off, the silence seemed unnatural. Griff strained to listen. He could hear the crackle of fire coming from the broken window and he could smell smoke. No one was shooting back.

Now was the time.

Stepping as quietly as possible, the Grand Lake posse slid out of the trees and boulders and moved carefully up the rocky slope. When he got closer, Griff could see fresh splinters and white pockmarks all over the front. They had done a good job of peppering the shack with bullets. If that didn't send the right message, nothing else would. He hoped the gang was ready to surrender, but in his gut he knew it wouldn't be that easy.

Griff kept his eye on the window. Everyone did. If anyone saw movement, he knew they were all going to shoot at the same time. But nothing happened. No one inside the cabin dared to look out that window. Griff knew they were smart enough to realize what would happen if they did. He was not surprised.

They got close enough to realize smoke was pouring out the window frame. It was thick in the air and several men started coughing. Ben Leavick and Griff moved slowly towards the door and as they did, they both nearly tripped. It was the body of Will Wyllis — the man they shot.

"This one's dead," Griff whispered to Ben. He looked over his shoulder at Merle. "Ready?"

Merle's cowboys spread out around him with their brand new Winchesters up. Merle himself stepped over Will and tried the door latch. Griff and Ben took positions on either side. Merle suddenly kicked the door open and began unloading his Colt. Griff and Ben did the same. Red Creek jammed his gun through the broken window and fired blindly around the room.

After a minute, they stopped shooting. Flames were raging everywhere in the cabin. Black smoke pitched out the open door and rolled up into the sky.

But there was no return gunfire.

Ben, Griff and Merle all knelt down to see beneath the smoke, which made their eyes sting. Griff saw the table in the middle of the room engulfed in flames. So was the wool rug beneath it. The twisted tree trunk the Mexicans had dragged inside lay in the middle of the room, absolutely roaring. The flames reached all the way to the roof. The heat it was throwing off was almost unbearable.

Griff scooted in far enough to see an unfortunate miner who, shot full of holes, had been dumped unceremoniously on the floor. Behind the bright flames, Griff noticed a big hole in the back wall. He knew immediately what happened. The gang tore a hole through the thin planks and then escaped into the night.

Earlier, Red Creek had snuck up and scouted around the cabin before any of the shooting started. He reported back to Griff what he saw. He also told him there was no back door — the only way in or out was through the front door. Griff chastised himself. If he had guessed they would bust through the building, he certainly would have sent men around back to catch them.

"Circle around!" Griff shouted. "Hustle!"

They all filed around the building, but no one was back there. Bill Ewing and his men were gone.

"By God, they won't get far," Griff announced.

"Gonna kill them for what they did!" Ben shouted, hoping to be heard.

The posse was geared up for a confrontation. Discovering the cabin was empty did not sit well. Merle's boys started shooting into the darkness, hoping some of their shots found their mark. There was nothing to aim at that they could see, but they fired anyway.

"Gonna hang you bastards!" Merle yelled, angry at being outwitted.

Once again, the mountainside was lit up like fireworks. Even Griff worked through all the rounds in his gun, caught up in the moment. He did not stop until the hammer clicked several times.

Red Creek came around the cabin. In one hand, he held the head of Will Wyllis by the hair. In his other hand was the long gutting knife he always carried. Everyone stopped shooting at once.

"Oh, me," Merle said quietly.

Red Creek just stood there in the flicker of the firelight. The cabin roof collapsed and a fireball plumed up into the air. Merle knew Red had been in the War back in the 60's — a sharpshooter or something. Merle himself had been in the fighting, as well, as a foot soldier. He had seen a lot of blood during that time. Seeing

Red with a head in his hand took him right back to Antietam. Merle lowered his rifle. His boys watched him and did the same.

At twelve thousand feet, there were so many stars in the sky it was hard to distinguish the constellations. The wind gusted, whistling freely along the ridge. It made the fire swell and roar like a train. By morning, Griff knew the cabin would be a pile of charred cinders. For now though, it was a heat source. The posse from Grand Lake silently gathered around it.

Red Creek held up the trophy in the orange glow.

"Got a pickle jar in the wagon," Roy Caldwell told him.

Chapter 24
Spring Gulch
Preacher's Glen

The blackened coffee pot sat in the coals at the fire's edge, steam puffing out. The fire was warm and all the boys of the B-Cross were grouped around it. Just above the flames was the potrack, but nothing hung from it at this late hour.

Hopper was lying quietly at Casey's feet. Without warning, he rolled onto his side, gave off a low groan and sighed profoundly.

"Me, too," Casey told him, and tugged lightly at his furry tail. Hopper opened an eye but otherwise did not move.

Rufe was the only one who wasn't there — he had been shamed into riding first watch. LG chewed on a stick. He squinted into the fire and hadn't said a word since the younger McGonkin left to saddle his night horse. After they got the cows settled down, they all pieced together what had happened to spook the herd. No one was pleased with the McGonkin brothers at the moment.

Emmanuel stood near the wagon with a flour sack tied around his waist. It was splotchy with congealed blood. So were his hands and forearms. Emmanuel had just finished gutting an antelope, which Gyp had shot earlier.

"Just dried apples an' mountain berries tonight," the cook said without apology. "Gonna have pronghorn tomorrow — be pleasin' for something different."

No one spoke.

"When ya want 'em, bedrolls in the wagon."

"Think we're all just waiting on that coffee," LG muttered. "Know I am."

Edwin got up slowly and yawned. He wandered over to the chuckwagon. He glanced back at the fire to make sure no one was watching him.

"Lost my damn hat," Edwin said to Emmanuel. "Got an extry?"

Shaking his head, Emmanuel reached into the back. He got a hold of an empty flour sack, like the one around his waist. He shook it out a couple times and handed it to Edwin.

"Tie this to ya head."

Edwin looked at him in disbelief.

"Pullin' my teat?" he asked in a half-whisper.

"Oh, no, done this muhse'f once out on the trail," Emmanuel said. "Head'll stay warmish."

The fire cracked and popped. The men were all sitting on their saddle blankets because the ground was damp and cold. Since LG had finally broken the silence, Davis decided it was safe enough to try his hand at conversation.

"Casey...what happened to your pup?"

Stirring, Casey inhaled slowly and sat up straight.

"Stepped on. He was just young. Didn't know which end of a horse gets up first."

Davis tossed a piece of dried apple toward the big dog. It landed on the ground right in front of his nose. He ate it without even lifting his head.

"Aw that's too bad," Davis said. "First saw him, thought he was part lobo...maybe ki-yote."

"Maybe he is, I don't rightly know."

A soft breeze blew up and whipped the flames around for a minute. Then the night grew calm again. Turning slowly toward Steve McGonkin, LG aimed a hard look in his direction.

"Next watch starts at four," he said.

Leaning close LG added, "Need me to *wake* you?"

The older McGonkin brother leaned away, careful to avoid LG's eyes. He knew the man was mad at him. It had been Rufe's fool idea to toy with that dead beeve. Of course, Steve went along with it, so what could he say? Sometimes that brother of his was dumber than a post. If Rufe *ever* tried to fool with dead beeves again, Steve was bound and determined not to join in.

"No sir," Steve replied quietly. "No need."

"Well, don't spook the herd when you crawl outta your hot roll."

"No sir, I won't."

"You bet you won't. Cut a pair of chaps outta your hide."

Steve got to his feet.

"Best get my bedding."

Shaking his head in disgust, LG stared holes in Steve's back as the man made his way to the wagon. The antelope skin Emmanuel had been working on was stretched across one of the wheels. It still needed to be scraped. Steve needed to reach between the water barrel and that wagon wheel to get his bedroll. He tried not to get blood on his shirt. His bedding was buried, but he managed to dig it out and then went off into the aspens. Normally, he liked to sleep by the fire. Not tonight. He wished he had some hot coffee in him before he turned in, but glancing back at LG he knew it was better not to wait around for it.

Emmanuel walked over to the ring of cowboys. He suspected the water would be hot enough to get some coffee going. The lid on the pot was flopping. One thing a good cook never did was boil the coffee. Davis told him that frequently, but Emmanuel always forgot to check the water until he heard the lid flopping — a sure sign the water was boiling.

Gyp sat on a stump warming his hands. He had taken the remuda ahead of the herd, following the chuck wagon through Spring Gulch all the way into the glen. As Emmanuel set up camp, Gyp set up a rope corral. The rope was half an inch thick, and he always stretched it taut four feet above the ground. That was the only thing holding the horses in, but it always worked. When the stampeding cattle came rushing into the meadow, Gyp's first thought was that the horses would bust right out, and then he would have a chore on his hands. But they did not bust out, which was a relief.

Emmanuel picked off the lid and poured fresh ground coffee into the boiling water. Cracking an egg, Emmanuel dropped it right in, shell and all, and put the lid back on. Davis just shook his head.

The cook yawned and straightened up slowly. He was ready for the summer. Emmanuel hated the winter. Especially up in the mountains, the cold temperatures always hung on longer than down on the plains. He hoped that last snowstorm was it, and warmer weather was on its way.

"Aw, crud!"

It was Steve's voice, out in the aspen grove. Emmanuel was the only one who heard, but he knew what happened. He had gutted the antelope back there, and the guts were piled between two trees. Steve probably walked right through the goo. No flies were out, but when the sun came up there would be a lot of them buzzing around. If there had been flies right then, perhaps Steve would have had some kind of warning. Since Emmanuel knew they would all be on trail again in just a few hours, he didn't waste time taking the guts further out.

No one else was in a talking mood, so Casey chatted with Davis.

"What outfit were you working for last?"

"Spent all last summer at Ferguson's ranch, up in Estes," Davis replied. "Worked till the wagon pulled off, the last of November. Lee was up there, too...at the Elkhorn. But you know how winter goes. Not much for a buckaroo."

"Don't tell me you signed on with the railroad."

Davis grinned.

"Took up with the Rio Grande, laying track down across the Bayou Salado," he told Casey. "Boy, they're probably up Trout

Creek Pass by now. Shoulda drifted south — cording mossheads on the Matamortos would be better than freezing my tail in Lake George. Miserable work."

Now that both Rufe and Steve were out of his sight, LG was starting to relax.

"Any work you can't do from a saddle is miserable," he said. "Ain't that right, Ima?"

LG kicked at Ira's outstretched boot.

Ira frowned and pulled his foot away. He had only known LG for less than a week. He wondered how long it would take for LG to get his name right.

Chapter 25
Ward

Even in the light of dawn, it was obvious the fresh snow was not going to last. Everything started dripping as the air warmed. It seemed like every few minutes another pine branch would shake off a clump of snow.

Julianna stood on the porch, bundled up beneath the stout eaves which overhung the front door. She loved mornings. It was so peaceful. Two robins flew down and landed in a fir tree. Their red chests were fluffy and they shook their feathery wings to flick out the moisture.

With a smile, Julianna watched them chirp at each other. Then they noticed her. Their little black eyes were curious.

"I have no crumbs for you," she told them.

From inside the house, she heard footsteps and low conversation. It was Samuel and Josephine, starting the day themselves. Julianna was an early riser, especially when she slept in a strange place. Their guest room was nice and the spring bed was comfortable — but it wasn't hers.

Julianna was about to go in and say good morning, but then she heard Josephine's voice rise. It was obviously an argument. Perhaps it was better to wait outside for a few more minutes.

Finally, the door creaked open. Wrapping a shawl around her shoulders, Josephine came outside and joined her on the porch.

"Domestic tranquility," Josephine announced wryly. "Head of the household...what purebred nonsense."

She stomped the porch — she was mad. Julianna gave her a hug and a kind smile.

"You're moving, then."

Josephine sighed.

"We're moving."

The two robins were still watching from their tree. After a minute they both flew down onto the wet grass, looking for worms to come to the surface. The snow was melting and they knew it.

Julianna took her hand and squeezed.

"Come on, let's walk."

The air was cool but not as cold as other mornings that week. The sky was getting lighter with each step.

"Let's get breakfast together one more time before I go home," Julianna said. "Away from Samuel and his Hilltop Mine."

They walked up the road and wound past the neighbors' homes. Other people were up with the dawn, too, but the two young women had the road to themselves most of the way. Above town somewhere, dynamite went off and shook the air. The first blast of the day.

They turned onto the main road and made their way uphill, breathing loudly with the effort. The Haw & Gee was still open — it had never closed. Like most of the mountain towns, Ward entertained its own gamblers and drinkers all night long. For them, the first detonation of the day was their dinner bell.

A wagon was parked at the top of the hill, where several men were busy leveling a tall pole with ropes and mules. Julianna and Josephine walked by, looking up to see what was going on.

"Telephone line," Josephine told Julianna. "Can you believe it?"

"It was only a matter of time."

"Don't have that in Horseshoe," Josephine muttered darkly. "Don't have a school, barely a post office. What am I suppose to do when the child comes?"

Stopping suddenly, Julianna grabbed her by the shoulders.

"A baby?" she asked. "Is that what's going on?"

Josephine nodded. She was in a bad mood, but Julianna broke into a warm smile and gave her a hug.

"Josephine, you could have told me you were having a baby! I'm so happy for you."

"Come on, I'm hungry," Josephine said. But it was hard for her to stay angry. She was angry at her husband anyway, for deciding to take a job at the Hilltop Mine and relocate the family to Horseshoe — without her say in the matter. Since he was back at the house, she decided to let it go. This may be one of the last times she got to spend with Julianna, and she did not want to waste it complaining about an obstinate spouse.

They went to the Halfway House for breakfast. At that hour, they had their pick of tables. Several Chinese men were there already, having their own morning meal. Their conversation was gibberish to the women. Coming out from the kitchen, Hugh waved them over.

"Something to eat for you?"

"For both of us, please," Julianna answered.

They made their way to a table by the big picture window. They looked out over the treetops and the steep green slopes. It was a beautiful morning, and Julianna could not believe her friend's news.

"Why haven't you told me yet?"

"If you would come to town more than once a month, I could tell you these things."

"I get here more than that," Julianna retorted. "What about Hazel? Vera?"

"Haven't said," Josephine said softly. "I've just realized myself, here, recent."

Hugh set down two steaming plates of eggs and beef.

The main door swung open and a tall stockman came in. Hugh glanced up from Julianna and Josephine to see who it was.

"Til Blancett!" he called. "With you in a moment."

Til waved. He stepped up to the bar and set his coat and gloves on top. He had slept later than he expected to. But the barn had been closed up tight — it had kept the heat in, but when the sun rose it kept the light out, too.

"Let me fix you a plate," Hugh told him and disappeared in the kitchen.

Til turned to survey the room. He saw the Chinamen talking among themselves, and the two women sitting at the window. He tipped his hat towards Julianna and Josephine.

Hugh returned from his kitchen with a plate and coffee. He set it in front of Til.

"Two bits?"

"Yep," Hugh said. "How's the B-Cross-C?"

"Moving out, actually."

"Thought you just moved back up there!" Hugh said, surprised.

"I did."

"Guess it has something to do with the Great Die-Up."

"Changes the game."

Til sampled the eggs. They were scrambled up and mixed with some kind of cheese. Usually Til ate hard-fried eggs. But that was because whenever he cooked eggs for himself, that was how they turned out.

"Tell Xin he did good."

Hugh snorted.

"That Oriental can't comprehend a bleat I say."

Chapter 26

The door eased open and Bill Ewing walked into the Halfway House. Vincent came in right behind him.

Before he got very far, Bill turned to look out the window. There they were, walking around in a tight-knit group: Poqito, Caverango, Granger and Lem were following Ned around. Bill grimaced. They looked like a damn circus troupe. Didn't they realize all the locals were staring at them? This was just a dinky little mining town. In a small town, you had to take pains to blend in — you don't want to stick out. Now here they were, trying to outrun a posse and these fools were making a spectacle of themselves.

"Traipsing along like mice and the piper," Bill said softly. "Tell those clowns to separate."

Going back outside, Vincent flagged them down. Ned saw and came right over — the others turned and followed along on Ned's heels. Still watching from the window, Bill shook his head at their tactless behavior.

"Get you a plate?" Hugh asked him.

Bill pulled off his wet leather gloves. His coat was damp and dirty. He took it off and hung it on a wall peg.

"Whatever you got on the stove."

Vincent came back in. He took off his own coat and draped it over his arm. His vest looked prim and clean, like he was out in his Sunday best. Bill smirked. That guy always looked proper. Even after getting shot at, burnt out, and riding all night in the wind.

"What about those pickle-nuts?" Bill asked him.

"Parsed out — two by two," Vincent said, pointing out the window. "Like Noah's Ark."

Bill turned and looked again. Ned had stopped and was standing in the street unscrewing his whiskey bottle. Lem and Granger were walking one way, while Poqito and Caverango were headed in the exact opposite direction. Across the street, a freighter was loading his wagon at the general store. The storekeeper was helping him with crates. They both had stopped to watch.

It was clear they needed to keep moving, but Bill wanted a hot meal first. It had been a long night, and they were not carrying many supplies. Hugh came by their table and set down plates and coffee cups.

Hugh took their money and went back to the bar. He paused in front of Til, who was still standing. He had remained where he was, standing at the bar while he finished his eggs and beefsteak.

"Ought to sit down to et, Til."

"Naw. Gonna be in the saddle rest of the day," Til replied. "This'll do fine."

"Telegraph's open by now."

"Hope that wet night we just had don't interfere with the connection any."

"Just a spring squall," Hugh said. "Not like we got three feet. That'd bring down the wires for sure."

The front door opened again. Ian Mitchell and Jim Everitt came inside. Ian carried a double-barreled shotgun. He set it on the bartop, just a few steps from Til.

Vincent and Bill noticed them come in. Who were these two? The posse? Had they gotten there already? That shotgun made Bill uneasy. But they both stayed seated, trying to stay cool and not draw attention to themselves. Vincent and Bill forked their eggs with one hand, while under the table they each took out their .45's and placed the guns in their laps while they listened to Jim and Ian talk.

"Leaving out this morning?" Hugh asked them.

"Jerk-line's all hitched," Jim said to Hugh. "Soon as we eat."

"Down to Gold Hill first, pick up their mail and such," Ian mentioned. "Why? Something to send along?"

Hugh reached into his vest pocket and pulled out a silver pocketwatch by the chain. He unhooked it and dangled it into Jim's palm.

"When you get to Boulder, just pass this on to John Meeker. Tell him it goes to my sister Lynn."

"Condolences," Jim said. "About your father."

"Means a lot more to her than me," Hugh informed him. "He was an old cuss. Good to the girls, though. I ain't going to the funeral, but this'll do. Family heirloom — take good care with it."

Jim Everitt turned it over in his hand. He opened the cover with his thumbnail. Inside was an inscription: *John Frederick Hughes, from Helena your loving wife: Absence from those we love is self from self.*

"Your last name is Hughes?" he remarked. "Hugh Hughes?"

Hugh stared at him but did not say anything.

"I'll make sure it gets to John Meeker, then."

Hugh nodded his appreciation.

"Thank you much."

Jim put the watch into his own vest pocket, patting it securely. Hugh nodded once more, and moved off to check on his other customers. The Chinese men were gesturing, trying to get his attention. They were pointing at their cups.

Julianna and Josephine watched Hugh bring out their coffee.

"Those Chinamen are hard workers, Samuel says," Josephine mentioned.

She looked around the room. It was still early for the Halfway House. Most mornings were quiet like this, whenever she stopped in for breakfast. A couple tired-looking gamblers came in and took a table. Other than that, it was just Vincent, Bill, Til, and the Chinese miners.

"If there were any Italians in here, we might see a fist fight," Josephine said. "Samuel tells me they don't get along too well with Chinamen."

"Why is that?"

"Don't know," Josephine said with a shrug. "Samuel just says they don't. Guess there are big fights up in Como, in those coal mines. Happens all the time. According to Samuel, Ward is pretty tame."

Chapter 27

Spring Gulch
Preacher's Glen

The sun was just starting to color the sky. Emmanuel knelt down and blew on the coals to see if he could coax a flame out of it. Morning was Emmanuel's favorite time of day. On the far side of the glen, he watched the moon floating over the Great Divide. The crescent had grown big and turned a rich yellow. It was suspended right over the ridgeline, getting bigger as it inched down. All night long he watched the moon. When he was driving the chuckwagon in the dark he saw it creep up over the trees in front of him, stark white like a fat thumbnail. Up it went, up into the cold windy sky and right over the top of his head. Now here he was, trying to get the fire back up for breakfast. The coals were still glowing and all it took were a few pinches of pine needles. Pine needles always burnt quick, hot and put out thick smoke. He added a few dead branches and the cookfire was going again. That big yellow thumbnail moon was almost touching the snowy ridge — like it was going to land right on top of it.

"Look at that, will you?" LG asked, with his normal wry grin. He pointed up at the ridge. Emmanuel was relieved that LG seemed to be back in a good mood. He had been fairly bent out of shape with the McGonkins. Or the McSpookies, as he called them now.

LG was an early riser no matter how late he stayed up or how little sleep he got. It was his habit to check on the horses as soon as he woke up — he even beat Emmanuel out of the bedroll most mornings.

"That moon gonna sit up on that ridge," Emmanuel told him.

It was chilly, but Emmanuel could tell it was going to warm up nicely before long. By the wagon, the McGonkins were still buried in their bedrolls. So were Casey and Edwin, and Gyp. Ira was off in the meadow riding the final watch for the night. When Emmanuel first drove the chuckwagon through there, the glen had a perfect layer of fresh snow all across it. It was beautiful in the moonlight. His own wagon tracks were the first thing to cut across it. Now, in the morning light, Emmanuel looked out. The fresh powder was completely churned up from the stampede. It was like a farmer had tilled the whole field.

Davis smelled the smoke. He was wrapped up in his blanket so thoroughly only his nose stuck out. Moving quick, Davis threw off his bedding, grabbed his boots and danced across the cold ground without even taking the time to put them on.

"Hoo hoo!" Davis called, poorly mimicking a train whistle.

Lee watched him go. He was shivering and had been waiting for the fire, too. He sat up, but unlike Davis, took the time to wiggle on his stiff frozen boots.

"What was that supposed to be?" LG asked Davis.

"Locomotive."

"Don't know why you would stoop to railroad work," LG asked him, mystified.

"Ferguson ran out of cow work," Davis told him.

"What's that ol' boy run up there anyhow?"

"Hereford."

Lee sat on a rock next to Davis and pulled his boots right back off his feet. It was only twenty quick steps from his bedroll to the fire, but Lee was sensitive about his bare feet.

"Ferguson didn't run outta no cow work," Lee explained with a knowing smile.

LG looked over at Davis, but the man just rubbed his toes and stretched his feet out over the flames.

"Heard about Aspen?" Davis asked LG. "They are blasting railroad grade right up the Roaring Fork even as we speak. Narrow-gauge."

"These are historic and industrious times," LG said in a disinterested tone. "Let 'er buck."

"Ferguson's got three awful purty daughters," Lee mentioned.

Davis examined the sole of his foot and picked at a corn.

Casey came up and sat down on a stump. He yawned.

"Wonder what Ferguson would do if one of the hired hands was to court one?" Lee continued thoughtfully. "A barn dance is only a barn dance when other folks are invited."

Suddenly, Davis reached over and cupped his hand over Lee's mouth. Lee jumped up and spat in the fire.

"Now my mouth tastes like your filthy toe corn."

LG looked over at the chuckwagon. Emmanuel was working the coffee mill. In the quiet morning, it was easy to hear him scoop coffee beans out and pour them in the mill.

"Grind that thing," LG called.

Off in the aspen grove, Gyp crawled out from his blankets. The horses saw him, too, and started nickering. Gyp went over to the wagon and dug around in the back. He found the grain pail and headed to the rope corral. There was enough grass to keep the horses busy, but Til gave him specific instructions. He wanted his remuda grained. So Gyp fed them grain every morning.

Steve and Rufe were both awake, but lying silently in their bedrolls. Neither had any interest in going to the fire and being berated. Edwin finally roused himself and came over. He held his hands over the fire.

"I don't see no church," he pointed out, apropos of nothing. "Why's it called Preacher's Glen if there ain't no church?"

"You need to confess something?" LG asked him. "You can tell me. I'm a peach at keeping secrets."

To the west, the moon had dropped below the Divide. To the east, the sky was turning a whitish blue as the sun came up.

"There's a preacher up in Estes Park that climbs them mountains," Lee mentioned.

Edwin glanced over at him curiously.

"Elkanah Lamb. Used to go inside the saloons, Bible in one hand — .45 in the other."

Ira rode in just then. He brought his horse right up to the fire and stopped. He looked down at LG.

"Cows a-stirring."

LG glanced back up at him, waiting for more.

"And?"

Shifting in his saddle, Ira looked blank.

Davis was not finished with his story.

"The good reverend used to guide folks right up to the summit of Longs Peak, for five whole dollars. His boy Carlyle is doing it these days."

"*Guides* them?" Edwin asked, confused. "People pay to climb mountains?"

"Hell, yes. Next season, you should hire onto one of the ranches up there," Lee told the boy. "I worked for WE James last season — he runs the Elkhorn ranch. You should sign on there yourself...peeling broncs, punching cattle."

Holding up his fingers, Davis began counting.

"There's five different spreads up in Estes," he said. "The Fergusons, the Lambs, Spragues, MacGregors, and Jameses."

Ira realized he was out of the conversation, so he turned his horse around and rode toward the aspen grove. He got down and let his horse nose through the frosty grass. There was no reason to untack his horse since they would be moving again after breakfast was over.

"I heard some Irish lord is buying up all the land," Casey said.

"The Earl of Dunraven," said Davis, with a frown. "Locals hate that ol' boy."

"Thinks high of himself," Lee explained. "Wants to own the whole dern park. Turn it into his very own private hunting preserve."

"Going to be trouble before that all pans out."

Edwin stood up straight, stretching his arms high above his head.

"I ain't interested in working for no damn Earl," he said with a yawn. "I *am* interested in some damn flapjacks."

At the chuckwagon, Emmanuel was rooting around the tool box. He hoped they would keep chatting because the coffee mill was bound up.

Chapter 28
Ward

Their breath blew out in white puffs, but the mules stood quietly and waited in the chilly air.

"Check Bitty's right front," Jim Everitt said. He worked along the harness buckles, securing them.

Ian Mitchell leaned down and softly pressed his shoulder against Bitty the mule's upper leg — to let her know he was there. Then he brushed his hand down the backside of her knee and fetlock, and took hold of the hoof. Bitty shifted her weight, and Ian lifted her foot off the ground. These mules were bigger than regular horses, some kind of draft cross — he wasn't sure what, though. Ian examined the sole, using a hoof pick to clean it out.

"Shoe's loose."

"Must of happened o'er night in the corral," Jim said. "Not like that yesterday."

Jim removed his hat and scratched his scalp. He walked around the mules and bent down to look it over. Ian held the hoof up so he could see.

"Have to pull it," Jim decided. "Tack it back on again."

"Either do it ourselves," Ian suggested slowly. "Or we traipse on over and get Hugh to pack us up some steak cuts...while someone else does."

Standing up tall, Jim stretched and groaned at the thought of horseshoeing on a chilly morning — in the shade nonetheless.

"My back *has* been rather tangy."

The men looked at each other.

"I'll get the farrier."

Gently, Ian set Bitty's hoof back down. The sun was high enough now to light up the top of the Halfway House. It was still early and still cold but smoke was already pumping out of the chimney. Jim headed down Main Street towards the blacksmith shop. Ian watched him go and began the process of getting Bitty out of the team. He removed her headstall and bit, undid the traces, and led her out from behind the singletree.

"He could have noticed this sort of thing *prior* to tacking up," Ian told Bitty in a tart whisper.

He led the big mule away from the stagecoach and tied her to a hitching post. The other mules watched closely, with their big ears perked up and listening. They wondered if grain was somehow involved in this turn of events. Ian rubbed her on the neck.

"Which one of these hambones was bothering you, huh Bitty?"

Bitty turned her large head and looked back at the other mules, which were still traced up.

"Yeah, I thought so," Ian said, following her gaze. "Buckshay... you wild ass. Let her alone."

A couple cowhands passed by and saw him talking to the mules. It was young Billy McCoy and his little brother Bobby.

"Mornin', Jehu," Billy McCoy said rather snidely.

"Scamper off, you skunks."

They laughed and went into the Halfway House. Ian shook his head. The McCoy boys had little in the way of social graces. Last time he drove through Ward, someone shoveled steaming horse turds inside the coach. Got the mail all cruddy. He suspected the McCoy brothers.

Ian patted Bitty on the neck and then decided to remove her collar. Grabbing it by the hame, he set it on the ground and propped it against the fence.

"Stand easy, we'll get that shoe tacked on right."

It was not long until Jim came back. He was walking with another man. It was the shoer, whose name was Zeke. Zeke carried a hammer, nippers, rasp, and wore a short leather apron.

"Move," Zeke said to Ian, rather bluntly.

Ian stepped away. Taking up Bitty's hoof, the shoer pinched it between his knees. He looked it over, nodding thoughtfully to himself. Using the nippers, he began to pry off the shoe.

Jim and Ian watched him work for a minute.

"Just leave 'er there when you're done," Jim told him. "Gonna be at Hugh's."

Zeke did not look up or even say a word. He was glad they were leaving. He preferred to work without the customers looming over him. Criticism was an irritation to Zeke and so were customers. Getting the job done well and right was always easiest when there was no one telling him how to do his job — when in fact he knew *exactly* what to do and how to do it.

After a moment, Jim Everitt realized Zeke was not going to answer. He shrugged, and he and Ian Mitchell headed for the Halfway House. It was time for one last decent meal before they headed on down the canyon.

"Way I figure it, we either pack out Xin's cooking or else gum on that johnnycake we get stocked with."

Ian shook his head and chimed in his salt.

"Grand courtesy of the Overland Stage."

They went inside. Ian Mitchell saw the McCoy boys. They were sitting at a table not too far away. At first, he felt like turning right around and heading back outside. They could just as easily get a meal over at the Miser's Brewery. But then almost as quickly, he decided to stay where he was and eat in there. Ian realized that if he could *see* the McCoy brothers, he knew right where they were. And if they were right there, then they weren't shoveling steaming horse turds into his stagecoach.

Chapter 29

Poqito and Caverango leaned on the fence rail. They were watching the hostler rope the horses in the corral. Of course, the horses did not want to get roped. They were giving him a run for it. Bill was getting antsy, waiting. They needed fresh horses, but this was taking far too long. The posse from Grand Lake could be riding into Ward any minute and he wanted to get out of there before they did.

Bill turned around and paced past the corral. It was hard to watch an inept hostler try and throw a loop when time was of the essence. Then he noticed the stagecoach parked nearby and the farrier running a rasp across Bitty the mule's right front foot. Bill marched over and looked over Zeke's shoulder.

"Where's that coach headed?"

Zeke had his head down and kept working. Zeke hated being interrupted by casual talk. Full concentration was important when working on a hoof. He might accidentally drive a nail into the white line, or quick a horse during a trim. That would be a shame and an embarrassment for a professional horseshoer to make a mistake simply because of idle conversation which he did not care for in the first place. Zeke glanced up to see who was interrupting him, gave Bill a disapproving glare, then went back to work.

Vincent watched all this. He walked right over and leaned so close to Zeke that Zeke could feel his breath on his neck. This was far too close for Zeke's preference. Didn't this fellow realize he was getting in the way? He sighed heavily. Zeke hated doing his work outside where anybody and their cousin could just walk right up and get in the way, or badger him with the same basic questions about horse hooves he'd heard a thousand times over.

"He said where's it headed?" Vincent reminded Zeke.

The horseshoer was getting irritated now. He knew he should have made Jim Everitt walk this dang-blasted mule right on down the hill to his blacksmith shop. He could have tacked this shoe on in privacy and not have to put up with irritating questions or people standing too close.

"When a body's talking to you," Vincent said to Zeke, "a response would be polite."

But again, Zeke did not say anything. Not saying anything was Zeke's way of letting people know their questions were unwelcome.

Bill watched Vincent's face start to get red. The veins in his neck started to pulse and stick out. It was the same look he had when they shanghaied the deputy in the Grand Lake courthouse — and Vincent had come very close to shooting the unconscious deputy in the head.

"Remember Grand Lake," Bill warned. "A quiet passage would have been preferable."

But Vincent did not move and his face was still red. Bill tried again.

"Put holes in a man, would be leaving a more *trackable* swath."

Zeke looked up at the two men, especially the one standing a little too close. He stopped rasping Bitty's hoof abruptly, midstroke. Zeke suddenly had a fluttery feeling in his stomach. Like the time last fall when he became so impatient with Hugh's Arabian gelding, who simply would not stand while he was being trimmed, that Zeke whacked the rasp in the gelding's side. It was a hard slap but the horse did not flinch — the gelding slowly turned his dark eyes and looked at Zeke in such a hateful way, it gave him the fluttery feeling in his stomach.

"Well verily, Bill, you may be in the right," Vincent replied, softening.

Without another word, the two men turned around and headed back to the corral. Zeke was still hunched under the mule, holding his rasp against Bitty's upturned hoof. Zeke wondered if he should just walk this mule right on down to the shop and finish up there. Why did he even leave the shop today? He knew better. Trying to tack a shoe on a mule, right here on Main Street was not even a gamble — it was a guarantee: a guarantee that he would be interrupted. When Jim Everitt came in, he should have told him to bring the mule down if he wanted the shoe tacked on.

"*Vamanos*," Caverango called to Bill. "*Quatro* cow horses, and *tres* fresh broke *mesteños*."

"Pay the horse trader," Bill instructed Vincent.

"And pick us the ones that are well busted," he added under his breath. "They can ride those mustangs."

Coming out of the General Merchandise, Lem and Granger saw everyone standing around the corral and headed over. They were carrying supplies they just bought.

"Got some rounds and shells here," Lem told Bill.

Granger had a sack full of groceries. Ned went up to him and pulled open the sack to see what he had.

"Your eye's all swolled up," Ned pointed out.

"Can see just fine," Granger replied, but in fact his eye was swollen and hurt like hell. "Fine enough to blast your guts all over this street."

"Surly...*and* a swolled peeper," Ned said. "You'll make a fine trail companion today."

Granger wasn't about to mention he had lost another tooth. It was bad enough his eye got mashed by the door. The worst part was that none of them even got a scratch. Except Will Wyllis, of course, who was shot in the gut and the head.

Lem and Ned walked off towards the corral gate. The Mexicans were leading out the new horses. Robins and bluejays were chirping up in a cottonwood nearby. Granger set the grocery sack down and collected stones to throw at the birds while he waited.

Bill looked down Main Street. The road was beginning to fill up with miners and townspeople, horses and freight wagons. The rising sun was getting hot, too — Bill looked up at the sky and squinted.

"Warming up."

Vincent nodded. He held his long-tailed coat folded over his left arm.

"We stay here any longer, gonna run our luck."

"I'll tell the boys to saddle up," Vincent said. "And I'll talk to that bronc-stomper — see which of these fine beasts Granger deserves. Make sure he gets a top choice."

Bill nodded, still squinting at the sky.

"Find one that lacks in girth, grace and finish."

Chapter 30
Spring Gulch

"When I was out a-ridin'
the graveyard shift midnight till dawn...
well the moon was as bright as a readin' light;
for a letter from an old friend back home."

LG's singing voice was clear and loud. It was a trail song.

"He asked me, why do you ride for your money?
Why do you rope for short pay?
You ain't gettin' nowhere, and you're losing your share;
aww, you must have gone crazy out there."

Riding point with Casey, LG turned in his saddle and checked behind him. He spotted Lee and Davis, one on each side of the cowline, only a hundred yards back.

"You boys are too far up," LG shouted. "Don't lose me any cows today. Get on back."

"Admirin' your fine tenor voice," Davis replied. But both of them stopped and let the cows walk by for a while.

Suddenly, Edwin emerged from the trees, passed Lee and Davis at a trot and rode right up to LG. The flour sack Emmanuel had given him was tied around his head like a turban.

"What's wrong?" LG asked him.

"Ira's driving me batty. Need a change of scenery."

"Why don't you ride drag with those McGonkin nitwits?" LG suggested. "With that handsome bonnet, you'd fit right in."

"I prefer company with a nugget in the brainpan."

LG nodded — that was understandable. The sky overhead was completely cloudless. Quite a contrast from the sleety weather they had the day before. All the trees were dripping and the layer of powder snow was starting to soak into the ground.

"Well, stay up here and chat with us a bit."

Casey looked over at LG in mild surprise. LG winked at him.

"Got you a little lady tucked away somewhere?"

Edwin immediately untied the flour sack from his head. He felt like a fool wearing it, but Emmanuel was right. It did keep his head warm.

"There was some heifers at the CK up in Glendive. Didn't catch my fancy."

"Glendive? Montana's a far piece."

Sitting a little straighter in the saddle, Edwin nodded nonchalantly.

"I git around."

"You ain't sparking no pretty schoolmarm?"

The boy turned red. He wadded up the flour sack and threw it at the lead steer.

"Hell. Girls was scarce at the CK. A cowman who managed to spear himself a steady girl, well — he was above the rest."

LG clucked his tongue sympathetically.

"Bottom of the herd ain't fun."

Edwin gritted his teeth and looked at Casey for help. But Casey was riding along, not saying a word. The boy shook his head in frustration.

"Damnation! Easier riding with the drags."

Edwin turned his horse and started walking away. Tilting his head back, LG laughed and waved at Edwin.

"I'm just playing. Don't go. You know the old saying...no cowboy can summer a girl or winter a slicker."

"I'd say we're closing out of Spring Gulch," Casey noted. Up ahead, the gulch made a southerly bend between the hills. LG took Specter up to a trot and went to see what was up ahead.

"Boy, that guy sure likes to get at me," Edwin said and spat on the ground.

Casey gave him a genuine, friendly look.

"He's just hooking his spurs in you," Casey told him. "LG wouldn't poke at you, if you weren't a prime favorite."

Edwin snorted.

"Gonna make a first-class fuss, if he keeps at me."

The day was turning out to be a nice one. It had warmed up enough already that Casey took off his winter coat and gloves, and tied them behind the saddle. At night, he knew he would need them again. But while it was sunny, he meant to enjoy it.

"We cowpunchers have to hang together," Casey said proverbially. "Or we will hang separately.

Chapter 31
Ward

"Union Station, stockyards. Stop. DR&G. Stop."

With a close-trimmed beard, studious eyes and circular rims, Mr. James looked like a serious telegrapher. He propped his arm on the table and poised his hand. He *was* a serious telegrapher and took every message to be as important as the one before. Whether it was an aunt writing her niece, a housewife ordering a percolator from the Montgomery Ward catalog, or a banker wiring funds to Europe, James gave them all his attention. He glanced up, ready for the next line.

"*Two thousand, thirty-three head,*" Til said.

Mr. James nodded and tapped out the message on the steel lever key. Til's eyes wandered out the front window. While the interior of this little shack was gloomy, he could see the bright sunlight through the window and looked forward to getting back out there. Til would never want to be a telegrapher himself. Just being in there made him feel cooped up. Glancing back at Mr. James, Til noticed the tapping had stopped and the man was ready for more. Til chose his words with care in order to convey the message in as few words as possible, to save unnecessary expense.

"Arrival by week's end. Rail to Wyoming. Stop."

Mr. James finished coding the information, then lifted his hand and wiggled his fingers.

"Til Blancett, B-Cross-C. Stop."

Til thought for a moment while the man tapped away.

"Well, that should about cover it."

The front door opened and another man came inside the dreary shack, wearing a dusty bowler on his head. He nodded at Til and leaned against the doorjamb with a loud dramatic sigh.

"Mercy me!" he said, removing his hat. The man had a distinct English accent.

Leaning up to see over the counter, Mr. James saw who it was and sighed unhappily.

"Another casualty to report, Coke?" Mr. James asked, although he said it blandly.

"Same cause of death as frequently found here," Coke informed him. "Miners typically die in the same manner. And as the coroner of a mining town, I have seen it many times: maimed and crippled!"

Til turned and sized him up. The man's hair was white and went down to his shoulders — along with his long white wiry mustache. Til looked at it in disbelief. It went from his nostrils all the way down to his chest. Til had seen some big mustaches, but none to rival this.

"Ain't why I'm here though, James," the Englishman continued. "Need to see about burying that fellow from last October."

"The one in the snowbank?"

The eccentric coroner with the longest mustache Til had ever seen, suddenly seemed to realize the stockman was standing there.

"So we were in the cemetery last October, you see."

"Summer tree?" Til asked, unable to follow the accent. "Where's that?"

"*Cemetery*. I'm British. Track with me now. Winter snows already rolling in, but the ground was still soft — soft enough to dig a grave. Couple of Germans digging the grave. Now here's the fascinating twist. Instead of dirt, up comes shovel-fulls of ore!"

Inhaling deeply, Til did not try to hide his disinterest. The man was standing right in the doorway. Til did not care to hear a story. He did want to get outside. The cooped up feeling was wearing on him, although Til had only been inside the telegraph shack long enough to send his message. He was done with the telegram now, and he wanted to step out in the fresh air.

"Well we staked a claim, the Germans and I!" Coke went on. "And the body was left in the snowbank until spring!"

Mr. James took off his spectacles and rubbed the bridge of his nose. He could tell that Til Blancett was not interested in the Englishman's story. For that matter, neither was he. In addition to this, Mr. James considered this his personal office. It was a place of business. Transactions were done and funds were exchanged here. He did not want Coke to chase off his clientele. If Til had a message to send next time, he might very well choose the telephone instead of the telegraph. The new telephone line was going to be a sore spot for Mr. James, he could already guess. It was important to retain all his customers to generate income. In this case, it meant intervening to help Til Blancett get out the door.

"Let the man go about his business, Coke."

The Englishman bowed at the waist, still smiling broadly, and reluctantly stepped out of the doorway. Til scooted by.

Chapter 32

Placing the crate gently down in the rear of the buckboard, Terrance Tillamook — the owner of the General Merchandise — turned to Julianna.

"There's your order, miss. Drive with care."

"Many thanks for carrying this out for me," she replied. "See you again next month."

"See you then," Terrance said and went back inside. His wife Joyette was waiting for him. Joyette made him feel guilty for not selling the girl any of the colorful linens she had been looking at the night before. But Terrance did not like foisting products on people and told her just that — for the hundredth time. If they liked something, they would buy it. Simple as that.

Julianna began tying down the crates and sacks. The rope she had was old and knotted, and it took a little effort to cinch it all down. She enjoyed coming to Ward. It was regularly just once a month for supplies, but she usually stayed longer to meet up with friends. Social opportunities were rare in Gold Hill. It was closer to home, but there were not any women her age there.

The air was fresh! It was already early afternoon. It would take a few hours to get home, winding down the stage road in Lefthand Canyon. She would get home right about supper time. The Commodore had mentioned that he intended to shoot squirrels while she was in town. She hoped he would skin and clean them before she got there. Not that she minded squirrel guts. It was mainly deer or elk that she liked to avoid. The bigger game was full of messy guts — and stank worse, too. It was just this past year that the Commodore finally started asking her to clean all the animals he shot, big or small. His knees and back were just too stiff for all that kneeling and cutting, especially in the winter when his joints gummed up.

Moving up front, Julianna double-checked the tack on her horse, a well-brushed appaloosa.

"Are you ready to go home?"

She rubbed his neck and walked to the side of the buckboard. Holding her skirt off the ground, she cautiously set her right foot on the axle step. It was always hard getting up by herself. She wished the store owner had stayed to help her in. Why these things did not have some kind of hand rail was beyond her.

Julianna grabbed onto the seat itself, and managed to pull up past the large spoked wheel and sit down.

"Impressive! In a skirt and all."

Julianna looked around. It was Josephine. She was walking up, and she was not alone. Vera, Hazel, and Ella (who had missed their dinner due to more colorful pursuits) were right behind her.

"I would've needed Samuel to help *me* up," Josephine told her cheerfully. "Plus, I require cushy seats."

Julianna wagged her finger at them.

"I thought the lot of you would be trailing after Mr. Holliday, ogling and swooning."

"That uncouth lunger?" Hazel asked.

"Shush your mouth!" Vera growled, and grabbed her friend by the arm. "He could be anywhere, listening!"

Julianna laughed.

"Ah, the terrors we tolerate."

"Ride safely," Josephine said. "I suppose we'll see you again?"

Josephine had not told the other women about her pregnancy, or the fact that she would be moving to Horseshoe soon. Only Julianna knew that, so far. The two women looked at each other, knowing this might be the last time they would see each other.

"Indeed," Julianna replied kindly. "I will see you again."

She unwound the reins from the wheel brake, released it, and called to her appaloosa: "Step up!"

The horse began walking and the buckboard lurched forward. Looking over her shoulder, Julianna waved at Josephine and the ladies of Ward.

"Step easy," she cautioned the appaloosa, as the road began angling steeply downhill. The horse moved carefully down the bumpy slope.

After a few minutes the trees closed in on both sides of the road, and Julianna could no longer see Ward behind her. It gave her a sad feeling, knowing Josephine would most likely be in Horseshoe before the end of the month. She wished they had more time together, especially now that she was going to have a baby. Julianna could easily hear the river running softly, off to her right. She could see it through the trees down in the ravine.

Several magpies hopped along the road in front of her. They chattered at each other and were picking at something on the ground. As she rode closer, she saw that someone had lost some oats. The road was pretty rutted in places and it would not take much to knock a sack over. She glanced back into her own wagon. The knots were holding. Nothing had come loose or spilled yet.

The morning was peaceful. Julianna's heart continued to feel a little heavy, still thinking about Josephine, Samuel and how things change in life. They had been friends for several years. They liked to meet up at the Miser's Brewery or The Halfway House for meals, tea, or desserts. How many times had they shopped together in the General Merchandise? Julianna knew that once Josephine moved to Horseshoe, she would be losing a close friend. Her closest friend, really.

She thought about what Josephine had said about her father. She had apologized later, but there was some truth in it. The Commodore could not make the ride into town anymore. Part of that was age, but part of it was temperament. He was indeed an ornery man, which invited criticism. She hoped that when she got home, there would only be squirrels waiting for her. If the Commodore shot a buck, it would be a messy evening.

Chapter 33
Spring Gulch

Weaving among the aspen and willows, the riders of the B-Cross plodded on slowly through Spring Gulch.

The final snowstorm of the season was gone. It had melted with the sun. They were all down to their shirt sleeves. Birds were out in numbers, lining the branches overhead. Hopper ran past Casey, hoping to catch one. He never managed to but it was amusing to watch.

Edwin was still riding point with Casey. It was hard to keep the cows moving, especially with the grass coming up underfoot. All the good stuff was in the bottom of the gulch. It was rich and green. The sleet and wet snow had done a good job making it grow.

Up ahead, where the trees got thick again, they saw LG. He had only been gone for a short time and was coming back at an easy walk.

"Much further?" Casey asked him.

"No, it's just up ahead. Keep 'em moving along," LG said, and then gave Edwin a look. "Hey, Head Sack. Go help Ima."

Edwin regretted ever putting on that flour sack. Instead of saying anything, he just turned his horse around and trotted back down the cowline, his central finger pointed up in the air. LG fell into step next to Casey.

"Tonight — gonna drag a lead line across his bedroll," LG said. "You yell *rattlesnake*."

Casey ducked down to avoid a low branch.

"You think I'm loquacious?" LG asked him.

"Loquacious?"

He thought about it.

"Bromidic, maybe."

"And you're a cantankerous ki-yote with a limp, a lisp and a drippy pecker."

"I don't got a lisp."

The gulch narrowed and the trees grew closer together. Casey dropped behind LG and let him lead, since he just rode through here a minute ago and knew the best path. The underbrush was so thick, the cattle were forced to funnel down into single file behind the riders. They channeled around a granite outcropping and down into a small depression. Casey knew any day now, this would be a flowing creek and all the runoff from the high country would come right through here. There was a wet seep running in the depression already. It wouldn't be much longer until this part of the gulch would be unpassable.

"If we tried this next week, we'd never make it through here."

"Yep," LG said. "Have to drive them cows straight through downtown Ward."

"Thank you, no."

LG pointed up ahead.

"Almost out."

The gulch finally intersected the stage road. They emerged from the forest and looked around. The seep they were following trickled straight across and disappeared over the edge into the ravine. LG looked down the slope and could see Lefthand Creek.

"Welp, here it is pard," LG said, pleased with his own guiding skills. "We made the canyon."

The herd trickled out behind them, one at a time. Casey's dog ran past them and began sniffing the fresh air. The slope was steep and LG hoped Casey was watching his dog.

"I ain't going after him if he falls in that creek."

"He ain't gonna fall in that creek."

LG knew right where he was. Ward was just up the road, maybe three or four miles. Taking the herd through Spring Gulch was not the most direct path out of the mountains, but it did route them around the little town.

"All them clunky miners banging around. Set off one stick of dynamite, which you know they would, and them cows are running."

"Well, we did not *quite* avoid that scenario, now did we?" Casey asked.

Edwin rode out into the sunshine and joined them.

"Hold up here for Ima," LG told him. "Get back on swing."

"Ira won't shut up about grizz, thanks to you," Edwin mentioned.

LG grinned and took off down the canyon to get ahead of the lead steer. Casey followed. They heard a horse whinny somewhere up ahead. Casey and LG's horses both perked up their ears, but they could not see very far ahead. The stage road curved sharply around a bluff.

Casey shifted in the saddle, angling his head to listen better.

"Something's going on."

Chapter 34
Lefthand Canyon

The bluff turned out to be a tall granite outcropping. There was a mound of hard-packed orange dirt at its base, speckled with quartz bits. Between the outcrop and the ravine, the stage road made a fairly tight turn. When they got around it, LG and Casey saw a stagecoach parked in the middle of the road. It was just sitting there.

"Bet they busted an axle," LG said. "Gonna back up this road with 2,000 cattle if they don't get this thing moving soon."

"Must of just happened," Casey reasoned. "Looks like Gyp made it through here already."

They could easily see that the remuda had passed down the stage road. The tracks were obvious and the stagecoach was parked right on top of them. Behind LG and Casey, cattle began pouring around the outcrop. Watching them come, Casey shook his head.

"I best hold them up."

He turned around and planted his bay in front of the lead steer, blocking his path. Both Ira and Edwin came into sight.

"What's goin' on?" Ira called.

Casey hooked a thumb towards the coach.

"Boy," Edwin said. "What dumby parked that there?"

"Won't be able to get around with all these cows," Ira reasoned.

"I'll go see," LG said.

He hoped to squeeze through the narrow gap between the coach and the ravine. There was a row of pine trees along the edge right where the road dropped off, and LG had to hunch down to get under the branches. It was like a little tunnel and he hoped Specter would just go on through without blowing up. The horse was pretty young — probably three years old. He liked to try and unseat LG whenever an opportunity arose. In LG's mind, this was one of those opportunities. He glanced down uneasily. If he did get chunked, the only place to go was down. It was a steep slope and a nasty tumble that ended in the running water far below.

The herd was bunching up. Ira and Edwin waded their horses through the cattle and sided up next to Casey. Between the three of them, they could block the width of the road. To Edwin, this was like watching a water tank fill up. The cows kept coming around the corner but there was nowhere for them to go.

"Like holding back the ocean," Edwin said.

"You can't hold the *ocean*," Ira told him. "It's all watery."

Casey hoped Steve and Rufe would figure out what was going on, and keep the cattle from turning up the road towards Ward. After going to all the trouble to avoid that town, Casey would hate to have to search for strays up there. If the McGonkins could just hold them in Spring Gulch until the road cleared, things would work out.

Coming around from the opposite side of the stagecoach, Bill Ewing, Ned, Poqito and Caverango filed out on foot. Bill glanced around curiously. He saw Casey, Edwin and Ira holding back the herd. The cows moaned and lowed, swishing their tails.

"Told you I herd beeves," Bill Ewing told Ned.

Chapter 35

Edwin was annoyed. His hat was gone. His scalp was sunburnt. And LG kept ribbing him about everything from girls to grizzly bears. Now all these cows were bunched up, noisy, and all he could smell was cow stink.

"Gotta get *through* here," Edwin called to Bill, raising his voice above the lowing. "Move that damn wagon!"

Bill turned to look at Ned, and Ned raised his eyebrows.

There was something about their demeanor that made Casey uneasy. The four of them lined up in a row. Casey twisted around in his saddle so he could face them better and wondered where LG went.

"You deaf? I said move that damn thing!" Edwin shouted again.

Casey gave the boy a stern look, but he did not notice. Edwin had taken to squinting since he lost his hat.

It made Edwin mad that LG took the herd through Spring Gulch. They could have trailed right down the canyon through Ward — it would have been twice as fast and Edwin could have bought a new hat in town. Plus he would not have to put up with Ira's constant fears about a grizzly bear that did not exist. But Edwin did not have a new hat. And he had to squint all day. And now these dummies were blocking the road.

"That's quite brazen," Ned said to Bill.

"Certainly is," Bill replied. "*Quite* brazen."

Poqito and Caverango stood there quietly, staring darkly at the cowmen of the B-Cross-C.

"Hey, little turnip. Recognize this fella?" Bill asked Edwin. "This here is Ned Tunstall."

"Ain't heard of him and don't care to," Edwin replied. "Ain't no *turnip*!"

Casey had a Colt .45 in the middle of his coat, which was unfortunately tied in a roll behind him. He started thinking about it. He noticed all four of these men wore gunbelts. All of them. Didn't Edwin see that? Maybe if he saw they were wearing guns he would shut his mouth so things wouldn't get worse and they could get their cattle down the mountain. Denver was still a fair distance away.

Ira sat his horse, listening, shaking his head. He twisted the end of his droopy mustache. He liked Edwin for the most part.

The boy was mouthy and had a salty tongue, of course, but sometimes Ira thought that was pretty funny — since the kid had a pudgy baby face. Without a hat, Edwin looked about twelve years old. Ira smiled to himself and barely held back a chuckle. A twelve year old with a salty tongue! What a thought. Of course, the kid was older than that, Ira knew. But the thought still made him want to chuckle.

"Ain't heard of Ned Tunstall?" Bill wondered. "Well...if I'm being honest, that don't surprise me none. Ned ain't his proper given name."

"Then why'd you say it, like I'd know?" Edwin said.

Casey cleared his throat. The boy heard it and looked over. Casey had a sour look on his face.

"Most folks know me as Charley Crouse," Ned announced and tipped his hat.

Edwin did not know a Ned Tunstall or who Charley Crouse was. However, seeing Casey's scowl made him wonder if he should — since Casey never scowled at anyone. Edwin hesitated.

"Charley Crouse cut the guts out of the Speckled Nigger," Bill explained. "Speckled Nigger ran the ferry on the Green River up on the far end of Brown's Park. Heard of Brown's Park, turnip?"

"I was drunk," Ned said in his defense.

Chapter 36

LG was stuck under the tree. Specter refused to take another step. It turned out he did not like enclosed places, nor did he like the sound of pine cones crunching under his feet. The horse stood stock still, no matter how many times LG jabbed his spurs in the gelding's side. This was especially embarrassing since LG prided himself on being a top hand. He hoped Casey and the boys had not noticed his predicament.

Bill's voice carried. LG heard everything as plain as day. Things were going south back there and here he was, stuck under a tree. He edged out his .44 caliber Colt Army pistol and looked at it. It was an old gun — the cap and ball style. He hoped it would fire properly. Or fire at all for that matter. With Edwin mouthing off like that, it sounded like he was going to need it. The .44 was his father's gun. He had been a lieutenant in the Confederate army. But, his father was dead now, and LG carried it mainly as a family heirloom. Since the Indians were beaten — Geronimo had surrendered just last year — the only thing LG needed a handgun for these days was for show.

"What's goin' on, Casey?"

That was Steve's voice. LG twisted around, trying to see through the pine needles. He could barely make out Steve — both he and Rufe were trying to get around the bluff but the cattle were in the way. The cows were bunched up so tight, a horse could not even get through.

From up on top of the stagecoach, LG heard someone shuffle around. Rising up in his stirrups, LG pushed his head slowly through the branches. Sure enough, there was someone on top of the coach. The man had a Winchester and was clearly trying to sneak into a good shooting position without being noticed.

Well, this is it, LG thought. Hope this fool horse don't buck, bolt or slip. He knew the .44 was loud as a cannon and didn't know how Specter would take to it. Probably not well.

Chapter 37

Steve could not believe his eyes. The herd was backed up like water in a dam — and cows were still coming, one after the next. Well, Steve thought, this was a pickle. At least half the herd was still strung out in the gulch, and Lee and Davis had no idea the road was blocked.

The McGonkin brothers had gotten tired of riding drag. Earlier in the morning, they swapped positions with Lee and Davis. Of course, trailing cattle through springtime mountain grass was not nearly as dusty as taking them across the dry prairies below the Front Range. Steve had done that more than once in his time, and being downwind of two thousand cattle was not his favorite chore. He mainly wanted to trade out of the drags before they got down there. Once they made it onto the plains, whoever was on drag would be breathing dirt and stink all the way to the railyards. Despite setting the herd into a stampede, and he felt bad about that, Steve had no intention of riding drag if he could help it.

Then he noticed there was someone on top of the stagecoach. The man had a rifle and was bringing it up at that very moment. Steve could not tell exactly who he had it trained on, Casey, Edwin or Ira — it was hard to tell. Reaching down to his rifle scabbard as fast as he could, Steve pulled out his own Winchester. He sat up straight and chambered a round.

"Dry-gulch!" he yelled, and fired.

The shot hit the top part of the coach and scattered wood chips everywhere. Too low, Steve thought to himself. He watched Bill, Ned and the two Mexicans duck when they felt wood chips sprinkle down on their hats. Steve knew his rifle sights were off. He wished he had taken the time to properly sight the gun when he had the luxury. Now he knew he had to aim high. Steve locked in another round.

On the rooftop, Lem got on one knee so he could aim better. He liked to take a good moment and aim so as not to waste a shot. He was pretty frugal with his shots. He even took a deep breath and exhaled purposefully before he fired. He knew he got Steve because the man flopped in the saddle and his rifle fell on the ground. There it is, Lem said to himself, and smiled. Take a good moment, no matter what is going on. Breathe in and ease it out. Otherwise you might waste a round. And why waste a shot when all it takes is a moment to clear your mind?

Chapter 38

Bill flinched at both shots, but was pleased when he saw blood spray up from Steve McGonkin's shoulder. Lem was an accurate long-range shot and Bill was glad he brought him along. Lem had been up in Leadville working for Big Ed Burns until December, which was when Bill rode through.

One night, they got to talking. Even though Lem was part of Big Ed's gang, he did not enjoy being penned up in the city with the rest of them. Lem was a marksman, he told Bill. He needed open, quiet spaces.

Leadville was neither open nor quiet. It was busy, full of smoke from the big smelters, and overrun with chattery starry-eyed miners. Sitting around a dank bordello in Leadville was what Big Ed cared to do, not Lem — so Bill mentioned if he'd like to come along. Lem did want to come along, *much obliged* he said. Bill was pleased. He liked to have at least one man on his crew that knew how to shoot a rifle spot on.

Rufe grabbed his brother's horse by the reins and dragged him back around the rocky bluff, out of sight. Bill sighed softly. Trying *not* to kill people seemed like a good thought back in Grand Lake, when the chips were down. But the circumstances had changed. So Bill pulled out his .45, took two big steps toward Edwin and shot him out of the saddle.

Edwin rolled backwards onto his bay's hindquarters. He slipped off and fell on top of the cows, his arms flinging around. The cows bawled loudly at the sound of all the gunshots — and their eyes got even wider when Edwin landed on top of them. He slid off and disappeared without making a sound.

Bill decided to just work on down the line. He pointed at Ira next and fired.

Like a winter wind, Ira's hat blew off in an upward draft. An upper chunk of his skull came off with it. Ira was a tall man. He swayed funny, then slowly buckled forward over his saddle horn.

Casey was shocked. He tore open his coat roll, got a hold of his .45 and took a shot at Bill. He missed and hit the stagecoach instead. Ned flinched, since it had come close to hitting his head. On impulse, Ned drew and fired back at Casey.

The cattle erupted. None of them liked the sound of the shots and they tried to get away from the gunfire. But the only way to go was back up the road. The embankment was too steep on the upslope, and on the other side was the ravine.

Chapter 39

Pressing his .44 caliber through the pine needles, LG held his arm out straight so he would not miss. He was close enough to begin with and the coach was not all that wide, but LG wanted to make sure. He stretched and pressed the barrel against Lem's kidney and pulled the trigger. Lem was too busy leveling his rifle to realize LG was right there. The man's torso shook with the impact, and he flew right off the coach top.

Specter immediately lunged forward. Between the narrow tree tunnel, the pine cones crunching underfoot and the gun going off in his ears, Specter had had enough. Somehow LG managed to stay on his horse. He almost got raked off by the thick pine branches, but hung onto the saddle horn.

"Whoa!" LG shouted.

Specter bolted down the stage road, past the coach and the mules hitched to the singletree.

LG knew he would have a bear of a time getting that horse to walk under another tree ever again. He made a grab for the reins. Specter slowed to a prancy walk, and LG glanced back up the road as he got the horse under control.

The mules were standing in their traces, watching. Bitty had her ears up. One was pointed at Specter, and the other was pointed back toward all the gunshots. But Bitty was a good mule. She had been used to guns going off. That was part of her training — after all, Ian Mitchell always carried a scattergun on the driving seat.

The other mules were just as calm. Even Buckshay stood quietly, though he pinned his ears at Bitty out of habit. The coach had been sitting in one place for too long, in Buckshay's opinion.

Chapter 40

There was really nowhere to go, but Casey popped his reins and kicked like crazy. Ira had been sitting right next to him, and Casey knew he was going to get shot next if he didn't move immediately. He ran his bay straight over Bill, knocking him flat on the ground. Poqito, Caverango and Ned scattered out of his way.

Casey turned and headed back towards the herd, hoping to find a gap now that the cows were moving. But there were not any gaps. The cattle were still pressed together, wiggling to get past each other and escape up the road. However, in their frenzy, they were locked up tight.

Casey heard Bill yell:

"Gone up the flume!"

A tuft of fabric popped up from Casey's shoulder and blood flecked his face. He didn't even feel it. Casey leaned over the saddle as low as he could. His horse Boot Sock whinnied, and both Dark Bay and Berry Picker whinnied back. The horses were trying to find a way out, too. Since they had nowhere to go either, Poqito and Caverango ran up and grabbed their reins.

Casey whirled around, taking it all in. No place to go. He edged his horse near the side of the road and looked down into the ravine. The slope was far too steep to get down — at least on a horse.

Everything felt so slow to Casey — his horse's black mane, waving; the rasp of his own breathing; the jostling cattle and the swaying treetops. Like water in a well, Casey heard the hollow clop of hooves and hide shushing against hide.

Come on, Casey thought, *come on!*

His horse was stalled between the herd and the ravine.

Gritting his teeth, Casey slid off. He could feel Bill pointing a gun at his back, radiating like heat off a stove. He did not need to see it to know it.

Bark spattered apart, just past his head. Bill had missed and hit one of the tree trunks instead. There was still time, then. If he could just slide down the slope and get to the river, Casey knew he would be okay.

Looking down, he saw the sunlight flickering on the cold water.

Chapter 41

Jim Everitt and Ian Mitchell were dead. Their bodies were sprawled on the embankment, right by the mules, staring up at the sky. Several large mailbags lay on the ground, too, dumped out and scattered.

Lem landed in a heap on top one of the mailbags. A fleshy twist of intestine oozed out of the big hole in his side. LG's heirloom .44 had in fact functioned properly after all.

LG trotted over to the stagecoach and looked at the bodies and the envelopes.

He heard another gunshot.

Blue powder smoke boiled up over the stage.

LG checked his loads. He had five left, but he didn't have another cylinder if he ran out. His shot was buried somewhere in his saddle bags — but there was no time to sit around re-packing, even if he could get to it. LG was still surprised the gun had worked at all.

Granger jumped out of the coach and stared down at Lem's body. Granger had several envelopes in his hands and looked confused. It had been a quiet afternoon up till then. Bill and Vincent had shot the drivers and they were all having a pleasant time going through the mail. It was like Christmas. They found a lot of gold dust and paper money. Ned even found a wad of cash on Ian Mitchell, and Bill took a fancy pocketwatch off of Jim Everitt. Now Christmas was spoiled and Lem had just fallen from the sky, deader than a fence post.

When he saw LG, Granger dropped the envelopes and made a grab for his own gun. In that moment, LG realized he didn't trust the .44 or the jittery horse he was sitting on. With a jerk he pulled Specter around and dug his spurs in. The gelding capered a bit, and then bolted down Lefthand Canyon.

Chapter 42

The ruts were bad. Julianna drove the buckboard along slowly. It was too rough to go any faster.

"New springs next trip," Julianna said tartly and gritted her teeth. The buckboard's springs did not seem to have any bounce or give. Coming down the road behind her, she caught the sound of hoofbeats and looked around to see who was coming.

It was Deputy Griff Allen, and he was leading the posse at a trot. All of them were on horseback except Roy Caldwell, who drove his own buckboard. As they got closer, Griff slowed and waved at everyone to slow down, too. The road was narrow, and they had to squeeze past Julianna to get by.

Griff saw the buckboard was being driven by a young lady, and even though they were on the hunt it was only right to be courteous — it was a narrow road, and perhaps she had a spooky horse. Griff saw no sense in startling the lady's appaloosa.

Roy was glad they were all slowing down. Like Julianna's, his buckboard had unforgiving springs and he was sore. A wagon had been voted a necessity for this manhunt. Since he owned a buckboard for his apothecary, which he regularly used for supply runs to Idaho Springs, Roy volunteered. But traveling at this pace, day after day, was rough...and he was starting to wonder if he could get someone else to drive it for an afternoon. Now that they were slowing to a walk, Roy decided he would ask around. Griff had kept a pretty unrelenting pace, and once they got going again there may not be another chance to talk to anyone until well after dark.

"Pardon us, miss," Griff said politely, as he eased by.

The posse filed into a line to get past. Julianna stopped her wagon while they passed. She noticed Griff Allen and Ben Leavick, the first two, looked pretty bad. Griff's face was bruised and his nose swollen. Both of Ben's eyes were black and drooped.

Julianna had driven this road so many times over the past few years that she never thought too much about her safety. None of these men gave her a bad feeling which was a relief. Except the last rider, just before Roy Caldwell's wagon went by — it was Red Creek Mincy. Julianna watched him uncertainly. Though he never looked directly at her, she felt her skin prickle. The man had dead fish eyes. Vacant, cold and empty.

It was a narrow fit for Roy's wagon, but he knew he could squeeze past Julianna's buckboard without scraping wheels if he got his own wheels up on the embankment a little.

"I'll get it by, ma'am. Don't you worry none."

Roy spent a good deal of his youth as a freighter — prior to the success he had had with the apothecary. Only once a month did he have to make the long trip down to the train depot in Idaho Springs. He preferred to stay inside where the woodstove was. The whole store stayed nice and warm all winter long, and Roy found that winters near the Great Divide were getting to be hard on him. But Sheriff Greer had been shot dead right up the street from his store.

When Griff announced he was setting off after the killers, all of the town leaders stepped up. Merle Hastings was a big ranch don — the man hadn't even hesitated when Griff asked, and even volunteered his cowboys and bought them all new Winchesters.

Roy had known Emerson Greer, of course — mainly as a customer, but the man had been their sheriff for quite some time and to get gutshot on a Sunday morning in his own office was a big blow to the community. So Roy offered up his buckboard. And now here he was, driving it down some narrow canyon, angling the wheels up a steep embankment.

Julianna held her breath while he inched past. Roy's old mule liked to start and stop in jerky movements, and it made her nervous to watch — especially since the ravine was on her side.

"This is old Clyde," Roy mentioned to her. "He's blind in one eye, but don't you worry none. As sure-footed as they come."

"I see," she said. But the information wasn't exactly reassuring.

Coming off the embankment, blind-eye Clyde successfully made it past her, and pulled the wagon back onto the road. By this time, Griff was back to a trot and the posse was almost out of sight. Roy would have to catch up if he didn't want to lose them. He sighed. There had been no opportunity to ask anyone about trading places. If this road was as badly rutted the entire way down the canyon, the next town they came across he would certainly invest in some springs that actually sprung.

Julianna watched Roy until he disappeared around the next turn. She released the brake and clicked her tongue. The appaloosa stepped forward in the traces, and they began moving again at a casual pace.

"Haw-over," she commanded. She wanted to get in the middle of the road. Parking next to the ravine had been a little nerve-wracking. She hoped no one else was coming up or down

Lefthand Canyon for the rest of the day. She just wanted to go home. Although there was probably a pile of squirrels waiting to be skinned, once she got there.

Chapter 43

They passed the first few strays on the road. Griff thought that was odd. He had not seen any cowpunchers, and the cattle were obviously loose. As the posse rounded the next bend, black Polangus literally covered the road, and they had to ease past at a slow walk just to get through.

"Lost herd?" Ben asked Griff.

They passed the outlet to Spring Gulch. Looking up the draw, Griff saw a lot more Polangus and some Durham in the trees, rooting around in the low grass. But there were no riders. Griff wondered whose cows these were. Riding up close to one, he read the brand. It was fresh burnt on the all the yearlings: B + C.

"Heard of the B-Cross-C?"

"No," replied Merle.

Griff figured Merle would know better than any of them. He was familiar with all the local cattle outfits, both big and small. But Colorado was a big state.

Up ahead, Griff saw the big granite outcrop. He led the way around the bend and saw the stagecoach sitting in the middle of the road. Several horses were standing near the ravine — they were saddled, too. Then Griff saw two bodies sprawled out on the ground. He rode over to take a look.

It was pretty clear these two were not getting up again. Ira's skull top was shot open and some brains were on the outside. Edwin was covered in dust and torn up pretty badly — Griff knew immediately it was from being trampled. Actually, he was surprised the kid wasn't worse off. He had seen men run down in a stampede and all they found afterward was a boot heel.

Griff looked around. He wondered what happened here. Whatever it was, it had just happened a little while ago. Fresh manure was everywhere, and the blood was wet and warm.

"They kilt some more folk! Damn them!" Ben cried out.

He was still outraged over how easily he had been overpowered in the sheriff's office. He should have *expected* the men they were hunting might circle back. Why wouldn't they? When they had their man locked up? Thick as thieves, the saying went. Ben should never have taken the task of tracking the getaways so lightly. Let alone josh and drink and cut up with Emerson, when they were on a serious manhunt. Maybe Emerson Greer would still be alive and Caroline Greer would not be a widow, and his own wife Meggy wouldn't have to console her every day. Now here were more dead men. Ben felt a wave of guilt.

"Check that coach," Griff told Red Creek.

The two of them got off their horses and went to have a look.

Roy stepped out of his buckboard awkwardly and stretched. His back and tailbone hurt. He needed to move around, so he went over to look at Ira and Edwin. They were certainly dead, there was no question there. They looked like cowhands.

"Probably shot down without no warning," he said to Merle, who was still in the saddle with a rifle in his hands.

But Merle was not listening. His eyes were working over the hillside. There could be riflemen up on that big outcrop, sighting them down even then. Or spread out among the trees. This was a good place to be attacked — the way the road bent around that granite bluff, it was a blind corner.

Roy realized he was not going to get a conversation out of Merle, let alone trade modes of transport, so he walked around to work out the stiffness. He looked down in the ravine.

"Griff!" he called out. "Got one in the river!"

He stood by the edge of the road and pointed.

Griff and Red Creek were standing over Jim Everitt and Ian Mitchell, and Lem's body sprawled out on the mail. Griff heard the tension in Roy's voice, so he hustled right over. From the road, they could all see someone was in fact lying in the creek. The bank had white crusty ice all along its edge, but the water flowed freely and loudly.

"Saw him move!" Roy shouted and pointed down at him again.

Merle snapped his fingers.

"Boys."

Three of his ranch hands slid off their horses and put up their guns. The slope was steep, but they worked their way down by grabbing tree limbs and brush for balance.

It was Casey Pruitt, lying face up in the water.

The young men got down the slope and checked him over. It was obvious that Casey had been shot a couple times. His clothes were completely soaked with blood and river water. Casey's eyes fluttered.

"He ain't dead!"

"Well, get him outta the water!" Merle shouted back.

Ben, Merle, Griff, Roy, Red Creek, and the rest of Merle's boys watched them lift Casey up to his feet. He was dripping, too weak to stand, and was barely conscious as it was.

"Mercy," Griff sighed.

They got Casey back up the slope and set him out on the ground. His skin was blue from lying in the cold water.

Griff heard a buckboard. He glanced up the road. It was the young lady they passed earlier. He raised his hands up and went over.

"Hold up, ma'am!"

Chapter 44

"He's coming to. Mister, how many were there? What did they look like?"

"Let him revive, Ben — for Pete's sake."

Ben was leaning right over Casey, shaking him by the shoulders. Casey had trouble getting his eyes to focus. He shivered suddenly, like a wave had just washed over him. He rolled over onto his side and began coughing.

"Stand back," Julianna told the men, in a commanding tone.

The coughing fit passed. Pushing up on his elbow, Casey tried to get up, but his left arm gave way and he fell on the ground. Painfully, he rolled onto his back and stared up at the blue sky. Julianna knelt down beside him and pressed her palm to his forehead.

"What happened?" Casey asked.

"You been shot," Griff told him.

Casey's shoulder felt like it was on fire, even though he was freezing cold. He had another hot spot in his chest, too. He felt around and discovered his fingers were wet with blood. He blinked and lowered his hand.

"Them murderers go on down the road then?" Ben demanded, impatient. "How many were they?"

But Casey was blank. Another wave of shivers ran through him and he folded his arms across his chest. He realized he was soaking wet.

"Did I fall in the creek?"

"Come on, mister!" Ben shouted. "Which way?"

"Hobble your lip," Griff told him, irritated. "The man's down. Give him a chance."

"They kilt Emerson Greer, didn't they?"

"I saw them," Casey said. He felt woozy but tried sitting up again.

"Don't know how many," he continued. "They shot..."

Casey's memory started coming back. He scrambled to his knees. Julianna stood up with him, holding his good arm for assistance. Griff stepped in to help, too. Squinting to see clearly, Casey looked around. He saw Ira and Edwin lying on the road and rushed over, falling to his knees. Casey squeezed his eyes shut.

"Oh, no."

Ben's face was red. It was hard to stand by watching when he knew the men they were after couldn't be far away. The question was, did they ride down the canyon? Or did they turn up Spring Gulch? There were fresh horse tracks leading back up the gulch — but it also looked like a whole herd of horses had ridden on down the road. There were hoofprints and fresh heaps of dark green horse manure everywhere he looked. They could have gone either way. Even Red Creek Mincy was not sure, and he had years of tracking experience.

"What can you remember?" Griff asked Casey.

He opened his eyes and stared at Edwin and Ira.

"Someone called Charley Crouse," Casey said, trying to think. "But some other fella kilt my friends, though. And a couple vaqueros...they all stood right there."

Griff shot a glance at Merle Hastings. They both recognized the name Charley Crouse, by reputation. Griff was sure the man was a horse racer, but he lived way up north in Brown's Park somewhere. What was he doing down here?

"Where's LG?" Casey asked them. He looked up and down the road. The stagecoach was still sitting where it had been. It was all coming back.

"Couple more around there, I'm afraid," Griff said, nodding toward the coach.

Casey got to his feet again. He had a sick feeling in his stomach. Heading slowly toward the coach, Casey prayed it wasn't LG or anyone else from the B-Cross. But Ira and Edwin were both dead, right back there. Who else would it be?

Julianna walked behind him, and noticed there was blood all over his back. They all followed him around the coach. Griff pointed out the stage drivers and Lem.

"Don't know these men," Casey said, relieved.

"I know these two," Julianna spoke up quietly. "That's Jim Everitt and that's Ian Mitchell. They work the stage line."

"So this other one...he ain't part of the cow outfit and don't work for the stage," Merle said, using the toe of his boot to roll Lem over. "Got to be one of the gang we're after."

Nodding, Griff scratched his chin and throat — he had several days of growth, and it was starting to irritate his skin. He looked up at the sky. The sun was going down. It was hanging just above the snow-covered peaks but as soon as it fell behind the ridge, it would start getting dark again. Griff looked around at everyone. Ben was impatient to be off and could barely stand still. Roy was clearly shocked by all this death and was sitting quietly in his wagon. Red Creek was unfazed, and stared cooly at Griff for direction. Merle went over to his ranch hands and began quietly instructing them to be wary and calm. They were young and obviously unsettled by all this. Griff had seen his share of death and knew what it felt like when you hadn't seen it before.

Griff turned to Julianna.

"Can you cook supper for a dozen hungry men?"

"I can and will, happily...as long as there is a bite left," she replied. "My home is just down the road a little further, in Gold Hill."

It was a decision that would not sit well with everyone, Griff knew that. The gang they were after had less than an hour's headstart. However, trying to tell which direction they rode was going to be hard. The ground was a criss-cross mess of horse and cattle tracks. Also, there was the problem of the dead cowhands. The posse could not simply ride off, as things stood. Griff believed in the importance of propriety and doing things right. After all, as a deputy he represented order and the good of society. Lawless men had the luxury of transgression — Griff did not.

"We need to bury these men."

Ben's face looked like it was going to burst, but he turned around and stalked off instead. Griff watched him go. None of them wanted to give up yet. But looking at Casey and Julianna and all the dead men on the ground, not to mention four mules standing in their traces — Griff decided it was the right thing to do. Then they could see what the morning might bring.

Chapter 45

Rufe rode back up Spring Gulch. He held onto one of the reins from his brother's horse. Steve was hunched over, gripping the saddle horn as tight as he could. After an hour of riding, they passed the last few cows in the herd, and almost collided with Lee and Davis.

"What happened?"

"Been waylaid!" Rufe shouted, without slowing down. "The herd's broke — forget them damn cows!"

Lee and Davis had heard the gunshots echo off the hills. Lee counted seven shots but Davis counted eight. They were arguing about it when Rufe and Steve came crashing through the underbrush.

The McGonkins wove through the pine and were gone.

Lee looked back down the gulch. The last few steers in the herd were plodding on slowly in the warm sunlight. A squirrel was up in a ponderosa chirping angrily at them. In the quiet and sunshine, Lee was confused. It felt wrong to abandon the herd. But Steve was dripping blood all over his horse's withers, and Rufe had certainly looked frazzled.

"What do we do?" Davis asked him.

Looking up and down the gulch, Lee wondered himself. What would LG say? What would he tell them to do?

Chapter 46

In the pitch dark, Emmanuel walked carefully so he would not trip and spill the coffee.

"Here you go," Emmanuel whispered and held out a steaming cup to Davis.

"Much appreciated."

Davis could barely make out Emmanuel in the dark. The black man was nearly invisible. He propped his rifle against an aspen. He cupped his hands around the mug and let it warm his fingers.

Emmanuel had been riding behind the drags that morning. Getting the chuckwagon down Spring Gulch was not easy. The trail they were following was barely a footpath, if even that — and the trees grew so close he wasn't sure he was going to make it. When Rufe frantically rode past the wagon with his brother in tow, Emmanuel wasted no time turning around.

Having spent his early years in the army, he knew how to doctor wounds. He always kept calomel, castor oil, bandages, needles and thread, and a good supply of whiskey in the cookbox. Once they got back to Preacher's Glen, he did what he could for Steve.

Moonlight made everything that was white waver in the dark like phantoms — aspen bark glowed, the snow on the ground lit up. Davis was just a dark shadow himself. The only way he knew Emmanuel was headed in his direction, was the flour sack around his waist bobbed like a will o' wisp.

After wrestling with it, both Lee and Davis had made the decision to leave the cattle and ride after the McGonkins. When they got to the glen, they found Emmanuel setting up camp right where they had the night before. Steve was in pain but conscious, and Rufe was agitated and couldn't sit still.

It was strange. They could smell the cow manure in the meadow all around them — but the herd was not there, of course. Davis took a quick sip and worked his jaw.

"Singy. Mebbe in an hour this'll be ingestible."

"You just keep readin' that dictionary," Emmanuel told him.

The cook turned and headed back towards the campfire. He had barely gone five steps when a gunshot went off in the trees.

Emmanuel dropped like a stone.

The gunshot echoed up and down the glen like thunder. Davis dropped his coffee mug and grabbed his rifle. He pointed it into the woods but it was too dark to see. He waited for another shot — the discharge would give him a target. But nothing happened.

He smelled gunsmoke wafting in the dark.

"Lee?" he whispered.

"Yeah."

"See where that came from?"

"Nope."

At the firepit, Rufe scrambled out of his bedroll, grabbed his gun and leapt behind a log. Steve was in no shape to move so he stayed where he was, lying flat on the ground.

The forest was silent. Even the crickets had stopped.

The fire crackled. It was down to a hot bed of coals and cast a deep reddish glow. A few steps from the fire and the night closed in. The crescent moon was out again, although a thin layer of clouds filled the sky. All the stars were gone.

Emmanuel got up and hustled for the wagon.

Another shot rang out. The gunfire was quite visible in that moment and without hesitation both Lee and Davis fired at it. Their own muzzle flashes were bright like lightning.

Emmanuel slipped and hit the ground near the fire, landing hard with a grunt. He did not stay there this time but got right up, scampering behind the first tree he could find. He realized the flour sack was glowing in the moonlight. No wonder they were shooting at him. He untied it and threw it on the ground.

The afterclaps were loud. After the sound faded, they heard a loud voice carry in the dark:

"That Negro's still flopping. You bean-eaters can't shoot worth shit."

Chapter 47

The Commodore's Cabin
Gold Hill

"Obliged, miss."

Merle nodded politely and accepted the ceramic plate. He sat back in his chair and placed it carefully on the tabletop. It was heaped with pan-fried trout, deer meat, fresh greens and syrupy canned pears.

The Commodore had not been able to shoot even one squirrel, as he had anticipated, so he spent the afternoon fishing in the creek. The catch of trout had come in useful. Julianna also had the groceries and supplies she purchased in Ward — and with the dried venison from the pantry, she was able to bring together a decent meal. She only hoped The Commodore would be able to maintain his composure and behave. She was worried. He did not get along well with unexpected company. Or any company, for that matter.

"This is all quite unexpected, and favorable," Roy Caldwell told her appreciatively. He seemed indecisive about which knee to lay his cloth napkin on. Living in the apothecary alone, his familiarity with supper table etiquette was rusty. In addition to this, he was feeling skittish in the presence of the young lady. The only ladies who entered the apothecary were either matronly or sickly — or both, usually.

Red Creek took his plate and stepped outside. Juilanna watched him go...privately relieved the man with the dead fish eyes was no longer in her home.

"He don't do well with enclosed spaces, ma'am," Griff cxplaincd, misunderstanding her look.

That is fine with me, she thought.

Merle's ranch hands were spread out in the room, sitting on whatever they could find — crate, footstool, hearth, wash bucket. Since they were the youngest of the group, it went without saying the grown men would sit at the table. Griff, Merle, Roy and Ben sat across from Julianna and her father — who looked leathery, feral and permanently windblown. They gave Casey the most comfortable chair in the room. It was the only one that had a seat cushion. He barely touched his meal. He mainly stared into the fire.

The large stone fireplace was roaring. Elk and deer horns and fox pelts were stacked in piles against the back wall. There were several old steel traps and a set of snowshoes hanging from nails. Griff looked around. He saw a gold-handled saber up on the fireplace mantle and glanced curiously at The Commodore.

"Sorrowful affair," Merle said, while Julianna finished serving supper.

"This is a heinous crew," Roy stated. "Leaving a kill streak all the way from Grand Lake to Boulder."

"For shit's sake," Ben Leavick muttered bitterly, and none too softly. He forked up a piece of deer meat and held it up. "Sheriff Emerson Greer is gutshot and dead. Now all these cowhands are murdered and here we are enjoying a fancy meal and a warm bed."

"Watch your language — we have a lady here," Griff warned, and looked apologetically at Julianna. She sat quietly, sipping hot tea.

"I seem to remember them knocking around our good deputy, as well. Why ain't you up in arms like I am? Why ain't we out on their trail right this very second? *We had 'em*, boys. We were *right there*. Now those murderers are halfway to Burlington!"

Merle cleared his throat and wiped his mustache with his fingertips. His ranch hands watched uneasily, chewing their food. Griff thought they looked quite similar to barn owls.

"If I may," Merle began, clearing his throat again. "We do not deny the rascality of that troupe. But they've led us far afield. And we've just gone and buried how many good folk?"

He looked around the room with a challenging look in his eye.

"Now their sign has been obscured by them Polangus. I can't make nothing out. Even in the morning light we won't know which way they went. Up that gulch or down the road? Them curly wolfs might have even split up and went *both* ways, for all we can tell. Like they did when they took *you* for a loop, Leavick."

Ben glared back but did not interrupt.

"We should consider our options," Merle said, pausing thoughtfully. "And obligations."

But that was too much for Ben. He dropped his fork on his plate with a loud clank.

The barn owls turned their heads toward the sound.

"Holy hell! Options? *Obligations?* What kind of talk is this, Griff?"

"It's real talk," Merle said sternly. "Real wives and real children and real business to attend. And God only knows if they're heading back up that way right now. May be doubling back to shoot up our town while we're looking the wrong way."

"Well, I'll be," Roy said and nodded.

Merle frowned severely. He leaned forward in his chair to convey the gravity of his words.

"Our wives and children are sitting up there...without *us* to defend them."

Ben's face was dark. He pounded the tabletop, making all the dishes clatter. It startled Julianna who jumped in her seat. Griff saw her jump, and pointed sharply at Ben.

"I feel it ever *bit* as you do, Ben! I worked close with the man for years, if you will remember."

Then Griff sighed, set his elbows on the table and rubbed his eyes.

"We can't expect everyone here to ride on forever," he continued in a resigned tone. "This posse has been riding for days now...and we're getting farther and farther away from our homes."

"And families," Merle added again.

He raised his hands up solemnly.

"*Vengeance is mine, sayeth the Lord.* We best let God Almighty remunerate this injustice."

"This ain't Sunday School, Hastings! We got to right this wrong!" Ben shouted.

"Hate it as much as you do," Griff said, softly.

"All of us agree they need to be tied down," Merle said. "We are not saying it ain't worth pursuing...we just can't keep going on like this."

The rancher placed his dinnerware on the table in a formerly manner and brushed at his shirt for crumbs.

"My boys and I are heading back to Grand Lake with the first light."

Sliding back his chair, Merle stood up. He surveyed the room one last time. Ben just shook his head. What else could hc say?

"Many thanks for the fixings, Miss. It was well timed. I shall retire to my bedroll, under the stars."

Merle went outside, and all his ranch hands filed out stoically behind him. They all left without saying a word.

For a long minute, the only sound in the room was Casey's labored breathing and the crackling of the fireplace. Julianna turned and looked him over, assessing his condition. He was pale as a ghost and still lost in thought.

Casey had not said a thing during the entire meal.

Neither had The Commodore. He was the only one who kept working on his supper plate, no matter which way the conversation turned. He even reached for seconds on the bread rolls. The Commodore hoped this group was thoughtful enough to leave some money behind for the food they consumed and the inconvenience they posed. The Commodore did not care for guests. Company in general was exhausting. He would prefer it if they all rode out immediately, and he almost decided to say just that. But he held his tongue. If he said anything of the sort out loud, he knew Julianna would have strong words for him.

The Commodore weighed his options carefully when it came to upsetting his daughter. He knew from experience that if he made her angry, it would upset his chances at dessert. And he knew she had bought fresh apples and sugar up in Ward in order to make a fresh pie. The Commodore liked apple pie very much. It was hard to restrain himself, but he managed to. He didn't want to jeopardize his chances at fresh apple pie.

Chapter 48

A bat flopped silently past Casey's ear and snapped at a mosquito. He tried to raise his arm to shoo it away, but it was already gone. He knew right away that he pulled something — his chest felt like it caught fire. But he said nothing since Julianna was standing right there. He felt his balance waver and took an awkward step to regain it.

"Easy," Julianna said, noticing.

She held the lantern high as they walked. The night air was very chilly, and they were both wearing winter coats. Julianna had offered him The Commodore's coat, since Casey lost his in Lefthand Canyon. She shivered, walking slowly to accommodate Casey's gait.

The kerosene lamp flickered steadily and quietly. The flame was yellow and it cast a good amount of light around them, causing shadows to dance as they moved.

"Much further ahead?"

"A little further," she told him.

The thin cloud cover had dissolved and the stars were out now, and bright. But Casey noticed a big dark cloud-bank to the west. It looked like a giant black blanket scrolling across the sky, eating up the stars.

"It's just up there," Julianna pointed out in a soft voice. "Watch your step, there's a low iron fence."

In the lantern light, Casey could just make out the fence in the darkness. Except for a few patches of snow the ground was basically dry. A thick bed of pine needles and moss made the footing feel spongy. Inside the fence were about a dozen tombstones.

Casey tried to look around, although his chest really bothered him whenever he twisted even a small amount. Tall conifers rose straight up to the sky, encircling the small cemetery. The moon was directly overhead and it seemed like all the trees were pointing straight at it.

"Your friends are over here."

Julianna's fingers were cold. She gripped the lift wire and held the lantern up as high as she could. She led him to two mounds of freshly turned dirt.

"I'll need to carve up some crosses," Casey said, more to himself.

Julianna checked on him from the corner of her eye, trying not to stare impolitely. Their breath hung in the moonlight.

"Edwin, you were just green," he said quietly. "Could've been a top hand one day...if you had the chance."

He shifted his weight and sighed.

"Sorry for you, Ira," he said, speaking to the other mound. "Never caused a fuss."

There were only two new graves. Casey noticed that.

"Where are the stage drivers buried?"

"Wrapped in a tarp. Deputy Allen thought it best to send them back up to Ward with the stagecoach. He's going to drive it up there himself tomorrow."

Julianna paused.

"That other dead man, the killer...they're taking him all the way back to Grand Lake."

They stood silently in the graveyard. Another bat flew overhead, snapping at the insects drawn in by the lantern.

"What are you going to do?"

"Not sure," Casey replied. "The B-Cross is ruined. The boys are dead. Maybe all of them, I don't know. I'm not sure what to do."

He reached up and covered his eyes with his hand. In the stillness Julianna heard him struggling to keep his emotions in check. She lowered the lantern to give him a moment.

Exhaling in one long breath, Casey wiped his eyes and stared at the graves.

"Nothing I could do. They fired on us without no call. Ira. Edwin. Dead like that, and I was next in line."

He swallowed hard and pressed his palm to his forehead, squeezing his eyes closed tight.

"It'll be okay," Julianna told him, her voice kind with sympathy.

"I thought if I got away," he whispered. "I could have..."

The treetops stirred and swayed. Looking up at the dark cloud-bank again, Casey could tell another cold front was coming in. There might even be more snow in the morning. Was this winter ever going to end?

"Can't let it weigh too heavy, Casey," she said softly. "Their dying wasn't on you. Those were hard men."

Julianna set the lamp on the ground and placed her hands on his forearm for reassurance. She could tell he was shaking, with cold or pain or grief. Maybe all of it.

"Times like this are hard to understand," she said. "But you have to play the cards you've been dealt. Sometimes they're bad cards...but you mustn't be broken by it."

They stood together for a few minutes, without speaking. Casey could not help but stare at the graves. His compadres were right there, under the dirt. *Six feet under*, the saying went. When just the day before they were trailing the same herd, drinking the same coffee, eating the same 3-day beans.

"You make damn sure you hold up now," she said firmly, sweetly. "Or they will have gotten you, too."

It was getting colder by the minute. She tried to keep from shivering too badly, since Casey was still lost in contemplation. The wind swirled down through the cemetery and cut right through her. Finally, she knelt and picked up the lantern again, holding her long brown hair back from the flame. Gently threading her arm through his, she turned to go. Casey let her lead the way.

"They brought in your horses," Julianna mentioned. "They're in the corral and the tack is in the barn."

"Appreciated," he said, in an automatic voice. But he didn't hear what she said.

Casey wondered what happened to everyone: LG, Steve, Rufe, Lee, Davis, Gyp, Emmanuel. He couldn't ride well enough to find out. He considered getting on that stagecoach and heading up to Ward with the deputy. Casey didn't know what to think anymore. He just knew he needed to lay up somewhere and heal.

Chapter 49
Lefthand Canyon

Specter's white face was bright in the moonlight. LG patted his neck. The moon was about to disappear behind that dark cloudbank rolling in. He figured he better get his coat on and grab a bite while he still had some light.

"Easy, boy."

The horse was breathing heavily. Behind the saddle, LG's coat was tied in place. He unrolled it and shook it out. Pine needles sprinkled on the ground as he did. This was the first chance he took to stop since Granger had surprised him. Or since he had surprised Granger.

LG knew he better not stay in one place for too long. Specter had surprised him by trotting confidently down the stage road in the moonlight. Now that they were losing the moon, LG wondered how the young horse would do in the pitch black. He would find out soon enough.

Ever since leaving the stagecoach behind, LG had been on the move. The stage road itself was the most direct path out of the chaos, and he had kept the black horse running hard for a couple miles. Then LG slowed down, alternating between a walk and a trot. He wanted to put distance between himself and that stagecoach without baking his horse. He didn't want to be caught afoot if they were riding after him.

Nothing but staying alive had mattered for the last few hours. Looking back up the dark road, LG listened. Hearing nothing, he slid onto the ground. He landed in a wheel rut and nearly twisted his ankle.

"I belong in a saddle," he told Specter. "That's why, right there."

Rooting around in the saddlebag, LG found a canteen and some salted pork. When he uncapped the canteen, he noticed the top was rimed with ice crystals. He shook the canteen a few times to clear it up. The water was very cold, but it helped. His throat was dry and sore.

LG had just wanted to get around the coach and chat with the drivers. How was he supposed to know it was a robbery and not a busted axle?

He took his gloves off and ran his cold hand through Specter's thick winter hide.

"Lord, help the boys."

LG realized Specter needed a drink, too. The canteen could use a refill anyhow. Lefthand Creek was just off the road, bubbling by. The ravine had thinned out considerably and he could easily walk down to the riverbank at this point. He started leading Specter down by the bridle.

Then he heard the hoofbeats.

Chapter 50

Til Blancett noticed one of his cows was loose on the road.

He almost rode right past the yearling, when he heard the swish of a tail. Polangus were hard to see in the middle of the night like this, but Til caught the scent of cowhide and manure. Whoever was riding drag was about to get their pay docked. Til needed every head to make this next sale count.

The stage road was the simplest route to the big city of Denver from Beaver Creek. Til had ridden it many times. He knew Spring Gulch came out just up ahead. He knew where he was. The temperature was falling though. He could hear the trees starting to sway. Til wished he had the moon or stars to see by — but they were gone now, too.

Several more cows were lying up against the embankment. He knew this because his horse shied away, trying to keep from stepping on them. Til could easily smell more manure the further he walked. He suddenly realized there were dozens of cattle bedded down all along the road. He could feel their presence.

"What in tarnation?" he muttered.

Til had bought a lantern in Ward, figuring it might come in handy with all this night riding. He got it out, lit it, and held it up high.

Cattle were everywhere.

He rode past Spring Gulch, since there were more cows up ahead. He went around the granite outcropping, which was just a big black tower at this time of night, looming over the road on his left.

Til slid off Bit Ear, so he could kneel down and study the road.

In several places, Til saw blood soaked into the dirt. It was obvious the cattle had been driven to this point but not a step further...like they hit a wall. It was odd to see so many hoofprints come to a sudden stopping point on an open road.

"Something happened — right here."

He saw wagon wheel tracks, hoofprints both shod and unshod, and a lot of boot tracks.

Leading his horse on foot, Til walked back to where Spring Gulch tied into Lefthand Canyon. He moved into the forest and held the lantern high. There were more cattle bedded down all around him, dotted throughout the underbrush. Their eyes shined like coins.

Chapter 51
Preacher's Glen

"I heet that cocinero!"

"If you *heet* him, then why'd he jump right back up like a jackrabbit?"

Ned was speaking to Caverango. Of course, now they knew his name wasn't really Ned. It was Charley Crouse. Charley didn't care though. It was better the Mexicans knew who he was. They seemed to be more compliant, especially after hearing what Bill had said about Speck William's guts.

"*Lo siento*, señor Crouse."

Caverango was nervous. Granger hated Mexicans — that was no secret. But Granger was just an impulsive fool. What if Charley Crouse hated Mexicans, as well? The man seemed impulsive, perhaps worse than Granger. But less of a fool. More cold than fool. Caverango wondered if he really did eviscerate some poor black man up in Brown's Park? For no good reason beyond a drunken rage? If so, it was possible Charley's bigotry ran the color spectrum. And *that* was what made Caverango nervous.

"I keel him. *Ahora.*"

It did not help his confidence that he couldn't see his hand in front of his own face. Perhaps Charley Crouse would choose the cover of darkness and the circumstance of an unkilled camp cookie as excuse to disembowel someone colored nearby. Someone colored — such as himself. Caverango decided the best thing would be to put some distance between himself and Charley Crouse.

"*Perdon,*" he whispered and tip-toed off.

He heard Charley chuckle behind him, somewhere in the darkness. Caverango paused to listen — he thought he heard a jagged knife being *swished* out of a sheathe. He began moving quicker to keep from being gutted like the Speckled Nigger. He extended both hands out and patted around in the darkness.

Tree trunk.

Tree trunk.

Brush.

Pine branch.

The further he got, the more relaxed Caverango became. Perhaps he would not get jabbed after all. He lamented silently for poor Poqito. Poqito was still back there, standing with Charley. Unless he reached a similar conclusion and had the good sense to sneak off in the night. Caverango wondered about it. Maybe Poqito *had* reached a similar conclusion. He sure hoped so. If they both got away tonight, they could break off from this gang. After all, there was a posse on their trail — and the posse was mainly looking for Bill and Vincent. They probably weren't even aware that Caverango and Poqito were riding with the gang. The two of them might even ride openly in the daylight, passing themselves off as regular vaqueros looking for work.

Between the tree trunks, Caverango spotted the soft orange glow of the campfire. He smelled the burning wood before he saw it. These gringos must not be anticipating any danger, he thought, or they would not have lit a fire. Caverango would never have lit a fire if his compañeros had just been bushwhacked and shot down. He would have ridden far away at once.

A gun went off and Caverango dropped to his knees. The rapport was loud. He held his breath. It had come from back behind him, where Charley and Poqito were — not from one of the *caballeros* up ahead. It came from behind. Close behind. He could smell the gunpowder.

Shuffling around, Caverango squinted into the darkness hoping to see something. He wondered if Charley had gone ahead and shot Poqito after all. The man always seemed to be sipping on corn whiskey. He was probably drunk right now. Poor Poqito.

Caverango heard a twig snap and footsteps rushing his way. Before he knew it, somebody ran right into him and they both went down together.

"Es me! Es me!" Caverango whispered tensely.

He could smell the familiar odor of corn whiskey. It was Charley Crouse.

"I figured so," Charley whispered back. His voice was nonchalant, but in that initial moment of uncertainty his hands had sought out Caverango's throat. He relaxed his grip and let Caverango breathe again.

"Time to run the gauntlet," Charley told him, quietly. "We been set upon from behind. Oh...and your Mexi friend is dead."

Both of them got to their feet. Charley held onto Caverango's sleeve as they stood there, panting.

"Alright, you ready?" Charley asked in the dark and slapped him on the back. "Rattle your hocks!"

He took off at a run, pulling Caverango along by his sleeve.

Both men ran directly towards the orange flicker of firelight. They ran right by Lee and Davis, who were unsure whether or not to shoot. They rushed past the smoldering fire and leapt over

Steve and jumped the big log. They sailed right over Rufe and disappeared into the night.

Chapter 52

Lefthand Canyon

“If you don’t shut up about them apple orchards I’ll reach over there and clock you,” Bill said to Granger.

“The hell you will,” Granger replied weakly.

Without the moon it was slow going. But since the stage road was an easy path to follow, they relaxed and let the horses pick their own way in the black night.

“He probably cut up some draw, back a’ways,” Granger went on. “Done euchered us...he’s long gone.”

“Vincent, what are your thoughts on all this,” Bill asked. “Should I clock Granger?”

“If you don’t, I will.”

“Hold up now!” Bill hissed.

They all stopped and listened. Bill thought he heard something besides the river and the cold wind. He held his breath. What was it? A deer moving through the brush? The crackle of a cookfire?

Silence.

A beaver tail slapped the creek’s moving surface, somewhere off to their right.

Bill angled his head to one side. That had to have been it.

“Wish I could hear better out of this ear,” he said sourly to Vincent.

“It was either I shoot and damage *one* of your ears — or I not shoot, and you could hear the judge crisp with *both* ears.”

Bill’s horse nickered.

Then they heard a horse burst into a gallop. They could easily hear the hoofsteps clattering down the road. They could not see to be sure, but Bill knew it was LG.

“There he goes!” Bill yelled.

Chapter 53

Bill was right — it was LG. He let Specter pull ahead at a dead run, even though he could not see a thing. He held the reins loose to give Specter his head. He certainly hoped the horse had enough trail sense.

Behind him, he heard guns go off. Muzzle flashes lit up the dark like lightning. With each flicker LG caught a glimpse of the road. Dark pines rose up to his right and left, walling him in. The only place to go was further down the road. LG's main worry was the wheel ruts. They were fairly deep.

LG brought his old .44 around and pulled the trigger. It fired. In that quick flash LG saw Bill, Vincent and Granger — clear as day for one split second.

They were right behind him.

LG leaned forward in the saddle like a jockey. Specter felt him shift his weight and pressed on even harder. The horse's breathing was loud, percussive. It was all LG could hear.

Time seemed to hang still.

LG wondered if it would be better to simply stop and shoot it out. Or run off into the trees on foot. But he knew that would be foolish for more than one reason. He rode on.

At that moment he heard a horse stumble behind him and go down. Someone just took a hard spill, LG thought. Almost at the same time, he heard horses squeal and somebody shout. He knew another horse had just wrecked — maybe all of them went down, he couldn't tell. Whatever happened, it sounded bad. But to LG's relief, the pursuit dropped off, and it was not long before Specter's hoofs were the only sound.

LG slowed him down to an easy trot. He was still expecting a wreck of his own and found it hard to believe he was still in one piece.

He strained to listen — no one was riding after him anymore.

The stage road was empty.

Chapter 54
Ward

Prescott Sloan drummed his fingers on the window sill.

"Okay, here it is," Mr. James told him. "From Boulder Station: *Stage no arrival, stop; if this be antics necktie social to follow, stop."*

Spinning around, Sloan took the two steps it took to cross the room and leaned right over the banister. He plucked the paper out of Mr. James' hand.

Mr. James balked in surprise. His wiry glasses slid down his nose and nearly fell right off. He was not used to anyone plucking telegrams out of his hand. That was quite rude! But then, he knew Prescott Sloan well enough to expect rudeness.

"Damn and blast," Prescott Sloan enunciated each word. He crumpled the paper in his fist.

Mr. James leaned back and scratched his head. Being a telegrapher could be boring much of the time. But sometimes things heated up. He wondered if it was better to hand Mr. Sloan his messages instead of reading them as they came off the wire. That *was* his standard practice, given that most folks were anxious to hear the message as it came in. It also gave Mr. James a bit of conversational fodder — it got pretty quiet in that tiny office. It was nice to chat with whoever came inside.

This particular message had come in earlier that morning, and Mr. James had stacked it on the pile like he normally did. When Prescott Sloan came through the door, Mr. James sorted through the stack until he found the right one, which took some time since a multitude of messages had rolled in that morning — which was unusual. Noting Sloan's impatient finger drumming on the window sill, Mr. James decided to immediately read it out loud. Now the testy banker was in a distemper. Perhaps Sloan took it as a breach of privacy, James considered. But as telegrapher, he read *everyone's* messages. He couldn't avoid it! From then on, Mr. James decided he would simply hand telegrams directly to the customer. He knew he would miss out on some nice conversation in the process, but he would also avoid any distemper as well. He sighed.

The front door was propped open a crack. The morning had turned out quite gray and gloomy, so Mr. James had the small woodstove going. However, in such a small building the room got hot quick. So he kept the door propped open enough to let some of it escape. He liked to be cozy for his telegraphy — not boil in a sweat lodge. Outside, through the cracked door, both Mr. James and Prescott Sloan heard the jingle of traces.

"That's them," Sloan grumbled. "The fools!"

Flinging open the door, Sloan marched out into the street. He did not bother closing it behind him, so Mr. James had to get up and come all the way around the banister to close it...and make sure it stayed open just a crack.

Sure enough, coming up the road was the stagecoach. But to Sloan's surprise, Jim Everitt was not driving and Ian Mitchell was not riding shotgun. Sloan's simmering anger turned into concern — concern for the leather pouch he had sent down the mountain.

At the Halfway House, Griff brought the coach to an easy stop outside the corrals. Bitty the lead mule twitched her long ears, wondering why they were back here again. But perhaps there would be grain, so she stood patiently.

"Who in the hell are you?" Sloan snipped as he walked up.

"Deputy Sheriff of Grand Lake, Griff Allen," Griff shot back. "And watch your tongue when you speak to me — don't care for salty language."

"You're out of your jurisdiction, deputy. Now where is Jim Everitt? And why is he not operating this coach?"

Griff jumped down and landed hard on the ground. He was tired. With his thumb, he pointed back at the stagecoach. He was in no mood for snippy bankers with silver hair neatly combed to one side. Griff was not tired — he was exhausted. They had Lem's body, and of course the head of Will Wyllis in a pickle jar. But Emerson Greer's murderers were still not caught. That stuck in Griff's craw, but there was a time for everything. And this posse had run its course.

Now all Griff wanted was a hot meal, a bath and a shave. He wanted to go home. He wondered how Bonnie was holding up. She did not do well when he was gone. She got lonely. Griff thought about her, all by herself in the kitchen, baking one of her terrible-tasting carrot cakes. He found himself thinking how nice it would be to share a slice of that terrible carrot cake with her, sitting next to the fireplace. The boys would be rambunctious, probably get in a fistfight. They were always like that when he came in off the trail.

Ben Leavick sat silently up on the driving bench. He stared vaguely up at the mountains and the low gray sky. That was how he felt: low and gray. Sloan ignored him, grabbed the doorframe and hauled himself up so he could see through the window. The entire coach rocked with his weight.

"Bang-up job, boys," he muttered darkly. "This is fine as cream gravy."

Jim Everitt and Ian Mitchell were lying inside, dead as could be. There had holes in their heads and blood caked around their faces.

"Who's this other man?"

"One of the Grand Lake Gang," Griff told him, matter of factly. "They killed your drivers."

Opening the door, Sloan stepped inside and wiggled his boots in between the corpses, in order to get his balance. Without any further comments to Griff, Sloan proceeded to rifle through Jim Everitt's vest pockets. Not finding what he was looking for, Sloan went on to check every pocket he could find — he even went through Lem's clothes.

Hugh Hughes came out of the Halfway House and ran over to the stagecoach. His sleeves were rolled up and wet from doing dish-work. Someone just told him the stage had come back in. That was odd. In fact, it had never happened before. Jim and Ian always drove the same circuit, every week. Why would they turn back?

"What's going on?" Hugh asked, looking worried. "Jim?"

Sloan stuck his head out the door and glanced at Hugh. He knew Hugh had been friendly with these men. After all, they ate a meal and slept at the Halfway House all the time. Sloan did not care one whit's lick about them, himself. He did care about his PO Box key. He climbed out into the street again and pointed at the doorway. Hugh looked inside.

"Why, they kilt the boys," Hugh said sadly. Then Hugh realized he had given Jim Everitt his pocketwatch. It was a family heirloom. He crawled up inside and began patting around at Jim's vest pockets, frantically.

"Ain't nothing there," Sloan told him. But he watched closely in case Hugh found something he might have missed...like the key he had given to Jim Everitt. Or the sizable transfer fee he gave Ian Mitchell to get it safely down to Soapy Smith in Denver — which was not in their pockets, either. And now Jim was dead, the coach was sitting in Ward, and the cash and PO Box key were gone. And apparently, so was Hugh's pocketwatch.

With a slow sigh, Hugh sagged down heavily in the doorway. He wiped his hands on the front of his apron.

"Took my pappy's pocketwatch," he said. "Meant for my sister. There was a funeral and everything. She was supposed to get that watch."

Griff had been a lawman all his adult days. It was not the first time he had seen men grieved over a loss of property or life. He had seen a lot of loss in the past month alone. Emerson Greer. These two coach drivers. The cowmen of the B-Cross-C. And two dead outlaws. Griff wondered what caused men to be so violent towards one another — especially toward total strangers. And it was almost always over monetary interests.

The sun was hidden. There was a chill in the air, but it was not cold enough to keep the flies from coming out. Several black flies zipped into the stagecoach and buzzed around the dead men's eyes.

"Thought to bring these two men up here," Griff told Hugh. "We're aiming to pack that other one out with us — hope there's an undertaker about."

"Talk to Coke. He's English," Hugh told him. "Fella with the mustache."

"Mustache?" Griff asked skeptically. Everywhere he looked he saw men with mustaches.

"You'll know him when you see it. Dern near touches his titties."

The rest of the posse rode into town at that moment. Griff saw them come into view, riding up the hill. This little mining town would be a good place to rest up, he thought — start back home in the morning. Their horses were worn and they all looked worn out themselves. Roy Caldwell drove his little buckboard just behind the group of riders...one hand busy with the reins, the other hand resting on the pickle jar.

Part 2

CHARACTERS

PART 2_

The IM Ranch:

Mr. Mulock – ranch owner, family patriarch; also owns the Cañon City Bank
Parker Mulock – eldest son
Edson Mulock – middle son
Peter Mulock – youngest son
Augustus Gaumer – cousin to Mr. Mulock, and cashier at the Cañon City Bank

Citizens of Leadville:

Horace “Haw” Tabor – affluent owner of The Tabor Opera House, Matchless Mine
Elizabeth “Baby Doe” Tabor – Horace’s eccentric wife and socialite
Big Ed Burns – local crime boss
Soapy Smith – Denver’s biggest confidence man & racketeer, with crime ties to Leadville
George Fryer – successful miner
JJ Brown – successful miner
Maggie Brown – JJ’s wife and rising socialite
Ben Loeb – local entrepreneur of baser things

Notable citizens of South Park & surrounding area:

Laura Blancett (Til’s wife)
Walker Blancett (Til & L aura’s son)
Sam Hartsel – owner of the Hartsel Ranch
Cassius – owns & oversees the Whale Mine
Chubb Newitt – runs the general store in Garo
Frank Stevens – owns Stevens Saloon
EP Arthur – Englishman, ranch owner

The XIT Ranch (Texas):

Sam Singer – runs “Singer’s Store, Merchandise”
Colonel AG Boyce – new ranch manager
AL Matlock – lawyer hired by the Chicago Syndicate to clean up corruption at the XIT
George Findlay – young Scot, working for Matlock
BH “Barbeque” Campbell – prior ranch manager
Billy Ney – “the Xmas hell variety”
Arizona Johnny – “the Xmas hell variety”
Frank Yearwood
Rollin Larrabee – bookkeeper

Chapter 1
Hall's Ranch
Lyons
Colorado

The wood sizzled and then popped. An orange cinder arced through the air and landed right in Granger's lap. He immediately jumped up and began slapping around at his pants. The cinder fell off and dropped near his feet. It looked like a dying firefly. Granger stomped it.

"Damn near burnt me," he muttered. "See that?"

Vincent and Bill were sitting on the ground, leaning back against the apple trees. The whole grove smelled like apples. Of course they saw the whole thing. But they didn't really care. To them, Granger was a circus clown who had long since overstayed his welcome. His nasally voice and tooth-whistle talk was really getting under Vincent's skin. Even Bill was tired of Granger. Bill always considered himself removed from the petty irritations of the lawless lifestyle. But after a full month dodging around in the backcountry with no one to talk to but these two, it was taking its toll.

Staying off trail was a necessary evil. After so much killing and robbing, Bill knew they had to lay low. He didn't let them ride into any town they came across. Not even for a quick meal at a local inn. Things were too hot. Plus Vincent had fouled himself up when his horse tripped. Even after weeks had passed, the man was still in a great deal of pain. What if some local lawman realized who they were? Vincent was dead weight. Granger was unpredictable. So Bill thought the best thing was to simply wait it out. Besides, he had instructed the rest of the gang to meet up at these apple orchards if things went wrong. And things had.

Bill pulled at a thin chain dangling from his vest. He took out his new silver pocketwatch. It was from the stage driver. After Bill shot him, he went through his clothes. It was a nice timepiece, even engraved: *John Frederick Hughes, from Helena your loving wife: Absence from those we love is self from self.* And sitting here under the apple trees, it was mighty useful. He could check the minutes and see exactly how much time passed between Granger's rants and outbursts.

"There was a time when I'd bellow at your fool ways," Vincent complained. "Now it's just deflating when you flap your maw."

He glanced over to Bill.

"How long?"

"Twenty whole minutes."

"Twenty whole minutes till what?" Granger asked them.

Vincent sighed.

"Go boil your shirt," he told Granger.

An owl hooted. It was in the tree up above the fire. Vincent could see it. It was just a small owl. He wished it was a big owl — a big owl that would swoop down and pluck out Granger's eyes. Or carry him away into the sky. But of course, that was a wistful thought. There were no owls in all of creation big enough to carry Granger away. Vincent shifted. Leaning against apple trees for the past week was as uncomfortable now as it was then. Especially since his whole chest ached. He wished he had a nice bed to sleep in somewhere. Really, it was insensitive of Bill to expect him to sleep outside night after night, knowing he was banged up as bad as he was.

Granger gave his lap one more defiant swipe and eased himself onto the ground.

The apple orchards. The moon was high and no one else was there but them. Bill sighed impatiently. He was a little surprised... surely, at least *someone* should have gotten here by now. Maybe Charley rode back up to Brown's Park. He had a home up there after all, and his own interests to look after. But surely the Mexicans had no better place to go.

He looked over at Vincent — his face was in the shadows, but Bill could see it was pale even in the dark. That guy sure took a hard fall back on the stage road. He got boogered up pretty good. It had been Vincent's horse that tripped that night. Bill was still a little put out. They were right on top of that waddie! Another minute and they would have ridden him down or shot the horse out from underneath him. But he got away. At that point, Bill knew the three of them better hole up. Let things cool off. That waddie rode straight into Boulder and stirred up the law...why wouldn't he? Probably roused another posse and came right back up the canyon. There was still the first posse coming down from Ward. They would have been boxed in if they had stayed on the road.

If it was Granger who had fallen, Bill would have just left him behind. But it was Vincent, after all. So he shot Vincent's horse — who was too hurt to even stand. Bill let him double up behind his saddle, then they cut up the first gulch they came to and rode off into the forest. And now here they were in Hall's apple orchards, bickering over stupid things said for the hundredth time.

"How much longer we gonna wait? If they ain't here by now *they ain't coming*," Granger told them. "Just them damn beaners and Charley Crouse, anyways. Lem's dead. Will's dead. We hold out here any longer, old man Hall is gonna find us for sure, and *we'll* be dead."

Vincent glanced at Bill from the corner of his eye.

"Turd's got a point."

It had been the topic of discussion for the whole week. The opinion swayed back and forth every night. Mainly, it was Bill who wanted to stay and wait. The pain was just getting worse for Vincent, even though he hated to take Granger's side on anything as a general principle.

Bill thought about it. Seven long days hiding in a grove behind the red sandstone hogbacks of the Front Range was finally losing its appeal. As had a week of eating apples and saddlebag-aged beef strips.

"It was a fine plan, don't get me wrong-like," Granger said, brightening. "Them Mex'kins probably split off for gall-damn Mazatlan anyhow. Gobblin' tortillas with little brown chicas. Catching the French Pox. And ole Charley, God knows he has a mind to do whatever he piss pleases."

"Why don't you go find *us* some tortillas," Vincent told him and started to chuckle. But he winced as he did and held his chest. Vincent knew his ribcage was bruised badly. He knew what cracked ribs felt like, but it had never taken this long to heal up before.

The fire hissed and crackled and another cinder skittered off into the dark. Granger glared across the flames at Vincent. That guy sure thought highly of himself. Granger was tired of the insults. But he seemed to be getting through to him now, so Granger held his anger back and tried again.

"Keep in mind ole John Hall now. He's gonna figure us out here soon," Granger reasoned. "Longer we sleep out here, more likely we are to wake up with buckshot in our asses."

Bill sat quietly watching the embers glow. Of course, Granger made the same statement every day. Bill had heard it enough times. He would rather watch sap boil up out of the backlog than listen to anymore of this same topic. However, Bill could tell Vincent was starting to side with Granger's opinion — which meant the man was in serious pain.

"Apples, apples, all week apples." Granger went on. "Get the backdoor trots while we're off among the willows."

Vincent coughed and his face scrunched up. He turned to Bill.

"Maybe we ought to consider riding on?"

Perhaps waiting in the orchards had run its course, Bill thought. It was true they couldn't stay there forever. But where would they go next? Well, Bill knew. He quietly took out a small buckskin pouch and held it up in the yellow light.

"Whatcha got there?" Vincent asked him.

"Picked it off the driver."

He unwound the twine and reached inside. He pulled out a short-handled key. He pinched it delicately between his thumb and forefinger and held it up to the light.

"Well?" Vincent prodded.

Granger leaned forward. He felt his heart beating but tried not to say a word. They had been riding together for a month, and Bill hadn't mentioned this. Obviously, Vincent didn't even know! To have big Bill Ewing reveal a secret key to him and Vincent *at the same time* made him feel like he was finally part of the gang. *This* is the inner circle, he thought. Bill, Vincent and me. Not even the infamous Charley Crouse! Granger took a breath and waited on Bill. He didn't want to say anything that might make Bill mad, or jeopardize his standing in the inner circle.

"It's a key," Bill said finally, twisting it slowly in the firelight. "A key to a Post Office box in Denver."

He reached back into the pouch and took out a piece of paper, rolled up tight. He unfurled it and read out loud:

"*To Soapy Smith. For the Tivoli. Courtesy, P. Sloan.*"

Chapter 2

Leadville
Colorado
10,152 ft.

"Cloud City!" the stagecoach driver shouted. He reached down and thumped the rooftop with the palm of his hand.

Harrison Avenue. The wide dirt street was busy. It was full of wagons, coaches and buckboards. Horses and mules pulled most of them — some oxen, too.

Casey looked out his window. Thousands of people were going about their day. It seemed like it was mostly men, miners, a sea of hats and mustaches in worn-out work clothes. Buildings rose up on both sides of the street, many two and three stories high. Most eye-catching, there were a surprising number of burros being led about. Some carried packs...and to Casey's surprise, some were even saddled.

"Look at that. Grown men riding donkeys," he said with a lop-sided grin.

Stepping into the sunshine, Casey marveled at how many people were milling about. He shook his head, thinking how noisy it all was. He was used to cows for conversation and tomato cans for something to read. Now here he was in the biggest mining city in the Rockies.

Behind him, Julianna extended her hand with falsified grace so the cowman could help her down.

"Many thanks to you, good sir."

Casey grinned ear to ear and grandly removed his hat with a broad sweep. His sweep nearly clipped some folks.

"M'lady, your township awaits," he said with an attempted accent.

Julianna laughed out loud at the way he said it.

"Casey! What was that? Welsh...or moonshine Kentucky?"

A wind blew up and whipped her long brown hair around her shoulders. She playfully gave him a punch in the arm.

Walking around the stagecoach, Casey got in line behind two other travelers who were waiting to get their own luggage. Up top, the driver loosened the knots that tied everything down. He handed down several other bags first, and then lowered a burgundy travel trunk to Casey.

Several coaches were stacking up in the street right behind theirs, loading and unloading passengers. The smell of horse sweat and smelter smoke was thick in the air.

"Boy, look at all this fuss," Casey said to Julianna.

"Leadville is certainly bustling. I already heard two guns go off."

"It's every bit like Denver...big," Casey continued. "Think I'd feel better if I saw some stockyards."

Julianna smiled and shivered a bit with the slight chill. It may have been June, but it was June at ten thousand feet in the Rocky Mountains. She pressed her hands deep into her coat pockets.

"Where's the Delaware?" Julianna asked a passerby.

"Corner on 7th," the man told her and quickly walked on.

Julianna and Casey each took a side handle and lifted up the trunk. They stepped into the flow of townspeople and made their way up Harrison Avenue. After a block, Casey was starting to walk stiffly.

"Not used to actual foot walking," he said with a wink. "Horseback — *that* I am accustomed to."

"That, *and*," Julianna spoke with gentle concern, "if my recollection is accurate, you've been shot two times and are still on the mend."

He pressed his hand against his chest, took a deep breath and winced.

"That does contribute."

All around Leadville, they could easily see immense mountains everywhere they looked. Peaks rose up on both sides of town. The western horizon was dominated by a large massif glistening white with snow. Someone told them it was Mount Massive on the ride in. And Mount Elbert. They were enormous, still caught up in winter conditions even though it was mid-summer down below. Long plumes of snow blew right off the summit ridges like streaks of cloud. To the east was the Mosquito range, which was not quite as jagged looking but still rose quite high.

Casey looked around curiously. These mountains were so tall the trees didn't even grow on top. A lot of mines were tucked in back there. Some were down in the trees and others were spread out along every inch of every creek — some were even way up on the summits. It was a different world than punching cows. The mining community was in full swing, which explained the proliferance of burros. Casey smiled again, wondering what twist of fate would lead a man to saddle a donkey.

The Delaware Hotel was three stories tall, red brick with a copper roof. The hotel was new and looked like it. The second and third floors all had tall narrow white-trimmed windows, floor to ceiling. The double-door entrance was built on the corner angle and just to its left, tall plate-glass windows gave everyone a good look at what the hotel store had to sell.

Julianna was excited. For years the nearest hotspot was Ward, Colorado. Not a cultural mecca by any stretch, but accessible. Perhaps even "accessible" was too generous a term, she thought. Julianna had never been to Leadville, and here the boom years were rolling along at full speed. It seemed to shine everywhere she looked.

Casey opened one of the solid pine doors for her, and they went up the entrance stairs to check in at the main desk.

"Welcome to The Delaware," said the clerk. "Rooms rented by the month."

"We'll take two. Uh, *separate r*ooms, please," Casey said chastely, and then added:

"What kind of preachers you got up here?"

Chapter 3

Hay Ranch
North of Garo
South Park

The ladder was rickety. Til shifted his weight gingerly. Looking off in the grassy valley, he spotted a spiral of smoke to the north. A steam locomotive was slowly chugging into sight. It pulled a short line of rail-cars, and from this distance looked like it was barely crawling through the grass.

Til hung his bucket on a thick nail in the roof's eave and called down.

"Here comes the train."

The bucket was full of wet clay, and Til's hands were covered in it. Taking care, he made his way down the ladder — leaving hand-prints on every rung. Stepping back for a minute, Til assessed his work as he cleaned up with an old rag.

"Chinkin' and daubin'," Steve McGonkin said admirably. "Are we really down to just this?"

"Are we ever down to anything?" Til responded with a carefree grin. "Always something."

The house was basically done now. It was the only building in sight on these gentle grassy slopes. They had spent weeks on it — a meticulous project. Til insisted that it should be plumb and square. He did not want a saggy looking home.

Behind the house, the west ridge rose up abruptly and cut off their view. But to the east, the valley was wide open and they had a clear line of sight. The McGonkin brothers even helped him build a large front porch so they could sit and watch the sun rise in the mornings. It also provided an easy view of the Denver South Park Railway running right down the valley.

It was a nice morning. Not too hot yet. Til took his hat off and ran his sleeve across his brow. Things were coming together. Finally! Quite a bit different, he considered, than the cattle drive earlier that year. Everything fell apart that day.

Stepping into the sunlight, Rufe McGonkin stuck his head out of the doorway.

"Hi-ya boss. Ready for the carryall?"

"Yep. Let's get the horses in their traces. Emmanuel in there?"

"Yessir, he is."

"Let him know to get some dinner rolling. I'm sure we'll be back by the noon hour."

Rufe ducked back inside while Til and Steve headed for the corral.

"I'll rope them horses," Steve volunteered.

The corral was the first thing they built. They made it out of lodgepole pine, fresh cut from the west ridge behind the house, stripped of all the bark. The rails were still sappy in spots. Every pair of Til's gloves were sticky.

There was a horse-drawn cart parked nearby. Its large spoked wheels were chocked into place. It was basically new. Til bought it some weeks back to help move timber and supplies. Next to it sat the B-Cross chuckwagon, all beat up by weather and a world of use. They built the house from the ground up, and all the while slept out at night and fed from the wagon.

Til smiled as he thought about it. It was the trail lifestyle. That was what they were all used to — and it was a hard habit to disrupt. Bedding down under the stars was how it had been for many years. Things were going to change after today, though.

Emmanuel came out of the house with Rufe. In the corral, Steve dropped a loop around one of the big black draft horses. Til had invested in a couple Percherons to pull the new carryall.

While he waited on the horses, Til looked across his new spread.

There were some cattle grazing on the tall grass — each running the *B+C* brand. They were the same Polangus and Durhams from before, but Til never did recover half of what they lost in Lefthand Canyon. Til and the McGonkins had gathered up a number of strays, but many were never seen again. It had taken several days to regroup, and the loss of half the crew was a hard blow.

He sighed, and not for the first time. It was just plain bad luck the B-Cross had driven their cattle right into a stage robbery. It even made the papers. "The Grand Lake Gang" was what they were calling it — the gang that murdered Ira and Edwin, shot Casey and Steve, and nearly ran Til's brand into bankruptcy. Lee and Davis had quit after that. No one knew where LG was. It had been an ordeal.

"Mrs. Blancett gonna 'preciate this fine home," Emmanuel said with a big smile. He clapped a hand on Til's shoulder.

"I think so."

Til sent a wire to his wife in Iowa. A couple years had passed since he saw her last. Til planned to have more for her by now — wealth from his cattle operation. But with the Great Die-Up, the entire West was in a ball of confusion. Plus rails and farms were eating up the open range, and times were changing as it was. And with the losses of crew and cattle, well...Til wasn't sure what to do. The answer might be raising pure-bred livestock. He knew Charlie Goodnight had been working on breeding techniques in the Palo Duro for several years now. Til was tempted to try the same. One thing he did know: simply collecting a hodgepodge of stray cattle, branding them and driving them north had seen its time.

The strays they rounded up in Lefthand were mainly Polangus, outnumbering the Durham they found. Til figured he could sell off the Durham and focus on Polangus. Breeding could be the game changer he was looking for. High quality stock would set him apart from other outfits, and he could get a higher dollar per pound.

He also knew it was good to be off the trail. Til was ready to settle down. The deaths of Ira and especially young Edwin brought his thoughts around to his own family, back east of the 100th parallel. Time was ticking away. He did not want to spend any more time without them.

"I'm all done on that kitchen table," Rufe mentioned. "I'll have all the tools put away by the time you get back."

Rufe helped Steve lead the Percherons through the corral gate.

"Now you got a place to set your plate down, Til," Rufe said. "I guess a man's batwings ain't the only plate he can eat off. Though I wouldn't know, myself."

"Well, a table is more rightly for a family," Til pointed out. "But you boys can keep eating off your chaps if you want."

The McGonkins got both the draft horses into their traces. Steve knelt down and unchocked the wheels.

"You're all ready now."

"Well, I guess I'll head on up to Red Hill and pick her up," Til said.

Soon, the carryall was moving north through the summer grass. By then the train had made some distance, but was still crawling as slow as the clouds above. Til knew he would be in Red Hill about the same time it pulled into the depot.

Chapter 4
Red Hill

The train eased into the depot. Steam hissed out in plumes. The sun was straight up in the sky and it was turning out to be a warm, pleasant summer day.

Til drove the carryall up to a wide watering trough near the stock fences. The two big draft horses knew what to do and dropped their noses simultaneously into the cool mountain water. Just over the fence, cattle lowed and clanked their horns. The scent of cow manure was strong but it was such a natural thing that Til didn't notice.

It was a busy time of day. Red Hill only had twenty-five permanent residents. The depot was the center of the town's life. It did not even have a Post Office. Til had to ride all the way down to Garo for mail or groceries. But when the train came through, a crowd could swell. At least a dozen freight wagons were parked nearby. Their teams were hitched and the drivers sat ready. Til was not far away from one teamster and called out neighborly.

"What have you?"

"Dry goods. I'll be making for Fairplay this afternoon. Alma, Dudley, Mosquito tomorrow."

"Mining camps all need to eat, I suppose," Til reasoned.

"That's the long and short of it."

The narrow-gauge train had large white lettering on the coal box behind the engine: DSP&P RR. The Denver South Park & Pacific ran all the way down from Denver into the Park, then kept going south to Garo, Weston and over Trout Creek Pass. For Til, the train had become a familiar sight. The steam whistle reminded him there was civilization beyond hay, cows, and home-building. Homesteading came with a different mentality than trail driving. Some days he got to feeling stuck and the steam whistle only made it worse sometimes.

Like most of the mountain trains, it was only a few cars in length. There were two passenger cars, one stock and four freight cars. The teamster nodded politely to Til and clucked his tongue. The other freighters all moved out to get in place by the freight ramps.

Til caught sight of several buckaroos saddling up their horses. It was an easy chore to load stock — after all, the animals were already in the holding pens. The only thing left to do was flush them up the loading chute.

Glancing up towards the depot platform, Til noticed the passenger cars were opening up. People began to pour out and their voices carried loudly. Backing the drafts from the water tank, he maneuvered the carryall around to an open grassy area. He set the brake and wrapped the reins around the handle.

"Be good," Til told the lead horse, whose name was Heavy.

Heavy turned to look over Til's shoulder at all the activity — and nearly knocked Til down with his draft-sized horse head. Til wiped the snot off his shoulder with a kerchief.

"Now I got horse slobber on my good shirt."

Making his way across the green grass and daisies, Til went up the steps and stood on the wide platform. He looked around at all the people — and there she was.

"Laura," Til said with a smile. "You are a sight."

Laura Blancett stood tall in a straight canvas-colored skirt and a wide low hat which shaded her face. Her hair was long and blonde, glimmering in the sunlight. She threw her arms around his neck and squeezed.

"Missed you, honey!" she said happily.

Til found it was suddenly hard to speak. He cleared his throat.

"You look lovely."

She smiled and pressed her palm to his clean-shaven cheek. She pinched the end of his mustache. It was longer than the last time she had seen him. It made him look older.

"Where's the boy?" Til managed to say.

"I sent Walker for the luggage."

They held each other tightly for a long minute. The other passengers milled around them.

"Two years, Til. That's such a long time," Laura said, seriously. "Any longer would be the ruination of me."

"You're my sweetheart, Laura. That's over now. Built us a home."

Their son came up just then. He was ten years old and already looked a lot like his father — although he was blonde like his mother.

"Poppa!" Walker shouted and wrapped his arms around Til's waist. "The whole train stopped so the ladies could pick wildflowers. I could barely stand such procrastination. I told the conductor how unreasonable it was. But he just ignored me, so we sat and sat."

Til grinned and put his hand on Walker's head. The boy may have my eyes, he thought. But he has the vocabulary and temperament of his mother.

"We won't stop for no wildflowers," Til assured him.

Chapter 5

Hay Ranch

Chili con carne, mashed potatoes cooked with onions, and warm buttermilk biscuits. Emmanuel laid it all out on Rufe's new hand-built kitchen table.

He attempted to do it with a mannered grace, or so he hoped. Emmanuel was keenly aware of Mrs. Blancett. A female presence was a rare phenomenon in a working cattle outfit, and cow crews were all he had known for many years.

Both Rufe and Steve also showed signs of critical self-awareness. Usually quite talkative, the brothers' conversation was reduced to baleful politeness. Fearful of faux pas, the cowhands busied themselves with the task at hand: eating.

Walker Blancett seemed fascinated by their clothes and gear. The Colt .45 held special appeal in his eyes. He wondered how he could get to hold one. He knew his mother would be uncompromising in her disapproval if he outright asked. Perhaps a more subtle ploy would work.

"Poppa, after supper may I see the stable?"

"Sure. Just a corral."

"Can Mr. McGonkin show it to me?"

Rufe and Steve looked up from their plates. First at little Walker...then at each other. Rufe pointed at Steve as if to ask, *you or me?*

Laura looked from the cowhands to her son.

"Perhaps. If you address Mr. McGonkin directly, he might acquiesce. Just do not be a burden or linger out there...they have their own business to attend."

Rufe forked a fat glob of mashed potatoes into his mouth. Steve saw it go in and realized his brother did not intend to reply.

"Sure, kid," Steve said.

Til poured a fresh glass of milk from a silver pitcher. He called into the kitchen:

"Emmanuel, come and join us. Sit down and have a plate."

Stepping out with a brand new ceramic coffee pot, Emmanuel looked uneasy about it but went ahead and sat down at the table.

"Til," Laura asked. "Catch me up on the B-Cross, since your last letter."

He sipped his milk and dabbed his mustache with a cloth napkin. He had bought cloth napkins, a cloth table cover, and all new dinnerware. Til wanted everything to be nice for his wife.

"Well. After the hassle in Lefthand, I gathered up as much of the outfit as was left. We swung a wide loop and brought in all the strays we could find. Drove 'em up here and bought this parcel of land."

Noticing that his young son was paying close attention to everything he said, Til nodded at the men around the table.

"They all ride for the brand. You can learn from these boys, Walker."

Walker nodded thoughtfully. But his thoughts were mainly about Colt .45's.

"Anyhow. I set upon to think this through," Til went on. "I come to realize, with the big Die-Up this last winter, the cattle industry is in for a change. Most everyone I been talking to of late has seen this as a passing hardship. But it's more than that. It's all changing."

"In what way?" Laura asked.

Emmanuel quietly began warming their mugs with fresh coffee. He had never seen the inside of a schoolhouse, but Mrs. Blancett seemed like an educated woman. She had a way of talking that made him self-conscious about his own choppy trail language.

"Past few years, population out here's been a jo-fired explosion. Dakota's nearly half a million folk now. Montana's all tripled up. Barbed wire is everywhere. And Colorado's headed down the same trail."

"The three G's," Rufe said suddenly.

Laura and Til looked over at him in surprise.

Rufe turned beet red.

"I won't bite, Rufe," Laura said kindly.

"Conversate, McGonkin," Til told him. He blew softly across the surface of his coffee and took an extremely careful sip — this was still Emmanuel's coffee, even if they were sitting around a dining table.

Rufe tried to remember what he was going to say. His mind went blank, and he realized his palms were sweaty.

"Biscuits are good," Steve mentioned to Emmanuel.

The cook gave him an overacted nod of approval. Emmanuel did not want to say anything embarrassing, so he decided to speak as little as possible.

"The three G's," Rufe said again. "God, government, and grangers."

Laura listened patiently and smiled again pleasantly to draw out whatever he was thinking. She knew all these men were uncomfortable around her. That was obvious the moment she met them. She realized they were not used to interacting with the female gender. Well, she intended to fix that. Engaging them in table talk was as good a way as any.

"Cowboyin's not the same now," Rufe continued. "Old days are over."

Til stepped in. Rufe's point was one thing, but his ability to communicate it in finer company was another.

"The days of big round-ups, big cattle drives and big herds — it can't go on like that no more."

"Where does that leave us?" Laura asked him. "People still buy beef. If the population is on the rise, it would seem the demand for beef would increase as well."

"It is, but it's that same population what's the problem. Homesteads, towns, fences. No more free range means no more long drives. That's where cattle get fattened up, is on the graze."

Laura considered what he was saying for a moment. She scraped her spoon slowly along the bottom of her chili bowl.

"So you think the money is in hay?"

"Yes, partly. People fence in their stock, the grass gets et up. They will need hay. I also plan on raising small herds here, and do it right. Focus on the *quality* of the stock. There's one man in the Park, Sam Hartsel, who's been experimenting with that. I aim to do the same."

"We need ownership of the land, water rights," Laura said, thinking out loud. "And fencing. And a lot more pure-blood stock."

Til sat back and looked at her. He smiled softly. She was certainly a lovely woman, and sharp as a tack. Even though the cattle drive was a failure — it made him rethink things. And now here he was, sitting at his own supper table, sharing a meal with his wife and son. If things had gone on fine, Til would be sitting on a rock in Wyoming at that very moment, eating out of a can.

"I'll need a desk," she mentioned. "A place to keep the ledger, tallies, bills of sale."

Til looked over at Rufe, who was watching the conversation's flow as if he were sitting on a riverbank.

"Manage that, Rufe?"

"I can build a desk," Rufe said and patted the tabletop. "I can do that. You bet."

Chapter 6

IM Ranch
Black Mountain
South Park

"You're looking for *work*?" Edson Mulock said suspiciously.

"Yessir," Charley Crouse replied with a starchy smile suitable for framing. "Me and this vaquero here. Just riding the grub line."

Edson looked over at his brother Peter. Peter Mulock looked back blankly. Both of them just sat their horses, not saying much. Charley realized this might be a hard sell.

"We been punchers at the King Ranch. Down Tejas way. Corpus. Heard of it?"

"Everybody *heard* of it," Edson told him, sharply. "What brought you way up here then?"

"Captain died a couple years back, ain't been the same since," Charley explained. He let the starchy smile fall into a look of pensive reverence.

Caverango was amazed at Charley's ability to pretend. Looking at him now, even Caverango wondered if what he was saying was the bona fide truth. And *he* knew it was a flat-out lie. But Charley pointed at him and went on with his tale.

"This hombre is one of the Kikeños: King's people. A top hand, staring you right in the face. Don't pass this ol' boy up."

What a story. Caverango wondered if Charley sat around thinking these things up beforehand. Surely he did. Otherwise he must be pulling it out of his hat. And who could pull something like that out of their hat? Caverango had never worked at the King Ranch, though he heard there were local Mexicans who did — locals who admired Richard King and rode for him out of loyalty. Caverango thought about Bill. And Charley. He wished *he* had someone worth riding for out of loyalty. As it was, Caverango wished he could put some distance between himself and Charley Crouse. The gringo was unpredictable and a little out of his mind. It left Caverango feeling that one day, he just might wake up with his own guts cut out and spilled on the ground.

Edson thoughtfully looked them over. He spat a stream of chewing tobacco on the ground. After a long moment of consideration, he relented.

"Well, come on then."

He turned his bay around and led the way. Charley and Caverango followed, and Peter Mulock came along behind. Edson led them along a well-used path that pointed straight across the open meadows at Black Mountain.

As they got closer, Caverango spotted the ranch buildings. Smoke trickled out of a chimney from a large frame house. Just behind it, the pine-covered slopes of Black Mountain swept up. It was a solitary mountain, surrounded by a good stretch of high prairie on all sides.

All morning long, Caverango watched big puffy clouds with dark flat bottoms collect in the sky. He had a fear of a being struck dead by lightning. Whenever clouds like that started building, he made it a point to get indoors — or at least off his horse. Especially when he was out in an open area, like they were now. The air was getting cool and a gusty breeze was picking up. Caverango hoped they would make it to the ranch before he got struck by lightning. The tall mountain grass began waving in the wind. A sure sign of a storm.

"That's the Big House," Peter mentioned.

The Big House was the headquarters for the IM. Edson took them right into the corrals where they dismounted and turned their horses loose. The wind was really whipping up now. It was obviously going to rain at any moment.

"Tack room's over there," Edson shouted above the wind.

They grabbed their saddles and hustled towards it. Cold raindrops started slapping at their hat brims. The tack room was a clutter of saddles and bridles and other things. They dumped their gear off and went back out into the rain.

"Father's inside," Peter said ominously, pointing to the Big House.

The sky was black now and the rain was coming down hard. Caverango was scared how quickly it got dark. He wanted to get where it was safe from lightning. Breaking decorum, he ran ahead of the Mulock brothers and Charley Crouse to get under the porch roof as fast as he could. If it lightninged, he didn't want to be the one to get blasted.

Caverango stood there panting as he waited for the others to catch up. Under the veranda he felt safe. He still wished he was as far from Charley Crouse as possible. Then he could truly feel safe.

True to its name, the ranch house was big. The sideboards were painted white and the trim was forest green. The roof was peaked in the middle. Beneath the peak, the whole wall was nothing but glass. The windows stretched from the floor all the way up to the ceiling. Whoever built this place spent a lot on those pricey windows. Charley figured that meant the IM was well off. Perhaps there was something worth stealing here.

The gold they got back in Kinsey City was still buried in that mineshaft up on the Divide. Charley was not sure who rode off with the gold dust and cash from Lefthand Canyon...he just knew it wasn't him. And getting shot at by a bunch of cowpokes in Spring Gulch was enough to keep him from going back to check. Which meant he was broke. Considering the fancy windows, the IM might be worth raiding. When the time was right.

Edson Mulock walked up to the front door and wiped his boots off.

"Come on in."

He opened the door and they all went inside. The foyer was gloomy. With the sky as dark as it was, the natural light did no good. Edson considered lighting one of the lanterns. But that would mean using kerosene during the day, which might be viewed as a waste by his father. His father hated wastefulness. He decided not to light one.

Thunder rumbled. They heard bootsteps echoing across the wood floor, and the patriarch of the Mulock clan came into the room. He walked right up to Edson with a deep frown.

"New hands?"

"Yes, pa," Edson said. He nodded toward Charley and Caverango.

"Say they're off the King Ranch."

Edson turned to Charley.

"This here is Mr. Mulock. Owner and operator of the IM."

Mr. Mulock stood a few inches shorter than Charley, graying at the temples. But he looked like a hard character. Charley stuck with his story.

"Just a couple of punchers," Charley explained.

Mulock began going through his overcoat, absently patting through the pockets one by one. He scowled at the floor thoughtfully. He finally found a cigar stub and examined it.

"Peter, fetch me some fire water."

Peter hustled off through an open doorway, disappearing into the shadows. Mr. Mulock suddenly raised his eyes and locked onto Charley. His gaze was direct.

"So you're riding the chuck line," Mulock said. His voice was brusque, no-nonsense. "Who's running the King now?"

"His lady," Charley told him quietly. "The Missus."

Peter came back into the room carrying a tin cup. Filing into the room behind him, a row of solemn cowboys also came in —

the only noise they made was the tinkle of their jingle-bobs. They fanned out. Caverango wished he had stayed out in the lightning. He wished he could leave right then and take his chances. Leave both Charley and his pretend stories far behind.

Mulock raised the cup and took a long sip. His gray eyes hovered over the rim, studying the two of them.

In one quick movement, he rang the tin cup across Charley's temple.

Crumpling against the door, Charley's knees drooped, but he managed to keep his footing. There was whiskey all over his face and shirt, and a raw red rash on his temple.

Mulock's cowboys stood around them, unmoving. They did not speak, flinch or blink. The ranch boss flicked his cigar stub across the room. It rolled beneath a bench and disappeared.

Outside the sky flashed brightly and the dim room was washed out for one silent moment. After a couple seconds the thunder caught up, with a rumble boom. Charley leaned heavily against the door for balance, and slowly straightened up — his hand pressed to his skull.

"Captain Richard King died two years ago. It went to Henrietta, yes," Mulock affirmed. Then he added: "But she don't run shit."

He held the tin cup loosely, twirling it by the handle. Caverango stood quietly, with his eyes fixed on the bench where the cigar stub rolled.

"*Kleberg's* running the whole jig," Mulock went on, his voice thick with derision. "*Has* been."

Hail began dinging off the rooftop. Slowly at first — then it really started coming down hard. Through the front window, all they could see was the gray haze of hail pellets bouncing off the ground.

Chapter 7

A hunched figure emerged from the hail with his arms over his head. He raced right up the veranda stairs. Edson grabbed Caverango by the arm and yanked him out of the way. The door banged open and the roar of falling hail became extremely loud. It was Parker Mulock. He took off his hat, which was damp and bent, and held his head. Parker had a headache from being pounded on the skull by hail.

"Parker?" Mr. Mulock said in surprise. "Why aren't you in Cañon City?"

"Pa, Augustus is right behind me."

Parker Mulock stood there, holding his hat with one hand and massaging his scalp with the other. Charley looked him over. How many more Mulocks were going to pop out of the woodwork?

Another ghostly figure appeared in the storm. He rushed across the yard and into the gloomy foyer. Unlike his eldest son Parker, who was sopping wet, Mr. Mulock's cousin Augustus Gaumer was wisely wearing a yellow slicker. He immediately hung it on a wall peg, where it dripped on the hardwood floor.

"Is it bad, Augie?" Mulock asked.

"It ain't good."

"Well, it sure as hell ain't good if you're here. Boys, let's move this into the great room. Build us a fire!"

Mulock marched across the foyer and through a wide archway which led into the dining room. Charley and Caverango felt as if they had been forgotten. None of Mulock's cowboys showed them any interest, and the Mulock boys followed their father without so much as a look back.

Caverango watched them go, feeling a ray of hope. They were simply looking for a free meal when they first saw the IM. That was what a lot of cowhands did — and most ranchers were happy to feed a wandering vaquero. But this did not feel right. It felt like some kind of lion's den.

"*Vamanos?*" Caverango suggested, beneath his breath.

Charley's temple was bright red from the swipe he had been given. Surely, thought Caverango, even Charley Crouse realized this was an opportune time to ride out. It was hailing like crazy — which would only aid their escape. The Mulocks would not try and ride them down in a hail storm.

"Naw," Charley said softly. He watched the group go through the archway. The dining room was the tallest part of the Big House. It was the room with all the windows. On a clear day, the Mulocks had a full view of the grassy prairie from their supper tables — all the way across South Park. At the present moment, of course, all anyone could see was hail.

"Walk out now, they'll cut us down for sure," he reasoned. "Follow of our own volition — they welcome us as one of their own."

He touched the side of his head gingerly, with his fingertips. There was no blood. He had taken worse hits to the head than this.

"Ol' boy's savage as a meat axe," Charley announced. He grinned suddenly. "Might be a crew we can tie to."

Caverango watched him stride off through the archway with a fresh spring in his step. With one last longing glance at the front door, Caverango scooted off after Charley.

This was his one chance to get away from both Charley Crouse and the IM. But Caverango's fears of sudden electrical death were too strong, after all. No matter what he told himself, he knew he couldn't go out there now. Not in a storm like this. Every minute the sky lit up. The thought of being blasted off his horse was worse than staying with Charley and the Mulock clan.

He wished Poqito hadn't been shot. If Poqito was there, then Caverango would have felt a lot better. As it was, he would have to wait to make his escape. Besides, Charley could very well be right — the Mulocks *did* seem like the type to chase people down.

Caverango didn't want to get shot, and he didn't want to get lightninged. So he reluctantly stepped into the gloomy dining room and took a seat next to Charley Crouse.

There was a large circular fireplace in the middle of the room, with an open hearth on both sides. The chimney seemed to go up and up and disappear in the shadows. Peter, the youngest of the Mulock boys, seemed to know his place and went right to work building a fire. He singled out a couple of Mulock's cowboys to help. They brought in loads of fresh split wood, kept dry beneath the veranda, and soon had the fire roaring.

Charley and Caverango sat quietly near the windows.

"Big trouble with the stocks. Half them mines are floundering, closing up," Augustus told Mr. Mulock in a sober voice. "We've got $200 thousand riding on it. All our eggs in the same damn basket."

"How much in the vault?"

"Pshaw," Augustus waved his hand. "Five grand in cash. The bank is *teetering*."

Mulock frowned and drummed his fingers on the tabletop.

"Get us some beers," he told Peter gruffly.

Peter hustled into the kitchen.

Charley perked up. What was this? They had just stepped into an interesting conversation! They might learn something useful. That something might even save them — or it might kill them. Either way Charley Crouse was paying close attention.

"At the end of the day, it's insolvent," Augustus explained. "Matter of time till it is broke. Collapse is imminent."

Mr. Mulock tapped his fingers on the table. He did not look pleased.

"This is timely then," Edson chimed in. "I happen to know for fact that George Green just sold the 63."

"When did you hear that?" his father demanded.

"Talked to him this very morning. Told me he's planning on making a deposit. Could be riding to Cañon even today. You can bet he'll want that holed up in the bank, quick as can be."

"Who did he sell to?" Augustus asked.

"Haver," Edson said. "Owns the Cleveland Cattle Company."

"Fifty thousand green," Mulock said, still frowning. "We're close-fisted on this, Augie. Don't you dare bet that out, you *hear me?*"

Augustus looked as if he was stung by a bee.

"I won't bet nothing out."

"You just slick up and be that dandy cashier you been all along. Keep receiving funds, like everything is fine. We need all we can reap now."

Mulock's face got darker as he spoke.

"I won't be the one sucking hind teat. I'll be in Mexico if this thing blows up."

Chapter 8
Whale Mine
Webster Pass

"A buckaroo don't milk no cows." LG said, offended.

"You look like you just ate a skunk," Cassius told him.

LG turned and looked at the cattle as if he was seeing them for the first time. There were only about fifty head total, spread out in the pine.

"We are short-handed," said Cassius. "Everybody's got to pitch in."

The Whale Mine was so high up in elevation, it seemed like there was hardly any air to breathe. LG caught himself wheezing when he walked from the bunkhouse to the meal hall. The prospect of milking cows also made him wheeze.

Cassius sighed impatiently while LG mulled this over. He knew LG was a cattle puncher, and like every cattle puncher he ever met, had no interest in milking cows. But Cassius was a realist.

"Rest of us are in the mine."

Avoiding Cassius' eye, LG counted through the local peaks. There was Sheep Mountain, Whale and Glacier Peaks to the south. Up north, he could see Handcart and Red Cone clear as day. All of them rose so high, half the time they were lost in the clouds.

"Would you rather break ore?" Cassius asked, getting irritated.

LG put his hat back on and squinted against the sunlight. In that moment, it sank in: he was not working for a regular cow outfit. It had no chuckwagon, no trail boss...not even a brand. This was just a no-name silver mine with some ratty-looking cows crapping in the trees.

"I would rather not break ore," LG muttered.

"Milk them cows, then," Cassius said. "And collect all the eggs, too. Take 'em to the kitchen."

The coop was situated next to the corral. It was full of squawking chickens. LG had to walk past it every day, more than once. Sometimes he would throw rocks at the hens to stir them up for fun. Now the indignities were stacking up quicker than he could say Jack Robinson.

"Be baking rhubarb cobbler next."

But Casssius had already stalked off. He had more important things to do than argue with LG Pendleton. There was a mine to oversee. When the cat's away, he knew all too well, the mice will play. And half these miners needed to be supervised closely. High-grading was a problem — it was all too easy to fill a tin lunch bucket with ore. Of course, he only paid the miners $2.25 a day. He knew they were getting $2.50 up in Leadville. But this was not Leadville.

The Whale Mine was remote. LG had been cutting through the backcountry for quite some time when he ran across it, several weeks back. Work meant three square meals and a bunk, and he was ready for those comforts. He had been through a rough spell, with too much on his mind to stay out in the backcountry any longer — with only his horse for company.

LG headed over to the paddock where the horses were kept. Specter was standing on the far side with his head between the rails, nosing for grass. The paddock had been picked over for so long, it was just dirt. But there was some tasty looking grass growing right outside the fence.

LG uncoiled his rope and stepped inside. There were about twenty horses in there. Like normal, they all scattered. Specter knocked his head on the rail trying to back up, but LG was not going after him. He wanted the dun instead and dropped a loop around its neck on the first try.

Even though Cassius had said there were other cowhands employed at the Whale, they were actually miners by trade. LG discovered they could sit a saddle — but that was about it. One of them, a freckly kid named John, was sitting on the top rail gnawing on an apple core. John had worked at the Whale all summer long. Now that an experienced stockman had signed on, John liked to spend his free time following LG around. He was impressed with LG's ability to throw a loop and whooped when LG caught the dun so easily.

"John-boy. Get the gate. I need you."

John slid off the fence and opened the gate for LG.

"Only got a few minutes," John told him, flinging the apple core into the paddock. "I'm on supper duty. Helping cookie on the butcher-block today."

"Naw, you're needed right here, pard."

The Whale Mine was owned and operated by two brothers: Cassius and Franklin. Well, Cassius ran it and Franklin mainly drank. No one ever saw him much. LG had never even met the man. The Whale produced a significant amount of silver ore. In fact, it had produced so well that the brothers built a smelter and a tramway to carry the ore. LG and John could hear voices carrying down the slope, along with the ring of mattocks.

A seasoned cowhand at the Whale was a rarity, so Cassius hired LG the moment he rode in. And for LG it had been nice up until that moment — being the top hand. Now the top hand was handling cow teats and fowl.

He saddled the dun and rode into the cattle pen, cutting out a cow and her calf. They bolted away together — the calf sticking close to its momma. The dun turned out to be a good cutting horse and took after them instantly. LG was surprised. These fellows may not have any real cowhands up here, he thought, but somehow they got a hold of one decent cowhorse. But the dun was rusty. She wasn't used to a real rider, he could tell.

LG shook out a loop and roped the momma. The cow did not like what was happening, and twisted and kicked.

"We best snub her. She won't stand pretty for us. Put your money on that."

LG pulled the cow into the round pen. He took her straight to the snubbing post and tied her head up against it. John ran off to find a pail. After a few moments she settled down.

John came running back with a pail. He held it out to LG.

"Here it is!"

"All you, bud."

John frowned. The camp cook was surely wondering where he was by now, and he was going to be mad if John never came back from his lunch break.

"Careful now," LG warned him. "Don't get stomped."

John set the pail on the dirt and slid it beneath the cow's udder with his boot. He squatted down but paused, wiggling his fingers uncertainly. John had been raised in New York. Milk came in glass bottles in New York. He glanced up at LG, hoping for some advice.

"What do I do?"

"Grab on."

John shrugged and reached in. Even though her head was snubbed against the post, the rest of her was free enough. Her hind hoof snapped out and caught him right in the forehead.

Chapter 9

"You'll do anything to get out of butchering," LG said.

John held a handkerchief to his forehead. It was soaked in blood. His hat was in his other hand — the brim was torn from the hoof strike.

"Got the skull cramps," John said miserably.

LG led him by the elbow to the bunkhouse. He took him inside and sat him on the nearest mattress.

"Am I gonna die?" John asked. "Feels like I'm gonna die."

He stretched out on the bed, looking piqued. His shut his eyes tight and kept the kerchief pressed against his head.

"Won't be no dead shine in camp tonight," LG assured him, patting the top of his head like a dog.

Cassius appeared in the doorway, obviously out of breath from hurrying.

"I heard John got his head kicked in!"

LG reached in his vest pocket and took out a small quid of tobacco.

"Yep," LG said and put a pinch in his mouth.

Cassius looked at John's blood-streaked face, then over to LG casually pinching off a bite of tobacco.

"I see you are wrought with concern over your fellow man."

"This is medicine," LG explained, holding up the package.

"*Climax Chewing Tobacco.*" Cassius said doubtfully. "Medicine?"

"Not only my favorite chew...makes a fine poultice."

"Think I'm goin' to die," John mentioned to Cassius.

Stepping over to the young man, Cassius reached down and lifted the handkerchief. John kept his eyes closed, fearing the worst. Dark sticky blood was all over his face. In the center of his forehead was a deep gash. The tear was several inches wide and the skin was bunched up.

"Got a good flapper there."

"Oh me," John moaned and pressed the handkerchief back on his forehead.

LG stepped over and lifted it again. He spit a glob of wet tobacco into his hand and liberally applied it to the wound, smoothing the skin into place as best he could.

"Stay," LG said to John, and then nodded at Cassius. "One more thing, hang on."

He left the bunkhouse and went over to the hay barn. On a dusty shelf in the tack room, he found a small can of *Thribble H Horse Liniment*. He took it and headed up to the kitchen. The cookie was there, working a lump of sourdough.

"Need some hot water," LG announced.

"On the stove."

A large cast iron wood stove dominated one corner of the room. The whole kitchen was uncomfortably warm, even with the windows wide open. Sitting on top was a blue ceramic kettle, steaming. LG found an empty drinking mug and poured some hot water in it.

"What happened to the kid?" the cook asked irritably. "You stole my helper, damn it."

LG set the liniment can on the tabletop and used a butterknife to pry it open.

"Well, you ain't got no help no more."

The cook paused over his lump of sourdough and glared unhappily at LG.

"John-boy took a hoof to the face," LG explained, and then paused reflectively. "Nicen up...people might like you more."

The cook ran a floury hand across his sweaty forehead, and then rested his palms on the countertop. He gave LG a forced, toothy smile.

"Can *you* gut that thing?"

"Cash got me milking cows."

The cook punched the dough, rattling the counter and a rolling pin fell on the floor. LG shook his head. Yet another cantankerous cook, he thought. Every other cook he ran into had a chip on his shoulder, it seemed — except Emmanuel. He had a good attitude. LG stirred the liniment into the hot water with the butterknife.

Cassius was standing in the doorway of the bunkhouse, looking impatient, when LG finally came back.

"Here, John-boy, sit up."

John sat up. LG handed him the mug.

"Drink it all."

Cassius left without saying another word and marched back to the mine. His constant concern over ore theft hovered over him like a cloud. LG watched him go and was glad he was gone. People got too pent up, in his opinion. Why live life pent up all the time?

"Tonight, you have to sleep with your head pointed north. If you don't, gonna wake up with the Ursa Majors and the gangrene-itis."

"Oh, me," John said.

"Just point your head north, you'll be fine."

John didn't know what the Ursa Majors were, but they sounded bad enough. And the gangrene-itis sounded horrible, as well. He wished he was back in New York.

Chapter 10
Texas Panhandle

"There...up ahead," Lee pointed out. "Must be the eatery."
"About time we happen upon it," Davis said, squinting to see through the heat waves piping off the plains. "I'm getting surly."
It was a one-story frame house, but it had a tall false front, which made it seem bigger than it was. The walls had been painted white at some point but had been successfully sandblasted by the prairie winds. Big black letters stenciled across the storefront read: *Singer's Store, Merchandise.*
A buckboard was parked in the shade. The mules stood sleepily in their harnesses, lulled by the Texas heat. There was one horse, a sorrel, at the hitching post out front. Clumps of white and blue sage dotted the area. Besides short grass and wildflowers, it was the only vegetation on these wide empty flats.
Inside, it was such a contrast from the bright sunlight that it took several minutes to get used to it. It was much cooler inside, too. They saw a long boarding table situated against one wall, and the rest of the room was cluttered with supplies and shelves. Three men were already there eating a meal. Lee and Davis walked over and sat down wearily. As they took their seats, the proprietor appeared from the back.
"Fifty cents," Sam Singer told them, wiping his hands on a towel. "Biscuits, pickles and beefsteak."
"Suits me well," Lee said.
"Keep the coffee coming," Davis added.
Sam Singer looked down at Davis sourly. Of *course* there would be coffee. Cowboys came through here every single meal, every single day. It went unspoken that he would serve up coffee. In fact, Sam Singer prided himself on good coffee. He ground it fresh every morning with a cast iron mill. And he rinsed the pot out good every night.
Glancing down the boarding table, Lee nodded in a friendly fashion towards the three strangers. Two of them appeared to be middle-aged, and the third seemed half that. One of the older men was dressed like a working cowman — from the wide-brimmed hat to the worn leather chaps to the rawhide gloves tucked in his belt. The other two wore dapper suits and, Lee imagined, were undoubtedly used to city lights more than starry nights.

"Sam, them was fine eats and a bellyful to think on," the cowman called to the store owner.

Sam Singer ignored the comment. He worked his way back to the table with two heaping plates for Lee and Davis. Sam rarely spoke while carrying hot plates. It was hard to do two things at once. At least to do two things at once, and do them both well. It had been over a year since he dropped the last plate while trying to carry on a conversation. And he hated dropping plates. It was embarrassing and wasteful.

"You boys riding for anyone?" the cowman asked.

"Looking for cow work," Lee replied and bit into a dill pickle. "Been up in Colorada punching for the B-Cross-C."

"Thought we might latch onto a wagon down this a'way," Davis told him. "Thought to check the XIT...or head on down to the King."

The cowman looked over at his city companions, but they were busy sopping up gravy with their biscuits.

"I'm AG Boyce," he said, and introduced his friends. "This here is Mr. AL Matlock and his colleague Mr. George Findlay."

"Afternoon to you," Mr. Matlock said in a sober Southern drawl, raising his gray eyes up from his plate. He looked them over thoughtfully, taking in their gear and demeanor.

"Hello there. And how are you?" Findlay added, in a surprisingly deep voice and an equally surprising thick Scottish accent.

Lee and Davis both looked straight at him, curiously. George Findlay was barely twenty years old and clearly out of his element. He kept glancing back and forth between Matlock and Boyce the whole time he sat at the table. Lee stared at him. He had a young boyish face, and not a hair on his chin — Mr. Findlay's deep voice simply did not match the look. Lee pondered the incongruity while he cut into his beefsteak. It was downright bizarre.

"I'm the new general manager of the XIT," Boyce continued. "Things there are...changing."

Matlock and Boyce exchanged a look of firm resolve.

Lee glanced up from his plate with immediate interest, but Davis was chewing mindlessly on a biscuit. He looked like a horse, with his jaw rolling around and his eyes half-closed. The two of them had been riding for too long in too much sun, and Davis was too sore and hungry to realize an opportunity was at hand. Of course, the pickle was fresh, the beefsteak well-seasoned and the coffee so tasty that even in the middle of this Texas heat Davis was enjoying it thoroughly. Emmanuel only knew how to scorch coffee. How many times had he told the man, *you don't boil the water.* You let it simmer, but never boil. And since they quit the B-Cross, neither Lee nor Davis had thought to purchase a coffee pot for their kit...which became a daily gripe.

Lee elbowed him.

"You are just the man we need to speak with, then." Lee said to Boyce. "Changing? How so?"

"Well now," Boyce went on. "Been a big change-up in management. And soon there will be a ranch-wide turnover of hands. We are in fact on our way out to the Yellow Houses headquarters right now to set this thing to spin."

AL Matlock studied them both closely. As a lawyer by trade, Matlock was in the business of distinguishing truth from lies. Experience gave him the sense to gauge a man's reliability in a relatively short time. He liked how the Good Book put it: *Ye shall know a tree by its fruits.* A fig tree produces figs.

"You boys interested in cow work?" he asked them.

"Yessir," Davis said, perking up. "Punching cattle, peeling broncs. Gather prairie chips if need be."

"May be part of it. We're gonna need ropers, bulldoggers, men to handle the irons and the knife."

"All that and more," Lee said, very genuinely. He could not believe their luck. Every single operation they rode through since quitting the B-Cross was no longer hiring. It was the middle of the season and most outfits had their quota.

"The B-Cross-C," Boyce said. "Beaver Creek. That's Til Blancett's outfit."

Lee and Davis both looked at him with surprise. The B-Cross was just a local brand in the backcountry of Colorado. There were a lot of small outfits tucked up in the Rockies. For a big Texas foreman to even be aware of the B-Cross was unusual, let alone know the fellow's name who ran it.

"Yes sir, it is. Mr. Blancett is a top notch boss."

"Why are you no longer there? Blancett turn you out?"

"No sir, we got along famously. Top hands on crew, too, but... there was an incident. Ran across some hard cases on the drive."

Lee's eyes fell to the table and he tapped his fork on the top of his biscuit. Some time had certainly passed since then. Lee tried to push it out of his mind after they cashed out with Til. Lee had not known the B-Cross boys long, but they all came to be pards pretty quick. It was hard to believe Ira and Edwin were bickering one day and shot dead the next. Lee wondered how Casey and Steve were healing up, and whether LG was alive at all.

Matlock was studying them both carefully.

Boyce leaned closer.

"Yes? Go on."

"Some bad men shot up the crew. Scattered the herd. Lost some of our boys to gunplay a'fore we even knew what the hell was goin' on."

"Still not sure the whereabouts of some of them," Davis mentioned. "It was an ugly time."

Davis ran a sleeve across his chin and pushed his plate away. The memory of Steve and Rufe galloping past came to mind. Steve's shirt was drenched in blood. Rufe kept shouting that his brother was shot. Davis could still see them, riding by like the devil was coming. Rufe was a mess of worry. They all made camp in the glen and waited for the rest of the B-Cross to ride in. But they never came. The raiders did, though, later that night. But just at the right time, Til appeared and flushed them out like quail.

"The whole crew about got wiped out."

Matlock softened and exchanged another inside look with Boyce. Boyce nodded his head, as if he were agreeing to some unspoken question. He turned toward Lee and Davis and raised his cup in a respectful gesture.

"You boys can tie on to the XIT," Boyce announced. "Come along with us. We're riding on as soon as we're done with our feed."

"Thank you sir," Lee said. "Much appreciated."

"Listen here," Matlock began. He paused and looked over the two cowmen again. Listening to them talk about the B-Cross, he could hear loyalty in their words. That was what he was looking for. Loyal men who rode for the brand. And men who could handle hardship, as well. With things as bad as they were at the XIT, hardship was not only expected. It was guaranteed.

"The XIT has in its employ some hard cases of its own. It's done up. That's why *I've* been brought on. Syndicate in Chicago hired me to fix it. And I aim to."

George Findlay sat quietly the whole time but was following the conversation closely. The Scotsman with the unsettling baritone voice nodded at the remark.

Boyce leaned back in his chair and began rolling a cigarette.

"The ranch is harboring all kinds of ilk. Gambling. Horse thieves. General lawlessness is rampant," Matlock went on. "I've surveyed the conditions myself. I was just telling Mr. Findlay here, on top of all this crud, last week I recognized Billy Ney. He's now *ranch boss* right under Barbecue Campbell. I saved Ney from a hanging down in Vernon a couple years back, you see. Thought I did right at the time but I recognized my error soon after. He's rotten. And him being at the XIT is evidence that something is wrong as wrong is."

"And Campbell is one hard-boiled egg," Boyce added. "He's the man who stocked the ranch with such deviant hands."

"I've reported all this to Chicago," Matlock confided. "They wanted *me* to take it over, but I'm a lawyer not a ranch manager. Mr. Findlay and I were sent to look into things, and I am appalled at what we found. Fact is, I'm lucky to have run onto Boyce...and lucky he was willing. Hell, I was just up in Colorado City last week. There's a man up there I had hopes would run this show. A civic leader. An experienced rancher. I told him he was the man of the hour. But know what he told me? He told me he's of greater value to his family alive than to be shot full of holes at the XIT."

He shook his head in disgust.

"If that tells you anything," he added.

Boyce puffed softly on his cigarette. Stories about the XIT were all over the Panhandle. He had been delivering cattle for the Snyder brothers up until the day before. On his way down from Colorado City, he ran into Matlock at a watering hole. Matlock laid it out as it was. Boyce knew he could do the job and signed on right there. He knew there was a chore ahead of him, and the thought of adding reliable men before they got there was a good one.

"XIT's got a mean reputation," Boyce said. "Call them *the Xmas hell variety.*"

Matlock set his coffee down and nodded.

"And we're stepping in. Turn that reputation on its head."

"Sakes alive, sounds like a first-class mess," Davis said.

"Well your man in Colorado City was right to be cautious. The B-Cross *was* shot full of holes," Lee said and spat on the floor. "Been through all that, and back again. If you need help count us in."

"Could use you," Boyce said, sincerely. "Need some good men. I'm angling to fire just about ever' man I see."

"There's still some honest ones left...men I can set store by," Matlock told Boyce. "Frank Yearwood, Earl Wright, Mack Huffman."

"You point 'em out to me when we get there."

Matlock's coffee was too cool now to be worth drinking and he poured it out the open window behind him. From the kitchen, Sam Singer saw him dump his cup and rushed out with the coffee pot. He had his own reputation to maintain: good coffee and timely warm-ups.

Chapter 11

Riding at an easy pace, Lee and Davis trailed along behind the buckboard. Mr. Matlock and George Findlay drove that, while AG Boyce road ahead on his sorrel. The sun was slipping below the horizon. The sunlight refracted off the clouds above, casting a rich evening hue all across the wide grassy plains.

They were on a defined path. The grass was worn away from use. Everywhere else, all they could see for miles was open prairie. In some places the grass rose up over the wagon wheels. They could see a long stretch of barbed wire fence up ahead.

"Lee, want to catch that gate?" Boyce asked.

Trotting his quarter horse around the buckboard, Lee went on ahead. There was not an actual gate, so much as a section of wire tied to a wooden post. He leaned low to unhook a wire hoop, which held the post in place. He pulled it back and they all rode into the Yellow Houses Division. Lee looked up and down the fence line. It seemed to stretch on forever.

With the fading sunlight, the evening was finally beginning to cool off. The breeze was hardly noticeable but they all welcomed it.

"We're in one of the Yellow Houses pastures now," Boyce told them. "We'll bed down under the stars tonight. Roll into headquarters tomorrow, come what may."

Beyond the creak of the buckboard was a vast silence — the quietude of miles and miles of grassland. Lee enjoyed this about Texas. It felt peaceful. Working up in Colorado's high country for so long, he had forgotten how big the sky was. In the mountains, he had begun to feel walled in and the change of scenery was welcome.

"I can really breathe out here," he said to Davis. "I think I spent one too many winters up there."

The sun dropped out of sight and the air took on a dim quality. Mosquitoes came out and hummed around them.

"We'll camp up there," Boyce announced.

In the growing gloom they could make out a windmill. It was nearly dark when they pulled up to it. A large wooden water trough circled out at its base, three feet high and sixteen feet across. Matlock noticed it was full of water and broke into a wide grin.

"Ain't like this everywhere," he commented. "The XIT is bone dry this year. Take it when you can get it."

George Findlay untacked his mules and led them to the tank. The mules drank, and then he hobbled them and let them graze. Both Davis and Lee staked their horses and shook out their bedrolls.

"Good thing we had a big dinner," Davis said. "Supper's in a can."

He opened up his saddle bag and rifled through it. Lee put his own saddle in the grass, laid down on his Navajo blanket, and pulled his bedding up to his chin. The grass smelled good. Some crickets were out and the frogs were croaking, too. Lee smiled to himself. This was what it was all about. The gentle lap of water against the tank's sideboards was rhythmic enough to lull him to sleep. He nodded off without waiting for Davis to open up the can.

"We're eighteen miles out from headquarters," Boyce said to Davis quietly. He took off his boots and made his bed in the back of the wagon. "At an easy pace, we'll be there by dinner tomorrow."

Boyce laid down and sighed.

"I met Til Blancett down in Dallas couple months back, at the stock show. Otherwise, I might not know the brand."

"Peculiar luck," Davis replied. But Boyce didn't say anything more.

Davis chewed on cold pinto beans and licked his spoon until it was clean. He walked over to the trough and filled his canteen with fresh cold water. He glanced back at the horses. His bay was just a silhouette — head arched toward the ground, grazing. The sound of the horses and mules cropping grass seemed loud in the stillness.

Matlock and Findlay were stretched out in their own bedrolls, sound asleep. Lee was out, too, and Davis could only make out Boyce's bare feet in the gloom — sticking out of the wagon.

Palming some cool water, Davis washed his face a little. He wondered how Til and the boys were doing. Things had changed after the shootings. The cattle drive was done for. Til was thinking about buying some land up in South Park. Settle down, he said. Said he missed his wife. The McGonkin brothers wanted to stay on, and so had Emmanuel. They left Casey to heal up at that girl's home in Gold Hill. He had been shot up pretty bad. Gyp moved on. No one knew what had happened to LG. That was the end of the B-Cross — as a trail driving outfit, anyhow. So that day both Davis and Lee decided it was time to move on.

Above him the sky was dark and the stars were really out, now. Davis appreciated the night sky. It was calming, reassuring. If God Above could make all those little stars way up there, give them each a place and a path to travel...well, the same could be said for him, he guessed. Even when things got so balled up he didn't know much *what* to think.

Chapter 12
Colorado
Leadville
Tabor Opera House

Only one gas lamp was burning at the moment. There were other light fixtures lining the upper room but they were all out, deliberately. Moonlight shined in through the 3rd-story windows and whitewashed the men inside. Horace "Haw" Tabor twisted the end of his walrus mustache and paced the floor. The other men in the room made him feel very uncomfortable, so he paced.

"Prescott Sloan just opened up The Pastime," Big Ed Burns informed him in a low voice. Big Ed's eyes looked like little marbles — little black marbles. Horace paused and glanced over at Big Ed. Those little black marbles stared back dully. It was unsettling, so Horace resumed pacing.

"It's over on State Street," Big Ed said sharply, watching to see how Horace reacted. Big Ed scowled. He watched Horace Tabor, the so-called Silver King of Leadville, pace back and forth across the dim room. Big Ed smirked. He knew Tabor had no stomach for this.

"Ain't that hard to figure," Big Ed told him. "Soapy Smith gives Prescott Sloan his whole stake in the Matchless Mine. In turn, Sloan claims he put a hunnert thousand in a PO Box in Denver. Well, hold the damn press...the PO Box is plumb empty. And now Sloan opens up a top-sawyer saloon right *here* of all places. Could only be stupider if he opened it in Denver."

Horace pressed his hand to his belly. The doctor told him it was an ulcer and urged him to lessen his work load. Relax. Maybe take a vacation in lower climes. But Horace had not taken the advice or the vacation. He shook his head at the bitter irony of life's twisty paths. He knew where this was headed.

"Can you count two and two, Haw?"

"I can count two and two," Horace replied. "Hell, I can count to a million with the Matchless alone. And I don't have any control over Prescott Sloan opening up a saloon in Leadville. Or closing his bank in Ward. Or hoodwinking Soapy Smith in Denver. Such machinations are not mine in origin, nor mine to wrastle against."

Big Ed turned around and glared at the other men standing behind him. There were three of them. They all stood silent as rocks, impassive — they were Big Ed's muscle. Not that Big Ed needed any muscle. His name was really a good description of his stature. He was a big man. But he always liked to bring the boys along anyhow.

Horace saw that Big Ed's men had their eyes fixed on him, and none of them seemed to blink. It was disturbing whenever he braved a glance in their direction. The mood in the room was unpleasant to Horace, and he did not like it. He hoped to dispel it soon and get home to Elizabeth. Have some buttermilk. Buttermilk might soothe his stomach ache.

"Aw, Big Ed, come on. Alright, what can I help with? I'm a busy man...a *respectable* man. I must keep it that way in the perception of this fine community."

Big Ed took a step closer to Horace, and Horace could smell the liquor. It was cheap whiskey. Up close, Big Ed's black marble eyes looked even smaller, like dark shadowy specks in his flat white moonlit face. Horace's ulcer was churning but he managed to stand up straight and maintain his composure. Surely the doctor had something more potent than chalky magnesium tablets for a man of his social and financial caliber.

"You keep being respectable," Big Ed told him. "Soapy's a-comin'."

"Here?" Horace asked, rhetorically. His mind began to reel.

"He'll be up. And so's his dander."

Chapter 13

Prescott Sloan was nicely dressed. But then he always was.

"Bucking the Tiger?" Doc Holliday asked him.

"Indeed. Follow me, sir."

Sloan led the man across the busy saloon floor and tapped on a solid pine door in the back wall. Holliday was certainly slight and frail looking — Sloan had heard the stories, but honestly he was a little surprised at how frail. The man' eyes were bloodshot from either lack of sleep or liquor or illness, Sloan could only guess.

They waited in polite silence for the door to open.

The Pastime Saloon was full of people. Since it first opened its doors, the saloon had never really closed. Sloan looked around the room, soaking it all in. Basking in it. Voices carried, bottles and glass mugs clinked. The bar was full and red-light girls were scattered around the room, painted up seductively. What a decision — to cut ties and leave Ward behind! Ward was a sleepy villa compared to the boomtown of Leadville. It was the new start Sloan needed. Especially since that PO Box key went missing.

Sloan turned back to the door and was about to knock again, when young Billy Barrister finally opened it from the inside. At that very moment, Holliday launched into a violent coughing fit. Sloan felt the hot moist air puff against his neck. Sloan cringed. Was the man's ailment something that could spread? A disease he could catch? Sloan slowly turned to face Holliday. But whatever he was expecting, perhaps an apology, did not occur. Holliday merely blotted his mouth with a white kerchief and looked at Sloan blankly.

"Welcome to enter," Billy Barrister announced in as formal voice he could muster. "Faro or poker, it's your game."

Billy tried to be as formal as he could when he opened the game room up. The young man's only job was to open and close that door. He heard Sloan knocking but happened to be standing by the faro table. The thing was...he was not *supposed* to stand by the tables. Mr. Sloan got angry whenever he discovered Billy standing by the tables, watching the game, because his job was to open and close that door. No one was able to open it from the outside, only from inside. Billy Barrister was trembling when he pulled open the door, but as soon as he saw Doc Holliday he brightened. Billy had lived in Leadville for several years and had worked at many saloons around town. He had the privilege of seeing Doc Holliday sit at card tables before.

Even though he never saw any scuffles or gunfights himself, Billy secretly hoped to. Everyone knew Doc Holliday shot Bill Allen in the wrist a couple years back, right inside Hyman's Saloon on 13th — over a $5 poker debt. Not long after that, Doc shot Constable Kelly in a duel on the street. The man died, Doc was charged, but was acquitted by trial not too long after the fact. Billy Barrister felt like he was watching history unfold whenever Doc Holliday walked into a saloon. And now here he was again. How fantastic!

So when Billy Barrister opened the door and saw Doc Holliday coughing all over Prescott Sloan's neck, Billy held his breath. This could be it! He watched Mr. Sloan bristle. What if he drew a gun? Or called him outside? But to Billy's dismay the tension slowly dissolved...and Mr. Sloan did not even utter a cross word. This was a surprise to Billy, since Mr. Sloan struck like a rattlesnake when someone said or did the wrong thing — like watching the game table when he should be opening the door.

"There is a seat at the faro table, sir," Billy mentioned, and held the door open wide.

Contagions were something that deeply concerned Prescott Sloan. He was a man of inordinate cleanliness. He washed regularly and wore only freshly laundered clothes. If the man coughing up spittle on his neck had not been Doc Holliday, Sloan would have boiled right over. But confrontation was not the wise course to take with Holliday — a person of mannered eloquence, southern mystique, and missing scruples. Even if the man *was* on death's doorstep.

Cordially, Sloan led the way in. Three ornately carved tables were spaced around the room and were filled with well-dressed men playing high-stakes poker. At the far wall was a green oval faro table, where a banker passed out chips — and cards with a Bengal tiger imprinted on them.

"Poker here, faro over there," Sloan explained. "Drinks are complimentary, of course."

"Rye. Just bring the damn bottle."

All the men stopped chatting and turned to take note. It was no mystery who had just walked in. Holliday had been in Leadville off and on for the past eight years.

"Thought you went to Glenwood last month," a man from a poker table said, in brisk German tones. His name was George Fryer.

Doc adjusted his lapels and sat down across from him.

"It *is* widely held," he agreed. "For the sake of perspicuity: I did, I was, and I shall likely return there again. Deal me in."

The other men around the table tensed up. They all recognized him. After all, Leadville had been a kind of second home for Holliday.

"Rumor puts you in Arizona as of late," Fryer said, unhappily. George Fryer had kept his eye on Holliday the moment he walked in the room.

"Rumors attribute me to many odd places, Mr. Fryer," Doc replied. "For the best, I suppose."

Sloan watched over the conversation curiously. He was sure he spotted Holliday himself, in Ward just a few months back. But he wasn't sure. Holliday was a dying breed, both literally and figuratively.

"My cousin said he sold you a ticket to Glenwood Springs in May," JJ Brown added. "Swore you boarded the train and ever'thing."

"Well," Doc noted slowly in his Georgian drawl, "Miracle cures are surely fancy. Yet if there is some truth to the sulfurous springs and their reputed regenerative properties...why should I not lend fate its opportunity?"

"Surprised you ain't been shot dead yet," George Fryer muttered.

"Fact of the matter is I anticipate gunfire outwitting consumption in regards to my own demise."

The German stared down at the cards in his hand. His complexion was getting dark. Suddenly he slapped his cards down on the table.

"Constable Kelly was a friend of mine!"

JJ Brown, who happened to be sitting right next to George Fryer, held his breath.

"Don't try it on, George," Doc patronized. "Been over now for quite some time. Besides, if you'll recollect, I did him the courtesy of asking prior if he was armed."

Billy Barrister and Prescott Sloan were standing near the table, and both felt it was a poor choice of location although neither moved.

"Prior to shooting him dead," Doc added cheerfully.

George Fryer went silent but sat very still. JJ Brown looked up and froze. The room became very quiet. Sloan felt a cold flutter in his gut. This is how it happens, he thought. Someone is going to die. Right here in front of me. Hell, I just opened this place a week ago.

Doc's face relaxed, and he chuckled softly. He carefully laid his cards down so he could cough into his kerchief again. George Fryer watched him closely. His complexion was still dark, but given Holliday's patterns of dispute, decided to pick up his cards again.

Billy Barrister quietly eased back over to the door and took up his position. Sloan watched him go and shook his head. The kid could hardly help watching these tables. Once the evening wound down, he would be sure to cuss that kid for not opening the door when he knocked. Maybe a slap or two. He walked over to the door to let Billy know what was coming.

But the sound of Doc Holliday coughing on his cards made him cringe again. The man was a lunger, rife with disease. Even syphilis, it was said. And here he was...coughing all over Sloan's poker table.

"Billy, after Mr. Holliday leaves get a wet rag and wipe down his seat," Sloan whispered on his way out. "And the table. And the cards."

Chapter 14

The treetops were hidden in the cool mist. Casey hung his hat on a damp limb and surveyed his work. He was pleased with how the cabin was coming together. The walls were made of rough-hewn logs, and he was taking the time to plane them down so they fit together perfectly.

"Stand, Mule."

The mule stood. He liked the mule. He named her Mule when he bought her, and Julianna chided him almost every day for his lack of creativity. But Mule stood patiently in her harness. She knew her name. Or more likely, she recognized the command to stand.

A thick hemp rope stretched up from Mule's harness to a big pulley. Casey had built a tall tripod out of lodgepole pine. He could move it where ever he needed. This made lifting the wall logs into place a whole lot easier. Casey was doing the work by himself — although he did have a few friends on the hill who helped out, now and then. But they were all miners with their own claims to work. He didn't want to impose if he could raise the home by himself.

The mist made visibility pretty difficult. Wherever he turned, he could only see a few hundred feet before the trees were swallowed up in the gray. He could easily hear the creek and voices carried. The rattle of river stones and silt being sifted in the placers was just background noise he no longer noticed. But on misty afternoons like this, all the sounds seemed louder than usual.

Hopper was lying in a pile of pine needles. Julianna also chided Casey about naming Hopper, Hopper. *The dog has a bad leg,* he told her. *He hops. Get it? Yes, I get it, Casey,* she would reply dryly. *Just doesn't seem like a lot of thought went into it. Well it did,* Casey would say. This conversation usually happened a couple times a week — ever since they said their "I do's" earlier in the summer.

Julianna's father, the Commodore, had kept Hopper down in Gold Hill while Casey and Julianna began their married life up in Leadville. It turned out the old man grew fairly fond of the dog. When they went back for a visit, he wept openly when it came time to go. He did not weep over Julianna or his new son-in-law. But he wept when they took the dog.

All around the city, the hills had long since been picked over for timber. For miles, it was nothing but tree stumps and mining claims. There were mounds of yellow tailings everywhere, and the creeks looked rusty from being worked so much. When he and Julianna first made the decision to move to Leadville, Casey decided he wanted to buy land well outside of town — where there were still trees. Plus, the air and water were clean out here. He wanted to be far from the big smelters and the big plumes of smoke they churned out.

It was his lunch break. He ate bread, an apple, yellow cheese, and some tasty salted pork. Julianna made sure he had good feed everyday, which was nice...especially after years on the trail. Some cooks did well, others did poorly. Like Emmanuel and his 3-day beans and boil-burnt coffee.

After a few minutes of resting in the cool mist, the chill crept in. Casey could not sit around too long on a day like this. He tended to overheat when he worked hard and preferred to be too cold than too hot, but at this elevation on a cool misty day, overheating was not a concern.

He got up from the stump he was sitting on and took the apple core to Mule. As soon as it was under her nose, she grabbed it.

"Watch my thumb," Casey warned her. Her main fault was that she had a tendency to mistake thumbs for carrots.

It did not take long to tie the haul rope around another big log. After he set this one in place, there were only a couple more left in the woodpile. Casey would need to bring down several more trees. That was certainly a process. He would have to fell one first, use a hatchet to chop off all the branches, then go back and saw off the stubs so the trunk was as even as possible. He would plane the bark off and finally Mule could drag it to the woodpile.

"Step up."

The slack came out, and Mule felt the weight catch the harness. With a powerful slow step, the animal surged forward and the log went up in the air.

"Ho, Mule."

Casey wiggled on his work gloves. He pushed hard to swing the big trunk around. It always took some jimmying to get it into place, but Casey knew exactly what to do.

It felt good to be working for himself now. For years, Casey had been riding for other people's brands. He never minded hard work, or working for other men. It was all part of life. He grinned as he thought about it. All those outfits he worked for, all those cows he branded. Sure was a heap of cowhide.

It was a wonder — life and living. He always imagined he would be cowboying for as long as he could sit a horse. Granted, it was not a very lucrative job. And a day's work could get fairly repetitive, mundane even, which was often the case. How many times had he been desperate enough for something to read, that he poured over old newspapers glued to the walls of a line shack? Or the label on a soup can — and read it again, many times over. But he never questioned it and never would. The life of a cowpuncher had been the right thing. He loved every minute of it. Even when he was bored out of his skull. He hoped he would have similar feelings about homesteading. He wasn't sure what he would do yet for income. Maybe open up a farrier shop. Shoe some horses. Julianna already had a job in town, which was a help while he built their home.

"Back," he told Mule. "Back."

She dutifully stepped backwards, and the log eased down into place. The tripod creaked under the weight.

Casey thought about all the places he had been: Beaver Creek; the stockyards of Denver and Cheyenne; the Iliff Ranch; Julesburg; Pueblo and Fort Bent; Hugo. He spent the better part of ten years cowboying on the plains of Colorado. One time, when he was maybe twenty years old, Casey rode a horse all the way out to Dodge City, Kansas. He heard so many stories about that town he just *had* to see it. But the railroads had left Dodge City so far behind it was just a husk of what it used to be. Most people seemed to sit around the saloons and yarn, and point to portraits on the wall. But times had changed for that old town. And times had changed for Casey.

He walked down to the creek to refill his canteen.

This far out from Leadville the creek was still clear and clean. The water around town was spoiled for drinking by the mining claims. Not this one. He knew there were a couple placer claims down the creek a half mile or so, but there was nothing upstream yet — which was half the reason he bought this particular parcel.

Casey took a quick sip. Boy, it was cold! It made his head hurt. All around him, the mist was still thick and gray. A stone's throw away, the creek seemed to just trickle right into nothingness...and disappear.

Sometimes Casey felt that life was like a creek. Or a river. A river he expected to cross and keep going. But it seemed the river had carried him away instead. He had not expected to be carried away by a river; he expected to make it across. And on to the other side. But one day he got shot off a horse. He could still see Ira's hat whipping off and the man's head-matter cough up in the air. Ira's eyes had been open, he remembered that. Open, trusting — like a kid. And Edwin *was* just a kid. Casey didn't remember even hearing gunfire. He just saw Ira's head flop back, and Edwin got knocked out of the saddle, his arms whipping like a rag doll. The poor kid rolled off his horse's croup and dropped into the herd. Casey remembered that, he remembered seeing the boy jostle and bump between the black cows, and then the black cows closed in around him like waves of the sea.

Casey looked over at Hopper. The dog was quietly studying the trees in case there might be a squirrel. His ears were pricked up. Casey smiled. It was good to have that dog back. And it was good not to be riding for a brand anymore — for the dog's sake too. He was definitely slowing down. *I guess if you only have three good legs, you're bound to slow down sooner than later,* Casey thought. And he was not a pup anymore, anyway.

Chapter 15

Julianna was in town watching the mist roll in over the rooftops. She could not see Mount Massive, which on a regular day dominated the western landscape. The people outside on the street walked past the window with hats pulled low, collars up, and scarves around their necks. The horses' and burros' breath was coming out in white puffs. Despite the weather, Leadville was still as busy as it always was — night or day, whether there was sunshine or blowing snow.

Being the new bookkeeper for the Tabor Opera House had been a wonderful find. The owners, Horace and Elizabeth Tabor, seemed like gracious people and welcomed her on board with surprising warmth — especially for being so effluent and cultured in a fast-paced town. They both had nicknames. Horace was *Haw* and Elizabeth was *Baby Doe*. Of course, Julianna started out calling them Mr. and Mrs., but some days Elizabeth would *insist* on being called Baby Doe.

The theatre scene in Leadville was lively. Julianna met a good deal of famous thespians in just a short time on the payroll. The frequent performances seemed to draw in big crowds.

Julianna found it curious that there were no actual operas scheduled at the Opera House. Filling the books were vaudeville acts, minstrels and dances, community and political meetings, theatrical performances by travelling troupes and local actors... but not a single opera.

In a couple hours, Casey would be bringing the buckboard into town. He made it clear he did not want her riding into Leadville by herself, for any reason. It made Julianna smile knowing Casey worried about her like that. She suspected it was partly because they were newly wed, and he was being protective. Perhaps, though, it could simply be realism. Leadville was not exactly a saintly place. And she noticed the city was made up mostly of men — miners working rough claims in a rough town, looking to get rich. And those that did not get rich got drunk, even drunker than those who *did* get rich. In a city revolving around silver, drunkenness and violence seemed to be close companions.

"We simply must have you and your husband over for dinner...this week's end," Elizabeth Tabor announced boldly as she swept into the office. Julianna was startled and stood up quickly, still getting used to Mrs. Tabor's surprising and often dramatic entrances.

Elizabeth Tabor was barely into her early 40s but had at least fifteen years on Julianna. The age and class difference gave Julianna the awkward sense that she was out of her element. And to complicate matters, Elizabeth "Baby Doe" Tabor had a duality about her — in some moments she was proper, well-spoken and demonstrably grand. Then in a heartbeat she would slip into personable colloquialisms and joviality as if she were talking to a sister. Julianna was never quite sure which version she would be talking to each day. The lofty aristocrat or the uncouth girl.

"Mrs. Tabor," Julianna said courteously, "My husband and I would like that very much. Many thanks."

"Just call me Baby Doe, remember? I don't care to be called his *Mrs.*" she insisted, quite down to earth. "I ain't ancient nor am I matronly. Nor am I Haw's previous marital attachment — *Mrs.* reminds me of that intolerable hag. And I hope you don't think me unapproachable. I like you Julianna. You're not like these Leadvillites, all prim and proper and capable of speaking about nothing but tea and the Sherman Silver Purchase Act. Now what was *your lesser half's* name again?"

"Casey."

"Why don't you and Casey come up to the house, then! It will be fun," Baby Doe said with a quick wink. "I need fun. We'll open up some wine. Haw just had a case of French wine imported, straight from the vineyards of Libournais in France. Merlot — yuck. But I've still got a few bottles of the Argentinian stuff in the pantry. Malbec! It's worth sharing. Say you'll come. Say it."

Julianna was struck by how familiar Mrs. Tabor was acting with her. It was actually quite nice. Imagine, Julianna wondered — to have a friendly and genuine conversation with someone of her own gender. Indeed, the city was overrun with males. The allure of bonanzas and lode veins brought an unending stream of fortune seekers.

And what of the women that did populate the town? They were just a small fraction of its inhabitants. The list of potential friends grew smaller the more she thought about it. Ruling out the "soiled doves" roving State Street, and the preening ladies on the prowl for rich husbands, the list dwindled quite quickly.

Although, Julianna *had* seen a few women around that might fit the profile. Over the past few weeks, she had been making a mental checklist. There were female teachers working at Central School up on Spruce Street. Possibilities there. A female doctor had a clinic up the road on Harrison. Then there was a printer across the street and a woman clerking at the Delaware. Julianna even noticed a couple lady-prospectors heading in and out of the assayer's. *They* must have spunk, she thought. But stranger than all, Baby Doe Tabor was befriending her. And the more she found out about Baby Doe, the stranger it became.

"I'll come! And so will Casey!"

"Splendid, splendid," Baby Doe exclaimed. She strolled to the window and looked out. "Haw is in a *tiff.* He'll need to blow off steam. His ex is coming to town next week, a tightly wound blemish of a wench."

Slipping back down into her chair, Julianna wasn't sure how to react to that one. Hag? Wench? She was starting to notice that conversations with the Silver King's wife might take unexpected turns at any moment. Baby Doe's eyes were scouring the streets, especially the collection of stagecoaches spewing their weary passengers into the misty street.

"Did *I* say that?" Baby Doe asked, clearly a rhetorical question, and spun around on a tall heel. "Perhaps wench is too kind. She already leeched my poor husband in the divorce. What more does that paunchy sow think she can get?"

Chapter 16

Arkansas River Valley
West of Cañon City

"Well, damnity damn — can't *believe* all this cash!"

That had become Granger's mantra for the last twenty miles. He was too excited to even sit still on his horse for any length of time. The animal was getting tired of his antsy movements and had taken to crow-hopping every mile or so. He immediately obliged with another series of crow-hops but was unable to unseat the filthy bandito.

"Shut up with the damnities, will you?" Vincent scolded him.

Vincent's chest pains were so bad now he could barely turn to cast the man a dour look. In fact, he could barely turn his head one inch to either side, and that was the full range of motion.

"It's painful enough just sitting my saddle," Vincent continued, his jaw clenched. "Listening to you say the same thing over and over for the past twenty miles? I won't tolerate it no more."

Earlier that afternoon they passed through Cañon City. Granger was so jittery about the one hundred thousand dollars cash that Bill thought it unwise to stop, even for a meal. He simply did not trust Granger to maintain his composure in public. Not only did they have to get through the town itself without some Granger-sized gaffe...in order to start up the pass they had to ride right under the walls of the Colorado State Penitentiary!

Somehow Granger kept it together, but Bill never let him have an ounce of talk time with any passerby as they progressed through. All afternoon since, Bill had been watching their backtrail for law. The tension was finally easing off, and with it the heat of the day.

They were heading west, following the Arkansas upriver. After leaving town they passed the deep canyon for which Cañon City got its name. The Royal Gorge, Bill thought bitterly, and its train wars. He had actually been rustling cattle in Beulah in those days. The Denver & Rio Grande was fighting the Santa Fe. He hired on with the D&RG as a gunfighter just to have an excuse to shoot at people. Boy, that was ten years ago, Bill thought.

Even in the foothills, this was still the high desert of southern Colorado. The short grass in the vicinity was mainly brown, even though it was a wet summer everywhere else. They were passing a lot of cholla and prickly pear, piñon and cedar. It was all spread out and they had a fairly unobstructed view in both directions. Bill was glad, so could keep a watchful eye on the trail and terrain around them. Traveling with saddle bags brimming with paper cash made him watchful.

Bill's eyes were never restful when he had so much money on him. In fact, he really didn't like to be so flush when horseback. At first he was tempted to find a mining shaft and bury it — like he did up near Grand Lake. But that had been gold, a substance that was not prone to decay. Cash on the other hand *was* prone to decay. It might become rotten if wet. Or burn. Or get eaten by varmints.

Sitting upright, stiff as a board, Vincent was the picture of discomfort. Bill knew the man would not be able to travel far or quickly. He was sure the man had more than just busted ribs. It had been weeks now, well over a month, since his horse went down and took him with it. If it was just ribs, he would be riding fine by now. Also, Bill had seen Vincent's chest. It did not look right. In fact his whole torso was black and blue — and a little bulby around the gut region.

At least they were alone. Many people took the train into South Park, so it could have been worse. They passed some freighters a few miles back, moving slower than they were. Up ahead Bill could make out a dozen riders moving west, in the same direction they were. There were a lot of birds in the trees, singing. Finches, he guessed. A crow kept cawing somewhere.

Ten *years* since those train wars, Bill thought again. That was a long time. Ten years of marauding. Well, professional marauding anyhow. He squinted up at the sun. It was arcing down in front of them. It had been blistering hot down in Pueblo yesterday and just as bad through Cañon today. The further they got into the foothills, and the higher the trail rose, Bill knew the general temperature would eventually get cooler.

Wouldn't it be pleasant to just drift off into obscurity? Get a little hacienda somewhere it was cool. On a river maybe...with some horses. Retire from the trail life. He had the money now.

Weeks on the move with just Vincent and Granger had worn thin. Vince he had befriended many years ago. He hated to say it, but the man was on his way out, with that bulby black and blue gut and whatever else was broken inside. And then there was Granger — both a fool and a liability. It was good to have someone like that to throw in with, of course. If something undesirable needed to be accomplished, the fool could do the errand. If a gunfight ensued, the fool could be sent in as a decoy or target, to draw out a shooter's whereabouts. Yet his inability to maintain posture when traveling with substantial amounts of money set the man squarely as a liability again.

"Bill. Might need me a doctor after all," Vincent said severely. "Prob'ly should have done it in Denver, got it over with."

"Aw, you heard Bill...we had to piss in an' piss out of Denver," Granger interjected. "No time to piddle around."

"I swear — I'll pull that blotchy little tongue right out."

"O, I'm all puckered."

Looking over at his old friend, Bill nodded thoughtfully. Healing would not come naturally now. True to what Granger said, Bill would never have stopped for doctoring in Denver. After all, they had *just* emptied out that PO Box. They had to get out of there. Then there was Colorado Springs and Pueblo — but with a potential pursuant in Soapy Smith and a hundred grand weighing on the mind, a sore test of Granger's ability to portray nonchalance, Bill was keen to pass on through the big cities as quick as could be.

"Maybe up in Chaffee County somewhere," he suggested. "Them hot springs in Poncha might do you some good."

Chapter 17

"Swap them saddles."

Bill's voice was tense. He stood by Vincent's bay, straining to hold the man's weight as he slowly rolled off. The white stripe on the horse's nose glowed softly in the starlight. Vincent was just a shadow — and just as talkative as one. He had been hunched over the saddle horn ever since the sun went down.

"Crimany! He's all stoved up," Granger whispered. He had just stolen three horses.

"I said swap them saddles."

They were tucked up near the trail in a stand of cedar.

They had quietly passed several other camps in the darkness, and Bill wanted to keep on passing quietly. He hoped to make Poncha Springs by sunrise. But Vincent was fading. And their troubles were piling up. Not only was Vincent on the decline, his bay had come up lame. The footing was rough. Bill's own appaloosa had lost a shoe a mile out of Cañon City, but he had no intention of turning back at the time. Granger's horse was the only sound one among them.

Bill knew their horses were spent, as well, thanks to this desert heat. Add to that the fact they'd been riding for days on end. He kept an eye out for replacements and saw a convenient thing: a group of cowboys snoozing around a large campfire less than a mile back. Granger may be idiotic in his banter and mannerisms, but his craft at horse stealing was valuable at times. This was one of those times. He retrieved three of the cowboys' horses without causing a stir. But Bill didn't want to boost the man's self-worth with too much praise. So he didn't.

It only took five minutes to swap the saddles. But it took nearly twice as long to hoist Vincent up on one — since he was unconscious. Bill *had* pushed him into the saddle on the first try...but Vincent slowly tipped right on over the far side. Bill scurried around to catch him, but it was too late.

"Would you get over here and help out!" Bill spat. He was on edge.

Granger heard Vincent hit the ground and glanced over curiously. He frowned at Bill's reproachful tone but came over dutifully. Together, they lifted Vincent back up and shoved him into place. Bill knelt down and picked up Vincent's squashed hat.

The crown was flattened evenly with the brim. Bill punched inside the crown and tried to reshape it, but it was mangled.

"Shoot. Vince won't like that," Bill said. As long as he had known him, Vincent always erred on the side of vanity in his dress. *To the nines*, he would always say whenever Bill made note of it. He wasn't a dandy, but Bill liked to josh him as if he were. Now Vincent's nice hat was crushed. But Bill supposed a crushed hat wasn't on the man's mind at the moment.

"Tie him on," he instructed and stalked off.

The sky overhead was dark and the stars were sharp. Bill lit a cigar and took a swig from his canteen. The water was still warm even though the evening had cooled down dramatically. What was he going to do? His plan had been to ride into South Park. Maybe up to Leadville. Or Aspen. That gold from Kinsey City was still buried up on the Divide. He could go back for it, although it was a fair piece in the wrong direction. Between the gold and the hundred thousand he now had, why not settle down? Go respectable. The memories about the railroad war had started him thinking. Vincent he could leave at Poncha Springs to heal up. Granger he could leave in a gulch somewhere, with a hole in his head. Then Bill could retire. Go about the business of happifying.

Bill puffed on the cigar while he unhaltered their spent horses. Even without halters, the horses just stood there. Bill clicked his tongue and slapped the appaloosa. The tired animals took a few steps. Bill waved his arms at them, but they didn't go anywhere.

"Wish we had some bacon," Granger lamented. He was going through their saddle bags looking for extra rope. But of course they had emptied out almost everything to make room for wads of cash.

"The tie strings — just use those," Bill said pointedly.

"Oh, yeah," Granger muttered and drew his knife.

He patted around in the dark until he found one of the tie strings on Vincent's saddle. Granger cut it off and threaded it through the gullet, then tied it around Vincent's wrists. The man was still out and made no noise, not even a groan. Granger tested his inertness by twisting Vincent's fingers several times while Bill wasn't looking. It was too dark to really see anyway, but he was worried Bill might notice. Granger heard the knuckles pop a bit, but Vincent did not react.

Since Bill was still trying to shoo their tired horses, Granger decided to wiggle off Vincent's turquoise ring. He had always fancied it. It took some jimmying and another knuckle pop, but he got it off and put it in his pocket for later.

Chapter 18

Hay Ranch
South Park

Laura Blancett put on a thick black shawl. Her ears and nose were cold. She wore thick wool socks and did not make a sound as she shuffled down the hallway. Til was out with the horses, as were the McGonkin brothers. Walker was still sound asleep.

Til had built a small bedroom just for his son, and when Walker discovered he would have his own room he couldn't believe it. Til kept ruffling his hair whenever he stood by his son. It pleased Laura to see her husband and son under the same roof again. Back in Muscatine, Iowa, surrounded by cornfields and low wooded hills, they had lived in a nice home. But it did not have separate rooms, just one big one. They did string curtains up for walls, but it only afforded a minor sense of privacy.

Laura decided the boy could use some extra rest after their long trip. Besides, there was no rush. Soon she would assign him chores to do every morning. Routines were important to Laura, especially as a mother. Children were apt to distraction and lazing about. She intended to instill a strong constitution in Walker. She wanted him to be responsible, considerate, and a strong leader like his father. But that could wait for another day or so. Today he would get to sleep in. In his own room.

On the trip out, Walker had been delighted by the trains. He loved the way the whole car rocked back and forth with the rails. More than once she woke up from a nap to see him inching up and down the aisleway...arms stretched out, like he was on a tightrope in a circus. When the train would throw him around, he would laugh like nothing was funnier. She tried not to scold him too much — boys needed to be boys. But several times he got tossed off balance and ran right into another passenger. It was not deliberate, she knew, but he always seemed to run right into the same white-haired old man who was constantly napping.

The man's eyelids fluttered, and he would sit up sharply and glare. By then, Walker was right back on his tightrope, giggling. Now that she thought about it, it probably *had* been deliberate. There was a healthy measure of mischief in that little boy. She was interested to see how far he pressed that mischief now that he had a father in his life again.

"Ma'am."

Emmanuel was sitting at the table sipping coffee in the shadows. He got to his feet when she came in the room. The sun was not above the horizon yet, although the sky was blue as a robin's egg. Laura smiled at him and motioned for him to stay seated — but he got up any way.

"Get some hot tea fo' ya?" he asked.

"Oh, coffee is perfect and I can fetch it myself, Emmanuel."

She was feeling good and enjoying the peaceful morning.

"You're a fine cook and a gentleman, but don't you feel like you have to jump up for me."

Not knowing what else to do, Emmanuel chuckled a little awkwardly and eased back into his chair. The large windows were open and let the morning air right in. The grass was green and waving and somewhere on the rooftop birds were whistling away. Laura went looking for coffee in the kitchen, then came back and sat down.

"Well there they go...hoss feedin' time," commented Emmanuel.

They could see the corral outside and all the horses circling and nipping at each other. Rufe came into sight with a burlap sack and a tin cup, reaching through the rails to dump scoops of grain into the feed troughs. The horses fought a bit, and the dominant ones were the first to eat. Rufe continued to dump scoops as he walked the fenceline.

"You was out east?"

"Muscatine. Right on the Mississippi," Laura said. "Going to miss those sunsets. The sun reflects right off the water, and you can see every color imaginable."

"If the clouds are thick up above, such as aft'uh a good rain, we get some real good sunsets. Like the Good Lo'd paint the sky with oranges."

Emmanuel shifted in his chair and kept blowing across his coffee. He would clear his throat after every sip. Laura could tell he was still uncomfortable with her — and being a basic stranger was no help. She knew most of these cowboys weren't used to company, but she felt a deep desire to make everyone there easy with her presence. This was her home now. And theirs, too, for as long as they would stay on.

"Where are you from, Emmanuel?"

He cleared his throat again and nodded thoughtfully.

"Been doin' cow work for quite some time," he said. "A'fore that, I was soldierin' down in Fort Concho."

"Where's Fort Concho?"

"Down in Texas, ma'am. I was with the 9th...'A' Company," he said proudly. "Cavalry."

He took a sip and glanced at her from the corner of his eye. Mrs. Blancett's blonde hair stood out brightly against her black shawl. She was friendly, and he appreciated the effort she was making. He found she was easy to speak with, which helped.

Emmanuel himself had been married once. But that was a long time ago and only for a short time. She died of small pox before they could have any children. It had been too short a time to get very comfortable speaking with ladyfolk. Soldiering and cowboying did not afford too many opportunities, after that.

"Muscatine. Never been there muh'self."

"Til came west a few years ago. Right about then a brand new business opened in town — making pearl buttons."

Emmanuel pointed at his shirt. It had large pearl buttons.

"Like these?"

"That's right. The boats bring in clams from the river. I would punch out buttons, straight from the shells."

Emmanuel grinned again. The sky was getting lighter every moment. He knew the sun was right behind the ridge now, about to pop up.

"I best get some eggs a-fryin'. Crew be coming inside soon." He pretended to tip a hat since he was not wearing one. "Ma'am, many thanks fo' the first rate con-vo-sation."

The cook disappeared into the dim kitchen. Even though it was hard to see in there, Emmanuel knew right where everything was. The woodstove had been going since 5 AM, and eggs would only take a moment. He liked to cook eggs. The coop was out back, and there were a dozen hens in it. They put out a good number of eggs every day. The idea of ranch life took some getting used to, but it was starting to sink in. There was a nice woodstove to cook on. He would not work out of a tiny chuckwagon anymore. He wouldn't need to set up and tear down a potrack every night.

Emmanuel took a bowl and went out back to collect some of those fresh eggs.

Chapter 19
Whale Mine

"I do hate chickens!" LG complained. Feathers were floating all around him. They were sticking to his shirt and hat. He sucked one in as he talked and began sputtering.

John stood at the hen house door with a small wicker basket in his hand. He watched LG sputter. John had two bruised eyes and a cloth bandage wrapped all the way around his forehead. The bandage was so thick he could not get his hat on. His hair poked up above it.

"Here, John-boy," LG called and tossed an egg towards him. The young man came out of his trance and hustled to catch the egg safely.

"Better run them up to Greasy Belly. He's one crabby ki-yote," LG told him. "And best walk light since you botched it yesterday. He may do you harm for averting your skinnin' duties."

"But I had a busted forehead!" John-boy replied, worried the cook would be mad. "Cow near raked my scalp off. That should be cause for exemption."

LG stepped out of the hen house and brushed the feathers from his sleeves.

"Now, don't get too close if he's got a skillet in his hand. Or a rolling pin. He had a rolling pin yesterday. Just set them eggs down and get gaited."

John-boy turned and hustled up towards the cookhouse. He slipped on a pine cone and lost an egg. It dropped and broke. But the boy kept trotting along until he disappeared inside the building. LG watched him go and chuckled.

It had been wise to sign on at the Whale — he had to get out of the backcountry. Being alone for weeks on end was hard on anyone, but it was especially hard on LG because he liked to be around people. He liked chatting with folks.

The moment Specter whinnied in the darkness LG knew it was all or nothing. It had been the tensest moment of his life...and survival was the only thing on his mind. After those men wrecked, he had a decision to make. He could have kept riding into Boulder. There might have been safety in such a public area. But it was also the middle of the night. The town would have been asleep, and LG didn't know Boulder all that well. The men chasing him may have known it better, caught up, and cornered him in some side street.

Going off trail had its own risks, of course. He could have run into underbrush too thick to get through. Or ridden into a box canyon — or right off a craggy bluff and broke his neck. But Specter proved to be a good night horse. LG was pleased with the horse's trail sense, but not his sense to keep quiet. But that was just a horse being a horse. Horses were herd animals after all and did not like being separated. It was just instinct to whinny when he heard another horse coming down the stage road. Unfortunately, it was also the worst possible moment.

To be safe, LG had avoided any burgs or settlements. If he saw chimney smoke or smelter smoke or campfire smoke, LG gave it a wide berth. People talk. And if his pursuers had any tracking sense, they might trail him right into some small encampment and find out what they needed from some conversation-starved miner.

The Whale had its own fair share of roughs. Being an isolated mine, with nothing to do but drink, LG had already seen some death since he hired on. That very week, a couple fellows drank too much and threatened Cassius himself. They pointed their guns right at him. Cassius backed down...long enough to go get his own guns and enlist some help.

Cassius told everyone he planned on taking the men down to the Fairplay jail in the morning. They locked the two men in the cookhouse storeroom. But sometime in the night, they were led out, lynched outside of camp and buried in the rocks. Maybe the jail talk was just for show. Maybe Cassius ordered the lynching, LG didn't know. The fact was he didn't know any of these people.

LG knew it was *possible* the stage robbers had picked up his trail — but after all this time it was unlikely. He had a good head start and made all kinds of loops in the woods. He even cut back over his own trail more than once. And now here he was, collecting eggs and milking wild cows at the Whale Mine in Weston Pass...giving some poor sucker a hard time for getting his head kicked in.

It was time to move on. Either back down to the plains, maybe Denver, or else up to the bigger mining towns. He would like some news about the B-Cross. He didn't know what happened after he lit out. LG suspected the crew was shot dead. There had been at least a half-dozen robbers. The boys were spread out with the cow line — if they had been together they could have made a fight out of it. LG himself managed to shoot that fellow off the stagecoach, but there was a lot of gunfire that day, and got chased off before he could see what was going on.

Chapter 20

Yellow Houses Pasture
Headquarters
XIT Ranch
Texas

When AG Boyce announced he was fired, BH "Barbeque" Campbell's entire face became red and veiny.

"I *just* bought several thousand head, Yellow Houses and Spring Lake pastures are packed...and you aim to fire half the XIT?"

Barbeque Campbell stood right up in Boyce's face. George Findlay was sitting in the buckboard watching solemnly. AL Matlock had a shotgun cradled in his arms.

Campbell was wearing a gun — but Boyce was unarmed. That had been a point of contention between Matlock and Boyce: Boyce refused to wear a gun. He had been a Colonel in the Army and hadn't worn a gun for several years now that the Indian threat was basically over. Boyce believed force of presence would be enough to keep things from escalating on the XIT. He served in the War and had no intention of pointing a firearm at another American in peace time. Boyce saw too much of that in the 60's and the years that followed. However, Mr. Matlock did not feel the same. And since Matlock had been the one to examine the conditions of the XIT firsthand, he knew words alone would not be enough for men like Barbeque Campbell.

It was late in the day, but there was still a lot of branding going on at the corrals. They could easily hear the bawling cattle. Lee and Davis got out of the wagon and moved behind Campbell. They had their gunbelts on, too — but no one was pointing a weapon at anybody yet.

Two men came around the corner of the house.

"Here comes Billy Ney and Arizona Johnny," Matlock said pointedly. "They're on my Xmas list."

"What's going on, Que?" Billy Ney shouted, wiping his forehead with the back of his hand. He was covered in dust and sweat. They both were. It was another hot June day in the Yellow Houses Pastures.

"They're firing me, Billy," Campbell shouted back. "Cuttin' me out. This is how they show appreciation for good hard work."

"It's done, Campbell!" Matlock spoke firmly. His gray eyes were sharp.

Campbell kept glaring at Boyce, bristling. He knew he was in a tight place. They must have watched and waited until he was far enough from his men. If they had tried this back at the branding chute, it would have played out differently. But Barbeque Campbell could see the odds were not so sunny at the moment.

"On the authority of the members of the Chicago syndicate, we are taking charge," Boyce announced. "You're gone, Campbell. Ride out today."

"Que?" Billy shouted again. He and Arizona Johnny stopped a little ways off. They had left their guns in the bunkhouse since it was a branding day. It was too easy to lose a handgun wrestling a steer or bending over the firepit to get another iron. Billy could not believe what he was seeing.

"Don't you worry none, Billy." Barbeque stared hard at Boyce. "I'll straighten this out."

"Set your gun on the ground, Campbell," Boyce instructed. "See that horse? Take it and go."

Barbeque Campbell eased down and set his Colt .45 on the ground. He straightened up slowly until he was eye to eye with Boyce again.

"Get on back there, Billy!" Campbell yelled. "Go help Earl. Finish up for the day. Guess I'm not on the payroll no more."

Billy Ney spun around and headed back to the corral. Arizona Johnny stood there a little longer, gawking. Finally, he followed Ney, and the two of them disappeared around the corner of the ranch house.

Barbeque Campbell set off towards the hitching post where a horse was tied to the rail, eyes half closed. Earlier, Boyce had put an old saddle on one of Campbell's day horses. If the man rode off and kept the horse, which he undoubtedly would, it would not be a major loss considering the circumstances. It was more important to get him to leave before the rest of his men knew what was happening. Billy Ney and Arizona Johnny were getting the crew riled up at that very moment. But without Campbell to lead them in some kind of upstart, Boyce was confident the tension would ease off.

Campbell untied the horse and climbed aboard. He walked the horse right past Matlock and Boyce, glaring down as he rode by.

"Here's your final pay," Boyce said and tossed an envelope up to Campbell, who caught it and looked inside.

"You had all this planned out. My horse...the money," Barbeque realized. He looked up at the ranch house window and saw a figure inside. It was Rollin Larrabee, the rotund bookkeeper, watching through the curtains. Campbell pointed at him with the envelope, shaking it angrily.

"I see you, Rollin Larrabee! You had time enough to get my pay together. You could have come out n' warned me instead. I see where you stand!"

"Light out...now!" Matlock demanded and pointed the shotgun directly at him.

"Oh, I will. You high-falutin' *bastard!*"

Barbecue Campbell, former general manager of the XIT Ranch of Texas, dug his rowels into the horse's sides and took off at a run. He loped out into the grass and headed due east. The sun was bright on his back and cast a long shadow out in front of him. Just then a group of hands came up from the corrals, predictably, led by Billy Ney and Arizona Johnny. Boyce went straight up to the group and addressed them sharply.

"Gentlemen. I am Colonel AG Boyce, and I am managing this ranch now. What I say happens. And I say Billy Ney is no longer foreman of the Yellow Houses division. Frank Yearwood is."

Boyce singled out Frank Yearwood, who stepped up and shook hands with Boyce. The rest of the cowhands began chattering. Some of them, like Albert Smith and Henry Higglesworth, were clearly pleased with Yearwood's promotion. Some were even relieved. But others threw hard looks. Billy Ney was speechless and looked around for some support.

"I would fire you right now, Mr. Ney," Boyce said, in everyone's hearing. "But with the pastures so full we need hands. Prove yourself worth something, and I'll keep you on. That goes for more than one of you here today. This is a warning against lawlessness. I will not stand for it."

"Thank'ya, Colonel Boyce," Frank Yearwood said gratefully. Smith and Higglesworth came up, and they both clapped him on the shoulder. The tension melted as the group of cowboys dispersed. Mr. Matlock tucked the shotgun in the crook of his arm again.

"These men ride for your wagon now," Boyce told Frank. "This is a bad time to change over, I know, but it *is* happening."

"Still got a lot of hard-cases need to be run out," Frank mentioned.

"Keep receiving cattle," Matlock told him. "Drive some north to the breaks in the Alamositas if you have to."

"After that," Boyce added, "I plan on firing most of this whole blamed crew."

Chapter 21

Arkansas River Valley
Colorado

"Eyelids all butterflyish," Granger observed, bending over Vincent who was lying on the ground. "Wake up!"

But Vincent did not wake up — although his eyelids were indeed fluttering like butterflies. Nearby, Bill sat hunched against a gritty boulder.

"I am afraid he won't make it to Poncha," Bill said with a note of sadness.

The sun had been up for an hour or so. He looked down at his old companion. They had ridden together through many rustlings, robberies and killings. But now, here they were. Vincent was dying. His face had no color, and the skin looked like it was stretched tight. Granger had been quiet for most of the ride. This was because he had been asleep in the saddle. Bill could hear his heavy slobbery breathing quite clearly as they walked their horses through the dark.

Bill always liked traveling under the stars. Summer nights in the high desert were cold. Even though temperatures could get pretty high in the day, it always surprised him how cool it could get once the sun went down.

Bill got to his feet and turned to face the rising sun. His hands were buried in his coat pockets. He sighed. Vincent was in bad shape. He would be dead soon. Probably within a day or so. There was no real point in riding on. Even if they made it to Poncha Springs, it would only get the local law asking questions. Why give them a reason to take interest? Bill squinted and saw a hawk gliding out in the distance. He wondered if there was a Hell. When his ma died, when Bill was just a boy, he listened intently to every word the preacher said at her funeral. He said there were Streets of Gold and Gates of Pearl up where she was going. But down below, on the wrong end of eternity, was a burning Lake of Fire. Bill glanced down at his friend. *Well, Vincent — it's the lake of fire for you, compadre.*

Granger was pressing Vincent's palm into a prickly pear. The thorns were long and slid right into the soft flesh. It was a new source of amusement for Granger: checking on Vincent's level of awareness. It began with finger twisting the night before. Now he was patting Vincent's palm into a cactus. It was some measure of compensation for the mean delights Vincent had taken in regard to Granger's own misfortunes.

In fact, to Granger, life seemed like a *series* of misfortunes. Ever since he lost his first tooth to an outhouse door, he spoke with a lisp. One of Vincent's mean delights had been poking fun at Granger's lisp. Then after Will Wyllis banged open the mining shack door, the ribbings got even worse. Two missing teeth made everything he said come out with a whistle. Vincent found that endlessly amusing. It sorely aggravated Granger. He hated to be made sport of. And now, look! Sweet recompense.

It was quite an enjoyable thing. Although it would be much more gratifying if Vincent was just a little bit lucid — so he could feel the pain Granger was inflicting. Maybe he could. Maybe somewhere deep down in there, even though he was unconscious, Vincent could feel the cactus thorns working into his palm.

"We're not riding further," Bill declared and took a small spade from his saddle. "Put up a rope corral and turn these horses out. Set up camp."

"Okay, Bill," Granger said plaintively. He decided not to irk Bill, in light of his sad demeanor. Of course, Granger himself was quite giddy over the fact Vincent was dying. The two had never gotten along. Perhaps, Granger supposed, Bill would be kinder to Granger now — once Vincent gave up the ghost.

"Gonna dig a grave. When I get back, help me move him up there."

Bill took off his coat knowing he would warm up quickly once he started to dig. Unbuckling his gunbelt, Bill stacked all his gear in the shade of a cedar. He took a canteen, a bottle of whiskey and the spade and made his way up a long low hill.

The sky was blue and cloudless. It was going to be a hot day. Once Bill hiked up the hill, the ground leveled into a wide plateau that stretched off towards several low, broken bluffs. Bill spotted a lone piñon tree ringed by cholla, not too far out there. The cactus had little yellow flowers budding on its tips. With all the pretty yellow flowers, Bill figured this would be as nice a place as any.

At least there was a little shade under the tree to work in. Bill set the whiskey and the canteen in the hook of the roots. He stuck the spade in the ground and was glad to find the soil was not too dense. It was a little rocky, but he managed to dig down. The grave needed to be several feet deep at least, to keep the wild animals from digging him right back up.

As he shoveled, Bill really began to feel blue. This could just as easily be his own grave. He stopped digging and used the spade like a crutch, resting in the morning sunlight. Bill was getting tired. Tired of the lawlessness which had been his life for so long. It was starting to seem like the right time to turn his life around. He didn't want to die in an unmarked grave in the high desert of Colorado — like Vincent, anonymous and forgotten. It wouldn't take much to change things. All he had to do now was get loose of Granger. Perhaps he would dig two graves.

Chapter 22

"Don't grab my waist, Mary," Charley Crouse said, irritated. "Hold onto the cantle or you'll be afoot."

"Don't call me Mary," Caverango retorted. "This *caballo es* bumpy."

Caverango was sitting behind the saddle, straddling the gelding's spiny croup and rocking uncomfortably with each step. He found it was much more effective to cling to Charley's waist than it was to pinch-grip the cantle or hold onto the tie strings. He had experimented with both, but when the trail got rough he realized it was safer to just grab onto Charley. But Charley Crouse did not like it when another man rode behind him. It made him feel awkward — and made him want to harm that person. Which was how he felt right then.

They were last in the line. They were following two other horses, which were also doubled up with riders. Peter Mulock sat behind his older brother Edson on an unlucky quarter horse. A lemon-faced ranch hand named Whitey Jones rode unhappily behind the eldest Mulock son, Parker, on a big Percheron cross. The haunches on the draft were beefier than a regular sized horse, and Whitey was feeling all stretched out. It wasn't natural and he was not enjoying himself. Whitey felt it was an indignity to have two cowboys ride on one horse. That morning, he started out on foot...until the sun came up and the temperature soared. It got too hot to walk.

In the lead — alone on his own horse — rode the family patriarch, Mr. Mulock.

And his face was grim.

"Shut the hell up, would you!" Parker shouted over his shoulder. He rode directly behind his father, studying the man's posture. He was worried his father was about to erupt. The man had a violent temper, and Parker knew what they were in for, should he erupt.

The Mulock boys had been raised under that temper and learned early to watch their step in times like this. Edson and Peter were keenly aware of the situation, too, and only muttered to each other in whispers. And of course Whitey knew his place in the pecking order, which happened to be near the bottom.

They had to wait for the sun before they could follow the tracks. It had not been too difficult once it was light enough to see. The hoofprints were of course unique and easy to spot. Every shoe was different to begin with and left its own distinct impression — but things were even easier since Mulock had employed the same blacksmith for the past twelve years. The blacksmith always punched the same kind and number of nail holes. In addition to all this, no one had been on this part of the trail except the horse thieves. Mulock was confident they would recover their stock before noon.

As it was, it was nearing noon. Whitey Jones had a look of extreme discomfort on his face and held one hand over his crotch. Over the last hour he had taken to moaning gingerly about his "bull scrote." Parker tried shushing him but found it increasingly difficult.

The tension Parker was feeling had started when they woke up to three horses missing. Between his father's mercurial brooding, Charley's complaints and Whitey's sensitivities, Parker wished mightily he had stayed home the day before.

His father's bank, The Cañon City Bank, was on the brink. But no one knew it yet —certainly not the clientele or the investors. It was a house of cards, Parker realized, and just a matter of time before it all fell down. As the firstborn, it was his lot to take the reins when his father got too old. So he was learning the business. Unfortunately, what he was learning was not good. And it had become clear to Parker that his hard-handed father was not interested in doing right by the bank.

Mulock's nephew and the bank's cashier, the one and the same Augustus Gaumer, was caught up in it, too, thick as thieves. Parker's main concern was a community hanging. The ranchers in South Park were stout and not easily taken by scheme or swayed by dysfunction. Hell, they hung their neighbor Ed Watkins for cattle rustling right there in Cañon City back in '83. That was only five years ago, and it could happen again.

"There," Mr. Mulock said, pointing.

Up ahead they could see the three stolen horses. They had been led off trail about a hundred yards and corralled in a stand of cedar trees. There were two men lying on the ground. One was napping in the shade. The other was sprawled in the hot dirt with his hand stuck in a patch of prickly pear.

Mulock looked up. The sun was overhead, and it was indeed the noon hour. Just as he figured it would be. Mulock liked to be precise. He liked to be right. What he did not like was horse thieves. He started to pull his rifle from the saddle scabbard, but then eased it back into place. This could be done up close. Mulock pulled out his .45 and cocked it. His eyes glinted with a certain satisfaction. With a tap of his heels, he walked his horse right into camp. The others followed behind and spread out.

Granger was having a nicc nap. He was tucked up in a shady spot with his hat pulled down over his eyes. He was having a pleasant dream where he owned a cantina. His teeth were all there, and he had neither lisp nor whistle when he spoke. He served whiskey, tequila and beer —all with a nice, unbroken smile. There was even a special bottle of high-end whiskey hidden in the back room for his favorite customers. Both Vincent and Bill were dead in his dream. Their bodies had been embalmed and were propped up on each side of the room. Granger liked to take shots at them, even though it was loud when a gun went off indoors. He always aimed for their teeth. Both Bill and Vincent had many holes in their heads. It was a nice dream.

Chapter 23

It was Vincent and Granger! Charley Crouse could not believe his eyes. He started to hoot and almost did. But then he realized it would not be wise to have Mr. Mulock associate him with two horse thieves. It was better to keep quiet about that. It had been a shaky process getting in with the old man to begin with — and it was still awful shaky ground to be standing on as it was. Charley did not need the pall of horse thievery to complicate the situation. He twisted in the saddle and gave Caverango a sharp glare to keep him quiet.

Caverango had never felt any particular affinity for either Granger or Vincent anyhow. In fact, Caverango was realizing how little he cared for the entire Grand Lake Gang and wished he could get away from Charley Crouse especially. And the Mulock clan was another dark pool that he wanted less of. But Caverango knew it was all about good timing. He was hoping once they got into Cañon City he could simply fade into the crowd and disappear. He felt he had a better chance at slipping away where there were a lot of people. Over the past few days, Caverango began to daydream constantly about sipping cervezas in Santa Fe.

Mulock took his horse over to where Vincent was laying. There was a smoldering campfire and a coffee pot in the coals. Saddles were strewn about, and there were bedrolls and coats piled in a heap. Looking around, he realized these two men hadn't even *considered* they would be tracked. They were bedded down right off the main trail, and certainly had not ridden far or fast with Mulock's horses. They were fools.

The man on the ground was clearly in no shape to travel. Maybe this was why they hadn't made a run for it during the night. He glanced over to Granger, who was still sleeping beneath his shady cedar tree. Mulock changed his mind again, uncocked the .45 and hooked it in his belt for safe keeping. Then he leaned over and eased out his Winchester after all. It would make a bigger hole.

"Bo-peep!" Mulock called out and pulled the trigger.

Vincent's body shuddered with the impact. His chest blew wide open and blood and bone spattered up in the air. The noisy blast jolted Granger out of his nice dream. He scrambled to his feet as quickly as he could. His hat fell off, and he squinted up to see Mr. Mulock pointing the rifle his way now.

Granger froze. Vincent was clearly dead as a stick. Granger hoped that somewhere deep down, before his soul fluttered away, Vincent felt the pain of being fatally blasted. Along with that prickly pear Granger stomped into his hand. It would be sad if Vincent got away without feeling any of those things.

"You stole them horses," Mulock stated grimly.

"Now, no, sir..."

Granger started to lie. He began working up a tale in his mind that might make sense. He didn't *steal* them — he was a prisoner himself and had been *forced* to steal them. Maybe even salt in some of the truth: they had money. A hundred thousand dollars! And Granger would give some of it to the old man. Hell, all of them could have a decent cut. Then Granger noticed the rest of the riders. He saw the Mulock brothers doubled up on horseback. And Whitey Jones and Parker on the Percheron cross. He knew these fellows must be mad as hornets — and mad at him in particular since he was the one who stole their horses. Of course, they didn't know the finer details yet.

Then Granger realized he was looking right at Charley Crouse and Caverango on the gelding with the spiny croup.

"Well, I'll be!"

Charley knew the moment it registered in Granger's brain. The scalawag was a slow thinker, which of course made him a prime target for razzing when they rode together and of course Charley razzed the man incessantly. But his slow thinking was a liability now and they no longer rode together anyway. Charley promptly drew his own Colt and shot Granger smack in the eye.

Granger wobbled and stumbled backwards into the shady cedar. His sleeves got snagged in the branches as he waved about. They watched the life go out of him.

Granger sagged dead in the tree, hanging like a scarecrow.

Slowly, Mr. Mulock turned around and fixed his stern gaze on Charley. The Mulock boys were in a state of absolute shock. They simply couldn't believe a green hand would presumptuously intervene in their father's affairs. Surely, there would be hell to pay! All three of them held their breath, and so did Whitey Jones — who also held his "bull scrote."

Charley Crouse holstered his gun and casually slouched in the saddle, crossing his forearms over the saddle horn as if he didn't have a care in the world.

Mulock sat silently for a moment and studied him closely.

Charley could not tell what the man was going to do. In Charley's short experience with Mr. Mulock, he knew this could go either way. Suddenly Mulock let out a guffaw. Then he glared at his sons who seemed frozen in place.

"What are you waiting for? Fiery chariots whirlin' down from the sky? Go get your damn horses!"

Whitey Jones immediately slid off the big draft and hit the ground hard, flat on his boots. He danced around for a minute like a chimpanzee.

"Yow! My feet are all tingly!"

Edson and Caverango dismounted with more care. As soon as the Mexican was down, Charley Crouse let out a sigh of relief. He was glad to have his horse all to himself again. There was nothing worse than backriding with a greasy bean-eater. If Mr. Mulock hadn't insisted, it never would have happened. And Charley knew better than to underestimate the old rancher. There was something in his look that made Charley hesitant to overstep.

"Pa! There's cash money in here!" Edson exclaimed. He knelt down to pick up one of the saddles...and noticed the bulky saddlebags.

Immediately, Mr. Mulock slid off his own horse and hustled straight over. He pushed his son aside roughly and flung open the saddle bag. Sure enough, there was nothing but cash inside. Glancing around at the other saddles, he noticed they all had abnormally swollen saddle bags.

"Boys," Mulock said. "There's more money here than I can count."

Parker was astonished at the find. His mind reeled. This was an unexpected turn of events. They had been headed to the Cañon City Bank before their horses were stolen — Parker was sure it was more than just a business visit. He suspected his father planned on cleaning out the vault, taking George Green's money and riding south. But this could save the bank! Between the cash-filled saddle bags and the fifty thousand Green had deposited for selling the 63 Ranch, the bank might actually stabilize and pull through.

"Pa, this sure will get us out of a hole. With Green's money and this right here, the bank will be okay!"

And no one will get hung, Parker added silently.

With a dry laugh, Mulock shook his head at his good fortune. He glanced up at his oldest son. So naive. The boy had no sand — Parker wouldn't make it in Mexico. He had too much of a conscience. He should have learned to beat that down, but if he hadn't figured it out by now it was too late in the game. I'll give him the ranch, Mulock thought. That'll be something at least.

The patriarch of the Mulock clan put a foot in the stirrup and got back on his horse. He was feeling quite pleased now. When he woke up to three stolen horses, he felt Lady Luck was standing hard against him. He was even rethinking his plan to take Green's money and ride off to Mexico. But he was not rethinking anything anymore. And now he had twice as much on top of that. Seems Lady Luck was on his side again.

Chapter 24

When Bill saw the shooting star, he thought it was a sign.

Lying flat out in the bottom of the grave, all Bill could see was the star-filled sky. Lying in a grave that he had dug himself was not an irony he appreciated. The spade lay across his chest. His fingers were cramped from holding onto it for so long. Like the greatest of fools, his guns were back at camp — but the spade would work well enough if anyone happened to peer into the grave. He might chop out a throat before getting shot.

Astrology was not Bill's forte. But that shooting star seemed to wake him up. Like it was telling him it was safe now. Someone upstairs was letting him know. Well, maybe.

From the bottom of the hole he could see nothing but rolling constellations and one silhouetted branch reaching out overhead, from the piñon pine growing nearby. The sun was long gone. He had watched it creep across the sky all day. At first, he checked his new pocketwatch every few minutes but that just made the sun creep slower. He gave up on that. Then, it finally grew dark and the stars began glimmering in the dusk.

The gunshots had been loud. The first one was a rifle, the second a sixgun. Bill knew immediately that the shots came from camp. And it did not take much rational thought to stitch the scene together. Vincent was an invalid and plainly ineffective in a gunfight. Granger was just a plain dummy. And now someone had done them in. Probably, it was the cowboys they stole the horses from. Another thing Bill noticed: the shots had been spaced out, unhurried. Which meant it was an execution — not a gunfight. They had been fools not to watch their backtrail, obscure the camp, or just ride as far as those damn horses would take them.

Bill's sense of self-preservation had been clouded by his emotions. It was one of those moments of neglectfulness...a lapse in judgment. Like Wild Bill Hickock, who just that one time took a seat at the poker table with his back to the door. For Bill Ewing, worry about an old amigo had blighted his rational mind. It could have cost Bill his life. If he had dallied around camp any longer, he might have been gunned down himself.

When he heard the two shots Bill instantly knew he was in a bind. He wasted no time and slid right down into the grave. It was gambly but what better options were there?

He had the whiskey, at least. It helped pass the day.

There were some coyotes yipping somewhere in the dark. They may have caught a jackrabbit. That was how Bill felt all day. Like he had been boxed in by a pack of coyotes, waiting for that final moment.

He sat up and peered into the darkness. There were no lights or fires that he could see. The camp was just down over the rise a stone's throw away. He hadn't heard a thing since around noon. Not even a horse whinny. Of course, he did not really expect to. They probably took everything after shooting his crew. At least they hadn't been diligent enough to notice there had been three horses...but only *two* men in camp.

It did not take long to walk back. Bill went along softly. He suspected the danger had passed — but he didn't want to make the same mistake again. He didn't want to walk into a bunch of angry cowboys with rifles and sixguns.

The starlight was bright enough that he could see down the short slope. The cedars and piñon pine were opaque black blobs which could easily conceal a man with a rifle. Bill himself took to the deep shadows, stepping from tree to tree quickly and quietly.

Vincent's body was easy to spot. It was lying where he left it. Bill could smell the blood and hear some flies buzzing around, even well into the night like this. Granger, on the other hand, was harder to spot. Bill almost jumped out of his skin when he stepped near the cedar where Granger was snagged — arms up like a ghoul.

"Aces and eights," Bill muttered. "Guess I drew a better hand than you boys."

All the horses were gone. So were his guns, his coat, and pretty much everything except the coffee pot which was still sitting in the charred coals. That hundred thousand was gone, naturally. Bill sloshed the flat coffee around and took a sip.

Chapter 25
Leadville

The cigar was so rich Casey felt his head starting to spin. He held it at arm's length and studied it. It was barely a quarter of the way burnt down and moving along very slowly. This was going to be a long evening. Maybe if I pace myself, he thought, I can get this thing used up.

Horace Tabor was working on his like it was made of candy, and so were Prescott Sloan and Ben Loeb — introduced to Casey at dinner as *The Famed Entrepreneur Benjamin Loeb.* Of course, Casey heard the man's name almost every time he rode into town. The man was an icon of wicked sins and ran the most talked-about bawdy house in Leadville. His black hair, thinning but not as far gone as Tabor's, was slicked down. He certainly looked the role of the deviant manchild, and Casey was uneasy trying to make conversation.

The whole night had been an awkward thing for Casey. He kept glancing across the parlor to catch Julianna's eye. Unfortunately, Julianna seemed to be enjoying herself.

"Maggie, where's JJ?" Elizabeth Tabor demanded briskly.

"Working another mine...where else?" Maggie replied. She took a sip from her wine glass and rolled her eyes. "The Little Jonny. It's been bought, you know. By the Ibex complex. He's doing the paperwork right now, he'll be foreman of that one next. Gonna quit the Louisville! But he *should* be right by my side, pretending we're fancy folks like I am. But I won't hold it against him too much. Someone's got to bring in the bread."

"All we ever talk about is mines, husbands...and mines" Elizabeth said to Julianna — with either a tone of apology or sarcasm, it was hard to tell.

Julianna laughed a polite but nice laugh. That seemed like the best reaction. Maggie shook her head in resignation and tipped her glass to get at the last swish of wine. She stood in the bay enclave with her back to the windows. It was a big bay window with three tall panes of glass. The sky was still bright with summer sunlight, even though it was well past the supper hour.

"Which mine does your fine husband work for, dear?" Maggie asked Julianna.

Julianna shook her head and glanced across the room. She could see Casey nodding along as the other men bickered and chortled. They seemed oblivious to the fact Casey had little to say. She could smell the aromatic smoke wafting in and smiled at her poor husband. Casey lit up hopefully when he caught her looking his way.

"He used to cowboy all over. But he's done with cows, or so he says. Right now he's building our home," Julianna told Maggie. She shrugged subtly at Casey and turned her attention back to the women.

Casey stared hard in her direction — no, no, no! Look back. Come on. But she was gone again. It was like he was lost on the ocean, floating along on a piece of wood and a ship just floated by...and disappeared on the horizon. He took another soft drag on the cigar Horace had given him and felt his stomach turn sour.

"Well if he's any good at it, he could make a living putting up shanties," Maggie noted. "All kinds of folk are moving into Leadville. Stars in their eyes. Although if he wants to work a mineshaft, JJ will hire him."

"Horace could easily get him on in the Matchless," Elizabeth added with a light slur and ran her fingertips across the extravagant pearl necklace she was wearing. With a glance down to her empty glass, she turned abruptly and headed for the wine rack. Julianna watched her stride almost aggressively across the room.

Mrs. Tabor was being aloof. She was remote and hard to talk with. When Julianna and Casey arrived for the evening event, it was Mrs. Tabor herself who grandly opened the door...and Julianna could see it in her eyes, who she was. It was Elizabeth, not Baby Doe. Tonight she was the condescending aristocrat, dainty yet stone, with a touch of morose and a splash of snide. And she was certainly in her liquor.

Elizabeth Tabor twisted a corkscrew around and around, her face pensive, lost in her inner world. Whatever was occupying the mining magnate's spouse, she was keeping it to herself. Julianna turned back to Maggie and considered her offer to get Casey a job in the mines.

Thinking back to her conversations with Josephine in Ward, Julianna recalled what a point of contention her friend had had with her husband Samuel. The mines were a strain on their marriage. She was always worried about his safety, and the pay for the average worker was low, too. Julianna was glad *not* to have mining as something to argue about with Casey. But she would never say that out loud, not to these women. This town lived and breathed mining. She wasn't about to say anything against it.

In the parlor, Casey was realizing the company was as bad as the cigar.

"How goes the Pastime, Sloan?" Ben Loeb asked in a caustic tone. Casey was glad Ben Loeb was ignoring him. The man's eyes just weren't right.

"Let me guess," Ben continued. "You think you're gonna make money on tail and titty. On State Street? Boy, that's *my* territory. And I got the corner on the whole damn market."

Sloan sloshed his whiskey around his glass in a gentle circular pattern.

Casey straightened up a bit, feeling a change in the air — like when a bronc was about to blow up.

"Loeb, you know something?" Sloan said slowly. He returned Ben's look and inched a step closer. "I *seen* your burlesque show. Better call it a burlap show and pass out burlap sacks to belch in. Your girls are so homely you gotta give away the tokens. The only market you've got cornered is the corner of ugly and shitfaced."

"Whoa, ho ho," Tabor said, trying to intervene. "Ben, you look like you need a top off."

"I need to top off this man's damn neck," Loeb said darkly. But he was smiling as he said it. It was a curious smile. Casey could not tell if he was in a joking mood or a violent mood.

"You ain't got nothing on me," Sloan told him, smiling himself. He clapped Horace on the shoulder and sidled up next to him. "Even if the Pastime rolls belly up, I've got a big stake in the Matchless. Me and Haw, we're thick. Soapy's out."

Ben's face fell for just a moment. Just as quickly, it bounced right back into that hard cast aloofness — but he studied Horace as if for the first time. Tabor's face flushed red and he shook his head quickly.

"Now, now," he fluttered and waved his hand around.

"Soapy's out?" Ben asked Horace. "When did this happen?"

"I know you was interested in his stake, Ben, but it all happened fairly quick."

"I just cannot *believe* Soapy would sell to someone other than me. Or sell at all for that matter."

"Perhaps you didn't know," Sloan suggested, "because you're not as savvy as you think. Maybe Soapy had his sights set a little higher."

"Man's a common bunko artist. Set his sights higher? Than me? I own Leadville."

"Not so common...the man owns Denver. And got a fair grip up here, I'd say. Certainly on your piddly nuts."

Horace Tabor cast a worried glance through the parlor doorway. The ladies were still grouped near the bay window, chatting among themselves. Horace was hoping on a fairly neutral evening. He hoped the social scales would have been balanced with Casey and Julianna mixing into this soiree. But who was he kidding? Himself mainly, Horace supposed. Between Ben Loeb and Prescott Sloan, things were bound to heat up at some point. He was hoping to keep that chestnut about the Matchless Mine to himself for a little longer. He wasn't sure how Loeb would react. But here it was, coming out.

"I may need to step out for a minute," Casey muttered balefully. He set his whiskey glass down on a bookshelf and made a line for the back door.

Uneasily, Horace watched him go. The door clicked tight and Casey was gone. Digging deep for some resolve, the Silver King pressed in between the two businessmen and whispered harshly.

"Gentlemen, there goes a pair of ears innocent to such banter. Can you keep it together for *one night?*"

Ben Loeb stared sharply at Prescott Sloan. Ben had run his own operation for quite some time and had seen his assets expand over the years. He was at the top of his game. And now, here he was staring at some slick banker from God knows where — with balls enough to open a saloon right there on State Street. Normally Ben would not feel threatened... *he* would be the one making the threats. But with the sale of Soapy Smith's Matchless stock to this primped up bastard, well, that was an oddity. Ben mulled it over. Who was this Sloan to move in so quickly?

"Oh, we're holding it together, Haw," Ben Loeb said passively, even cheerfully. "Just a couple dogs pissin' over a bone."

Feeling more and more secure with himself and his meteoric rise in Leadville, Prescott Sloan decided to voluntarily check his tongue. What an unexpected pleasure. Digging it in to the all-too famous Benjamin Loeb. This was where kingdoms were made! Sloan smiled. Here he was, among the upper echelons of the criminal elite. Sloan had played his hand well tonight. Old Ben Loeb was on the downslope now, and the man with the queer eye was just starting to realize it.

Sloan felt on top of the world. He knew this was where he belonged now. No more doubts or regrets about Ward. There was money to be had here in Leadville. Sure, Soapy Smith was the big crime boss in Denver these days. Oh, he had quite an operation going on down there. Judges, cops, politicians on the graft. The man did it all: rigged gaming on the streets and behind closed doors, lottery and stock scams, bad auctions. It was fortuitous

Sloan had met him at all, and even more to be in a position to fund the next big thing in Denver: Soapy's new gambling hall, the Tivoli Club. Sloan had seen the blueprints himself.

It was a major move, to buy out Soapy's stock in such a high-producing mine. Not only did it cut Soapy's hold up here, but it gave Sloan the leverage and finances to step up to the top of Leadville's underworld. He would run things in Cloud City. And it wouldn't take long. This would be Sloan's empire. And men like Ben Loeb would either submit, get run out...or get plowed under the dirt.

Chapter 26

The sky was finally losing its light. Mount Massive and the entire ridgeline grew dark in silhouette — the sun was somewhere back behind it all. Casey was glad to be out in the open air. He turned and realized he was only a couple steps from the big bay living room window. There was Maggie Brown just through the glass, chatting and acting rather animated about something.

Casey stepped closer and glanced in, over Mrs. Brown's shoulder. Julianna was right there, but she hadn't noticed Casey outside the window. She stood with a wine glass in her hand. She sure looked pretty in that new dress.

At first, he hoped to catch her eye. But quite suddenly, Casey felt guilty. Julianna was having a ball. Why spoil that? He stepped away from the window and leaned against the corner of the two-story house. The cigar was still in his hand, smoldering. He checked to make sure no one could see him and then hurled it as far as he could.

Since the day he bought his patch of land, Casey allowed himself to merely focus on the simple things. Stripping the bark off a tree trunk. Notching a corner. Mixing mortar. He set up a big canvas tent, and they left their comfortable room at the Delaware behind. It was no luxury, but it was their own. Plus, Casey could only handle living in the city like a dandy for so long.

Getting out to the country was good. And Julianna liked watching their home come together — there was progress every time she came home. Casey liked to see her carefree smile, so he worked hard to get something done before he went into town to pick her up from the Opera House.

Seeing the Tabors up close was a little too much. Casey wondered how someone came to be a big shot in a town like this. And do it above board? He knew where those fellows stood. Sloan and Loeb were clearly men of darker machinations. Casey had thought the Tabors were sound, the way Julianna talked about them. But who would invite men like that into your home? Unless you were caught up in it. From the minute the parlor talk started, Casey wanted to light out of there.

Gee, it was good to be out in the fresh air! He surveyed the street. There were other houses, most of them had a Victorian flair — purple, baby blue, white, pink even. It was quiet outside. Most folk were probably getting ready for their bunks.

Casey reached in his pocket and pulled out a crinkled envelope. The day before, he stopped at the post office on his way into town.

It was a letter from Til. He had a new spread on the south end of the Park, which he was calling Hay Ranch. Haying and cattle. Not a big *range* operation, but a small *ranching* operation. Working to get quality beeves made sense. Genetics and breeding were the name of the game now. Casey opened it back up and skimmed down to the post-script:

"I almost forgot. LG rode through here day before. He is riding out to Sam Hartsel's place to look for work. Told him about you up in Leadville. Says he wants to pay you a visit."

He flicked the letter with his finger. Casey wasn't sure what to think about that. This was the first time he'd heard anything, hide or hair, about LG. He wasn't even sure that LG was in Colorado anymore. Or alive.

Casey crumpled it into a wad. LG had ridden on — he hadn't even looked back. Ira and Edwin were cut down. Casey was shot and left for dead. And LG just lit out. It really ate at Casey the more he pondered it.

Pay me a visit? Why? To see the scars on my chest? Well, I ain't dead. No thanks to you, compadre.

Looking up, Casey noticed the first stars. Just faint, but they were there. He sighed and smoothed out the letter. It wasn't the first time he had crumpled it up. He pressed the letter back into the envelope and tucked it back in his pocket.

One of the ladies inside laughed. It wasn't Julianna; he would have known her laugh through a dozen walls. Casey straightened his necktie and checked the buttons on his vest. He knew he could only stay outside for so long.

Turning the knob, Casey stepped back into the parlor. It was dim inside. Horace Tabor was busy getting lanterns lit. Sloan and Loeb were nestled in padded armchairs near the fireplace, bristling at each other with watery eyes and whiskey refills. Casey didn't care. He wanted nothing to do with those devils. He had a home to build — good clean honest work — and couldn't wait to get back to it.

The cowman just kept on walking and didn't say a thing. He made his way through the parlor into the kitchen entry. The women had moved on from the bay window by then, and were seated at the table. There was a deck of cards — it was rummy and coffee was in the air. Julianna noticed him leaning in the doorway and waved sweetly. Casey smiled softly at her.

Chapter 27

XIT Ranch
Spring Lake Pasture
Texas

Frank Yearwood squinted at the sunset. The sky was full of flat-bottomed thunderboomers but the rain was still bottled up.

He liked the feel of the wind when rain was coming. It was fresh and smelled good after a long day in the white Texas heat. After such a blistering week working the branding chute, it felt particularly good. With the sun going down the clouds suddenly blossomed across the sky, coloring in like a well-painted portrait.

The last of the August sunlight took on a golden glow. It made the thin grass look richer and thicker than it did during the hot afternoons. Frank could see across the plains pretty far. The landscape felt bone dry. Large patches of prickly pear stuck up in places. Whatever wildflowers had come up in the spring were long gone now. Frank's favorite time of year was when the bluebonnets and paintbrush covered the hillsides.

"They're circling in," Lee told him.

Small pockets of cowboys were slowly riding in, pushing cattle towards a center point up ahead. The three of them had cut out a dozen head themselves and were easing their way forward. Davis was riding a stone's throw off, keeping them pointed in the right direction and picking up whatever strays they happened upon.

A pulse of lightning flickered and hit the plains off to their right somewhere. It took a couple seconds between the sight and the sound. Above them the sky rumbled, rolling right over their heads.

"Whoa, hope no one gets cooked," Frank drawled without much worry. "I expect to have about 1200 steers collected by the time all of us pull together. We'll run a tally when we pass into the Black Water pastures. Then we can take 'em all up to them breaks in the Alamositas. Maybe on up to Rito Blanco if need be... course that means crossing the Canadian."

"Twelve hunnert four-year olds," Lee contemplated. "In this pasture alone? The B-Cross ran about 2500 total. And that was the whole mixed herd...mommas, babies and all."

"Well actually," Frank said, squinting again at the sun. It was hovering about an inch above the western horizon. It would not be long and it would be gone. "There's around thirty thousand in

Silver Lake alone. Which is plumb too many on this end, what with water so scarce this year. They all can't stay here."

"Thirty *thousand?* Gee whiz, that's a bunch of beeves. How far off is the Alamositas?"

"We got a ways. It'll take a few days of easy walking. Just ain't much water between here and there."

Lee was trying to wrap his mind around three million acres. He had seen some barbed wire running across the open spaces, but he was surprised how far spread out it all was. The pastures were subdivided and even those subdivisions were sprawled out enormously. All this open space was just the opposite of the mountain life. But, the high country was a place of rugged beauty like none of these Texas cowpokes had ever seen — and probably never would. If they were lucky, some of these men might catch a glimpse of snow-topped peaks from a distance, on a cattle drive to the north.

As for his pard, Lee was not sure how bad Davis would miss those same peaks. *That ol' boy sure did relish all that a lot more than me,* Lee thought. The heavy snows and the bitter cold really take its toll on a body. And yet, he knew winters in the Panhandle would not be any easier, really. *I may need to drift on further south before then*, Lee reflected.

A few fat rain drops plopped down from the sky.

"Wish it would rain," Frank said. But even with clouds like this, the rain might pass on by.

Frank Yearwood was relieved the syndicate had brought in Matlock and Boyce to fix the XIT. The morale had really been dragging. There was a lot of theft. Gambling was everywhere. And with it came violence. Frank knew there were men working for the ranch who had been run out of other parts of the country, men that Barbeque Campbell had deliberately brought on.

The sun dropped off the horizon and the wind picked up. All the cowboys were moving in good time and had all the steers bunched up by nightfall.

Frank decided to put both Billy Ney and Arizona Johnny on first watch. They might be too tired to cause any trouble come morning. The rest of the crew staked their horses and got out their bedrolls. With the gusty wind, Frank was uneasy with a large fire, even if it sprinkled. The grass could catch with just a spark. And these parched conditions were too bad to risk a prairie fire. He had seen plenty of prairie fires and knew it took a lot of hard work to get them under control.

They did get a small bed of coals going...just big enough to heat a coffee pot and warm some canned chili.

"Chuckwagon be waiting for us up yonder a'ways," Frank mentioned. "Get a real meal in you all, tomorrow night."

He dug out the can opener and started notching off lids.

Chapter 28

Frank sat straight up. He flung off his old wool blanket and froze stock-still. He cocked his head a bit and listened.

It was pitch black and there was no moon and there *should* have been. The stars were gone. He couldn't see a thing.

Then the sky lit up bright — so bright he had to squint, and the landscape was bathed in black and white. *Boom.* The sound split the sky and made his chest hurt and his head ring.

Frank got up as quick as he could get to his feet. He grabbed the wool blanket and ran a few steps.

White light exploded again and he didn't need to see to know what was coming...he could feel it. Above the throbbing in his chest and the dull humming in his ears, the drum of the running herd shook right up his legs.

"Huh-yaw! Go on! Go on!"

Frank made as much noise as he could and waved the hell out of that blanket.

Lee and Davis both jumped out of their bedrolls, slapping around frantically for their boots.

The steers came running.

Loose of their wits and barreling along blindly, the herd parted around Frank and poured past their camp. The noise consumed Frank's shouts, but he kept yelling and waving the wool blanket. Dust was everywhere and all he could hear were horns clanking and hooves pounding and bellows and snorts as they all blew by.

Davis's horse was thrashing around on his side, feet kicking at the air — he was still hobbled. He wasn't hurt, but tripped himself when he spooked. As luck had it, he had been standing in rein's grasp from Davis's bedroll and was safe from being trampled by the cattle. Davis was hunched over his horse cooing *easy easy,* trying to grab those reins without getting struck in the face by a hoof.

Lee's horse was gone. He had staked his horse, and in the chaos it must have pulled up the stake and ran.

The steers were gone now and the danger along with it. Frank put his fingers in his mouth and let out a long sharp whistle.

His bay whinnied, out in the dark.

Frank went out looking, and it didn't take long to find the horse. Then he was up in the saddle tearing across the prairie in the pitch black.

His eyes couldn't adjust to the dark with the electric sky cutting apart every few seconds. Frank's ears were ringing pretty good, but it helped that he could see where the herd was.

In one burst of brightness, he caught sight of Davis riding wildly ahead of him, chasing after the herd.

Ten minutes of hard riding passed before Davis realized Frank was behind him. That was all he needed. He knew he wasn't alone out there and figured, between the two of them, they could turn this herd in. Quirting his horse, Davis pushed to get up with the lead steers.

Leaning into it and hoping his horse wouldn't trip up, Davis rode up alongside the stampede.

In what light he had, he could see the leaders a short distance up ahead. But in that light he also saw them go off into an arroyo. They just disappeared — right off the edge. So did the steers following them. They just plowed right over.

Davis snapped his reins and leaned back hard into the saddle, angling away from the herd as he did, in a wide arc. White slobber strung off his horse's bit, eyes wide and mane waving.

The sky lit up again. The ground shook with it. Davis managed to get his horse stopped but he looked on, horrified.

The stampede was a dozen animals across at its widest — but they just charged on, following the tails of the steers in front of them. Row by row, they dropped out of sight like dominoes off the edge of a table.

"O mercy!" Davis shouted. He sat there, aghast.

Frank Yearwood pulled up next to him, and they both sat their saddles watching with every lightning pop. The noise was loud — the thunder and the rush of the herd. Being so close to the arroyo, they could hear the sickening thud of cowflesh.

Davis could not believe his eyes.

"What the Sam Hill!" Davis cried.

He pulled his hat off and whipped it helplessly across his thigh. His heart was pounding.

Then the stampede was running on. Past the arroyo. On the far side.

And on into the night.

Frank shook his head slowly, his face set. He said nothing.

The sound of the running herd faded with the distance.

Maybe Frank had seen this before, but Davis never had seen anything like it. He couldn't believe what he was seeing. The draw was full of dead steers. Full of them. They piled right on top of each other, right on up till it was so full of dead steers the rest of the herd ran right across to the other side and kept on going.

"Sakes alive," Davis spoke softly. His voice was raw from the hard run and all the dust he breathed in. "Sakes alive."

Chapter 29

"Like Moses," Lee said and raised his arms up. "Partin' the Red Sea."

The other cowhands were milling about the chuckwagon eating black beans, beefsteak and dried banana chips. The fire beneath the potrack was smoldering. A dutch oven was seated in the gray dust and chunks of smoldering manure. The lid was off and half the sourdough biscuits were gone.

Frank Yearwood knelt down and plucked out a second biscuit. He had missed breakfast — they all had, riding after the herd like they did. By the time dawn came around all the riders regrouped and crossed the draw. It took a while to catch up with the loose herd. By then the stampede had ended all by itself, and the steers were grazing. The riders swung out in a wide loop and brought them back together again — and now here they were, eating biscuits.

"We would have been trampled to bits, Frank," Davis said solemnly. "Owe you one."

Some of the hands wore permanent scowls, ever since the week before. Barbeque Campbell may have been gone, but he still had a good number of loyal men in the crew. Frank knew it and could tell who was with him and who was against him. No one had to guess that Arizona Johnny and Billy Ney were against him. They weren't with him in spirit...and that morning they weren't with him in person, either.

Frank looked around the group.

"Johnny or Ney turn up yet?"

Albert Smith and Henry Higglesworth were two good men. They stood by, tiredly spooning up black beans.

"Ain't seen 'em yet, Frank," Albert said.

"That storm rolled in on their watch," Henry muttered. He was salty. Most of them were. The entire experience put them in a sour mood.

"Maybe they got it," Albert suggested. "Run down to pieces."

"Well, ain't seen their horses around though," said Frank. "Probably still in the saddle."

"Squally night. Mebbe they just rode off," Henry added, walking his fingers in the air. "Simple as that."

A sea gull flew over the chuckwagon. Davis craned his neck and watched in wonder as the bird floated slowly overhead. It was the top of Texas in a late summer drought and there wasn't any sea for a thousand miles, but look at that. A sea gull. Circling over the chuckwagon.

One of the new young hands, Kenyon, rode in and got off his horse. He stepped up to Frank and pointed off across the low grass.

"I believe that's Arizona Johnny, sir."

They all turned and watched him ride in.

"Sun'abitch!" Arizona Johnny snarled as he parked his horse by the chuckwagon. "Them cows busted loose, and it ain't my fault, Frank! Ain't my fault on that!"

He slid off and hit the ground hard. He marched over, shaking his fist toward Lee and Davis.

"Boyce's crew! Saw you light a cigarette, you sun'abitch! It was one of you."

Arizona Johnny was fuming. His face was flushed.

"Where you been, Johnny?" Frank asked and frowned. "Needed every hand we had to bring them steers in this AM. And I could'a used both you and Ney. Where is he?"

"Oh, you think it was on *our* watch, so it must o' been us, don't you?" Arizona Johnny spat at the ground, his eyes narrowing. "This ain't on my back, Yearwood!"

"Didn't strike no match," Davis stated firmly.

"Didn't strike no match neither," Lee added, just as firmly.

Johnny's face wound up tight and he glared at Lee.

"Boy, I'll fix your flint."

Spinning away from Frank, Arizona Johnny took two quick steps and lashed out with his fist. It landed hard in Lee's chest. He fell in the grass, his plate went flying, and beefsteak and black beans splattered down his pants.

Tossing his own feed plate aside, Davis charged and tackled Arizona Johnny around the waist. But Johnny did not go down. He made fists out of both hands and swung them down hard on Davis's back. The wind whooshed out, but he did not let go.

Then Arizona Johnny produced a small knife from somewhere and jabbed it into Davis's back. He pulled it out and stuck him several more times before Frank could get there.

"No more o' this nonsense!" Frank growled. He drew his handgun and thunked Arizona Johnny on the head with the gun butt.

Dropping wobbly to his knees, Johnny let the knife fall out of his hand. Davis slid to the ground, face first. Blood oozed from his back in several places. Then he rolled over to face the sky, wheezing.

Henry, Albert, Kenyon and the cookie were all standing at the chuckwagon, watching. Cookie was holding his own plate of bean-soaked biscuits, his fork halfway to his mouth. He just held it there, watching the fight.

Lee scrambled to his feet and went to check on Davis. He pressed his neckerchief over the worst of the wounds to soak up the blood. Arizona Johnny hunched over and pressed his hands to his head.

"Don't get your dander up, Johnny," Frank told him. "No one lit no match. It was lightning that spooked that herd."

"You know all there is to know, don't you, Yearwood?"

Looking pained, Arizona Johnny got up and slowly angled toward the chuckwagon. He strutted past the men standing there — past Henry, Albert, and Kenyon — eyeing them toughly as he went by. Arizona Johnny paused in front of the cook. He grabbed the plate right out of the man's hand. Cookie just handed over his fork without saying anything.

"Hell, Frank," Johnny said, chewing with his mouth open. "You in Boyce's pocket, huh? Course I knowed that. Need to hash this out?"

Frank held up his Colt.

"I'm heeled," Frank pointed out, waving the gun a little. "We can hash this out."

Johnny plucked up a bean-sopped biscuit. It was a big bite, and he stood there chewing for a long moment, looking like a coiled snake. Frank sighed. He undid the hammer and holstered the handgun.

"Just get on outta here, Johnny. Go cash out at headquarters. You're done for. Tell Billy Ney the same. I don't want to see neither one of you again."

Davis lay on the ground, his breathing was labored, but his eyes were clear. He glared at Johnny but did not speak or try to move. He was hurting pretty bad.

"Know what," Johnny said finally. "Sick o' this shit."

He pressed the plate flat against the cook's chest, smearing black beans and sauce across his chest. The plate peeled off his shirt and fell to the grass. The cook did not move an inch.

Arizona Johnny put a foot in the stirrup and pulled up heavily onto his horse. Sitting up straight, he grabbed the reins and clicked his tongue.

"Boyce thinks he's got Barbeque all tidied up. Boy, he gonna kick up a row a'fore this is all done."

And with that they watched Arizona Johnny ride off into the afternoon. The sun was overhead, pale yellow and hot. It was another dry August day in northern Texas. All that lightning and wind…and no rain came of it.

"Well, I'll be," remarked Albert Smith.

He went over to help Davis. Together with Lee, the two of them got Davis up to his feet. Albert checked him over. Davis was certainly in pain, but the stabs were not all that deep really. He knew the man was going to be sore for a few days. Blood had been spilled, but he would heal up.

Chapter 30
Hartsel Ranch
South Park

Samuel Hartsel's hairline was pretty much gone up top. What was left was short-cropped and white, and so was his neatly trimmed beard. But his eyes were dark and sharp. He also stood a little too close to LG when he spoke.

"Shorthorns — the whole herd," Sam Hartsel told him proudly. "Purebred. What do you think about that, sir?"

"Why, that makes good sense," LG replied. "Pure stock makes for high quality beeves, and high quality beeves makes for a purty penny."

"You understand what we're about, then."

When LG rode in to Hay Ranch earlier in the week, Til informed LG all about Sam Hartsel's operation and his theories on pureblood stock. Til was aiming to try the same thing, he said. Sam Hartsel was working on it. Charles Goodnight was working on it. And it did seem to make good sense — LG could get on board. As long as he had cattle to punch and a horse to ride, LG was game for anything. It sure had been good to see the old B-Cross crew. Til, Emmanuel...and even the McSpookies.

Mr. Hartsel leaned in even closer to emphasize what he was saying. He was well above LG in height, thin framed and stern in opinion.

"I was the first rancher here in the Park. Bought up 160 acres, right here between the two forks of the South Platte. All started with just twenty head. In '64, boy, there was no one around and I could graze 'em up and down the Park without worrying...without worrying about cross-breeding, you see."

LG realized he was in for a sermon. But he was expecting it, after talking to Til. LG knew it was wise to pay attention if he hoped to sign on. The Hartsel Ranch was a crossroads of sorts, and that's what LG wanted. The Whale Mine had worn him down quick. There was nothing to do up there but drink and gamble and listen to the same miners prattle on about the same pipe dreams night after night.

"Then I went and bought me a hundred and fifty more. Two bulls and the rest were cows. Brought them in from Missour'uh myself. Took time. Took persistence, you see. Built this place up. Sawmill. Hotel. Blacksmith. Wagon shop and trading post. They all come right through here, yes they do. From Currant Creek Pass to Wilkerson, they all roll through here. Still do, you see."

Hartsel put both his hands on LG's shoulders and looked him straight in the eye.

"Then my brother disappeared. Found the skeleton under a tree — his horse too, all bone-dry and crumpled in. Lightning, you see. Struck him dead. Then a tich later, I got took by Cheyennes. Killers. Not like the Utes, you see. But a little ingenuity got me shut of that situation."

"I see," LG said.

Nodding, he wondered where this was all going. LG was good at talking, but not so good at listening, and had to force himself to. And Sam Hartsel was a man who could fill up a room all by himself. Maybe even more so than LG.

"Then ranchers started moving into the Park: cows, horses, a few grangers. And the plagues! Locusts in '74. Grasshoppers in '76. Know how many cows are grazing out there right now? Fifty thousand! Fifty thousand cows...and there's thousands of horses and sheep, too. *Sheep!* Used to be a time when I had all the grazing land I needed, and keeping pure stock pure was cherry pie. Does it sound like cherry pie to you?"

"No, sir. No, sir, it does not."

"Well, hell if it is. 'Cuz it ain't. This ain't cherry pie. But I aim to keep them Shorthorns *pure*, young man. If even *one* of them low breed bulls gets to poking around in one of my pastures, there will be hell to pay I can assure you."

By that time, Sam Hartsel was leaning heavily on LG's shoulders. He looked at LG closely, studying him, as if he could see right into his mind. The man must have seen what he was looking for, because Hartsel's face suddenly relaxed and he grinned softly. He unclamped his shoulders and LG felt like a spell had been broken.

"I'll cut you $2.75 a day. Plenty of good chow here, only the best. Eat all you want, and you get a nice room in the yellow wing all to yourself."

Then Hartsel snapped his fingers as if he just thought of another selling point.

"And we've got *hot running water*. You heard me. We pipe it straight inside the house from the hot spring. Get you a warm bath every night if you want it. How about that now?"

LG realized he had the job. He took off his big hat and ran his fingers through his crusty hair. It had been awhile since he had bathed at all, let alone in warm water.

"Shoot, I may never leave."

Hartsel chuckled and clapped his hands. He looked past LG and spotted a stagecoach coming across the low grassy hills. He immediately set off towards the hotel. LG turned around to see what he was looking at. The coach was just a speck heading right toward them, pitching up a dusty cloud.

Hartsel waved without looking at him.

"Got customers, I best head in. Keep them Shorthorns *pure!*"

The hotel door closed with a bang, and LG was left to figure out what was next. He could smell the river and hear it bubbling by. The cattle were grazing on the far side. It wasn't a bad place to be. Better than milking and collecting eggs for $1.50 a day. Now he was heading up Sam Hartsel's stock operation for nearly twice that — plus hot baths and free sit-down meals.

Taking a look around, LG took it all in. There was the hotel and trading post. He could hear someone hammering away in the wagon shop, and smoke puffed out of the blacksmith's. A sizable group of folks were strung about, coming and going on the wide thorough way. Freighters, passengers, cowboys. LG could even see a railroad grade. Two pretty ladies walked by in colorful skirts and carried shade umbrellas. Yes, this was a bit more his style.

LG led his horse to the nearest hitching post.

Part 3

PART 3

Notable Brown's Park residents:
Speck Williams – ferry operator
Mary Crouse – Charley's wife
John Jarvie – runs the store on the Green River
Mexican Joe Herrera
Asbury Conway
The Hoys
The Bassetts

Chapter 1
Grand Lake

Ben Leavick was not a drinker — anymore.

It was four in the afternoon. Daylight shot through the doorway each time someone stumbled out the door. It made the room light up and the drinkers inside squint. It also made it feel like the seediest place in town.

At least, that was how Ben felt each time the door swung open. He glanced around at the drunkards of Grand Lake. This wasn't a place he would typically step foot in, but this wasn't a normal day. Well, truth be told, he hadn't had a normal day since Sheriff Emerson Greer's death. Even though the world kept on moving, Ben's world had not. A hollow feeling settled in the bottom of his gut and stayed put. So he figured, no, he hadn't had a normal day since then so why should entering a seedy saloon in the middle of the day make him feel out of place? Everything was already out of place.

Ben did not touch alcohol for any reason. He didn't want to lose his sharpness, even dull it, for a single moment. What if he needed to be sharp? Any time, anything could happen. Like when Em got shot dead. They had been on the trail for bank thieves. Just riding along through the snowy rocks. It had been quiet in the high country that day. The pine trees were frosted over — the branches sagged but held their loads. It was still winter back then, snowy and bitter cold especially when the sun was blocked by that thin cloud-cover, as it was that day. No one knew, but Ben knew: they had a bottle with them. Greer drew on it some. Ben drew on it some. That was how they lost the tracks. If they were thinking clear, they would have seen that the riders had circled around. *Back into town*. That was how Emerson got shot. And how Ben got beaten down with just a few hard whacks to the skull. But no one else knew that — no one but Ben Leavick and the late Emerson Greer, and the knowledge was becoming harder and harder to keep bottled up inside.

The glass in front of him was just Vin Mariani. Caffeine and some cocaine. He was waiting for it to kick in and wash out his headache.

Em and Ben had been amigos for a long time. They had lived in Grand Lake for about the same length. They both had youngsters about the same age. Caroline, Emerson's kindly wife, was staying over at Ben's place ever since the shooting — his own wife Meggy was a consolation while Caroline grieved.

Meggy was an oak. Not only for her bereft friend, but for her own husband though she never knew the whole of it. Ben scowled. A lot of long nights and silent supper tables had gone by. Poor Meggy. And poor Caroline. Losing her husband to such senseless killing. Absolutely senseless. The love of money was like kerosene — the fuel of so much evil. The Good Book was right on that one. What was wrong with this crummy world, Ben wondered, that people murder other people like that? Over coins.

"Two of them turned up dead," Red Creek told Ben quietly. "Down thereabouts of Cañon City."

Ben nodded and rubbed his eyes with his knuckles. He scraped out some sleep crumbs and wiped his hand on his pants. His sense of hygiene was going downhill. Meggy gently tried to help but never said anything about it out loud.

"Can't catch no decent sleep," he explained to Red Creek. Red Creek merely stared at him. He had deeply bloodshot eyes, much worse than Ben's.

All Ben's private thoughts would stir up every night he blew out the bed lamp. Even after a hard day's work. Meggy would pass off into sleep quickly — she always did, no matter the day or its happenings. Not Ben. He would lie awake. Even when he was completely worn out, his mind kept working.

Red sat across from Ben, passively. Ben always wondered if the man got his name from a creek somewhere or if it was on account of his eyes being bloodshot all the time. Ben rubbed his own eyes again. He didn't want to have red eyes like Red Creek. Meggy would have something to say for sure.

Behind them at the bar, Otto was clinking glasses around. There was a card game at the next table over. Several men, including some of Merle's cowhands, held cigarettes and sipped at shot glasses every now and then.

"Well, about damn time they flub it up," Ben said grimly.

Red took off his hat and set it on the table. His hat brim had lost its shape many years ago. His hair was thin. It was almost gone around the crown and what was left reached down to his shoulders and looked greasy.

The trail had long since grown stale. This was the first hint the Grand Lake Gang was still out there. From his coat pocket, Ben pulled out a stack of cash money wrapped in brown paper sacking. He slid it across the table. Now he was part of it — part of that senseless world which killed people over money.

"I'll ride on out there, then," Red Creek said.

"Ride on out there," Ben echoed.

Red Creek *was* a drinker. He picked up his whiskey and raised it up as if making a toast. His red eyes focused on the wall behind the bar. Ben did not have to turn around to see what he was looking at. He knew what Red was looking at. Up behind Otto, next to the big mirror, was the big pickle jar containing the head of Will Wyllis.

Some people said it was rather macabre for a civilized town like Grand Lake to have a man's head in a jar, on display for all to see. In Ben's private opinion, he was glad it was there. It kept the memory of what happened alive. Otto's story became more polished each time he told it to someone, and it seemed every time it got a little shinier, too. Ben didn't care if the details got all flowered up or what the retellings sounded like on the street. It just meant the legend of Sheriff Emerson Greer stayed alive.

Ben wasn't going to forget. There was such a thing as *justice* in his mind. He aimed to get Emerson Greer justice. On one hand, that could mean posses and arrests and courthouses and all the legal loopholes that came with it. Or it could mean sending Red Creek Mincy out to finish it quickly, with certitude. Too much time had passed, in Ben's estimation, for judges and courthouses to have anything good to go on. Criminals got away with things at the bench after too much time passed. Memories could fog. Witnesses might disappear.

Will Wyllis looked out of his pickle jar. The formaldehyde was getting cloudy. There were some floaters in there. Red Creek finished his whiskey and left the saloon. Otto watched him go and came over to the table.

"What's the word?" Otto asked Ben.

"Justice."

Chapter 2
Leadville

It was clear in Julianna's mind: Casey was sour. Her husband's face was flat and he wasn't being conversational. Whatever was going on in his head was not making it out his mouth. He was just flat as could be.

"Casey, you better buck up."

They were crowded in and Casey hated being crowded in. The buzz of a thousand voices was eating right through his head. It had taken quite a bit of persuasion on Julianna's part to get him into town for this. Persuasion...meaning arguments. And then pleading. Finally she plugged the guilt angle and *that* got the horses in their traces.

Leadville was all decked out for the Colorado Midland. It was the first and only wide-gauge track being built in the mountains. It had made it as far as Buena Vista earlier in the year. Now the rails came straight into town.

Grandstands were built just for the day, and obviously the whole town was out to see the train roll in for the first time.

"Don't these people have claims to work?" Casey complained.

Vendors were out in great numbers. Julianna lost count of how many they passed, although it turned out to be a good thing. She was able to buy Casey's tolerance in the form of cooked meat on sticks.

"Any excuse for a party — that's Leadville," she said lightly. "This town just can't sit still."

Even though she was acting passé about it, Julianna was actually having fun. Leadville was fun. She liked it. If only Casey could enjoy the occasion. They didn't make it into town for social events very often. She turned to Casey, who was still sour.

"He's coming," Julianna told him in a firm voice. "*Buck up.*"

"You said that already."

"Well, buck up and I won't have to."

The sun disappeared. Heavy clouds rolled off the big peaks and were sailing right over the city. Casey knew what they were in for. Looking around, he knew most of these people were not ready for any kind of weather besides the summer sunshine. They were ready for a nice day and a reason to cheer. On cue with that thought, the crowd's chatter suddenly swelled up into a roar.

"Here she comes!" several folks shouted, pointing down the line. They could see the steam engine, just rounding a distant bluff.

"Gonna rain," Casey predicted.

"Just find a seat," Julianna said with a sweet smile. "Quit acting poopy."

The grandstands were pretty full already, but they managed to work their way up and find seats. They had a pretty plain view of the train tracks stretching off to the south. Coal smoke billowed up and seemed to mix with the dark sky. Julianna leaned into Casey as the wind suddenly whipped up. Thunder boomed, metallic and loud. The crowd cheered.

"What are they clapping at? Can't wait to get stormed on?" Casey asked her, and rolled his eyes. "These cuckoos."

"They're just having a good time with it. Do you need another frankfurter? The concession is right down there."

But neither one of them got up. The wind gusted strongly again and they shivered with it. The two of them leaned in closer, and Casey put his arms around Julianna. She smiled up at him, hoping his mood would improve. She worried though. LG was on board that train. The two of them hadn't seen each other since last April, the day the B-Cross scattered. Casey had gotten the letter from Til, but that was it. LG himself never wrote. Julianna knew this was going to be hard for her husband. He didn't talk much about it, and she knew he had mixed feelings.

It was close to twenty minutes of shivering before the inaugural Colorado Midland passenger train from Denver finally eased into Leadville. It blew its steam whistle several times and the crowd responded loudly, waving and yelling. From the windows, people leaned out from the cars to wave and cheer back.

Then the rain came down — heavily.

It came down hard just as the train settled to a stop at the depot. People began looking for whatever cover they could find. The grandstands thinned out quickly. Many people even huddled underneath the grandstand itself for shelter. Casey and Julianna stayed where they were for a little while watching passengers step off the train into the rain. Casey had brought his slicker, of course. He was never caught off guard when it came to the weather. He opened it up and held it over both of them, as cold water sprayed down and splattered off the benches.

"Let's head on down," Julianna told him, speaking loudly over the rain.

She held onto Casey's arm as they worked down the slick stairs. The ground had turned to mud. It was pretty easy to get to the platform now since most of Leadville was bunched up under eaves and awnings, and anywhere else they could find.

"There he is," Casey said and pointed.

LG had his own slicker on, and he stood tall in the rain — his big hat kept his head dry. When he saw Casey, he grinned his old LG smile. Casey found it hard not to smile back. Casey had almost forgot about that. Wherever LG went, whoever he met, people were drawn in by that good ol' boy charisma.

"Hey pard!" LG shouted. "Hoo hoo! Can you believe this luck? Caprice of the skies. What a gully washer! Just like old times."

LG walked right up to Casey and grabbed his hand. In the middle of the handshake, LG locked eyes on Julianna. He lifted his hat just high enough to tip it politely. Rainwater poured onto the ground.

"Now, *shoo-ee*, what in the world?" LG said. His grin got even wider. "Anymore of these? Or is this one freed up?"

"No, she is not freed up," Julianna replied just as playfully. "You have *got* to be LG Pendleton. I'm Julianna Pruitt."

"Keepin' company with this fella?" LG asked her, pointing at Casey. "Why, he's ugly as a mud fence and you're purty as a cottonwood in spring."

"Aw, he's not so bad," Julianna said with a laugh. She tugged at her husband's sleeve. "When he smiles, he dappers up."

"Course I'm just jawing...this pal of mine has been over the trail," LG told her in earnest. "Greatest fella I ever knew — and everyone that ever rode with him knows it. So I guess I could see why. Makes for a fine pairing."

LG glanced around at the citizens of Leadville, huddled and hiding from the rain. The grandstands were completely empty now. Many people were in the depot office waiting it out. The rain was still pounding the ground and LG, Julianna and Casey could not see much beyond where they stood. The town itself was hidden in the downpour.

"Quite the frolic," LG noted.

Chapter 3

Soapy Smith stood motionless in the narrow doorway. He watched the rain pounding down on the platform. He scratched his black beard. It felt like he was standing behind a waterfall. The platform was made of thick pinewood planks and the rain drummed along its topside. It made a beautiful hollow sound.

Soapy liked rain.

When his grandfather took him to the Holiness camp meetings, back when Soapy was just a youngster, there had been a lot of hymn-singing and hand-raising. Sometimes, an evangelist would get up on a tree stump and holler about sin. The thing that stuck with Soapy was how water washed sins away. People got dunked under water and then God did not hold their transgressions against them anymore. Being a man of sin, Soapy liked to think that rain was God's heavenly water. It was His clemency being poured out from Heaven. So he liked it when it rained. It rained in Denver every afternoon in the summertime. But even with rain every afternoon, Soapy thought it might be smart to move somewhere it rained a lot more frequently, just in case he got strung up or shot someday. The hot fires of damnation might not be such a difficulty if he happened to die on a rainy day.

Soapy Smith seated his fedora nice and tight on his head and stepped out into the elements. The rain shook the brim pretty good, but it was a sturdy design. Rainwater immediately began rolling off, onto his shoulders and back. He was also wearing a long black overcoat. Soapy knew he would be soaked before he took more than a few steps. Big Ed better be out there and he better be quick.

Big Ed Burns *was* out there. And he was quick. Hustling through the cold rain, Big Ed scurried right up to Soapy.

"Ho there, Soapy," Big Ed said and pulled out a newspaper from inside his jacket.

Unfolding it partway, he tried to hold the newspaper over Soapy's head like an umbrella. Big Ed was big, so he didn't have any trouble with the gesture. But the rain was coming down so hard, the paper immediately sogged through. Before he had escorted Soapy Smith the twenty steps it took to get inside the depot office, the newspaper was pulp.

As soon as they were inside, Soapy Smith pushed Big Ed off.

"Your breath reeks of spirits. It's repulsive."

Big Ed blinked his black beady eyes, trying to gauge Soapy Smith's mood.

"Yeah?" he asked and cupped his hand over his mouth.

It was true Big Ed enjoyed spirits. In fact, he had taken several nips in the AM to start his day. Perhaps his breath — in the close quarters of a makeshift newspaper umbrella — was offensive to Soapy. Big Ed was never quite sure about Denver's biggest crime boss. Sometimes he could act out quite violently. At other times, even in similar circumstances, he might be peaceful as a dove. He hoped the man was in a peaceful mood.

Big Ed Burns reached out and awkwardly plucked a soggy blob of newspaper off Soapy's shoulder. The black overcoat was very damp. Bits of pulpy newspaper dotted his shoulders and had collected on his fedora.

Soapy looked down and noticed all the gooey bits.

"This is my Sunday coat."

"It's not Sunday," Big Ed replied and then took a quick step back in case it was the wrong thing to say. But Soapy seemed fine. He even smiled softly, as if he was remembering something.

"No Ed, it is not. It is not Sunday."

Uncertainty crept into Big Ed's mind once again. Better to try and change the topic.

"What do you want me to do about the banker? And his new establishment?" he asked in a hushed fashion. Of course, now Big Ed felt leery about his breath odor, and was not quite sure how to strike a good balance between volume and proximity.

Other train passengers were standing all around them in the building, waiting for the rain to slow down. Big Ed glanced around furtively. Soapy watched him — he found Big Ed's attempt at discretion mildly amusing. No one was paying attention to them, and Soapy didn't care if they were. Good fortune was his. He could feel it in the rain.

"We'll have to spill his blood. There is no forgiveness of sin without the spilling of blood. That's in Leviticus."

Big Ed stood up a little straighter, surprised at Soapy's uninhibited reply. They were in public, after all. There were people two feet away, chatting about the weather!

Ed was a big man. Soapy always thought he looked like an elephant: a big man with small dark eyes — roundish, not from lard but power. The man's ears were even too big for his lumpy pink head. Soapy smiled again. Ed's comedic body shape and his violent persuasion were a paradox of sorts. Perhaps that's what made him one of Soapy's favorites. Soapy liked paradoxes.

"The boys will want to see you," Big Ed said a little bolder, since he saw that Soapy was being bold. "And Haw knows you were headin' to Leadville at some point, he just don't know the when. I thought we could make it a surprise visit."

"Sure, sure. Let's make a nice surprise out of it," Soapy agreed.

Chapter 4

"Why, hello there Prescott," Horace Tabor said with aplomb.

Sloan blew across the surface of the small saucer, and stole a quick glance up as he did. He had just poured coffee from his cup into the saucer when Haw approached him. It was a habit that Sloan picked up living in Ward. The cowboys that came through used to stop in the Halfway House for meals. They all seemed to share the same habit of pouring their coffee from the cup into the saucer. Then they would blow on it, sipping directly from the saucer. He found it curious the first few times he witnessed the ritual.

Being a banker and a businessman, a transplant from the East, the cowboys of the frontier caught Prescott Sloan's attention. Maybe it was the romanticism of living in the West. The Indians were no longer roaming like they used to. Geronimo and his Apaches had been caught the year before and were down in Alabama now. Even though Sloan despised the filth associated with horsemanship, he also admired the working cowboy. They knew who they were. They were proud of it. There was a dignity in most of them, directly related to their lifestyle and the earth. He liked that. So he started pouring his own hot coffee into his saucer.

"What can I help with, Haw?"

"I have an invitation for you. To a private banquet at the Matchless Mine. Well, *in* the Matchless Mine."

Sloan daintily set his saucer down and looked up at Horace. He had heard about these things. The Silver King of Leadville was rumored to throw elaborate underground soirees, especially when some kind of major load had been discovered.

"I am intrigued," Sloan said and gestured at Tabor to seat himself.

"What's the occasion?" he continued. "Strike something new?"

"Now, I'm not telling anyone outside a few close acquaintances," Horace confided. He sat down across the table. "You know, I'm not even a prospector. When I first got to Leadville, I opened up a general store. Supplying all these dreamy miners... *that* was where the money was."

Sloan waved at the barkeep, held up his coffee cup and pointed to Tabor. The barkeep came right over with another hot cup for Horace.

"I remember these two fellas came into the store one day. Nothing special, just a couple boys with a small claim. So I grubstaked them. Some tools, food for a week. I had seventeen dollars invested in those two when it was all said and done...in exchange for a third of their profits."

"I dropped more than that on faro just last night," Sloan mentioned.

"That was the Little Pittsburg out on Fryer Hill. That little thing was putting out ten thousand dollars worth of ore. *Per day.*"

Tabor picked up his coffee and took a small sip.

"Then I sold out for a million," he said, eyes twinkling. "Promptly after that, it quit producing. I got out just in time. Good Fortune was on my side."

"Sounds like I need to grubstake some miners."

"Never hurts to take a gamble on someone else's hard labor. Now truth be told, most of these folks come here starry-eyed and don't find anything to squawk about. Seen it a thousand times over."

"It's all a gamble," Sloan pontificated quaintly. "So much of life is."

Horace studied him. He wondered how good Sloan was at reading people. Now, Horace considered himself to have a well-developed poker face. And he played exclusively with high rollers, both in cards and in business dealings. But Horace was particularly nervous this day, walking into the Pastime Saloon, right inside the hornet's nest, and setting out the bait. Horace felt if he just kept talking, he could get it done and get out the door.

What kind of fool would be so brazen as to steal a hefty stake in one of the most talked about mines — from Soapy Smith! — and stick around town? Was the man so confident? Or did he have some kind of reputation in Ward that hadn't made it into Leadville yet? Maybe a criminal infrastructure or a gang of his own? If so, Horace Tabor hadn't seen anything yet. He had been paying attention, too...there wasn't even any kind of security around the man, which was unusual for someone playing such a high stakes game.

Perhaps the man was just a lucky fool, and thought he had successfully pulled one over on Denver's most notorious confidence man and gangster. But even a fool should be thinking of repercussions, no matter the luck up till the present hour. The man moved to Leadville! He had been there all summer! Opened a saloon! He should have gone to the Argentine. Or some far off corner in Europe and changed his damn name.

"Shaft Number Six. I thought it was done producing, played out," Horace continued. "But my boys took one last chance. Another twenty-five feet down and wouldn't you know? One more rich mineral deposit...the nature of which I shall not reveal. Until the banquet! Tell me you'll come."

"Of course. Name the time and day, I'll be there."

Horace stood and drained his coffee cup in a couple big swallows. It was barely lukewarm. He wasn't sure why Sloan was pouring it delicately into a saucer and blowing on it. The man had his quirks.

"Saturday. Come out to the Number Six at sundown. Ride the bucket down. It'll be a hoot."

Sloan got up and they shook hands. He gave Haw the relaxed, condescending smile of a social aristocrat. Sloan was almost giddy, but he kept it bottled up and played it cool. In just a few short months, here he was, rubbing elbows with the top players of Leadville. He ran his own saloon. He was part owner of the Matchless Mine. This really was the Cloud City. He felt like he was in the clouds.

Chapter 5

Garo
South Park

When the morning sun came over the hills, the dew lit up like it was made of diamonds. The air was cool and fresh and grasshoppers popped away from Bit Ear as he plowed through the meadow.

Til enjoyed mail runs to Garo, mainly because he needed time on his own. Every now and then he could feel it building — he needed to get out and calm his spirit back down. The business of ranching, even the bustle around the house, took a subtle toll. He needed to get out on a horse and just ride.

Up ahead, the sun was burning through the mist and he could finally differentiate the small town of Garo from the dark mass of 39-Mile Mountain off in the distance behind it. Garo was only an hour's ride south. There was nothing in between but the grass and the hills. It was convenient to have Garo so close. Chubb Newitt ran the general store and had a good selection of supplies. It was also the post office. The store had been built next to the train depot, right on the platform. Newitt's store was the hub of this little town and all the local ranchers stopped in frequently.

Leaving Bit Ear at the hitching post, Til climbed up the stairs. He was not the only one on the platform, at least a half dozen people were milling about. Til knew them all by name — they all lived in or near Garo. It was seven o'clock on the nose. Mrs. Dittmore, the station agent, was just opening up the depot. She propped the door open and began sweeping.

"Morning, Mrs. Dittmore," Til said and tipped his hat.

Ignoring him, Mrs. Dittmore seemed too intent on her sweeping to be bothered with pleasantries. Til passed on by and headed inside Newitt's store.

"Howdy, Til," Chubb said pleasantly. "Train'll be by soon. Expecting visitors?"

"Naw, just the mail."

The mail came on the train, which arrived daily by 8 AM and then passed back through later in the afternoon. Til was anticipating a letter from his partner on the Wyoming range, Jake Barlow. With the Great Die-Up, the cattle business was still in a mess of uncertainty. Til considered selling his half of the Wyoming plot to Jake, if Jake was interested. After all, it had mainly served

Til as the winter pasture for the B-Cross cattle. Those days were over. Til could use the funds to expand his operation at Hay Ranch.

"And how's Mrs. Blancett?" Chubb asked him.

"Adjusting to the country life wonderfully."

With a smile, Chubb waved Til over to the counter. He opened up one of the glass candy jars and scooped several cherry candies into a brown paper sack.

"That's for your boy, Til. Tell him it's a welcome-to-Colorado gift."

"Many thanks, Chubb, I'll pass that along. He'll right thank you next time he's in town."

"School house opens up this month. My boy Billy is his age, and I expect they'll get along fairly well."

"I expect they will."

Outside a steam whistle echoed. The train was bearing down on Garo.

"I'm gonna need some sugar, cinnamon and flour. Not more than I can fit in a saddle bag."

The whistle blew a second time and the sound of the locomotive pulling in was loud. The engine blasts were rhythmic, hissing. Til walked to the doorway to watch it come in. More people had gathered on the platform, all waiting on the train. It was a small train, with only a couple passenger cars and a few storage cars behind those. The passenger cars were almost full. Mrs. Dittmore, the station agent, came out and stood there watching — wearing a sizable frown.

"Garo Station!" the conductor called from inside the train.

The windows were all down. Til could see people's faces looking out on the small town. He knew most of them were headed for the big cities: Fairplay, Alma, Buena Vista, Leadville. Garo was certainly not one of those towns, not by a long shot. The train eased to a stop and steam blasted out like a dragon's sigh. That's what Walker would say, Til thought, and broke into a fond grin. His boy had started turning everything into tales about knights and dragons. Cowboys were knights, trains were dragons. He wondered what the cherry candy would become once he got it home.

"Tickets, please."

The conductor stepped out into the sunshine. A couple folks were boarding but the rest were just there, like Til, waiting on the mail. A postal rep stepped off the train with a mail bag, and they trailed after him like the pied piper. Til joined the troupe, which led straight into Chubb Newitt's General Store and Post Office.

Outside, Mrs. Dittmore's pitchy voice suddenly rose an octave.

"Ma'am, that's what is meant by *produce*," the conductor was saying, rather defensively.

"Lettuce n' cabbage! Lettuce n' cabbage!" Mrs. Dittmore shouted, peculiarly.

The conductor, whose name was Benj, was starting to look confused and stared at her ruefully. Til and the others stepped right back out to see why Mrs. Dittmore was so excitable at 8 AM. There was something in the lady's voice that was unusual. Everyone knew she was a widower. Her husband died nearly ten years ago, and the elderly woman had been living alone ever since. Chubb Newitt himself checked in on her throughout each winter, bringing her supplies. She was typically a reserved woman, though brusque more often than not.

"Morse code! Lettuce n' cabbage! Morse code, lettuce n' cabbage!" said Mrs. Dittmore.

Benj the conductor glanced around, unsure what was happening. He was used to Mrs. Dittmore dressing him down with insults about telegram contents and freight reports. However, her response today was more bizarre than irritating.

"Lettuce an' cabbage!" she said one last time for emphasis and poked him in the sternum.

Then Mrs. Dittmore retrieved a well-oiled revolver from the folds of her skirt.

"Oh, Lordy, no!" Benj cried out, and jumped off the platform into the grass.

Til, along with the townspeople of Garo, were so startled at this turn of events that no one reacted. Not Til, nor Chubb Newitt or Frank Stevens, or EP Arthur or his oldest son Will — they were all glued to the platform like a nativity scene. It was very unusual to see Mrs. Dittmore screaming about lettuce and cabbage, and even more unusual to see her retrieve a revolver from her skirt.

The elderly widower pressed the gun firmly against her cheek and pulled the trigger. The gun went off, and she collapsed immediately.

Off in the grass, Benj the conductor continued to run evasively. He thought for sure Mrs. Dittmore was shooting in his direction. The Garo Station stop was his least favorite of the day. He preferred the drunken gamblers and sweaty swindlers of Fairplay to the morose glares of Mrs. Dittmore at Garo Station. He knew she despised him. She received his daily telegrams from Denver with unrelenting criticism as to their specificity. But the constraints of telegraphy were such that he *had* to be categorical, rather than itemized. And that was standard practice! Lettuce and cabbage could be conveyed under the term "produce." It was neither necessary nor helpful to delineate any further than that — but Mrs. Dittmore was not very cooperative when it came to telegrams *or* delineation.

Chubb stepped over to check on the woman. He knelt over her and studied the wound.

"Yep, she's gone."

"Fancy that...she was mad as a March hare," Mr. Arthur said, who was British. "I did not expect to see that."

"Cantankerous woman," stated Frank Stevens flatly. "Don't surprise me none, though. She was getting plain distracted there towards the end."

He shook his head sadly, but knowingly.

"Sick as a horse," Frank added, tapping his temple. "In the head."

Til took his hat off and held it over his chest. The rest of the men followed his lead and did the same. There were no other women on the platform, it was just the men that morning. The sun rose steadily in the sky and the summer heat was starting to set in for the day.

Benj the conductor, who had run up and over the nearest grassy slope, slowly made his way back.

"Is she dead?" he asked, still concerned that he was the intended target.

"Chubb, I hate to be untimely," Frank Stevens asked. "But can I collect my mail?"

Chubb shrugged. He walked back inside his store with Frank Stevens right behind him. Til glanced at Mr. Arthur, his closest neighbor in the valley. The older Englishman seemed unfazed. Mr. Arthur nodded thoughtfully.

"Bloody crazy."

"Both," Til replied.

Chapter 6

Hay Ranch

Rufe and Steve were quite interested to hear that Mrs. Dittmore shot herself dead on the Garo Station platform. After a quiet summer of bunkhouse construction, windmill building, digging fence post holes and cutting hay — any news caught their attention.

"She did *what?*" Rufe asked.

"Done herself in."

"What kind of gun did she use?" Steve asked Til.

"Just a Colt, I think."

Caring housewife and mother that she was, Laura immediately shooed young Walker out the front door. He was not interested in hearing about Mrs. Dittmore's demise once Til produced the cherry candies. On a normal day, Laura would have confiscated the cherry candies and placed them in a jar for measured dispersal. But today was not a normal day. She just handed the small brown paper sack to Walker and pointed him out the door.

"Jewels for the court of King Arthur!" Walker shouted with ostentation. He marched outside, leaving the door wide open. But no one moved to close it.

"Til, why in the world would Mrs. Dittmore do such a thing?" Laura asked.

She was horrified to hear what happened.

"We done fed already, Til," Steve said in a hopeful tone. "Mind if we cut out? Just down to Steven's saloon, catch up on the latest news about all this."

"We done fed," Rufe reminded him.

Til waved his hand at them. The McGonkin brothers flew outside and made straight for the corrals.

"I can't believe she just *shot* herself," Laura said quietly and placed her hand over her mouth.

"It was just one of them things," Til explained. "Happens. Now and then."

"Not in Muscatine, Iowa!"

Laura looked at Til with fresh eyes.

"Is this what the frontier is like? Women shooting themselves in public with Colt six-guns? In broad daylight? On a train platform full of people waiting for their mail?"

Til shrugged.

"Now that I think about it — it wasn't a Colt. It was a Smith & Wesson."

Laura began pacing the room, clearly upset and getting more so. Til watched her with growing apprehension.

"Surprised that old thing went off at all."

His quiet morning ride was over. Part of him considered following the boys down to Steven's. But he knew as soon it crossed his mind that riding off would not sit well with Laura. He decided not to mention it.

"Why aren't you more upset about this?" she asked incredulously. "I hope I never get to the point where I want to point a gun at myself!"

"You won't, honey."

"Things can get pretty lonely out here Til. It's just me and Walker most of the day. You go out to work with the hands, and I don't see you until dinner. Emmanuel spends half his day chopping firewood and the other half drying antelope meat. And beyond that, I haven't seen another lady since I unpacked. It's too quiet sometimes."

"I know. I know it is."

To the contrary, Til did not actually think it was too quiet. In fact, in his opinion, it was a fairly boisterous ranch. Between the jabbery McGonkins and Emmanuel's trail songs and Walker's kid habits — it was a plumb full house.

Laura put her hand on her hips and gave her husband a firm look. Til waited, not sure what was coming.

"I need something, Til. To keep my mind busy."

He sat down at the kitchen table. The sky was still blue outside. It wasn't even dinner time yet.

"Alright, then," Til said.

Laura stared at him darkly, her thoughts racing about. Til knew she had made a nice jar of fresh lemonade. The sugar he bought in Garo was sitting on the table right in front of him. He had gotten that far with his purchases — before the conversation derailed. He glanced past her towards the kitchen. What if he just ducked in there for a moment and brought the lemonade jar out here? He could stir in the sugar while she talked.

"The school house," she mentioned. "Maybe they need a new teacher there."

Til almost said it, but he didn't: Garo needed a new station agent.

"That may be. We can ask on it."

Laura was still wrestling over why. She didn't know Mrs. Dittmore. In fact, she'd never even met the woman before. Laura had only been to Garo once since moving to Hay Ranch. And that was a grocery run. Perhaps she had seen Mrs. Dittmore that day, but Laura did not remember if she had. She couldn't put a face with the name.

It would be nice to have other women to talk to. Being around all these males was a little tiresome for her. The conversations tended to repeat themselves and revolve around the same topics: horses, weather and hay prices.

Being a school teacher would be a good fit. She could continue to watch over Walker, and have something to fill her time, as well. She was not sure how well the boy would do, cooped up in a schoolhouse for lessons. He was an active boy. He had trouble sitting still through a meal.

Laura decided that yes, she *would* look into the Garo schoolhouse. Even if they only needed an assistant, it would be a welcome distraction. It would give her a chance to meet the other children's mothers, too. It would be wonderful to make some friends of her own. The ranch life had become rather lonesome. Perhaps that was Mrs. Dittmore's problem — being lonesome. Living alone, working out of a train depot, taking telegrams and watching for cinder fires as the trains went by...Laura could guess that had *not* been a good job for a bereaved widower.

She looked at Til, who sat there staring at the bag of sugar.

"Go get the lemonade, Til."

Til slid from his chair and went into the kitchen.

Chapter 7
Garo

Being that his clothes were in such a state of disarray, Bill circled the small town of Garo hoping it was someone's laundry day. He was in luck. Several clotheslines were strung about. A new shirt was the main thing that interested him — given the fact he had just been shot. He found one and tried it on. Green plaid was not a color he would normally wear but it would do.

Bill's feet were still sore from walking out of the Arkansas River valley on foot, but his main problem was a new hole below his left clavicle. Stealing a horse in Guffey could not have been easier. However, riding away from Guffey proved to be more difficult. If the shooter had been a bit more spritely in his response time, Bill might have taken a worse hit.

In addition to this, the horse he stole was not the best pick for an effective getaway. It was an old gelding with a swayback and lost its wind after less than a mile. It was the only horse he saw in Guffey, so he took it. Bill continued to ride the poor beast for the better part of a day before getting off.

He had been worried the shooter might chase him down, but no one ever appeared on his backtrail. Maybe the old gelding was not worth the recovery effort. The old horse had such an unpleasant trot — if it was Bill's horse that was stolen, he would have thanked the man who did it.

If there had been a saddle, Bill might have been happier with the situation. He had looked but didn't find one...not even in the run-down barn by the corral. In fact, he did not find any tack whatsoever. Bill had to fashion a halter from a length of rope he found where the corral gate should have been. Bill started thinking about it. Perhaps the swayback's owner was not giving chase because he couldn't. Perhaps he was too poor to own a second horse — or even a saddle. Obviously, the man was too poor to afford a proper corral gate.

Bill began to worry about him. Maybe the fellow was too old, or maybe a cripple, which would explain the slow response time and poor aim. Maybe the swayback was the only livestock the man owned. Bill decided he would let the horse wander home on its own, once he reached the next town. So he did. He let it go once he reached Garo. It was strange...Bill never had much of a conscience before. He wasn't sure where these thoughts were coming from.

Bill's newfound conscience did not hold him back from peering in through windows. He checked all twelve homes in town. It did not take long to find an unlatched door and a flour tin with coins buried in the flour. People always tended to choose the same hiding places for their valuables. It was enough to buy a train ticket, head back to Grand Lake, dig out the saddle bags buried on the Divide, and move on.

Bill could barely believe the hundred thousand in cash was gone. Some angry rancher was a rich man now.

The fear of being shot down like Granger and Vincent was gone. And the shot he took in Guffey had passed all the way through his shoulder, so he wasn't too worried about dying. The first creek he came to, Bill packed it with mud. It would work until he could get some proper doctoring. Distance was the most important thing at this point.

The sun was starting to arc down to the west. The hottest part of the day was over and he hoped it would cool off soon.

Bill stepped over the train rails and climbed the platform stairs, but discovered the little depot shack was empty. He looked around. There was a general store — perhaps the station agent was in there. The door was open and Bill walked right in.

"It was unexpected, that's all I can really say," Chubb Newitt was saying to Steve and Rufe McGonkin, who stood at the counter.

Rufe was eyeing the candy jars.

"It was *not* unexpected," Frank Stevens told them. "Tumbleweeds are best left to themselves. And she was a-tumblin'."

"How much are them cherry ones?" Rufe asked Chubb. Ever since Til gave Walker that brown paper sack full of cherry hard candies, Rufe had been anxious to purchase some for himself. The ride down had been a long hour of contemplating those cherry candies.

"Your station agent here?" Bill asked, from the doorway. "I need to buy a ticket."

"Nope, she's dead as a doornail," Chubb replied. "Talk to the conductor. Train be through in half an hour."

"In hard times some folks grin and bear it," Frank continued, turning to Steve. "Others shoot themself's. Mrs. Dittmore was the shoot themself type. Stuff like that tends to well up over quite a spell, I'd say. And that's what happened. Got the habit of dwelling on unhappy thoughts. The straw that broke the camel's back... was vegetables."

"Fudge, Frank," Chubb cautioned. "I been out to see old missus Dittmore every now and again, especially in the snows. I don't think it's wise to speculate about her mental disposition."

"Naw, it's purty clear she husked her brains out over vegetables."

Bill turned and headed back outside. His nerves were jumping. He recognized those two cowpunchers! Lem had shot one of them in the shoulder. When was that? Just a few months ago? Bill didn't have a gun. He didn't have much of anything at the moment. And he was wounded. In fact, he was wounded in the same place: the shoulder.

He didn't think the punchers recognized him. They were too busy chatting. He hoped. Either way, it was best to stay out of sight until that train rolled in.

Bill hustled back down the platform steps and out into the grass. There wasn't much to Garo. Not many places to wait for half an hour. Bill swallowed nervously. If those cowpunchers were here, what about the rest of their crew? They could all be in Garo! What if he bumped into another one? Or what if the shirt he was wearing belonged to them? Or any of the locals loafing around the platform? He didn't want to run into the man who owned it.

There was a saloon down the way, Steven's Saloon, but Bill decided against going inside. Since it was the only saloon in town, it would be the one place everyone would go to congregate. Bill saw that the schoolhouse was empty. He walked around back and sat in the shade, leaning against the wall. He checked his watch. A half hour wasn't too long to sit in the grass and wait.

Bill hoped he could get on the train without any hassle.

The minutes dragged by, but no one came around. When the train finally chugged into the station at four o'clock, Bill waited until it was fully parked before he went over. He glanced at the general store as he crested the stairs. The door was propped open and he could hear the cowpunchers were still inside, talking.

"Ticket, please," the conductor asked him, stepping off the train.

"I need to purchase one."

Then Chubb Newitt and Frank Stevens came out of the store and walked over.

"Well, Monroe. Got to do your own ticket work now," Frank told the conductor.

"Heard about that," Monroe replied, and not unhappily. "Benj wired the rail office from Fairplay, ever'body knows."

"Scared Benj so bad," Frank recounted, "he ran all the way to Guffey before he got around to stopping."

"Benj has a big pot belly," Monroe said thoughtfully. "I'm sure the exercise did him some good."

Chubb noticed Bill and bobbed his head proudly.

"Told you...half an hour. Trains roll in here on time."

Bill took out his pocketwatch and opened it.

"You are right. It has been a half hour on the nose."

Frank looked down at the watch in Bill's hand.

"That is one fine timepiece. I been needing to order one myself, Chubb. That one there looks like a special-order timepiece. Montgomery Ward?"

"Sure was," Bill said. Of course, he didn't know who bought it or where it came from — beyond the vest pocket of the stage driver he killed.

"Let me look at that," Frank said bluntly, holding out his hand.

Bill raised his eyebrows but handed it to him. If he wasn't so determined to get on the train unnoticed, Bill might have given this blunt man a fist to the face. He didn't like intrusive people. And he did not like to pass around his personal objects. Such was the price of blending in.

Steve and Rufe stepped out of the store, not ten paces away. Bill dropped his eyes down to the watch in Frank's hand — he felt a sudden urgency to board that train.

"Absence from those we love is self from self," Frank read aloud. "That is pure poetry. Hell, I don't even know what that means. John Frederick Hughes, your wife must actually care for you. How 'bout that, Chubb? Wife buy you a fancy pocketwatch yet?"

"Well, no," Chubb admitted sheepishly.

Bill reached out and snatched the pocketwatch out of Frank's hand, turned abruptly and got on the train without another word.

"Scared him off," Frank said to Chubb.

"Cuz you're nosey, Frank."

Chapter 8
Ward
The Halfway House

"Was meant for my sister. Family heirloom!" Hugh Hughes said and shook his head bitterly. "Doggone thieves made off with it!"

"Describe it."

Red Creek took another bite of beefsteak. Hugh's face got flushed the more he talked about what happened.

"Silver, with a real nice chain — ties to a button. Inscribed, got my father's name. It says: *John Frederick Hughes, from Helena your loving wife: Absence from those we love is self from self."*

The beefsteak was tough. It was probably left over from the dinner hour, unsold and sitting in a frying pan. And it was well into the afternoon, in between the meal hours. He shouldn't be too surprised. Red Creek submerged his next bite in the gravy and let it soak. From his coat, he took out a notebook and wrote it all down word for word.

"That's Shakespeare," Hugh said, proudly tapping his finger on the tabletop.

Red Creek forked the beefsteak and decided it needed more time in the gravy.

"My pap passed on in April," Hugh continued thoughtfully. "Funeral was down in Boulder and that pocketwatch was supposed to get to my sister. Poor girl had her heart broke when the old man died. Absolutely broke. Pap had gave it to me, hell I'm the eldest, but I knowed it meant more to Lynn. Never made it. The stage was robbed!"

Hugh's face became flushed again as he spoke.

Giving up on the beefsteak, Red Creek took one last whiskey shot and got to his feet. He glanced across the room at the big plate glass windows. The pine and fir were deep green and covered all the hillsides as far as he could see.

"If it means anything...couple of 'em are dead now."

"You find that watch, it'll mean something."

Adjusting his hat, Red placidly looked him in the eye. The barkeeper was angry, he could understand that. People got attached to things. Red used to be attached to things. Not anymore. It had been many years since he felt sentimental about anything or anyone. His sense of what normal life was had died in the War.

"See what I can see."

Red went out into the fresh air and took off his overcoat. It was cooler inside the eatery than it was outside in the sun. His horse was down in the corral, so Red set off for the tack room where his saddle was.

Ward was a hectic little mining town, especially in the midstride of summer. The snow was all gone and the ground was soft enough to dig at with a pick-axe or shovel. Everywhere he looked Red saw miners scurrying around...from the placers to the assayer, from the smelter to the bank, from the saloons to the gambling halls.

Getting to Cañon City, which was quite a long distance from Ward, would require riding down Lefthand Canyon to get out on the plains. The last time Red Creek went through there was the day the posse called it quits.

His appaloosa was rested from an afternoon in the corral and ready for the trail again. Even though it was mid-afternoon, Red started down the stage road. He rode through the night. It was almost dawn when he left the foothills behind and rode into Boulder.

By the time the sun came up, Red was loading his horse onto a freight car and getting his ticket punched. Except for the description of the pocketwatch, the trail was cold in Ward. But he knew it got warm again near Cañon. The two dead men found on the trail to Poncha Springs were part of the gang he was after — one matched the description of the false newspaperman "Judas Furlong."

The train was the best way to eat up those miles.

Chapter 9

XIT Ranch
Yellow Houses Division
Headquarters

"A hunnert an' fifty thousand head. Hereford, Shorthorn, Angus. Three million acres and a boat-load of fence. A gall-damn finishing ranch in Mon-damn-tana and I've got Barbecue Campbell sittin' a horse outside *my* door looking for the OK Corral."

AL Matlock was in a fit of outrage. He always thought of himself as unflappable. But this was too much. After all he had done to clean up the XIT, it had come to this.

"The biggest cow operation in the nation itself — and a bunch of deviants are here to hamstring it."

AG Boyce was prying back one of the thin curtains with his fingertip. He was calmly watching the riders outside to see what they would do. Boyce had been through the War beginning to end and recognized that old gut-feeling of chaos swelling up. He spoke evenly, without turning around.

"There's ten of them. Plus Campbell."

"What about those peckers Bill Ney and Arizona John?"

"Yep, they're out there."

In the archway leading to the kitchen, George Findlay — the quiet young Scotsman with the unsettling baritone voice — leaned calmly against the wall and lit a cigarette.

"Richard King would roll over in his grave if he saw what was going on here today," Matlock ranted and waved his arms angrily. "*He* never had any mutinous events transpire down his way! No sir, he got blessed with a faithful friendly town to do his cow work. Respect. Honor. Not like the Xmas variety I got saddled with."

He glared across the room. Through the thin cotton curtains, he could make out the hazy shapes of horse riders lined up, sitting out there…waiting.

"Skunks!" he shouted. "Got the numbers on us? Well, bully for you!"

Matlock heard the click of a firearm and turned to see George Findlay checking over his gun's action. Matlock shifted his eyes over to Boyce — the man still carried no gun, which was a foolish disposition in Matlock's opinion. He pulled a Colt .45 from his own belt and held it out.

"How about a six-iron, Boyce?"

Turning from the window, Boyce waved him off.

"We'll see how this pans out."

"Principles don't stop lead. Go in heeled, man."

Boyce ignored him and walked casually past Findlay into the kitchen. It was early, the sun was barely up and the house was dim. The woodstove was still putting out some warmth. Boyce got a tin cup from the cupboard. Taking the percolator off the stove, he poured himself some hot black coffee.

"Cup, George?" he asked.

Findlay merely nodded.

Striding away fiercely, Matlock left them to their coffee and went into the sun room. Davis was sitting on a low couch. His shirt hung open and Matlock could see bandages had been wrapped clear around his upper body. Davis was busy feeding shells into a shotgun. He glanced up at Matlock with a sparkle in his eyes.

"Oh-ho-ho! I ain't a-nappin'!"

"Fools are lined up like ducks in a pond. You can take half of them with that scattergun by yourself."

Davis grunted and got to his feet unsteadily. His back hurt terribly but he was determined to stand and fight with his bosses. Like any loyal cowman, Davis believed in riding for the brand — besides which, Campbell and his boys were clearly bad eggs. Davis could not stand for such epic disloyalty, even with stab wounds. Not when he could step up and do something about it.

"Yearwood's out in Black Water with the whole damn outfit," Matlock noted sourly.

Davis's back was sore. The stabs he had suffered were shallow but left him feeling out of sorts. As luck would have it, Lee was off with the crew in Black Water, too. It was just the four of them at the ranch house headquarters. Even Rollin Larrabee the bookkeeper was not present. The day before, Rollin had asked one of the freighters for a ride in to Tascosa. Davis almost went with him. It was tempting to visit town for some kind of distraction but whenever he moved or twisted, the wounds burned like fire. He could guess what a jostly wagon ride would feel like.

"If I had suspected Campbell of commencing a *coup d'etat* we would have stocked this house with guns and trustworthy men to operate them," Matlock told him.

"I expect so."

"Well, this is Boyce's show now. I never wanted to head this thing up. Let's go see what he wants to do."

Together, they went back into the great room. Boyce looked Davis over, assessing his condition and abilities. He took one last sip of coffee and set the cup on the table.

"It's time to see to these aggravators."

Boyce went to the front door and opened it wide, stepping out into the morning air.

Matlock came out right behind him, followed by Findlay and Davis.

Boyce went on down the stairs while the other three fanned out along the porch — facing down Barbeque Campbell and his ten gunmen. Barbeque Campbell was in the middle of the line, five men to each side. He slouched in the saddle and wore a snide complexion.

"Looky here, fellers. The bruisers finally come out to play. I don't like to be kept waiting."

AG Boyce stepped directly in front of Campbell's horse, arms crossed. Matlock rested his palm on the grip of his .45. Findlay stood quietly, while Davis took several slow steps further down the porch.

"What in God's name are you up to, Campbell?" said Boyce. "I told you to ride out."

Campbell saw Boyce was not armed, so he trained his attention on Matlock.

"Here to end your administration, Matlock. Don't need a damned *lawyer* telling seasoned cowmen how to run cattle," Campbell called. "I'm still range boss to these boys."

"You ain't range boss to anyone now," Matlock replied sharply.

"He is too range boss!" Arizona Johnny said, lamely.

Matlock looked over at Billy Ney who wore his classic condescending leer. Matlock knew that look. He hated that look.

"Should've let them hang you back in Vernon, you skunk."

"Prob'ly," Billy replied.

"Got the bulge on y'all," Arizona Johnny said, bristling. "Would think you might take more kindly with your words. What with the numbers on our side. Make 'em dig their own graves, Cue!"

"Ride out now and we won't cut you down," Matlock told them.

Laughter rippled up and down the line. Barbeque Campbell made a show of rubbing his eyes as if to clear the sleep out.

"Wake up, Matlock! I *knowed* we snuck up on you right early, but come now! Crawl outta your bedroll. Open your eyes. Fireworks are about to pop and you should be awake for the show."

Boyce stood still, watching the riders laugh at them. They had the advantage and they knew it: eleven to four. Campbell looked like the cat that ate the canary.

"Know what I figure? This whole outfit is mine...you and Boyce ain't got no play here. You been meddling and I seen enough!"

Leaning his arms across the saddle horn, Campbell's eyes narrowed.

"You're a damn meddler, Matlock. And I don't kin to no damn meddlers."

He smirked again.

"And no gotch-eared Colonel's," he added, and spat at Boyce who was standing in spitting range. It splatted onto Boyce's vest. All ten gunmen broke into laughter and Campbell smile devilishly.

That was enough for Colonel AG Boyce. His face went dark and he took three quick steps towards Campbell's horse, reached up and pulled him directly out of the saddle. Campbell was a large heavy man, but Boyce had a lot of sinewy strength and Campbell came off like he was made of straw.

He hit the dirt hard, which knocked the wind right out of him. Barbeque Campbell laid flat on the ground and not one of his gunmen moved or even made a sound. Except Billy Ney, who pulled out a .45.

"Drop that gun!" Findlay shouted grimly.

Findlay had his gun out as soon as Boyce went for Campbell. Davis leveled his shotgun on the crew at the same moment. Matlock drew two Colts and held his arms out straight, pointing one at Arizona Johnny and the other at Billy Ney.

Campbell's men were shocked. They just sat their horses. Seeing the way Matlock was staring at him, Billy Ney immediately dropped his own gun in the dirt.

Arizona Johnny blanched. He was amazed. He couldn't believe that a man as small as AG Boyce had the capability to yank a big man like Barbeque around like that. Campbell had always been a force of nature in Johnny's mind. It was hard to comprehend, seeing Boyce make such short work of him.

In the silence, they could all hear the sound of AG Boyce pounding Barbeque Campbell's face with his fist, repeatedly. After the first few swings, his knuckles came up bloody. It became clear after a few moments that Boyce was not stopping. Matlock, a little surprised himself at Boyce's fury, tried to call him off.

"Colonel!" Matlock shouted, his guns still pointed at Arizona Johnny and Billy Ney. "Colonel!"

Boyce stopped pounding Campbell. He was breathing heavily from the effort but the trance was broken. He glared up at

Matlock, then around at the horsemen. He looked at his bloody knuckles and wiped them slowly on Barbeque Campbell's shirt.

"Get him out o' here," he muttered.

Two of Campbell's crew dismounted and hoisted their beaten leader to his feet. His face was ground up nicely and his nose was angled crookedly.

"Bunged him up good!" one noted mildly. It was more of an observation than an objection. He found himself on the ground, eye to eye with Boyce — and the man still looked pretty volatile. They moved quickly to get Campbell up across his horse.

"I would suggest riding out immediately," Matlock announced.

They took to their stirrups and got back on their horses without any talk.

"If I see any one of you inside an XIT fence," Boyce told them, "I will have you shot dead."

He walked in front of all their horses, studying them one by one. Boyce's voice was low.

"You are a sorry lot. Maverickers and brand-burners. Gamblers. I will forget neither your faces, nor what has transpired here today."

AL Matlock and George Findlay and Davis watched over the riders from the ranch house porch. The three of them kept their guns aimed as Boyce walked down the line. When he was satisfied, he pointed at the horizon.

"Get out of my sight!"

Chapter 10
Leadville

The day Casey finally got the roof in place, he made a big show of picking Julianna up and carrying her right through the front door. Breaking down the canvas tent was a happy occasion in itself. It was a drafty tent when the wind blew. And it was a stuffy tent when the sun beat down. And a leaky tent when it rained. The two of them folded it up neatly, laid it in the back of the wagon and went inside to eat their first supper indoors.

In the beginning, one of their first major purchases had been a woodstove. Casey had to cut a hole in the tent roof to vent the stack. The day he bought it, it required three men to get it out of the wagon. Once the home was finished, Casey had to move it again. Julianna was still at work that day and all his mining friends were busy mining. But dragging the woodstove inside was easier than unloading it — he just hitched the stove to Mule and let her do all the work. He was glad Julianna was in town at the time. She might not have appreciated having Mule in the house.

Julianna smiled. She loved having a home. It had been less than a month since they moved in. What a full year! A new husband, a new town, a new cabin. She stood by the woodstove tending a simmering pot.

"You'll like this," Julianna told LG. "It's an old family recipe."

As she stirred the stew, LG winked to Casey.

"You're feeding two lifelong stockmen *squirrel*?"

She took a long-handled wooden spoon and tasted the broth.

"All these hungry miners around, you think there's any big game left? In these woods?" she asked. "If we want deer or elk, Casey has to make a special hunting trip. Or we buy beef at the butcher shop."

"Little things are chattery," LG commented, shaking his head. "Won't be chattering no more, I guess."

Casey thought *that* was ironic. LG himself was as prone to chattering as any squirrel he ever came across. He went over by Julianna and opened the stove belly to check on the fire. The coals were red hot, but he went ahead and put in another log.

"It's better than Emmanuel's sour beans," Casey said, and got a prompt whack from the wooden spoon.

"And his burnt boiled coffee!" LG added.

"Only good thing he made was them sourdough biscuits," Casey said, suddenly nostalgic.

Casey was doing his best to be friendly with LG, but Julianna could tell it was forced. Her husband was running out of pleasantries and cattle statistics. She found herself casting side-glances at Casey, wondering what was going on in his mind. She could guess. LG and Casey had ridden together for years...they were compadres. But LG had ridden off while the rest of the B-Cross crew was being gunned down and no one knew where or why and now here he was, sitting across the table, joshing about Emmanuel's culinary failures.

That was also the day Julianna met Casey for the first time.

She could remember it quite vividly. She was heading home after a visit with Josephine, driving the buckboard alone through the canyon. There were supplies in the back, mainly kitchen sundries: baking soda, flour, canned foods. Apples and sugar to bake pie. Her father, the Commodore, was always more amenable when she baked fresh pie. Julianna preferred it when he was amenable. She passed several magpies at one point, bickering over spilled oats. Then a posse rode by — grim men on horseback. They were after killers, the deputy said. Killers, it turned out, who robbed a stagecoach that very morning not five miles down the road. By the time she got there, the men were pulling Casey out of the creek.

"They say Doc Holliday's up in Glenwood Springs now," LG informed them. "Wastin' away."

Casey went back to his seat and sat down with a sigh.

"Yeah, I guess."

Julianna watched him from the corner of her eye. She was nervous. She just wanted Casey to *talk* to LG. Like she did with Josephine. If there was ever anything between them, they would talk it out. Casey and LG had been together for three days but hadn't gotten past bovines.

The stew had thickened and was basically done. Julianna took a dish cloth and wrapped it around the pot handle. She carried it over to the table and set it down carefully. Steam roiled off in thick wisps.

"You know, I saw him once," Julianna mentioned. "All the way back in Ward, before I met Casey. I don't know *what* he was doing *there*. Probably passing through on his way up here."

Casey went and got a chair for Julianna, then went to find bowls and spoons. Earlier, Julianna had made a loaf of wheat bread to go along with it. She said a prayer over the meal and gave thanks.

"So, how do you like squirrel?" she asked LG, after they had all tasted it.

He held up his spoon to show her.

"Is this the brisket or the sweetbreads?"

The tea kettle started to whistle and Casey got up from the table again. They had several lanterns going now that the sun was gone. Hopper was lying on the floor directly behind Casey's chair, watching closely for a soup spill or perhaps a tasty bread crust.

Up on a shelf, Casey found the tin can with the tea leaves and sprinkled some into the hot water to let it steep. Julianna was fond of tea and had trained him how to make it. Training him to enjoy it had proved unsuccessful, however. He told her it tasted like tree bark. But Julianna liked it, so Casey fixed it.

Chapter 11

Lanterns were hanging from the timbers above the ore bucket. Electric arc lights were suspended from a spider web of wires, too. Between the lanterns and the arc lights, a fairly bright glow illuminated the ground around the Matchless Mine.

It was after sunset and the sky was a deep purple, speckled with pinpricks of starlight. Prescott Sloan rode up on his black mare and dismounted promptly. Several well-dressed grooms were stationed there. One immediately stepped up to hold the mare's reins while Sloan got down.

"Welcome to the Matchless. The gala is being conducted below ground, in Shaft Number Six," the groom announced rather cheerfully. "This here is Shaft Number One. Number Six is just a short walk down that path. Follow the string of lights and you'll come right to it. Enjoy the evening, sir."

Sloan smoothed his pant legs to make sure they weren't bunched up around his boot tops. He opened the saddle bag. The banker-turned-businessman was starting to think of himself as a top-tier socialite. A personal invitation from Horace Tabor himself! An eighteen year-old bottle of Scotch seemed appropriate to help seat his style. He removed it from the saddlebag and examined it to make sure it had survived the ride from town.

The summer night was cool. At ten thousand feet, even summer nights frequently required a jacket and neck scarf. Add to that the meal would be served underground. Sloan unrolled his coat and put it on, along with gloves. He left the mare for the groom to take care of and followed the string of arc lights, cradling the Scotch in the nook of his arm.

The path led down a steep pile of tailings. Sloan took his time, carefully working down the slope. It was more than a little steep. Couldn't they have chosen an easier approach for dinner guests? If he dropped that Scotch, Sloan would not be in a pleasant mood.

When he reached the bottom of the tailings Sloan relaxed. The lights led out into the darkness, lighting up a footpath. The entire area was a wasteland of spent gravel, yellow mounds and waist-high tree stumps. In the dusk, the Number Six was just a silhouette of timber beams reaching up into the sky. There was a small shack nearby where the motorized hoist was stationed. Thick cables ran out of wall slots up to a pulley, high in the timber frame above the shaft itself. Just like Shaft Number One had, there was a large ore bucket suspended over a dark hole in the ground. Except this one was not lit up as well.

So, this was the shaft where Horace Tabor was hosting a fancy dinner soiree? Sloan was disappointed for some reason. The light string led right to the ore bucket...but other than that, there were no lanterns or bonfires or musicians or champagne to mark the spot. He looked around in the darkness.

Sloan heard a door creak open and an attendant came out of the hoist shack.

"Am I in the right place?" Sloan asked him.

"You most certainly are! Welcome, welcome! If you'll step into the bucket, sir. This...is...the Number Six!"

He waved his hand over the ore bucket grandly — as if he were introducing Grover Cleveland instead of a dank hole in the ground. Sloan scowled disdainfully.

The bucket was large enough for a man to crouch in comfortably. Sloan stepped in carefully, while the attendant kept it from swinging around too much. It took a moment of shuffling to get his balance, and he was especially careful with the Scotch.

"I suppose I'm in."

"Yes sir," the attendant replied. "We shall begin lowering you presently. Enjoy your fantastic evening!"

The boisterous attendant disappeared in the hoist shack. The fellow needed a shave.

There was a loud metallic bellow and then a low grating sound. A bell rang twice. The heavy ore bucket jerked into motion and began its slow descent into the earth. Sloan quickly balanced the Scotch on his lap so he could grip the bucket with both hands.

There was an arc light attached just overhead. Whenever Sloan looked up he had to squint. It was a harsh light. But there was nothing more to see anyway. The purple night was framed in above him, but that little square patch of purple sky got smaller and smaller as the bucket eased lower and lower into the depths of the Number Six.

About fifty feet down, it came to rest on the ground with a gritty bang.

Everything was pitch black except for another strand of electric lights trailing down a corridor. Nearby, Sloan could tell someone was leaning against the wall having a smoke. The orange tip of a cigarette bobbed in the darkness. Sloan waited expectantly but the man did not make a move to assist him.

"Gonna steady this damn bucket?" Sloan asked, frustrated.

The orange tip glowed brightly and the scent of tobacco breezed by. Sloan suddenly felt that something was off. He glanced up the ore shaft but couldn't even make out the tiny patch of purple sky. He got out carefully and looked around. It was extremely dark in the mine, except that strand of little bright lights. The ceiling was low. He heard water dripping.

"Where's the shin dig?" Sloan asked.

The man flipped a switch that was wired to the rocky wall. A bell rang once, echoing off the walls. The ore bucket scraped heavily off the ground, slid up the shaft and was gone.

"Follow the drift," the man said, pointing down the corridor. His voice echoed.

Sloan stayed close to the glowing light strand, moving tentatively. He couldn't see anything else. The little lights turned down a narrow passageway. Sloan took care not to hit his head or drop the bottle. Behind him, he could hear the attendant's footsteps padding along slowly.

Sloan glanced back nervously but kept moving.

Up ahead, the light string led through a rectangular doorway — the doorway emitted a warm welcoming glow. It was a relief. Sloan stepped through into a wide mine chamber.

"Sloan...you made it."

There were half a dozen men leaning against the wall waiting for him. Sloan glanced around. Several lanterns were lit, hung on nails in the timber roof supports. But this did not look like a party. Sloan was confused. He was expecting a banquet table, live music, pretty girls serving beer and steak. But there was none of that.

Horace Tabor was standing behind one of the timber supports, chewing on his thumbnail. Sloan recognized Big Ed Burns and several of his entourage heavies. It was Big Ed who had spoken. Prescott Sloan immediately became wary. He turned around, only to see the bucket attendant filling the entryway — still toking on that orange-tipped cigarette.

"What's this?" Sloan demanded.

"Why, it's a banquet," Big Ed said. "Come hungry?"

"Haw, I don't understand," Sloan said, trying to catch Horace's eyes.

Another man came out of the shadows and walked right up to Sloan.

"I felt quite the fool, when I opened up that PO Box expecting to find a hundred thousand in cash."

Sloan became pale.

"Soapy Smith!" he said.

"Yes, good memory, good memory."

Soapy reached out and took the Scotch out of Sloan's hand. He examined it curiously.

"That's eighteen year-old Scotch," Sloan pointed out, his mind racing. "All yours, Soapy. So good to see you here! Perhaps we can dine together this evening. Be pleased to hear how the construction is going on the Tivoli."

"Ain't a banquet tonight," Soapy replied. "We're having a revival."

"A revival?"

Soapy tossed the bottle at Big Ed, who scrambled to catch it. Sloan watched helplessly as it soared through the dim light, cringing. But Big Ed caught it.

"You know a man can live without sinning?" Soapy asked, and gave Sloan a peculiar look. Sloan did not like it.

"I remember my granpappy took me all the way out to Manheim, Pennsylvania. There was this big tent meeting. It was a Pentecost, for sure. There was a preacher there...I can picture him to this day. Stood on a stump, holding his Bible-book high. Know what he said? He kept saying *you need the Holy Ghost!*"

Sloan tried again to catch Horace's eye. But Haw Tabor was absorbed with the condition of his thumbnail.

"Do you have sin in your heart, Scotty Sloan?"

Soapy suddenly grabbed a hold of Sloan's lapels with both hands and shook him violently.

"*The PO Box* was *empty!*"

Sloan flopped around in Soapy's grip. He pulled Sloan close — so close their noses touched. Sloan stared at him with wide eyes but did not try to break Soapy's hold. The mine chamber was silent, except the drip of water somewhere.

"The stagecoach was robbed!" Sloan explained. "Right there, just outside Ward. The key was stolen! I sent down another one. Tell me you got that key, Soapy!"

"Where is my money?"

He proceeded to give Sloan another good shaking.

"Haw?" Sloan pleaded, reaching out towards the Silver King.

But Haw Tabor was not looking very kingly at the moment. He stood where he was, with a sad look in his eyes — as if he were watching a theatre production at the Opera House. Thinking that made it easier for him to digest what was going on. This was all just a play. The curtain would come down and he would be home soon, crawling into bed. His wife Elizabeth would be dead drunk and passed out on the bed already.

Horace reached into his pocket and produced a vile of white tablets. His ulcer was flaring up, and he expected it would only get worse as the evening progressed. No sense waiting for a private moment to take his medicine. Better give it a head start, before the belly acid really started to burn. The magnesium only helped quell it so much, anyhow.

Prescott Sloan *had* thought it was odd that Soapy Smith never sent word about the money, one way or another. It was a hundred thousand dollars after all, quite a large transaction. Sloan had indeed sent his spare key down the canyon as soon as the stage was operating again. Of course, that didn't happen overnight. It took time to rehire stage drivers who weren't afraid to end up dead.

There was only one explanation. He knew Jim Everitt and Ian Mitchell had been killed by stage thieves. From what he learned, it was the same men who killed a sheriff in Grand Lake and rode off with a haul of gold from the Kinsey City bank. Between the bank gold and the stagecoach heist, why would they risk everything to see what was in a PO Box? That didn't make sense. Sloan could guess they found the key easily enough. Rummaging through pockets was standard procedure for any robbery. But it was just a key! A posse was on their trail and there was no time to waste. Why would they travel all the way into the big city of Denver, all the way to the Post Office, just to see what was inside? They had plenty of gold and a posse to outrun. It made no sense.

"Why didn't you tell me it was cleaned out?" Sloan asked Soapy Smith, gently. "I could have provided a loan, or a forward of some kind. Or just signed over your stake in the Matchless, right back to you."

"How dull do you think I am?" Smith asked, his eyes getting hard.

He slapped Sloan across the face, splitting his lip.

"Ow," Sloan stuttered. He could taste the blood. "You busted my lip."

Soapy turned toward Horace Tabor, Big Ed, and Big Ed's crew. They were standing there quietly, watching and waiting to see what he would do.

Prescott Sloan was afraid now — afraid Soapy Smith wasn't interested in money at this point.

"Haw? Does this man need to be baptized?" Soapy Smith asked.

Horace felt cold in his stomach. Being a businessman in Leadville meant conducting business with all kinds of people, including men of shady repute. That was just the nature of the game. For the first time in his career, Horace knew this could be the moment where things took an ugly irreversible turn. And here he was, caught up in the thick of it. Horace didn't necessarily *like* Prescott Sloan. He didn't know him well to begin with, of course, but the man's character from the beginning was obviously questionable and Tabor had sensed that the first time they met. But dislike didn't mean Horace wanted to witness the man's abuse. He fumbled open the vile again and thumbed out several more magnesium tablets.

Chapter 12

The harsh glow of the electric lights made the walls look black and glittery. Small bits of quartz in the dark rock seemed to shine like stars in the night sky.

Soapy Smith dragged Prescott Sloan across the cold floor by the collar. Sloan slid along, trying to keep his footing but he was completely off balance. Soapy pulled him over to where Horace was standing.

"Sign that," Smith told Sloan.

Horace held out a legal document and a pen.

Sloan slouched to his knees and looked at the floor. Soapy rapped him on the head with his knuckles until he looked up again. Wincing, but without another word, Sloan took the pen and paper. He signed his name without even reading it.

Plucking the document from his hands, Soapy looked it over. He relaxed and gave Sloan a sullen smile of satisfaction. He patted Sloan's head softly, smoothing his hair down.

"You just signed your stake over to the Silver King," Soapy Smith told him. "Horace, this thing is all yours now. The ore. The income. But good with the bad, too...got some skeletons in the closet."

He handed the document back to Horace and roughly took hold of Sloan's collar again.

"Well...one at least."

He pulled Sloan across the floor to the far end of the chamber where the light string came to an end. In the glow of the last bulb, Prescott Sloan could plainly see that the floor dropped away.

Swinging Sloan around, Soapy shook him one last time.

"Help me! Haw!"

But Big Ed Burns, Horace "Haw" Tabor, and the Burns gang merely looked on. Sloan could feel the emptiness below him.

"Say hi to the Holy Ghost."

And with that, Soapy Smith let go.

Prescott Sloan disappeared down the dark shaft. The Number Six was fairly deep, and it took a few seconds before he hit bottom.

Horace quietly folded the paper and tucked it in his coat pocket. Now he owned the *entire* stake in the Matchless. Soapy had just sold it to him, and no longer held any interest in it whatsoever. Horace was glad of that — this was all too much. He decided right then to cut all ties with Soapy Smith. Horace wanted nothing more to do with things like this.

Soapy ran his fingers through his short black hair and stood up straight.

"All yours now, Tabor. You owe me a hundred thousand."

"Sure, sure," Horace said quickly. "Get it to you tonight."

"No, let's make it two hundred thousand."

"Two hundred...that's fine, that's fine," Horace agreed nervously. "You know, I own the Bank of Leadville so we don't have to wait for the morning tellers to show up. How about that?"

While he was trying to add a little levity to a tense situation, an after-hours withdrawal also meant Horace wouldn't have to explain what he was doing to any of the bank employees. This was a transaction he didn't want anyone to know about. For all people *would* know, Prescott Sloan's name was on the sale's receipt for the Matchless Mine. Of course, if anyone ever found Sloan's body in the bottom of shaft Number Six, the jig would be up.

"What do you say to a bite?" Soapy said. "I want me a nice thick tender steak."

Horace kept looking down into the dark shaft. He couldn't believe it. And he couldn't believe Soapy Smith wanted to eat after this. Horace was not feeling well. He was certainly in no mood to eat after what he just witnessed.

"Good thing this shaft is played out. Fill it in, Horace. First thing in the morning. But right now, we dine. Ed, what's your favorite restaurant in Leadville? Now, don't say the Pastime."

There wasn't any sound coming up from the darkness. Horace was hoping it had been a quick end. He hoped Sloan wasn't down there alive, with a broken leg or something. It was likely the man broke his neck and simply died. Horace hoped so. That was an easier thought to live with.

"Ooo!" Soapy said, snapping his fingers. "Nearly forgot! We have eighteen year-old Scotch."

Soapy led the way back. Big Ed stayed close to Horace the whole time, studying him closely. Big Ed knew that poor Haw Tabor was a softy. He wasn't cut from the same cloth. Big Ed put his hand on Tabor's shoulder and squeezed. Horace glanced over at him and smiled weakly.

"Let's go celebrate," Big Ed instructed.

They all went back into the drift shaft and followed the string of lights back to the ore bucket. One by one, they rode up to the surface. Each time the bucket went up, the bell rang once. Each time it came down, the bell rang twice. Horace was the first one to climb in.

Chapter 13
Continental Divide

The wind whistled across the boulders on the ridge. The rocks were loose in places, so Bill crossed the talus with care. The last thing he needed was a twisted ankle.

The town was only a few miles back. Of course, he gave it a wide berth when he rode through. The good people of Grand Lake would string him up in a heartbeat. Bill barely made it out of Garo, a mere handful of houses and a pathetic train depot in the middle of nowhere, without being recognized. And he had never even *been* to Garo before!

If those two cowmen had come just a few steps closer, or turned around at the right moment, they surely would have recognized him. How couldn't they? After all, it was Bill's gang that robbed the coach, shot their pards, and scattered their herd.

Bill kept a close eye on his backtrail. Once again, he was riding a stolen horse. This time, it was from Kinsey City just the day before. He didn't know what it was about Kinsey City, but it sure was an easy place to steal from. First the bank...now a big bay horse from some alfalfa farmer. The best part about Kinsey City was that no one knew his face — Bill had worn a neckerchief over his nose for the bank robbery, so he felt confident passing through that sleepy little burg any time of day.

He even dropped by the local inn again for a cup of coffee, trout and rice dinner, and a big slice of mountain raspberry pie. He remembered that from when he robbed the Kinsey City bank — the pie. The raspberries weren't in season in April, but somehow they had rhubarb available. Perhaps it came in on a freight wagon, who knows. But it was good pie. Both times, Bill made a point of thanking the inn matron. She should know.

He left the horse in a thicket of charred pine. Curiously, the trees all along the ridge were burnt. Almost all of them had been reduced to blackened stumps. Even the rocks were sooty. Bill wondered if lightning had set off a wildfire since he was here last.

The fact that the forest was burnt meant he could be spotted easier from a distance. Especially once he got above timberline. Looking around, Bill was a touch nervous about being afoot. Granted, this was a lonely stretch of the Continental Divide, but there were mines up here every so often. And the citizens of Grand

Lake seemed like fairly vitriolic folk — after all they did send a posse to run him down.

The inn matron in Kinsey City talked about a jar on display in Grand Lake. Apparently, poor Will Wyllis had his head chopped off and pickled. Bill liked his own head where it was and intended to keep it there...thus the wide berth around Grand Lake.

The more he looked around, the more Bill's nerves frayed. He knew the mine where they buried the gold was along this ridge. Somewhere. But nothing looked the same. The wildfire really affected the landscape. None of this seemed familiar although he knew it should.

The worst part, Bill realized, was that all the trees up here were burnt to stubs! Vincent had taken pains to set a marker. He stabbed a big butcher's knife in the side of a pine tree to point the way. Fifty paces uphill from the knife. That's where the mine was. The mine they took great pains to conceal.

Bill wondered what happened to half those guys. The Grand Lake Gang was what they had come to be called. Of course, none of them were from Grand Lake. And their achievements in theft ranged much further in terms of geography. That was simply where they gained the most notoriety, when Vincent killed the sheriff.

Bill began to realize he wasn't going to find the mine entrance. Those two saddle bags were gone. Full of gold coins and bars! He rubbed his eyes and tried hard to remember. Was it the Mexicans who brought the bags down into the mine? Or was it Will and Lem? Or Granger? He seemed to remember they were all there that night, crowding around him in that narrow, steep shaft. Did they merely cover over the entrance with brush? Or did those Mexicans bring the whole thing down? It was cold and dark that night, Bill could remember that easy enough. Granger was stirring up some trouble — he despised Poqito and Caverango, for whatever reason.

Of course, Will Wyllis was dead. Bill saw him get shot in the mine shack doorway, right there in front of him. The posse must have sawn his head off. Now it was on display in a jar in a saloon in the same town where they shot the sheriff. An eye for an eye, I guess.

That had been quite a full night. Bill wondered what became of his crew. Vincent and Granger were dead near Cañon City, he knew that firsthand. Lem got shot right off the stagecoach roof back in Lefthand Canyon. That damn buckaroo shot him. Taking Granger and Vincent along, Bill tried to ride that cowboy down. Then Vincent's horse spilled and that was the end of it. The

Mexicans he couldn't account for. Or Ned, whose real name was Charley Crouse.

Bill first met Charley Crouse up in Brown's Park a few years prior. Brown's Park was a little valley in the northwest corner of the state full of rustlers and thieves of all sorts. It also was a quiet little ranching community with lush green grass in the summers. A pleasant place, Bill reflected. I might have to head up there again.

The mining shack was nowhere to be seen. But that was no surprise since it had been on fire when they rode out that night. And even if it hadn't burned to the ground, the wildfire that ate up this ridge would have finished it off. Either way, he had no landmarks. The mine with the gold-filled saddle bags was somewhere up here. But Bill Ewing knew he wasn't going to find it.

Chapter 14
Garo

"What did it look like?"

"Sterling silver...with a chain," Chubb Newitt replied.

"It was engraved," Frank Stevens added.

That was what Red Creek wanted to hear. He was starting to put it all together. At first, he wasn't sure who he was after. Which one of them it was. The Grand Lake Gang was hard to identify as to who was who. Back when it all started, and the posse had the gang boxed up in a mine shack on the Divide, Red took the time to count their horses. There were eight of them.

He got a decent look through the window, too, and even though it was dark Red Creek got a good idea that eight was about right. He crept all the way up to the window, which was not hard since they hadn't posted any guards. There were seven inside and one outside checking on their horses. The moon had been out — although the clouds were moving at a fast clip and the light came and went. Red used to be a sharpshooter in the War. He fought for Lee at Antietam. And he was the marksman who shot General Sedgwick in the face at Spotsylvania at 800 yards. That blue coat was so arrogant. Couldn't hit an elephant, indeed! Red Creek still had the rifle. It was a .45 caliber British Whitworth, and it went everywhere he did.

Ever since Sheriff Emerson Greer was killed in Grand Lake, Red Creek had begun to feel his blood stir again. He felt purposeful. Ever since the War, he felt numb towards civilized people, civilized conversations, and the mundanity of the civilized world.

"Had his name writ on it...something Hughes," Frank told him, staring thoughtfully out the general store window.

"And there was poetry, too," Chubb mentioned.

Opening his notebook, Red Creek looked over the description Hugh Hughes had given him.

"*Absence from those we love is self from self.*"

Both Chubb and Frank lit up, nodding in surprise.

"Why, yes, that's it," Frank affirmed.

"What did this man look like?"

"Well, a white fella. Clean-shaved. Dark hair, I suppose," said Frank.

"Tall, though," Chubb added.

"You're a short little bugger as it is, Chubb — every person is tall to you," Frank chastised him. "And husky...you are Chubb, not that fella with the watch."

Red Creek knew then it was not the Mexican. And it could not be Charley Crouse, whose face he recognized through the cabin window that night. Charley was blonde.

This meant he was trailing the very man Emerson locked up in the courthouse prison back in Grand Lake.

There were eight to begin with, in Red's count. The horse-checker Red beheaded up on the Divide that first night. The second they found dead near the stagecoach in Lefthand. One of the Mexicans was shot and killed by the B-Cross in Spring Gulch that same day. The one who broke Bill out of prison, the false newspaperman called Judas Furlong — who dressed like a dandy — was dead down near Cañon along with the gap-toothed fool. That left one Mexican still alive, and the blonde-headed Charley Crouse. Neither of which matched the description.

Red Creek knew it had to be the one they called Bill.

Griff and Emerson got the man's name when they arrested him...although what his real name was, was any man's guess. Red Creek reasoned Bill must be the gang leader. He seemed to be the most crafty, save for maybe Charley Crouse. But Charley Crouse no longer interested Red Creek. Red wanted the man who shot Emerson Greer. After all, Ben Leavick had paid him to hunt down the killer and that's what he aimed to do.

"And he was wearing Harold Chalmers' green plaid shirt. Took it from the clothesline," Chubb said in an excitable tone. "Mrs. Chalmers put out the word, thinking it might have blown off the line. It didn't — the thief jacked it."

"I thought the shirt looked awful familiar," Frank said thoughtfully. "You see, Harold comes into my saloon most Saturday nights. I own the Stevens Saloon. Right down there."

These two men were gabby. Gabby people irritated Red Creek but he *was* learning new facts as they jawed on. If he had to listen to their ramblings to learn just one or two new facts about Bill, he would tolerate it.

Already, this had been a profitable stop. He knew who he was after now. He knew Bill was wearing a green plaid shirt. He knew he had been shot by an old rancher down in Guffey, although it clearly wasn't slowing Bill down any. In addition he took the northbound train, the Denver South Park Railway, right out of Garo. The outlaw stood in this very spot at four o'clock in the afternoon not three days prior. The hunter was closing in.

Red tried to guess where Bill might be headed. Perhaps Como. Or any of those mining towns: Tarryall, Hamilton, Jefferson City. Or on to Denver itself.

Red Creek had already ridden quite a circuit looking for this man. He had ridden from Grand Lake to Ward. He had taken the train from Boulder to Denver to Pueblo. He'd ridden horseback through Cañon City, up to Guffey, and on into Garo. That was a big loop...just to hear Bill was circling back towards Denver.

But no matter. Red Creek was patient, if nothing else.

Chapter 15
Leadville

LG held up a ceramic jug triumphantly.

"Moonshine!" he whispered.

Casey looked back at the cabin. In the window, he could see the orange glow of hot coals in the woodstove. But the lanterns were out — Julianna was probably sound asleep by now.

It was late. But the evening was nice and there were several big stumps on the porch to sit on. Casey usually sat on one every night. Being used to long cattle drives sleeping under the stars, Casey was drawn to porch-sitting.

Julianna usually joined him, but since LG arrived Julianna rarely came out to sit. Casey knew why. She was giving them "space." Space to talk. Every night that week, late at night, Julianna would whisper to him about how important it was to "talk" to LG. Casey let her go on about it, but mainly because she was pretty and sweet and he didn't like arguing with her. He had no intention of talking to LG about anything.

"Got this in town."

"Open 'er up," Casey said to LG, quietly. "And keep your voice low."

The cork came out with a hollow pop. LG had spent the afternoon in Leadville and Casey was glad for some quiet time. LG went to buy his train ticket since Casey suggested he better buy the ticket a day early — the Colorado Midland was a new spectacle and people were coming and going every day since they laid the tracks, he said.

"Heading out tomorr'a," LG mentioned.

They sat in the dark rolling cigarettes and passing the jug.

"Love these things," LG mentioned, looking at his smoldering cigarette. "Reminds me of all them trail drives. Always had a smoke. Especially when I was nighthawk."

Casey threw him a look.

"When were you *ever* nighthawk?"

"Oh, I rode the graveyard shift," LG said with a little indignation. "Many a time. Many a time."

"Must of been a time when I was rep'n for another brand."

LG reached out for the jug. Casey saw him reach but took another quick pull before passing it over. An owl was hooting up in a tall pine, just in front of the cabin.

"I remember the time, down near Walsenburg, I was on the midnight guard. Hardest rain you ever seen. Hail, too. Got soaked to the bone. After it let up, tried to light a cig but them matches were so sogged."

"Who were you riding for?"

"The 4W...Jacob Weil, down in Purgatoire. We brought them cows all the way up from there, grazed 'em the whole way."

The moon was starting to rise up over the Ten-Mile Range. It was just a crescent.

"I spent a summer in Walsenburg," Casey said. "Back in '83. I put in some hours at the feed store. But dry goods didn't suit me none. That was my last time living in a proper home. Till now."

LG handed the jug back over again.

"So, what'll you do here? This ain't exactly a finishing ranch."

"Nope," replied Casey. "I'm hitched now. I can't ride the range no more. Plus the range is closing up fast. Won't *be* no range."

Blowing smoke rings, LG got quiet.

It was true, LG knew. Homesteaders *were* eating up the open range and stringing wire. They both knew it wouldn't be possible to drive a herd up to Montana before too long. What with the railroads built up everywhere, it was easier to simply ship the cattle where they needed to go. LG could see that. He didn't like it. But he could see it coming as plain as day.

"Gonna shoe," Casey told him.

"Ain't a bad idea," LG responded. It made him think about his own future. "You know, managin' for Sam Hartsel ain't too bad. But, I been thinking...mebbe I'll sign on as a brand inspector down in Colorada Springs. Or Denver. Enjoy the city life for a spell."

"Looking at a store downtown here," Casey went on. "Right on 3rd. I can shoe horses right off the street."

The alcohol was stronger than Casey expected. He was feeling it now. The stars were extra twinkly. He could see the North Star up above. Casey pointed at the Big Dipper.

"Ladle creeping up on midnight now."

"Surely is," LG said, and grinned thoughtfully.

The constellation rotated around the North Star like a clock face. That's how they always knew when their shift was over. His grin faded. He wasn't sure if he would ever point cattle up the trail again or ride nighthawk on a long drive. He could stay on at the Hartsel Ranch as long as he needed, and oversee the breeding program. He wasn't sure, though. He wasn't sure what he needed. LG wasn't too sure about anything anymore.

"Hey, pard."

Casey looked over at him, expecting the jug. But LG was still holding it in his lap.

"I feel cruddy — how I lit out."

Casey turned back to the night sky. He was feeling the buzz of the alcohol. Each time he turned his head the stars seemed to move around.

"Once I realized what was going on, I shot that ki-yote off the roof," LG continued softly. "I heard shots back there, but I was on the wrong end of the wagon."

Casey leaned over and took the jug out of LG's lap. LG didn't seem to notice.

"I just had my ol' Navy .36, cap and ball…not a quick-shootin' gun. Clunky. And then they set upon me. The only route I had was on down the road. Was all I could do."

The owl continued to hoot somewhere above them. He took a breath.

"Could have rode back later," Casey pointed out, after a minute.

LG looked up at the treetops. He didn't know what to say. Or why he didn't ride back after he shook those riders.

"They shot me," Casey said. "Almost killed me. Like they killed Ira. And Edwin. Right there in front of me."

Casey took another swallow and set the jug on the ground in between them. The owl was hooting again but he couldn't tell where it was now. Whenever he turned his head one way or the other, the trees seemed to bend.

Chapter 16

Garo

Driving the carryall through the tall August grass was pleasant. Til got two good cuttings this season, might even get a third if the weather would hold. He was thoroughly enjoying the ride and the morning air was enlivening.

The draft horses were walking quietly and seemed to get along with each other. That was not always the case. They liked to bicker. Especially Bear, the swing horse, liked to nip at the lead horse, Heavy. Heavy had a lot of bite marks on his neck. But today they weren't bickering. Just walking nicely.

Til knew the pleasant summer days would be over soon. Autumn came early in the high country so he always savored the easy weather.

Laura sat next to him, her arm hooked around his elbow. Her long blonde hair was blowing with the light breeze. Little Walker came along behind them on a gray Arabian mare, riding confidently.

It was Laura's first day of work and Til thought it was a fair enough occasion to take her into town himself. He figured it would give her a chance to think ahead without worrying about anything else — not even the bickery drafts. Laura had been almost too excited to get any sleep the night before.

Chubb Newitt sent word the week before that the Garo schoolmarm had up and moved to Fairplay, without much notice. The school year had already begun, and Garo was suddenly without its teacher. Laura, of course, was beside herself and accepted the role without hesitation.

There were enough children in Garo and the outlying ranches to justify both a schoolhouse and a teacher's salary. The schoolhouse was only a few years old, but in that short time a half dozen young ladies passed in and out of the occupation.

Laura found that curious. According to Chubb, none of the children were happy about attendance. He said it was because they had a different teacher each year, sometimes more often than that. He didn't know why, but he guessed the glamour of the big mining towns lured them all away. Watch out, he warned her, for the small town blues.

Or perhaps, Laura suspected, it was because certain people's children were unruly and disruptive. Oh, she had met Chubb's son Billy — and he was no petunia. She knew temperamental boys were capable of grand feats of insubordination. And in Laura's opinion Billy Newitt seemed capable of chasing off inexperienced school teachers single-handedly, through pure malaise.

She smiled at Til, who smiled back.

"I'm so pleased!" she told him. "Initially, I was only hoping to assist with the school. Or start a library. But look! It's all come about so quickly, so unexpectedly. How wonderful!"

"Better than making pearl snaps?" Til asked, joshing her.

"Better than making pearl snaps," she said and dug her finger in his ribs. "Although, which man in all of South Park has the most dazzling shirt snaps?"

"I do believe it's me."

He puffed out his chest. Laura laughed at him.

"Such a peacock!"

Chapter 17
Kinsey City

The river sounds were loud here. Muddy Creek and the Blue came together not fifty feet away, and then joined the Colorado River just beyond. The water was not particularly high this time of year. Even though it wasn't September yet, a couple cottonwood trees already had a handful of yellow leaves.

Riding up to the Kinsey Inn, Red Creek studied the area from the saddle. Calling this place a *city* was a tad fallacious, he thought. If he had sneezed, he would have ridden right through and never saw it. There were a lot of cattle grazing about. Across the river from the Inn, he saw a calving barn, a corn bin, the defunct Kinsey City Bank, and Kremmling's Store.

Red Creek slid off his horse, led him up to the Kinsey Inn's hitching rail and wrapped a rein around it. There were a couple other horses grazing outside, tacked up but grazing unattended. Maybe this was a nice quiet town where people let their horses wander around while they got a bite to eat. But Red wanted his horse where he could see it. Especially with his Whitworth in the scabbard. He could simply carry it inside — but he didn't want to make a spectacle of himself.

He headed up the stairs onto the veranda. The door was propped open and flies were buzzing in and out of the windows. Maude, the bulgy inn matron in a plain blue dress, was chatting with two men at a table. When she saw Red Creek come through the door, she hustled right over.

"Afternoon, dear! Mutton is the meal of the day. Does that suit you?"

"Suits me fine."

Maude saw Red check over the two men talking quietly at the table. She nodded their way.

"Them's the brothers," she said in a singsong voice.

Red Creek looked at her blankly. It was clear she expected him to recognize who they were.

"Aaron and John Kinsey. I thought you might be here to sign on. They're recruiting cowboys to rake alfalfa."

"No, ma'am."

"Sit over there then, and I'll bring you some nice hot coffee and a plate of chops."

Maude disappeared in the back, the big blue dress swishing around her portly frame.

Red leaned back in the sturdy chair. Someone knew how to build furniture up here. The table was stout, too, he thought, and must weigh as much as a heifer. The two brothers *looked* like brothers. One had dark hair, the other light brown...but each had the same mustache, wide set eyes, and monotoned voice. They were talking about the merits of alfalfa.

Maude returned with coffee, a steaming plate, and a carefree grin. The mutton chops smelled good. Red had been living off of jerked venison and a lot of fresh fish. Red was pretty good at catching fish. He carried fish line in his saddle bags and usually fashioned a pole out of branches he would find. But he liked mutton when he could get it.

"There you go, hun!" she said, but was in no hurry to leave. She liked to see men eat. It made her feel like she was doing what she was put on this earth to do: feeding people.

"Ma'am, I was wondering. You seen a feller come through here recent, in a green plaid shirt with a nice pocketwatch?"

She pursed her lips and put her hands on her hips.

"Surely did. Not a couple days ago, if I remember rightly."

The Kinsey brothers turned in their seats, abruptly ending their dull talk.

"Friend of yours?"

"Afraid not," Red replied. He could tell they were interested, but not in a kindly way. He decided to be straightforward.

"The man's wanted. Right up in Grand Lake, actually. Been tracking him all over the state...and here he's looped right back to Grand County."

Aaron and John stared at each other, raising their eyebrows in the same manner at the same time.

"He was very complimentary about my raspberry pie!" Maude exclaimed.

"He also helped himself to a horse from my corral," Aaron said bitterly.

"Are you sure it was him?" Maude asked.

John looked at her and sighed loudly.

"How many times we got to go through this, Maude?"

"Was the only visitor we've had, recent," Aaron reasoned. "No one else has passed through."

"Makes the most sense," John agreed.

Kinsey City was small — just the inn and Kremmling's store, the tiny bank and the brothers' alfalfa ranch. Red figured it would be better just to speak freely and see what the locals knew. This wasn't much of a town and folks seemed open enough. He bet anything unusual got around quickly.

"Well, I'll be!" Maude said, and slid into a chair at Red's table. "Are you a bounty hunter?"

"Yep."

"Man stole a horse," Aaron reiterated, leaning forward on his elbows. "Just a quarterhorse. Big bay. White nip on its nose."

"Sock on his left hind. All the way up to his hock," his brother added.

Red Creek made a show of pulling out his notebook and scribbling the information down. He did not really care about their horse, and he wouldn't spend any effort bringing it back. But the description might be useful. Ben Leavick had paid him to hunt down the Grand Lake Gang — these people had not. The stolen horse was their responsibility.

"Tracks led due east," Aaron mentioned. "We're short-handed this season. Rowed up alfalfa all week long. Trying to get it in the barn a'fore any rains come in. Or else I'd chase that sun'bitch down myself."

"We *surely* woulda chased him down," John chimed in and banged his fist on the tabletop.

Maude wore a look of absolute surprise and began fanning her face with a napkin.

"Just can't believe it! I fed the man my good raspberry pie. He paid for it, too. I didn't suspect the man was a horse thief or I never would have served him any raspberry pie."

"I'm sure you wouldn't have, ma'am" Red said.

"You *hang* that sun'bitch horse thief," Aaron told Red Creek.

"*Hang* that sun'bitch," John echoed.

Another man strode in through the open doorway. It was Rudolph "Kare" Kremmling, owner of Kremmling's Store across the river. He walked up and rubbed his hands together excitedly.

"Who's getting hung?"

"The feller who ate Maude's raspberry pie. And then stole my dern horse," Aaron said.

He also robbed your bank, Red thought, but decided not to mention it. What if that information stirred them up, and they invited themselves along? Red didn't need the company.

Kare had watched Red Creek ride up to the inn and decided it was as good a time as any for supper. His store was empty at the time. Of course Kinsey City was pretty empty most of the time, generally speaking.

The Kinsey brothers' moved in and set up their ranch a few years back, but it was Kare's store that brought people in. Then one day the brothers decided to nominate the area "Kinsey City." Kare was flabbergasted — he found that irritating. Hell, he found the brothers irritating. If this was a city, it shouldn't be named after a couple alfalfa farmers. No one went to the Kinsey's for anything *except* alfalfa. They came to Kare for everything else...for supplies, for mail, for fancy ceramic dishes and Chinese teapots. They came to Kremmling's Store. When Maude wanted some rhubarb earlier that year, who was it that freighted it in? Kare did, special order, just for her.

"You ain't got your horse back yet?" Kare asked Aaron, and pretended to be shocked. He knew they hadn't but decided to rub salt in the wound.

"Had to rake...a'fore the rains come in," Aaron said, his face getting red. "Got to be dry to rake alfalfa!"

John's face also got red.

Kare smiled a secret smile. He was pleased to get their goat.

Chapter 18

Brown's Park
Colorado
Pots Creek

"Why, Bill Ewing, I am tongue-tied!" Mary Crouse exclaimed. "Charley told me you was buzzard feed."

Mary stood in the open doorway, hair pulled back in a tight braid. Her sleeves were rolled and her forearms white with flour.

"Where is that presumptive warbly-eyed sack o' corn?" Bill replied with a gallant bow.

"Racing," she answered. "And he ain't got warbly eyes. Just one...it's only a *bit* warbly-like."

"As I am only a *bit* thieving-like," Bill told her. "Racing... against whom?"

"Matt Rash, trail boss for Middlesex."

"Don't know him."

"Lots change when you're gone for so long, Bill."

"Charley dope his horse?"

Mary's smile dropped into a scowl. She stood up tall in the doorway and folded her floury arms.

"Charley don't dope no horses. Fair an' square as always, Bill Ewing, and don't you think crosswise again, no two how's or what's about it!"

He realized his chances at a warm meal were suddenly slipping away. Bill struck a professorial pose and gave her an indignant look.

"Of course not. I was just funning you."

"What do you want, Bill?" she asked tartly.

"I'm back for good, Mary. Do I scent the famous Mary Crouse dumplings? Is that what I smell?"

He leaned to one side to look past her shoulder and sniffed the air. Knowing he meant no harm, Mary softened a little and let him in.

"Charley be back when the race is won. You can stay for the evening meal, if you're of a mind."

"Obliged."

The cabin was not a large place. It had been built in a stand of tall cottonwoods, which peppered the air with white puffs like snowfall.

"What else is new?" Bill asked, taking a seat at the table.

The small windows were open and cotton tufts blew in, dotting everything. Mary went back to kneading.

"Charley and Overholt opened a saloon and livery. Down in Vernal."

"A saloon for all them *Mormons?* Mormons don't drink. Guess that's like selling stripes to a Zebra. I am impressed at his entrepreneurial spirit."

"Ten dollar words don't impress me none. And they don't cook dumplin's."

The woman had always been a whipper snapper, Bill knew. But she was easy to get along with. He liked to get her feathers up — it was all in good fun. Bill had been raised in the Park, but went on to spend more time on the trail than in any one place. Now, with everything that had happened, he was thinking Brown's Park would be a good place to settle again.

Bill got up and went to the window. He liked the fresh breeze. It also brought in the sounds of the horses, grazing just outside. Charley was known to breed and raise horses.

"Bassett's still on Pablo Springs?"

"Where else would they be?" Mary replied without looking up from her dough. "John Jarvie shut down the post office in June. Hear that?"

The afternoon was pleasant. The sky was blue with just a few wispy clouds stretched out overhead, but it wasn't going to rain today.

"They told him to look into bad money orders. Meaning that shady ol' Kraus up in the Vernal office. Jarvie said he weren't no spy...so he bagged up the books, inkwells and even the pens, sent it all in and quit."

"Oh my," Bill said, genuinely surprised. John Jarvie was a fixture in the Park. He ran the only supply store for seventy miles. It was in the Utah half of the valley, on the north bank of the Green River. Everyone knew where it was.

"He's still running the store, though?"

"Yessir, still runnin' his store."

Brown's Park was well known for being chock-full of rustlers. It was a narrow mountain valley over thirty-five miles long. Half of it was in Colorado and half was in Utah — and it was an easy ride up to Wyoming through any number of draws, which made escapes convenient on those occasions when lawmen chose to ride into the Park. Which they rarely did.

Of course, there *were* some honest people living there. John Jarvie was one. Herb Bassett was another. In Brown's Park, the code was to live and let live. Rustlers ranched side by side with common folk and no one batted an eye.

"So, how can Charley just walk back in here after what he done to Speck?" Bill asked in a conversational tone. He held his breath. Maybe Mary wouldn't blow up over the comment.

She didn't. She was rolling out the dough with a rolling pin.

"Speck's alive and fine!" she said and laughed lightly. "Don't know *how* that rumor took, but the man's still working the ferry. Happy and hale."

Bill raised his eyebrows. He heard that Charley gutted poor Speck Williams, who ran the Green River ferry. Speck's real name was Albert — a black man who was once a slave. His skin was so speckly that people called him Speck.

Everyone knew Charley had been talking about building a toll bridge downstream, some day at least. That would not sit well with Speck since the ferry was his livelihood, so it made sense that there might have been a fight. Of course, Bill knew John Jarvie actually *owned* the ferry...but Speck ran it. Still, Charley was a little off and might have gutted him over a dispute.

Mary Crouse was good friends with the Jarvies and got along with them fine. She told him to forget about the toll bridge but Charley would not let it go.

"He didn't gut the Speckled Nigger?" Bill asked again, just to make sure he heard right.

"Nope."

"Nobody did?"

"Nope. Why would he? Why would anyone? Speck's the nicest fella in the Park."

"But Charley's been riding the outlaw trail with me since spring! Why would he do that then?"

Mary sighed and shook her rolling pin at Bill.

"Sometimes Charley gets to feelin' all cloistered up. Especially after a slow winter. When he gets to feelin' that way, I tell him to ride out or by Jove I may end up whackin' the man with this here pin and splat his brains."

Bill nodded.

"Charley *can* be a bear."

Chapter 19

Charley Crouse was pleased with himself and kept plucking at Mary's waist when she walked past the supper table.

"C'mon, Mary! Tell them what a great racer I am. Twenty-one new cows to add to the ranch. That Rash boy can sit a saddle but he ain't no match for me!"

"Hush, I'm busy makin' a meal for three extry folks I wasn't plannin' for."

The table was fuller than usual with the unexpected company. Charley was there and Mary had been expecting him. But Bill was unexpected, as well as Mexican Joe and his lawyer and ranch partner Mr. Conway, who had ridden home with Charley and the twenty-one cows.

"Poor sucker," Charley went on. "Tells me the Middlesex is done for. The Great Die-Up done it in."

"Kid's job is spent, winter's comin' on, and you took his twenty-one cows in a horse race?" Mary asked, but not in a really interested way. None of the locals liked it when the Middlesex company came into the valley. But the young trail boss seemed like a good egg to Mary. He had merely tied to the wrong wagon.

"He didn't have to bet all twenty-one!"

"If he needs work, he can sign on here for the winter," Mary told him firmly.

"Fine...he can work his own cows, what I just won!"

Bill watched Charley with interest. Out on the trail, Charley was stone cold, moody even. Here at home, Charley seemed cowed down by this sweet whipper snapper. Bill was privately amused, but at the same time wasn't sure what was what.

"So Speck ain't dead?" Bill said to Charley.

Charley sat back in his chair and pulled out a pipe. He tamped in some tobacco and lit it.

"Everyone thought you killed him."

"Everyone?"

"Well, that's the word," Bill said.

"Haven't seen you since we parted ways in Lefthand Canyon," Bill added after a moment. "Thought the posse got you."

"Hell, no. I went after them waddies Lem was shootin' at. But one of 'em put a hole in Poqito, so I lit out."

Bill watched him re-light his pipe. Charley had only ridden with him since Kinsey City. The papers had called them the Grand

Lake Gang since Vincent shot that sheriff barely three days later. But they weren't so much a gang, as acquaintances who threw in together for a short spell.

"Yeah, that was a bad day," Bill admitted. "I rode out with Granger and Vincent and we headed on down the Front Range. Until them boys got plugged."

Charley smiled at that and gave him an odd look. Bill thought it was a little unsettling.

"I *know* they got plugged. Hell, I plugged that gap-tooth myself."

"*You* shot Granger?"

If that was true, Bill thought, Charley may very well have killed Vincent, too. Bill had been digging a grave for the man when he heard the shots. Why on earth would Charley shoot them? Bill started feeling uneasy about Charley's unpredictable nature. Add to that, Mexican Joe brought several jars of whiskey, one of which Charley had mostly imbibed by himself.

"How did it happen?" Bill inquired, trying his best to act disinterested.

Charley snorted and waved his hand.

"Aw, them fools stole horses from a feller I was riding with. But they didn't make it far."

Since Bill was not sure about the full truth of the matter, he decided to keep mum about his own whereabouts at the time. How would Charley react if he discovered Bill had been right there the whole time? It had been Bill's call to steal the horses that night, too.

Suddenly Bill wondered about the one hundred thousand dollars he had stolen from the Denver PO box. Charley must have it! Bill's stomach fluttered at the thought. He glanced around the room. It was likely the money was right here in the house somewhere. Probably in a closet, or under a mattress. In a cabinet, maybe.

"Joe, how many hombres have you shot for horse stealing?" Charley asked.

"I don't know," Joe replied.

Of far more interest to Mexican Joe was the big platter of beef which Mary put on the table. They had been sitting there for over an hour, smelling the meat and the stew cooking on the stove and all the good kitchen smells.

Mexican Joe was in the mood to eat, not talk about how many men he killed. He was mainly into rustling these days anyhow. Joe liked the Robin Hood ethic of Brown's Park. And he hated the big white ranch outfits that passed through — or the ones that tried to stay. Those big operations made Joe's blood boil. He hated the Middlesex company and didn't care that young Matt Rash lost his cows in a horse race to Charley Crouse. He hated the 2-Bar up on Cold Spring Mountain. His own people, the Hispanics living in the West, were getting driven out by the white outfits. Often, they just pushed right in and took over the good grazing areas. Joe aimed to do something about it. Maybe he would get back to killing again, after all.

Conway was a lawyer from Wyoming and a glassy-eyed drunk. But he was always that way, and Joe didn't think twice about his state. He never saw him without a shot, nip, or flask in his hand.

"Conway, pass the gravy bowl," Mexican Joe said, speaking slowly to get his request into the man's foggy head.

The gravy bowl seemed to move when he reached for it, but Conway managed to grasp onto the ceramic dish. Seeing a gravy dish that seemed to move by itself was no odd thing to Conway. It would be odd if it *didn't* move. That would mean he wasn't drunk enough.

Chapter 20

Red Creek waited for the sun to drop down behind the western hills. Then he could be sure his field-specs would not reflect and give away his position on the ridge.

Through the binoculars, Red could see right down into Brown's Park. The Green River wound through the valley. The bottoms were lush with late summer grass and cattle were everywhere. Red surveyed several log homes. He was close enough he could smell the woodsmoke from their hearth fires.

A couple days prior, he rode into John Jarvie's store, which sat right on the river. The man had a rich Scottish accent, white hair and a big white beard — even though he didn't look old enough to have white hair. But he was helpful. And Red Creek was coy. He spun a tale about being a cowhand looking for work.

Jarvie gave him the rundown of the valley. Who was who, what was what. The bigger family operations were probably the ones to start with, Jarvie suggested: the Hoys and the Bassetts. There were a couple bigger outfits, the Middlesex and the 2-Bar...but the Middlesex was shutting down, and people didn't care much for the 2-Bar.

"Most other folks in the Park run small herds," Jarvie said. "No need for hired hands, and too poor on cash money even if they had the need."

There were shelves of dry goods and various supplies and sundries. There was also a row of whiskey barrels, all of which were tapped. Red walked over and took a closer look.

"I sure wouldn't mind some good rye," Red told him. "Been horseback for too long."

John Jarvie produced a couple glasses and poured two. There was no one else in the store, and Jarvie was in no hurry to lose his company too soon. Some days were busy. Other days were slow. This was one of the slow days. And John Jarvie liked people. He liked to chat and the summer days were hard to sit through sometimes.

"What's your name?" Jarvie asked him.

"Blue," Red said. "Blue Sedgwick."

That was Red's private joke. It was a reference to the fact that he shot General Sedgwick in the face back in the War — he blew a hole in the man's face.

"You might know a buckaroo pard of mine," Red explained. "Rode up here recent...not sure where he's staked out. Name's John Frederick Hughes, but he goes by different names now and again, if you get me. I call him Bill."

John Jarvie grinned. Of course he understood that. Most of the men who lived in the Park were living with new names, old names, or different names.

"He's a white fellow, clean-shaved, dark hair," Red explained — as if describing a friend. "Last I seen him, he was wearing a green plaid shirt. And he carries a nice pocketwatch with some poetry etched on it."

Red took a sip of his whiskey and smiled approvingly. He wanted John Jarvie to lower his guard as much as possible...and to think Blue Sedgwick was just another rustler or horse thief rolling through.

"Bill's riding a big bay quarter horse with a white sock, last I saw him. White nip on its nose."

Details were important to Red. That's why he wrote everything down in his notebook.

"Your man is up on Pot Creek staying at Charley Crouse's place. Yeah, that's old Jesse Ewing's son Bill. Came through last week, methinks."

Red adjusted the focus on his binoculars. He used them back in the War and kept them ever since — just like his British Whitworth rifle. Red could make out the entrance to Hoy Draw, winding up through Diamond Mountain. The mountain was covered with cedar trees. The quickest and easiest way was also the least suspicious, should he catch any attention.

That was because the night before, Red noticed a couple different campfires burning up on Diamond. Given the reputation of the Park, he figured they were just common outlaws hiding from the law. But that meant a discrete crossing over Diamond off-trail was out of the question.

Through the course of the day, Red Creek watched the Hoy crew ride in and out of the draw. Their cattle were grazing down in the river bend. According to Jarvie, the Hoy ranch was up that draw. And just past that was Pot Creek. Later tonight, after it got dark and the Hoy punchers were sacked out in their bunkhouse, Red would walk his horse right up the draw. He would ride by the Hoy Ranch in the cover of nightfall and head on up to Pot Creek. There had to be a good perch up on a ridge where he could spend some time watching Charley Crouse's front door.

Chapter 21

Little Minnie Crouse ran around the kitchen table screaming. Only Bill seemed to be bothered by it. Both Charley and Mary were finishing their breakfast as if it were quiet as a church. It was clear the girl was only acting her age and was ready to start the day her way. Every morning Bill spent at the Crouse's home, Minnie ran around the table and screamed the whole time.

The early sky was pale and clear. Bill was feeling good. It felt good to be off the trail. He knew he was in the right place now. It was time to go straight, start over clean. Except to maybe rustle a few cows from the 2-Bar, to get a herd started.

Bill's father used to have a mining claim in the western end of Brown's Park, but it never amounted to much. Old Jesse Ewing was not an easy man to be around, anyway, which was half the reason Bill left the valley so many years ago. In fact, his father used to take advantage of so many people that no one in the Park wanted anything to do with him. Bill hoped people around here nowadays wouldn't hold his family name against him.

Jesse went through so many mining "partners" over the years that Bill eventually just walked away, having deciding he had witnessed enough abuse. One poor black kid signed on — back when Bill was still a teenager himself. He remembered it well. His father worked that poor kid to the bone but never paid him a cent. Cheated him out of his earnings, quarreled him off the claim. The old man spent everything that came out of the mine on liquor and fancy restaurants. Of course, no one got to enjoy any of that except old Jesse Ewing.

But that wasn't the end of it.

The poor black kid got thrown in the Green River Jail soon after that — only to find his cell mate was his former mining partner Jesse Ewing. He made him kneel down in the cell so he could balance his supper tray on the kid's back. Then late that night, Jesse took one of the kid's boots and beat him senseless.

Bill was glad the old man was dead and gone. He was a violent man and downright mean. As a result of his family reputation, Bill decided to avoid the Utah end of Brown's Park. That's where his father's claim was. The Colorado end offered a fresher start.

Charley Crouse had meanness in him, too. Bill had seen some of that on the trail. It was not as thorough or unmasked as Bill's father, but Charley had a volatile nature nonetheless...if the mood was upon him. Seeing Charley now, in his home, with a small girl running around the table screaming — it put Charley in a better light. Not to mention, it seemed Mary Crouse held an influence over him. Perhaps family was Charley's saving grace. Bill hoped so. He hoped little Minnie Crouse would grow up without the meanness that Bill grew up with. Bill sighed. This was certainly the right time to give up being an outlaw. He was getting downright sentimental.

There was still the issue of the hundred thousand dollars Bill had rightfully stolen. And Bill, being flat broke, was keen on finding it. Charley had not left him alone since Bill arrived for dinner that first night. He was starting to worry Charley might suspect something. But surely he couldn't possibly know Bill was there the night Granger and Vincent died. Bill hadn't told a soul.

"Ready?" Charley asked him.

Setting down his coffee cup, Bill nodded his thanks to Mary and the two of them headed out the front door. Outside, they could still hear Minnie's scream as she rushed around the table.

"Mexican Joe still sacked out?" Bill asked.

"Naw, they both rode out before the sun came up."

The dewy grass filled the air with a crisp moisture. It smelled good.

"Let's ride down to Pablo Spring and chat with Elizabeth Bassett," Charley said. "Herb's wife. She's in charge, you know."

"What about Herb?" Bill asked.

"Herb ain't got no sand. Besides, he's religious. Elizabeth runs the whole thing. They run the Z-K brand, mostly Durham cattle. Rustled to get by at first, but now it's her thing. She can get you started."

"What about the Hoys?"

"Naw, they're fairly up and up. Elizabeth and the Hoys got a feud going, too. I ain't too keen on the Hoys. I back the Bassetts."

Falling backwards, Bill felt like he'd been kicked by a horse. He landed on his back pretty hard in the wet grass and slid a few feet, right there in front of Charley's porch. His ears were ringing. Charley himself hunched over and covered his head with his arms, and ran back into the house without another word.

The strange thing was that there *was* no horse. Not anywhere near, at least. They were grazing off near the small barn. Charley fed them grain every morning and told Bill grain was a good guarantee none of them would wander off too far overnight. Fences cost money, and that's half the reason Charley had settled on Pot Creek. It was a nice enclosed glen with the stream running through it, but far enough from Brown's Park itself that the horses could roam free and he wouldn't worry about them being stolen.

Bill could not breathe very well. He was gasping. He wondered why he was gasping. Had Charley hit him, knocked the wind out? Bill tried to sit up but couldn't. He could barely lift his head and when he did he saw his shirt was bloody. What worried him more was the big hole in his chest.

Leaning back in the grass, Bill gave up trying to move. He could not feel his legs. He couldn't feel much at all, actually. The sky above him was still clear. The sun's first rays were just starting to color the top of Diamond Mountain. It was a rich, vibrant yellow. Bill always liked sunup.

The last time Bill was lying on his back watching the sky like this, Granger and Vincent had just been shot, and he was hiding by the Arkansas River sipping whiskey in a shallow grave.

Then Bill noticed clouds had covered over the top of Diamond Mountain. He was surprised how quickly the clouds came in! He hadn't even blinked and there they were.

Suddenly, the whole backside of the mountain was gone.

It must be an early morning fog but it was moving lightning fast.

The fog was white and floated over Bill — it was all he could see.

It was chilly, too.

He wondered if Charley could bring him a blanket or a coat. A cigar would be nice.

"Charley...get my coat, would you."

There were cigars in his coat.

Epilogue

Sangre de Cristo Mountains, Colorado

Chapter 1
Leadville

The sign hung fairly straight. Casey was glad, since he spent so much time painting the letters. He stepped back and put his hands on his hips. Julianna smiled broadly and clapped her hands.

"*Pruitt's Practical Horse Shoes*," Julianna read out loud. "That has a shine to it!"

Casey decided to lease out the store he had his eye on — the one on Third Street. He was worried it wouldn't last long, with all the businesses starting up and dying down in a busy city like Leadville. Someone else could have gotten it before he did. So he made the leap and scraped up the lease money. Plus, he was finished building their log home and needed to put his hand to something new.

It took a couple weeks to get things ready. He ordered supplies from New York and had it shipped in by rail: a hot forge, an anvil, hammers, tongs, rasps, nails, standard shoes, straight steel.

Horace Tabor helped out by giving him a line of credit. Casey had been cowboying for the last twelve years of his life and only managed to scrape together enough savings to buy the land they were living on. Julianna had some family money, enough to cover the lease but not enough to invest in shoeing supplies. It was her suggestion they ask the Tabors. Julianna still worked at the Opera House and saw Mrs. Tabor frequently. Julianna waited until Baby Doe was in her Baby Doe mood, and things came together quickly at that point.

"Are you happy, Casey?" she asked him.

He couldn't help but smile. Julianna had that effect on him. Her enthusiasm was like a light, shining bright every time he saw it.

"You bet," he replied and gave her a hug.

"Stay here, I'm going to walk up to the Post Office," Julianna told him.

Casey looked up and down Third. Like all the main roads in downtown Leadville, it was a bee hive. Folks were coming and going — carriages and people on horseback kept flowing by. This was a prime location. Casey had cut out the people door and put in a big sliding barn door, so horses could be brought right in from the street. Plus, it just looked right.

He knew he better get started on this shoeing business anyhow. Julianna was with child, and raising a family would incur extra expenses. Plus hc wanted to raise his boy with a skill. Shoeing was a good one to have, since everyone relied on horses and mules at some point in their day.

Chapter 2
Hay Ranch

It was late in the day when Davis rode up through the tall green grass. The wind was blowing strong and he held his hand on his hat to keep it from blowing off. Til and Emmanuel were on the porch sipping lemonade. Walker balanced on the corral fence and aimed a whittled branch at the approaching rider as if he were sighting a rifle.

"Ho, the house!" Davis called.

Til couldn't believe his eyes. He waved him in and called above the wind:

"Ho, the rider. Come on in!"

Davis slid off into the soft grass, loosened the cinch strap and took off the bridle. Til had sunk a hitching rail out front, but Davis just cut him loose to graze. The horse wouldn't go far.

"The prodigal has returned," Emmanuel said and grinned.

Til welcomed him with a firm handshake.

"Dang, son. Where you been?" Til asked, and looked around. "Where's your pard?"

The wind swelled continually, causing the grass to whip and ripple in the gusts.

"Way down south," Davis told him.

"Well, come on in out of the wind."

He held the door open and let Davis and Emmanuel go in first. Til liked to make sure the door closed tight. It wasn't a perfect latch and had a tendency to come loose in strong winds like this.

"Where's those McGonkins?" Davis asked.

The house was dim inside, even with all the curtains pulled back. Clouds were streaming by, blocking out the sun, and the house creaked in the wind. There was a tall grandfather clock against one wall — it was as tall as Til. He had ordered it the previous month from Montgomery Ward, to make the place more homelike for Laura. He let her pick out anything she wanted. It was fun to watch her pore over the magazine for hours, dreaming about each item that caught her eye. It wasn't everyday they had enough money to special order something. The clock was what she settled on, so that's what they got. It ticked loudly.

"The brothers are down in Garo," Emmanuel told Davis. "Shoot, you prob'ly rode right past them to get here."

"There's a boy on that fence," Davis said and pointed out the window at Walker — who still sat on the corral rail. His hair whipped around with the wind. Walker aimed the branch at a train puffing along in the distance.

"Don't get too close if you want to say *how do*... he couldn't keep his eggs down this morning," Til explained. "Mrs. Blancett is here for good, too. She's down in Garo, herself. Teaching."

"How was it down south?" Emmanuel asked.

Davis shrugged tiredly.

"It was a change of scenery. Thought I'd check and see if anyone down there knew how to cook beans proper."

"Shoot," Emmanuel said. "Muh beans is second t' none!"

"Shoot — they're downright inedible."

Davis pointed out the window at Walker.

"Probably fed that kid right there 3-day Dutch oven beans, didn't you?"

"Got him out of school for the day," Til mentioned dryly. "He ain't complaining."

Emmanuel ducked into the kitchen long enough to come out with the lemonade pitcher and another cup. Til pointed Davis toward a chair but he had no desire to sit down just yet, although he accepted the lemonade gladly.

Davis was feeling sore. His stab wounds were almost healed, but his back still bothered him after a long day in the saddle. He had been on trail for several days. Sleeping out didn't help either. One of the first things he thought when he saw Til's new frame house, was how nice it would be to sleep in a real bed.

"There's sugar in here," he said after the first sip.

"We ain't on the trail no more," Til said with a smile.

"Where's the rest of the boys?"

"Not too far off. Casey's up in Leadville...married now."

"Casey got hitched?"

Til nodded.

"To that girl who helped pull him through," Emmanuel said.

"Julianna," Til reminded Davis.

"That's right, I 'member her now. Boy, that was a mess of a day, wasn't it."

The big grandfather clock struck a chime.

"LG is just a few miles south, bossing the Hartsel ranch," Til went on.

"*He* ain't hitched," Davis wondered. "Is he?"

Emmanuel brayed liked a donkey and shook his head, as if that was the most ridiculous thing he had ever heard. Til and Davis laughed, too, but more at Emmanuel's reaction than anything else. After their humor wore off, Davis did not ask about anyone else. They knew where Edwin and Ira were. There wasn't much to say about that now.

"Lemonade's surely good," Davis commented.

The lemonade was good. Laura made it, and knew just how much sugar it took to sweeten it properly. Til glanced out the window, down toward the far end of the valley. The grass was still waving around like crazy. It was about time the school day was over. Laura would be heading home soon. Til hoped those two bickery drafts would walk fine for her in this strong wind.

For more information about the author, visit his official website:
www.markmitten.us
Talk about it on Facebook:
facebook.com/SippingWhiskeyInAShallowGrave

Made in the USA
Charleston, SC
05 August 2014